THE MYSTI
LILY OF THE VALLEY

Robert Connolly

ARTHUR H. STOCKWELL LTD
Torrs Park, Ilfracombe, Devon, EX34 8BA
Established 1898
www.ahstockwell.co.uk

© Robert Connolly, 2021
First published in Great Britain, 2021

The moral rights of the author have been asserted.

*All rights reserved.
No part of this publication may be reproduced
or transmitted in any form or by any means,
electronic or mechanical, including photocopy,
recording, or any information storage and
retrieval system, without permission
in writing from the copyright holder.*

*British Library Cataloguing-in-Publication Data.
A catalogue record for this book is available
from the British Library.*

This is a work of fiction. Names, characters, places and incidents are the product of the author's imagination and any resemblance to actual persons, living or dead, events or locales, is purely coincidental.

ISBN 978-0-7223-5110-9
*Printed in Great Britain by
Arthur H. Stockwell Ltd
Torrs Park   Ilfracombe
Devon   EX34 8BA*

CHAPTER ONE

THE FIELDS OF HOME

Where wandering byways and
hedgerows mark the boundaries
of fertile fields,
and early mayflowers on
hawthorn trees proliferate
with extravagant ease,
I used to wander with faithful
friends in boyhood days to see
the wild apples, damson plums
and brambles develop their
plentiful yields,
whilst here and there and
everywhere about wondrous daffodils,
daisies and dandelions loudly
summoned the joyful honeybees.

And now in adult years I
sometimes stray down memory lane
to live again those happy hours
of not so long ago,
and feel the wistful nostalgia
that oozes from the artful
composition of a poem,
as I linger in a favourite haunt
embraced by the soothing fragrance
of crowding bluebells that dissipate

the remnants of lingering sorrow.
And I spill silent teardrops
for the needless hardship of past
poverty and the nostalgic joys of nature
among the boyhood fields of home.
And as for emigration it was
a forced leap out of the
frying pan and into the fire,
with zero consideration for the
sudden imposition of my state
of distress,
as bigotry was piled on top
of hardship, and slavery was the
art employed for every hireling
of alien tongue and ragged attire
and the hidden truth was the
unknown stigma that imprisoned
me and rendered me stateless.

But I would read and write
and thru my pen tell my tale
of woe,
when a baby boy was born and
denied the formalities of registration
and he grew up lacking legal
credentials and was trapped in a
state of limbo,
where he struggled with the vagaries
of life and was denied access to
the study of higher education.

Abandoned to his plight in the
stagnant realm of society
he bravely descended into the
explorative depths of deep thought
and succeeded in his quest for
enlightenment,

discovering aspects of truth
of diverse variety.
And he claimed the rewards of
the deep thinker's scientific
efforts thru divine entitlement.

Now where can true contentment
be found if not indeed among
the fertile fields of home,
where I could wander free again
with my love and faithful
friends among life's abundant
diversity?
And there to dwell and fulfil
our dreams inspired by the
wondrous petalled eyes of God
beneath heaven's dome,
where the colourful flora and
fauna is the Earth's richly
endowed university.

"Well now, I think that should suffice," the composer and reviser of the self-analysis poem, Paul Attanagh, a writer and a restless man seeking a place of contentment to settle down in life, assured himself verbally. And after a pause he added, "Yes, among the fields of home – that is where I believe we will find contentment: the homeland where I grew up, the village and region of Attanagh [which was also the name he wrote under]." He then addressed his two female Border collies, Bonzie (two years old) and Fleurie (eighteen months old). Both were sat on a large travel rug busily and contentedly exercising their teeth on a hide chew each, close to the armchair in which Paul was sitting.

"I wonder what you two bosom friends will make of the fields of home?" he asked thoughtfully.

Both dogs stopped chewing and looked up at him with tails slowly wagging, indicating their lack of comprehension.

"I know you don't understand, girls, but I'm sure you'll both like the place I have in mind, where I used to live until I grew up to adulthood. So we will be leaving this rented cottage tomorrow morning after a pleasant, enjoyable week thanks to the fine weather with which we have been blessed."

Maura, his wife of less than two years, found the break quite relaxing too and he intended sharing his idea with her as soon as she had finished hanging out the washing and returned.

"In the meantime let us prepare tea and home-baked apple pie to please her, girls."

He spoke aloud again, and the second time the dogs knew exactly what he meant, having heard the words many times in the past. They responded by dropping their chews, approaching Paul and each placing a paw on one of his knees as a token of their bonded affection and understanding. Paul gently fondled their heads, reassuring them of his love for them.

Then, rising upright from his armchair, he said, "I had better put the kettle to work."

Moments later the rear door of the cottage opened and Maura entered. She was lovingly greeted by the dogs standing upright on their hind legs with their front paws on her apron. She embraced Bonzie and Fleurie and received a faceful of affectionate licks in return.

"Oh, how lacking we would be without the presence of you two best friends, Bonzie and Fleurie," she uttered whilst fondling the dogs' heads.

"The kettle's nearing boiling point, Maura. What's your choice – tea or coffee?"

"Oh, tea ninety-nine times out of a hundred for me, Paul. And thanks for the effort."

"Well, it's only fair that we should share life's burdens, and I have no complaints about doing exactly that, Maura."

"I am well aware of that fact, Paul, and I appreciate it too. As a matter of fact I don't harbour any complaints concerning your efforts of engagement."

"Well, that is a pleasant compliment that I can not only equally return, but surpass on your behalf, my love."

"I don't doubt your ability, Paul, but I do doubt my worthiness of your appraisal of me."

"It's my way of expressing how your thoughtfulness, faithfulness and caring and sharing qualities appeal to me, and I am just simply being honest, which, itself, is also another one of your outstanding qualities," Paul stated whilst placing a slice of apple pie in each of the two dogs' bowls.

He then sliced them into more manageable pieces before placing the bowls in a reserved space close to the rear door of the cottage and watched as both dogs made swift work of devouring their tasty treat.

"They seem to have the same love for home-made apple pie as you and I do, Maura," Paul casually remarked.

"Yes, agreed. Apart from cats I can't think of any creature that would refuse quality home-made apple pie," Maura suggested.

Paul instantly endorsed her observation. "I can't remember ever having considered that fact before, so that's a point of interest to your credit, Maura, that I will not forget," he assured her as he poured some cooled tea into each of the dogs' bowls.

The dogs lapped contentedly. He then put two plates, each containing a slice of apple pie, on the table followed by two mugs of medium-strength tea, and Maura and he sat down to enjoy their morning snack whilst Bonzie and Fleurie returned to the travel rug and their hide chews to continue what had been temporarily interrupted.

"Did you notice any unusual feathered visitor to the food containers in the garden whilst hanging the washing out, Maura?" Paul asked, hoping for a positive report.

"No, Paul, and I did deliberately delay quite a bit with the thought in mind of catching a glimpse of something surprising. I did hear the echoes of woodpeckers drumming along the banks of the close-by wandering stream, and I heard the distant unmistakable call of the green woodpecker several times plus the nostalgic operatic notes of a number of song thrushes spread out near and far and the sudden short bursts of song from a tiny wren. And what a brave, dedicated little maestro the wren is! I did, of course, enjoy the arrival and departure continuously of our regular feathered visitors."

"Yes, you did enjoy what you heard and saw and one has to be grateful for that," Paul commented. He continued: "I would have joined you, but I felt a pressing need to complete the revision of the self-analysis poem, and I am glad to announce that I have managed to do that."

"Well, congratulations! Will I be invited to read it, or is it private to you, Paul? If the latter, I will abide by your wish." Maura expressed her feelings.

"But of course you can read it, Maura, my love. We don't harbour secrets from each other – we are carers and sharers."

"Yes, of course – that's fine, then, Paul. I don't want to give you the impression that I am being nosey," she explained.

"No, no, my love. The thought never entered my mind. You are welcome to read it. And besides, it was my intention to ask you to do just that anyway. I hope you understand it. If there's anything you find difficult to unravel just point it out to me and I will endeavour to explain in simple terms what it means. How does that appeal to you?"

"That sounds fine to me, Paul. I'll read it after we have finished this break – unless that's too soon?"

"No, it's not too soon, Maura. And after you have read it I have a suggestion to make that concerns all four of us." And after a slight pause he said, "Are you prepared mentally for our departure tomorrow morning?"

"Oh yes, Paul. I never get deeply attached to a place until I feel that I am free to bond at my leisure with the area I choose to settle in. It has been a pleasant week that we have spent here," Maura happily remarked.

"I am glad to hear that, Maura, because that is relevant to the suggestion I just alluded to and which I will reveal to you after you have read the poem. I will take the dogs down along the stream for a little ramble whilst you read and contemplate on what I have written. Is that OK with you, Maura?"

"Yes, of course. That's thoughtful of you, and Bonzie and Fleurie will be delighted with the exercise."

The dogs stopped chewing at the mention of their names and looked up expectantly at their bonded owners.

"Who's ready for a ramble?" Paul asked.

Both dogs dropped their chews and went directly to the umbrella stand in the front hallway, where lay their double-chained lead. They returned with it dangling from both their mouths and with wagging tails indicating their delight.

"OK, then, girls." Paul addressed the dogs as he stood upright from his chair and, looking at Maura, added, "We'll be about twenty minutes or so, Maura."

"I'll be looking forward to your return," she acknowledged with a smile.

Paul delayed returning from the ramble so as to give his wife time to mentally digest the self-analysis poem, and the three returned just after a half-hour had passed. After changing the dogs' bowl of water for a fresh supply he sat down on a chair by the kitchen table, where Maura was still seated with the written poem spread on the table in front of her.

"I believe you will now be aware of where I was thinking of looking for a permanent place to settle?" Paul remarked to his wife.

"Yes, indeed, Paul. The fields of home where you spent your childhood years seem to be mentally calling you back. Well, that's how I read it," she commented.

"Yes, you are right, Maura. It must be a nostalgic yearning for the past and its associated memories. I want you to see the area and I want to know how it appeals to you. I hope you will be impressed by it and might like to settle there, but if it's not to your liking we can try another setting elsewhere. What do you think, Maura?"

"I will follow where you lead, Paul, and I hope that I will find the area as appealing as you do." Maura kept the hope alive.

"I remember a thatched cottage on the side of a country lane about 100 metres off a tarmac road, and there were other cottages dotted along the lane on both sides at about fifty-metre intervals and all with a half-acre to two acres of land to cultivate. The one I most remember, and would have loved to live in, was sited on a slight bend in the lane. Gardens on either side of the cottage stretched to about thirty metres, and the garden at the rear extended to about fifty metres. There was a large damson tree in one of the side gardens and a Bramley apple tree and Victoria plum tree in the rear garden. I always admired that cottage when passing during my boyhood years. It might still be the same now, and if it is and up for sale that's where I would like us to settle, if, of course, it also appeals to you. Does my description appeal to your nostalgic imagination, Maura?" Paul asked with an air of excitement.

"It certainly does, Paul. I can visualise the scene and I am hoping too that it still is a reality and up for sale." She shared Paul's wish.

"Am I to take it, then, that you are agreeing with my suggestion to travel south-west to the region of Attanagh and the fields of home on leaving here tomorrow morning?"

"Of course, Paul, unless you want to leave me behind," Maura joked with a laugh.

Paul laughed too and assured her that there would be no likelihood of that happening since they were bonded souls and the dogs were likewise bonded spirits.

"I liked the way you set the scenery in the first verse of the poem, and then as it advanced it became a self-analysis. I had the distinct impression that it was a personal self-analysis and that you actually experienced what you wrote about. Is that true, Paul, or am I exaggerating?"

Paul fell silent for a moment before replying, "Yes, you are right, Maura – it is true. I was reliving sorrowful incidents of my earlier life when I felt that I was being punished for something I knew nothing about, but I don't want to go into details of the past now, simply because I don't know the reasons and there's no way I can ever discover the truth about the past. I suppose that is what is most annoying about it. From time to time I will probably divulge aspects of my past to you. You might find some of my history upsetting, but I don't want you to lavish any sympathy on me as I don't like to wallow in self-pity."

"Understood, Paul," Maura agreed. "I could feel the sadness oozing from your words and the anger too," Maura revealed, and she promised that she wouldn't press him for information.

The remainder of the beautiful day was spent sitting outside with the dogs, enjoying the fine weather and natural beauty of the countryside as well as wandering at their leisure along the banks of the nearby stream meandering through the woodland in gentle, endless flow. Bonzie and Fleurie loved the rambles, like all dogs, as did Paul and Maura walking hand in hand. They were long-time lovers of spring even before they first met. The dogs' fascination with the scents of other dogs and creatures of the wild had always triggered Paul's mental explorative capabilities of discovery. He watched the dogs' undivided concentrated efforts. What, he asked himself, is so interesting about the scents they encounter? There must be important information in those scents, otherwise they wouldn't bother with them.

He addressed Maura – not only his wife now, but his partner in everything: "I would love to be able to see into the dogs' mental instinctive processes when they are comparing the differences between the scents of creatures they encounter during their wanderings, Maura. I wonder if they have the instinctive ability to match a scent to a distinct memory of a known animal, or do they merely judge the size and degree of danger of a species by the strength of its scent? What do you think, Maura?" He invited his wife to speculate.

"Wow!" she exclaimed. "You really do delve deep into your mentality, Paul. I have never even considered such queries about the instinctive mental processes of dogs. You have just introduced me to a heretofore dormant subject, Paul, that I may well develop an attachment to," Maura confessed.

"Well, Maura, my love, what's the purpose of accumulating knowledge and developing intelligence if one is not going to put both to use?" Paul asked with a smile.

"Yes, agreed, and I understand the logic. And I am obliged to bow to logic, so tell me more, Paul."

They both stopped and Paul looked her in the eye and smiled. They embraced and he kissed her sweetly and said, "I hope you will not think that I am trying to pressurise you into becoming scientific, Maura, as that is an art I would not indulge without your approval," he assured her.

"I believe that I know you well enough to trust you implicitly, Paul. Because I am devoted to you, I really would love to learn all I can about natural science and I promise to be a good student." Maura declared her love and her thirst for knowledge.

"Well, what a pleasant surprise! I am delighted with your declaration, Maura. But remember, I too am limited in my knowledge. I don't know everything, but I do make logical speculations on mysterious subjects. I suggest we start with your first lesson right now, Maura. What wild flowers do you recognise on our pleasant ramble?" Paul casually asked.

"Well, I can see bunches of late-flowering daffodils here and there and some clusters of field daisies plus lots of dandelions and lots more leaves and flowering stems pushing up through the soil."

"Good – and well observed, Maura! Do you know anything about dandelions?" Paul quizzed.

"Apart from the fact that most people look upon them as troublesome weeds in their gardens, no, nothing," Maura truthfully replied.

"Well, no doubt you will be surprised by my description of them as beautiful wild flowers – in my opinion they are the queens of all the wild flowers and possibly the most successful worldwide. And if true, that would imply they are the most ubiquitous. It's perhaps because they are so widespread and plentiful that they are looked upon as a weed, but the honeybees love them for the copious amount of nectar and pollen grains they produce. From these raw materials their beehives are not only constructed, but filled to capacity with nourishing honey. And who doesn't love honey? There is more about the dandelion that I will reveal to you later, but that is enough for you to mentally digest on your first lesson. Have you been a little enlightened by that piece of knowledge, Maura?" Paul asked out of curiosity.

"Yes, I'm really impressed by the successful dandelion. I now feel guilty for having labelled it a weed in the past, which was an insult to its beautiful flower. I am looking forward to learning more about it soon," Maura enthused. She added, "I hope it will forgive my past ignorance."

"It will forgive you, Maura, and will always greet you with a golden smile," Paul assured her. "You will develop a deep respect for the beautiful dandelion when you learn about the ingenuity of this inspirational wild flower, and thereafter you will reserve a special niche for it in your memory banks."

"That sounds quite intriguing, Paul. I will be wondering now until the next lesson what it is that could be so important about a common dandelion. It's mysterious and therefore challenging." Maura expressed her growing interest.

"That's good, Maura. That's the right attitude to adopt, and I hope you will discover the answer before I reveal it to you. That would really delight me, but somehow I doubt you will succeed – not because you are not intelligent, but because of your self-confessed lack of knowledge of the dandelion at the beginning, which was quite honest of you. One learns from being honest, and the more one learns the more knowledgeable one becomes. Would you agree, Maura?"

"That's certainly so, Paul. Nobody knows anything at the beginning of life – that is the starting point without restrictions." Maura philosophised with ease and was congratulated, embraced and kissed by Paul.

Bonzie and Fleurie were just a few metres ahead of Paul and Maura, and they returned at a trot side by side. Each was holding one end of a thirty-centimetre baton of wood in her mouth. They had found it in the grass, and now they dropped it at Paul's feet.

"You saw that, Maura. They want me to throw it for them to chase," Paul commented.

"Yes, that can be the only reason," she guessed.

Paul picked up the length of wood and duly obliged by throwing it about twenty metres ahead of them, and the dogs chased in pursuit of it.

"I think those two dogs will be speaking our language in no time," he remarked, smiling in amusement.

Maura laughed aloud and uttered, "Now, that would be something. I wonder how their speech would sound?"

"Well, what they did proves they are capable of thought processing, even if it is in a disjointed form," Paul speculated.

"Yes, I am forced to agree with you, Paul," Maura endorsed.

The dogs returned with the wooden baton to repeat the enjoyable act again and again during their stroll until Paul decided they had exercised enough. He hid the baton in an inside pocket of his jacket and the dogs accepted it was the end of the game. They were probably tired of the chasing to and fro.

"After dinner today, Maura, we may as well start storing our non-essentials away in our camper van in preparation for tomorrow morning's departure," Paul suggested.

Maura remarked, "Would you believe it, Paul, I was just about to suggest the same to you! Isn't that strange?"

"Well, I expect you will have heard the old adage 'Great minds think alike.' " And he laughed lightly.

"Yes, I've heard it in passing, but don't you think 'like-minded minds' might be more appropriate?" Maura proposed.

"Exactly so, Maura, but then some people would argue that both sayings are more or less the same. And is the point really worth discussing?"

"I agree, Paul, it's not worth the effort."

"The human race should concern itself with important things like making sure the grass keeps growing," Paul remarked casually.

After a thoughtful pause Maura asked, "Why is that so important, Paul?"

"Because if the grass were to stop growing it would probably mean the end for all life when one considers the number of animal species on Earth, including the human race, that depend on grass for survival. And remember cereal grasses are included in the mix," he revealed.

"I've never thought that deeply into the subject of survival, Paul, but I do feel the temptation to in your company," Maura confessed.

"I will consider that a compliment, Maura." And he embraced and kissed her warmly.

When he released her from his embrace she exclaimed softly, "Wow! You've lost none of your romantic prowess, Paul. I enjoyed it," she stated encouragingly.

"I'm glad to hear it, Maura. It makes me feel as proud as a cockerel ready to crow from its perch. And now I suggest we return to the cottage and snack on some of that home-baked apple pie with tea. And what do you girls say to that?"

He addressed Bonzie and Fleurie and they pranced about in delight with barks of agreement.

CHAPTER TWO

The following morning, Friday, after a stroll along the endearing stream, an exercise for all four beneath a sun-swept blue sky punctuated with slow-pacing iceberg-like cumulus clouds reminiscent of a dreamy upside-down seascape, they had breakfast consisting of porridge, which the dogs also liked, followed by thick slices of bread from a still-fresh unsliced loaf bought the previous day. Rashers of fried bacon were placed on the lavishly buttered bread slices with fried tomatoes spread on top of the rashers. The dogs' slices of bread were fried and rashers only were placed on top; then the whole was cut into manageable pieces for them to devour and all was washed down with satisfying, wholesome tea, which the dogs also appreciated although a bowl of fresh water was also placed at their disposal.

After breakfast Paul and Maura completed the loading of the camper van and locked it. Then both they and the dogs ended their stay with a final ramble along the tree-lined bank of the stream to admire the scenery and what wild flowers there were in bloom. A proliferating multitude of fragrant bluebells were spread out beneath the bud-studded branches of awakening trees along the woodland stretch, and they were being continuously serviced by crowding honeybees in buzzing song.

On their return to the camper van, Paul and Maura decided to leave their freshly filled peanut container as a parting gift for the wild birds and as a reminder to the next occupants of the cottage not to forget their example. They stopped briefly at the managing couples' residence at the entrance to the park to surrender the cottage keys and to express their satisfaction with their accommodation and the enjoyment of the picturesque setting.

Bonzie and Fleurie occupied the central area of the van, where the deep-pile rug was laid down for them. The separating panel between the cab and the rear of the van was about a metre high with a central door for access. So the dogs and Paul and Maura were always in sight and contact with each other. On the completion of farewells and best wishes, Paul, sitting in the driver's seat, guided the camper van out of the park and headed in a south-westerly direction towards the flowery mountains and the region of Attanagh.

After an hour's driving, during which time Maura and the dogs had been lulled into restful sleep by the gentle vibrations of the vehicle, Paul reduced speed and turned off the main road into a signposted picturesque lay-by picnic area for an exercise break and refreshments. The lay-by was simply 100 metres or so of twisting bends that had been part of the original road but had been abandoned and replaced by a straight stretch of newly constructed road. The highways departments of local councils had been engaged in road-safety improvements around the country in recent years, and the construction of straight stretches of road to replace dangerous bends, such as the abandoned one where Paul had now parked the camper van, was an example. As soon as he switched off the engine Maura and the dogs awoke. Maura, of course, wondered where they were and why they had stopped.

Paul explained the situation to her and ended by saying, "So the original knots of bends, such as these ones, were simply turned into rest areas for travellers."

"Oh, I see. And what a good idea!" Maura commended the decision and added, "One sacrifice for three advantages – now, that has to be good."

Paul smiled and asked, "Would you like to explain your logic in the commendation, Maura?"

"Certainly! The clusters of bends were set aside as rest havens and replaced by straight sections of road. That helped to reduce the growing number of road accidents and at the same time was beneficial in shortening journey times, and the abandoned bends became safe havens for exercise and rest." Maura defended her statement.

"Well, congratulations! That was well summed up, and it places you in the lead again for the wine allocation this evening, Maura," Paul conceded with a laugh. Then after a thoughtful pause he added, "The road planners deserve to be congratulated too. However, the good intention to solve one problem unintentionally created another and a far more dangerous one," Paul told his surprised wife.

"That's like saying the project is both right and wrong at the same time. Am I right in thinking that, Paul?" Maura asked, confused.

"No, I am not saying that, Maura, my love. I'm merely thinking ahead and considering the circumstances arising from the misinterpretation by drivers of the well-intentioned plan. I suspect time will reveal the unfolding truth that I will explain as follows: the bends on main roads are being gradually side-lined and, as you remarked, this is helping to reduce accidents. At the same time it is helping to increase speeds, which reduces the time spent travelling from place to place. As bends are phased out, drivers are tempted to travel faster to reach their destinations sooner and they begin to develop a false sense of security until they become involved in an accident at high speed and then the truth is laid bare. Speed is the supreme killer, as explained in Einstein's equation of relativity, $E = mc^2$, and the problem is generated by peoples' mentally blind attitude to speed. You will have to think a bit deeply about my explanation, Maura, and you are free to ask any questions you wish to," Paul concluded.

"Well, I have seen the resulting devastation when vehicles have been involved in road accidents on TV, but I don't quite grasp the meaning of Einstein's $E = mc^2$ equation." Maura confessed her lack.

"Yes, I didn't expect you to understand it as it explains in the briefest form the ultimate consequence of collisions at speed. Road accidents, although major events to us, pale into insignificance when compared to the ultimate devastation of nuclear bombs."

"Do you mean like the annihilation of most of the city of

Hiroshima that ended the Second World War, Paul?" Maura asked, full of interest.

"Yes, exactly that, Maura. And well remembered! It proves that you have lively memory banks to draw on when the need arises. Congratulations!"

"Thanks for the credit, Paul. That makes me feel good and gives me a mental lift," Maura enthused.

"Good! You are worthy of it, Maura," Paul assured her.

Maura thought to herself for a prolonged moment and then excitedly remarked, "Now I'm beginning to see the significance of what you meant by the straightened roads leading to vehicles being driven faster without due consideration for the growing danger of the increasing speed. Am I thinking positively, Paul?" she asked, almost convinced about her mental calculation.

Paul looked at her eye to eye, smiling. He reached over to her from his seat, embraced her and kissed her with loving passion as Bonzie and Fleurie silently looked on.

After that loving embrace he spoke, saying, "My darling, you are absolutely right. Congratulations again." He kissed her several times in quick succession and remarked, "You must feel good about your endeavour, Maura. And so you should," he proudly reminded her.

"Well, Paul, I would be lying if I were to deny it; but, like you, I don't advertise my feelings. My reward is embodied in the feel-good factor of the deed, whatever it may be. You do understand, don't you?"

"Of course, Maura. I am well aware that we have similar natures, and I feel certain that is what attracted us to each other when we first met in the livestock market in Attanagh town eight years ago."

"Yes, I remember it well," Maura reminisced. "I had accompanied my mother there. She was hoping to find a bantam with a clutch of chicks for sale, but she was unsuccessful. She was as fascinated by the cute, colourful fowl as I likewise was. I remember tripping over something and was in the act of falling when I was caught in the embrace of someone that turned out to be you, Paul, and the rest is recent history."

"Yes, well remembered. I believe we fell in love with each other at the moment of that incident, when our eyes met. It must have been the collision of traits that we both possessed, caring and sharing, and I have always wondered since whether it was accidental or divine intervention. Have you ever harboured similar feelings, Maura?"

"Oh yes, and just like you, Paul, I too remain in a mental state of limbo regarding the answer," she revealed.

"Well, it was a magnetic moment and an equally magnetic memory that we will celebrate with a bottle of Chablis, Sauvignon Blanc or Beaujolais this very evening in memory of that memorable moment."

Bonzie and Fleurie remained quiet, probably unsure of the mood of Paul and Maura because of their conversation, but they overcame their doubt and ambled forward to the partition between the cab and the rear area of the van. Standing upright on her hind legs, resting her front paws on the panel top, Bonzie uttered a stifled squeal to draw attention.

Paul glanced sideways and fondled their heads whilst addressing them: "So, did I wake you girls from your cosy nap too? It's OK. I'm just going to explore a bit further along and then we'll stop for exercise and refreshments. So just relax, Bonzie and Fleurie."

He started the engine and put the vehicle in motion at a slow crawl forward whilst Maura continued to fondle the dogs' heads and spoke to them as a mother would to children to humour them. Paul noticed a small building ahead and stopped within ten paces of it, parking the camper van under a tall, stately beech tree whose branches were beginning to break into bud. The tree was part of a long but narrow woodland stretch. The original roadside verge overlooked cultivated fields, and the ground beneath the trees was covered with flowering bluebells – a wondrous sight – and their fragrance lingered in the languid air, evoking nostalgic childhood memories of both Paul's and Maura's past. The small building was a thoughtful addition, providing toilet facilities for travellers, erected by the local authorities. Paul released the dogs and remembered to take their double-chained lead in hand in case the unexpected should crop up. He then secured the camper van and the four ambled along a winding path through the magical woodland stretch.

Paul and Maura, hand in hand, breathed the heavenly fragrance of the bluebells.

"Oh, if heaven is anything like this it will be the fulfilment of a dream to look forward to!" Maura exclaimed in wishful expectation.

"Yes, indeed, Maura; and if this embracing scene is an aspect of heaven, who wouldn't want to look forward to the journey to heaven's realm when age reaches the stage of restricting a body to immobility in their earthly home," Paul mused thoughtfully.

Bonzie and Fleurie were captivated too by the scents of animal species that had recently trespassed in the pleasant woodland and left their individual odours in their wake. On their return both Paul and Maura used the toilet facilities in turn. The dogs would have to rely on their natural instincts when responding to the call of nature, and that wouldn't pose a problem to them.

Refreshments were in the form of sandwiches the pair had prepared the evening before, and Maura had managed to bake an apple pie in addition. They had also prepared meat sandwiches for the dogs (sausage and chicken), and how they enjoyed them! They had been sliced into manageable pieces. This was followed by a slice of apple pie each – a treat they never refused – and all was washed down with cooled tea, which they had developed a penchant for although there was always a bowl of fresh water available if they should prefer that.

After their appetites were appeased it was time for relaxation in their collapsible chairs. Bonzie and Fleurie sat lengthwise on the ground beside them and gave their attention to the two hide chews provided by Paul.

"Wouldn't it be just wonderful to have a cottage or bungalow in a setting similar to this landscape? We could sit there and relax between daily tasks accompanied by the equally relaxed dogs," Paul remarked wistfully.

"Let's just hope that we are lucky, Paul, when we come upon that thatched cottage that you longed to live in when you were a young boy," Maura reminded her husband, and she added, "It might still be there and possibly vacant and even for sale as you also imagined."

"Well, Maura, I do confess to being a dreamer at times, but stretching a dream that far is way beyond my usual limit. Still, you meant well and you deserve credit for that, and there is a possibility of it being as you suggest." He paused for a moment and then remarked, "I don't think I have mentioned the following to you before: from time to time, over recent years, I have dreamt of the thatched cottage and I distinctly remember seeing wild lilies of the valley in bloom under the damson tree in the side garden each time I dreamt of it. The strange thing is I can't remember ever having seen lilies of the valley in bloom there during my boyhood years. Can you think of a logical explanation for that addition to the scenery in my dreams, Maura?" he asked his wife.

Maura thought about the dream mystery for a lengthy moment before replying, "You might consider my explanation a feminine intuitive stab in the dark, Paul, but nevertheless I will give you my opinion. I think it might have been a childhood innate wish or childish dream. Perhaps you had seen lilies of the valley growing in the wild, and you imagined having them growing under the damson tree if your family members and you, perhaps through a stroke of good fortune, ever occupied that cottage. What do you think of that theory, Paul?"

Paul thought about the suggested theory before thoughtfully answering, "Are you suggesting, Maura, that a dormant wish in my memory banks is evoked when I dream of that cottage of my childhood years?" Paul simplified Maura's effort.

"Yes, Paul, that is exactly what I am suggesting, just as you have described it in a nutshell," Maura endorsed.

"Well, yes, Maura, I can see the logic in your assertion. Congratulations to you again. You will be entitled to drink nearly all the wine in the bottle this evening due to the number of congratulations you've received over these last twenty-four hours, so I had better buy two bottles instead of one to be sure of getting my due share," Paul stated with an outburst of laughter.

Maura responded in like manner.

When the laughter had run its course, Paul remarked, "This

period of thoughtful contemplation must have been inspirational in your life, Maura. I hope you are enjoying the experience. Inspiration develops the habit of generating itself in different forms, just like wild flowers, when one both deliberately and accidentally creates the mental platform whereon it can display its creative art," Paul stated with conviction.

"Yes, I believe you, Paul, because that is really what happened when I thought about the road-straightening programme that the highway authorities indulged in to reduce accidents and increase speed, as you explained to me. It was so enlightening and mentally uplifting." After a thoughtful pause she asked, compelled by curiosity, "Do you rely at times on inspiration when writing, Paul?"

He looked at her, smiled and answered with loving generosity, "The mental flowers of inspiration burst into bloom whenever I choose to trespass into the realm of thought, Maura. If they didn't I would never finish anything."

"Oh, how I would love to have such a mentality. Do you think—"

"Yes, I do, Maura," Paul interrupted her. "You have already begun to develop an inspirational trait that will gradually generate the mental flowers of creativity," Paul predicted, smiling.

"Wow, Paul! You certainly know how to lift a human spirit to dizzy heights," Maura mentally applauded.

"Well, I have never professed to being a fortune teller, but I simply judge people by their ability in their chosen field of interest. You induce me to think along the lines of creative potential – and there you have it, Maura, my love."

Paul delighted his wife.

"You are an unselfish soul, Paul. You have qualities that I have always admired and always will." Maura expressed her feelings.

"I can assure you, Maura, that the feeling is mutual and I pray it will always remain so even beyond our physical existence."

Maura stretched her hand across the intervening space between their chairs to Paul, and he gently grasped it.

With hands locked she uttered, "I believe we are bonded soulmates, Paul."

"There's no doubt about that, Maura."

After an eye-to-eye smiling pause Paul suggested that it was time they were moving on and she agreed.

She remarked, "Bonzie and Fleurie have been so diligently engaged with their hide chews that both have fallen asleep with their chews still in their mouths."

"They know how to relax, Maura, unburdened by worry, but they'll be instantly awake when we start packing things away."

The sound of cutlery and crockery proved him right, as they got to their feet with wagging tails, dropping the remains of their chews, which Paul retrieved and washed clean for later use. He then collapsed the chairs and stored them with other bits and pieces in the camper van. What little waste there was went into the waste bin by the toilet building within a metal cage. Paul and Maura used the toilet facility in turn as one remained outside with the dogs until the other returned. Paul then ambled among the trees with the dogs to encourage them to relieve themselves of whatever they needed to. On their return Paul invited the dogs to enter the rear of the camper van, and when they had obeyed his instruction he secured the rear doors. Paul and Maura climbed into their front seats and a couple of minutes later the vehicle with its crew of four rejoined the main road at the other end of the pretty rest-site bend and headed again south-west. The dogs approached the dividing panel and stood upright with their front paws resting on top of the short door.

Maura fondled their heads and Paul remarked, "They probably want their unfinished hide chews. They're in the well that was originally an ashtray there on the dashboard."

"Are you serious, Paul?" Maura asked, thinking he was joking.

"Ask them, and if I'm right one of them will utter a stifled bark and wag her tail and try to lick your face!" Paul suggested.

"Do you want your unfinished chews, girls?" Maura asked, still fondling their heads.

Bonzie responded just as Paul predicted, and both wagged their tails and flicked their ears. Maura passed the chews to them, which they gently accepted. Then they retreated to their thick rug and lay down lengthwise to continue their demolition of the chews.

"How did you know that was what they wanted, Paul?" Maura asked, her curiosity piqued.

Paul glanced at her and replied, smiling, "Experience over the years plus the fact that standing on their hind legs and resting their front paws on top of the half-door is not a comfortable position for them. I just deduced from that logical thought that they wanted something. That was my simple deduction based on the reality that there is a reason for everything. That was my conclusion, rightly or wrongly," Paul explained in detail.

"Yes, I agree. It's an interesting calculation. As you said, there is a reason for everything, Paul, but would that include instinctive reactions too?" Maura posed the question, eager to hear his opinion.

Paul thought a moment to himself before deciding on his answer: "Well, I feel obliged to say yes, Maura, simply because instinctive reactions are usually associated with survival and the animal instinctive reaction is faster than the speed of thought. But then, some people would see that as a bone of contention, and that is when logic has to be carefully employed. Even then, logical conclusions can be bones of contention as well, so one is compelled to delve deep into thought and tread carefully at the point of speculation," Paul elaborated.

"Yes, I understand your logic, Paul. I like to hear your explanations about subjects because your expressions are easy to comprehend and mentally digest," Maura endorsed.

"That's very kind of you. I'll treat your remark as a compliment, and I believe that will help to slightly boost my allocation of the wine this evening," Paul responded with a good-humoured laugh.

And Maura joined in.

They stopped again after just over an hour's drive on another abandoned bend off a straightened section of road, primarily for exercise and relaxation. The dogs had dozed off again between stops, but were instantly awake when Paul brought the camper van to a halt and switched off the engine. He then climbed out of the cab and went directly to the rear and unlocked the door to allow the dogs out in excited mood. Paul pointed to the trees and the dogs moved in that direction, but hesitated to make sure that he was following in close proximity. Maura, in the meantime, began preparations for tea brewing and afterwards visited the toilet building close to where the camper van was parked; Paul was also obliged to use the toilet on his return with the dogs. When all four were relieved of their physical needs, a pot of tea was brewed and the dogs again ignored the bowl of water placed on the ground for their benefit. Instead they made their preference for tea known by making stifled friendly whines whilst almost touching Paul's and Maura's mugs of tea, held in their hands, with their noses. Paul responded by brewing another pot of tea and pouring some into each of their bowls. When the tea's heat reduced to a tepid state he put the bowls down in front of the dogs and watched as with wagging tails they quite contentedly lapped the contents. they licked Paul's and Maura's hands when finished as though thanking them.

"How's that for intelligence, Maura?" Paul remarked to his wife.

"I think it's absolutely marvellous how dogs and other animals can use their instincts, Paul. They never fail to impress me."

After the tea break the four wandered for fifteen minutes along the woodland trail among the trees that bordered the abandoned bend, and on their return Paul and Maura relaxed in their chairs for another half an hour whilst the dogs worked on their unfinished chews.

Paul asked Maura if she wanted to drive for a while, but as she wasn't familiar with the roads she was reluctant and said so, adding, "I'd rather not, Paul, but if you're tired or bored I will."

"No, I'm not tired or bored, but I don't want to seem selfish either. So just remember, Maura, any time you feel like driving just say so and I will willingly relinquish the wheel. Is that understood?"

"Yes, understood, Paul," she replied with a smile.

Soon after departing after their break they crossed over a bridge spanning a river bearing the sign 'River Barrow', and Paul remarked to Maura with a feeling of satisfaction, "We are now among the fields of my home and yours, because the River Barrow, the gentle wanderer, meanders through both of our homelands. You are aware of that fact, aren't you, Maura?"

"Oh yes, Paul, but I haven't managed to accumulate a knowledge of flora and fauna of the region like you have. Do you think I will succeed in emulating you?" she asked wistfully.

"Yes, I do believe you will, Maura, and you will enjoy the experience." Paul boosted her confidence.

"Oh, I can't wait to get started," she enthused.

"You had your first lesson with the dandelion flowers, Maura, and the second lesson, I believe, will be when we arrive at the site of the thatched cottage, which is not far away now!"

CHAPTER THREE

It was a mere ten-kilometre drive from the River Barrow bridge to the turn-off on to the formerly unmade Valley Lane, now tarmac-surfaced, where the thatched cottage of Paul's boyhood days stood just off the first bend, 100 metres distant. He felt a surge of excitement tempered by the possibility of disappointment, and it was the latter that manifested itself as the camper van rounded the bend and Paul brought it to a halt on the wide lane-side verge. He stared in silence at what was in his boyhood days a picturesque country cottage with colourful cultivated gardens. The burnt-out blackened ruin of that pretty cottage was now surrounded by brambles and wild species of grass and young shrubs. Paul stared in subdued thoughtful mood and didn't utter a word until Maura had commented. She was full of sympathy for her husband as well as being personally deflated. Having had the 'reality' memories of Paul's childhood vividly described to her by Paul, she had mentally looked forward to being captivated by the cottage itself.

She offered her heartfelt commiserations to her husband on his evaporated dream and tried to comfort his feelings by suggesting, "We are sure to find something similar in the region, Paul."

He turned to her and remarked, "Strangely, Maura, I am not personally devastated by the scene, but truly I am more disappointed for your sake, especially after building up your hopes. I feel obliged to apologise to you."

"No, Paul, you mustn't feel apologetic. Such events, I imagine, happen regularly all over the world. They are just part of the vagaries of life," Maura stressed.

"Yes, I agree with your logic, but I can't help feeling a bit guilty nonetheless. . . . . Look there!" he interrupted himself. "The damson tree is not only still there, but it is in full bloom. I can feel its spiritual greeting. And there, to the right, more daffodils are in full bloom. It is time for your second lesson. Let's get out and look around.

Both climbed out of the camper van's cab, then Paul unlocked the rear door to allow the dogs out. He attached the lead chains to their collars as they were so close to the lane and he was aware of the danger from passing farm vehicles as well as other traffic.

"I'm sorry, girls," he said, addressing Bonzie and Fleurie, "but I can't take the risk of either one of you – or even both – being injured or possibly worse."

"I feel likewise, Paul, and was just about to say so." Maura also made her concern known.

"Well, Maura, that's how strong the bond is with man's best friends on Earth. They become part of you – just like children."

"Yes, that's a fact, Paul, strange as it seems," Maura agreed. "There's only one heartbreaking drawback to bonding with a dog, and that is the dog's short lifespan compared with that of a human being," she reminded him sadly, fully aware of the disparity.

"Yes, I know how you feel concerning that fact, Maura, but the way the complex system of existence is designed means it has to be as it is in order for existence to keep functioning," Paul understandingly acknowledged. He continued: "To understand how the complexity of life works, one has to delve deep into quantum mechanics, particle physics, the composition of matter and the Universal Mind of Creation, Maura. One aspect of truth, however, is paramount, and that is that all pulsating forms of life are dependent on struggle. That is the key to existence, and the varying lifespans of all forms of life are tied into that network of struggle. So we have no choice other than to accept God's divine plan – after all, it was God who created existence," Paul concluded.

"Yes, and what a beautifully designed world He created, with an abundant diversity of animal and plant life, of enchanting scenery and endless varieties of colourful flowers and fruits. Yes, we have no cause to complain." Maura spilled her praise.

"I'll go along with all that, Maura. And I have just noticed an ideal arrangement of dandelions with which to explain some additional information concerning those endearing flowers. Give me your hand, Maura," Paul instructed.

She complied and he guided the dogs along the route he wanted to follow. When they reached the flowering area Paul pointed to several clusters of dandelions in various stages of growth, from not yet in bloom to faded flower heads and the miraculous clock heads familiar to all adults from their childhood days when they scattered the tiny parachute-like botanical filaments into the air with a puff of breath and shouted their delight as the breeze carried them away on its invisible wings. He reminded Maura of her childhood memories and then, using the specimens, showed her each phase the dandelion flower passed through, eventually resulting in the miraculous clock head of tiny parachutes. A yellowish-orange coloured seed is attached to the bottom of each independent parachute, and the seeds of the globular clock of parachutes are attached to what was the flower head. All the parachutes are attached by the weakest connection – so weak that they can be released by the softest puff of breath.

Paul then gently plucked one of the parachutes from the clock head and held it up in front of Maura's eyes, saying, "That tiny yellowish-orange end below the chute is an individual seed that is transported through the air by its chute, and wherever it lands on Earth that tiny seed will give birth to a new dandelion plant. Is that not a miraculous event, Maura? Plus the fact that its tiny carrier, its chute, inspired the advent of the parachute, invented by man!"

"Oh my, my, Paul! That is a wonderful piece of knowledge!" Maura exclaimed, and she added, "And to think that I always looked on the dandelion in the past as a garden weed, but now I am beginning to understand why you see it as the queen of all the wild flowers. What a miraculous plant it really is! To my eyes now it is suddenly beautiful, and I reiterate my shameful ignorance of its importance. Its wonderful clock head of seeded parachutes following its ever joyful golden flowers is an ingenious work of art. Oh, what shame I feel for my past sin!"

"Well, I'm sure all these dandelions around us here will have spiritually heard your confession of regret, Maura. As you can see, all those in bloom are expressing their joyful approbation of your confession and welcome you into their midst." Paul raised her feel-good level of mental contentment and then he brought her attention to the flowering damson tree, again from a different angle: "From here the damson tree in flower looks even more beautiful. It's more like a heavenly deity, wouldn't you agree, Maura?"

"Yes, indeed, like a true replication from the Garden of Eden and an endearing presence. How beautiful!" Maura remarked, deeply impressed.

"It has hardly changed since my boyhood days, or so it seems," Paul said. "Come – let's make our way closer to it."

He took Maura's hand as the dogs, still restrained by their lead chains, led the way through the overgrown wild grasses.

On reaching a more advantageous viewing area, Paul stopped and, staring ahead, said to Maura, "What do you make of that, Maura?"

She was fascinated by the mass of white flowers covering the crown of the damson tree.

She answered, "Oh, Paul, I don't think I have ever seen a tree with such an abundance of flowers. It's just gorgeous."

"Yes, it certainly is an extravagant display of floral beauty, but I was referring to the ground beneath the tree," Paul remarked, pointing to the area in question.

Maura brought her gaze to the ground and exclaimed, "Wow! They are lilies of the valley in bloom."

She looked at Paul amazed, and she was about to speak when he spoke her thoughts: "Yes, my dream has come true, Maura. Was that what you were about to say?"

"Yes, exactly that. What a strange coincidence, Paul!"

After a brief silence, Paul spoke: "I have just realised a great truth, Maura. It wasn't really the thatched cottage that was calling me back, but rather the pulsating forms of life that create the landscape – the flowering damson tree, the fragrant Bramley apple blossoms over there behind the ruin, the Victoria plum tree in flower too, plus the berry bushes obscured by overgrown wild plants and all the wondrous wild flowers, like the dandelions, daffodils, bluebells, hedgerow primroses, the hooded arums, buttercups, field daisies and numerous others. Nature's family of living entities are still here just as they were in my boyhood years. They are all around us, embracing us and welcoming us back to the fields of home. That's what it is, Maura, and I can feel it in my blood through my spiritual self. Do you understand, Maura?" he asked, embracing her.

She emotionally felt his exuberance and reacted in unison: "Oh yes, I do, Paul. I can feel the surge of joy that emanates from your body. It magnetises me too. Yes, it's the welcome home from nature, Paul."

The dogs felt this as well, and they stood upright on their hind legs with their front paws resting on Paul's midriff as he and Maura fondled their heads lovingly.

After a pleasant prolonged moment Paul said, "If this site belongs to the local council it might be on their sales list, Maura. If so, what do you say to us buying it and having a bungalow constructed on the site and returning the landscape to its former glory, as I remember it from my boyhood years?"

"Oh, I think that would be wonderful, Paul – a boyhood dream fulfilled, and we would be an integral part of it. I like the surrounding area and the scenery and I would love to be a part of it." Maura expressed her feelings.

"Our next stop will be the council offices in Attanagh town, which is only five kilometres away. I will make some enquiries there, and in the meantime we will just have to keep our fingers crossed," Paul concluded with an air of confidence.

"Can we have a look at what used to be the rear garden with its Bramley apple tree and Victoria plum tree, plus whatever also grows there, Paul?" Maura requested, eager to see all there was to see.

"Of course. Give me your hand again, Maura." And, addressing the dogs: "Come on, girls – let's take a look at the back garden."

The dogs led the way, helped by Paul's prompts.

Both the Bramley apple tree and the Victoria plum were also covered with flowers, but the apple tree was the main attraction because of the appealing fragrance that its flowers breathed into the languid April air.

"The fragrant apple blossoms take all the plaudits in spring, but the Victoria plums and damsons take all the accolades in autumn with the sublime taste of their soft fruits," Maura was quick to remind him.

"Yes, true, Maura, but don't forget those outstanding home-baked apple pies by courtesy of the Bramley apple throughout the year." Paul returned the Bramley apple into the limelight again.

"Oh yes, true, Paul, and isn't it wonderful how nature seems to deny in one sense and compensate in another?" Maura highlighted nature's balancing act.

"Yes, Maura, you've struck gold there because that's a good conversational topic for future interest. It seems as if nature likes playing games with its dependants and who knows, but it might be the manner in which it encourages us to experiment!" Paul speculated as he detached the lead's chains from the dogs' collars, feeling they were now far enough away from the lane and knowing that Bonzie and Fleurie wouldn't stray more than a few metres from him and Maura.

"There are gooseberry and blackcurrant bushes and raspberry canes here in this spacious rear garden too. As you can see, they have been joined by wild plants, such as stinging nettles, thistles and rosebay willowherb, Maura, but we could soon have the garden under control again if we can secure ownership of the site," Paul added. "That small field beyond the rear garden as far as that boundary hedgerow fifty metres or so away was part of this property too. It may have been rented, but then again it may have been owned by the occupants at the time."

"Paul, I am beginning to feel a strong attachment to this overgrown, forsaken and yet joyful setting; and I am already praying that the property is not only in council hands, but for sale as well." Maura revealed her secret wish.

"Well, I'm glad that we are on the same wavelength regarding the inviting site, Maura, and I even feel good just being here again and being enlightened by the pulsating liveliness of nature's dependants and their flower-filled attraction in welcoming greeting.

The affinity I used to feel with this setting in my boyhood years – though I was too young to understand it then – is still strong in my adult life now, and I do understand the nature bond. Everything is as I left it, except for the absence of the thatched cottage, which wasn't really a living part of the pulsating reality that surrounded it. But the family that lived in it were, and I wonder why they never tried to re-establish themselves in their ideal setting," Paul mused thoughtfully.

"Yes, the same thought crossed my mind, Paul, but I suppose we will never get to know the answer to that. Still, it's water under the bridge now, so to speak, and we have to look forward." Maura put the question to sleep.

"Have you been aware of the distant sweet notes of birdsong drawing ever nearer, Maura?" Paul asked. And before she had time to answer, Paul continued: "They are the exquisite notes of a song thrush echoing from the hedgerow across the small field, and there now close by another is answering from among the flower-covered crown of the damson tree. And now the mellow notes of a blackbird joins the chorus and the notes of robins. And listen also, Maura, to those short intermittent spirited outbursts of love song from a tiny wren. The whole area is a carnival of sights and sounds of joy. Can you feel that vibrant affinity with nature, Maura?"

"I can indeed, Paul, just as you described it. I believe in your dream this boyhood memory of yours must be the ideal setting for us to put down roots and be bonded in unity with nature and its harmonious existence with all its joyful dependants." Maura committed herself to the realisation of Paul's dream.

"Yes, that sounds good, Maura, and well expressed. I believed you would like the area, but to be a bonded part of it I wasn't sure. I feel sure now that you would like to settle here, and I will make enquiries and hope that our dream will be fulfilled. So let's sit a while here beneath the fragment blossoms of the Bramley apple and breathe the inspiring breath of the tree's spiritual self as it bathes us in its balm."

When they found a suitable spot to sit, Paul withdrew two hide chews from a pocket and offered them to the dogs. Each gently accepted his offering and they settled themselves down beside Paul and Maura to exercise their teeth.

Paul embraced Maura, saying, "This is to assure you of my loving devotion to you, Maura."

And they kissed the kiss of love.

CHAPTER FOUR

Before leaving the site of the blackened ruin of the former thatched cottage, Paul, Maura and the dogs had tea and biscuits. Then, after inviting Bonzie and Fleurie to enter into the camper van through the rear, which they did without hesitation, Paul secured the door and climbed into the driver's seat. He buckled his seat belt, as Maura had already done ahead of him. Then he started the engine and reversed the vehicle several metres, turning into the opening with closed gate that led into the small field behind the remains of the cottage. On stopping, he engaged a forward gear and turned left towards the road junction 100 metres away, where he turned left again on to the main road leading to Attanagh town, five kilometres distant.

"It's only ten to fifteen minutes' drive from here, Maura," Paul reminded his wife.

"That's quite a convenient distance from the town for socialising, and yet far enough away for seclusion, wouldn't you agree, Paul?" Maura posed the question.

"Yes, Maura, I agree now that you've drawn my attention to the fact, but previously I hadn't given any thought to that aspect of the location. I must admit your power of observation is growing by leaps and bounds, and that is a rewarding mental asset," Paul commended with a smiling glance.

"Well, I must also admit that's due to the fact that I have access to a reliable source of inspiration, which I will always be grateful for," she unselfishly conceded with a returning smile.

"I couldn't claim my reward for helping to point you in the

right direction since it's you – your spiritual self – that has to do all the mental configurations to impress your intellect, Maura," he reminded her.

"Oh, that's a deep dive, Paul – too deep into the abyss of your ocean of thought for my mental comprehension, Paul. I will just keep nibbling beneath the surface for a while yet, and by degrees I will trespass a little deeper," Maura cautiously restricted herself.

"I understand your consternation, Maura, but I'm sure you will be pleased to know that you are pointed mentally in the right direction and you will grow more confident as the future unfolds," Paul assured her.

"That is enlightening news, Paul," Maura enthused with a sweet smile.

At the same moment Bonzie and Fleurie silently came up to the partition and stood upright on hind legs with paws resting on top of the panel.

Paul briefly fondled their heads with his left hand without taking his eyes off the road and said, "You know what they want, Maura. They're in the dashboard well."

"Oh yes, of course."

She fondled their heads and passed the partly demolished hide chews to both dogs. They rewarded her with licks of affection before returning to their rug and settling down to work.

Paul commented on the fields of home just beyond the winter-trimmed hedgerows on either side of the road, where he spent many of his boyhood days in seasonal slavish toil, thinning sugar beet, swedes, and mangold seedlings in spring and planting potatoes manually – back-breaking work for juveniles and adults alike. In high summer he would weed the half-grown potato haulms where sturdy thistles grew defiant among the rows, and in autumn he would harvest the mature potatoes – another back-breaking task that punished the body. Equally tough, if indeed not more so, was the hand-pulling and snagging of the mature sugar-beet roots in late autumn with frost-cold hands. The reward for this slavery was a pittance, but spring and summer provided lifetime-lasting memories. The hardships, for Paul at least, were compensated by the sights and sounds of nature, including seeing leverets surviving alone among the developing crops. The spiritual presence of God was embodied in the wondrous notes of joy that spilled from a diversity of feathered minstrels, including the simple but joyous double note of the cuckoo, which heralds spring, and the corncrakes' incessant grating calls, which kept the April and early May nights awake. Paul could not but nostalgically recall the pulsating encyclopaedic artefacts of nature supervised by the unseen universal mind of God.

"Wow! Wow, Paul! You had a tough time of it during your boyhood days and you don't seem bitter about the treatment doled out to you in your early life. Did you just accept the hardships of your past life as payment for the knowledge you have accumulated during that time and since? Am I on the right track, Paul?" Maura asked, intrigued.

"Yes, Maura, I agree with your assessment. I have no regrets and I am not vindictive. So I can mentally bathe in the nostalgic atmosphere of the past."

Paul steered the camper van into the car park adjoining the town council-office complex in Attanagh and parked close to the entrance of the building.

He turned the engine off and addressed Maura: "Have you any complaints about staying in the van and keeping the dogs company, Maura, whilst I go in and enquire about the site of the cottage ruin?"

"Not at all, Paul. I was even ready to suggest that had you neglected to," she answered, smiling, and added, "I will go back in there through the door in the panel and sit on one of those collapsible chairs and humour the dogs when you have left us."

Bonzie and Fleurie abandoned their chews and approached the partition, sensing a change in the status quo.

Paul fondled their heads and addressed them as one would children: "You girls be good now until I return." After kissing Maura he opened the cab door and slid out, saying, "I'll be as quick as possible."

He closed and locked the cab door and gesticulated to Maura to press the locking device on her door too.

On entering the building, he glanced about looking for an 'enquiries' sign, and on noticing it he went directly to the counter, which was supervised by a young woman.

She greeted him with a smile and a "Good afternoon. Can I help you?"

Paul smiled, greeted her in turn and asked for directions to the office or department that dealt with property and land sales. He was directed to a nearby corridor, where the office in question was the third door on the right. The door bore a sign which read 'Land and Property Sales'.

He thanked the assistant, walked the short distance to the office and knocked gently. On being invited in, he opened the door and was confronted by a friendly-looking man of similar age to himself, sitting behind a desk on which several piles of documents rested. The man greeted him cordially and invited him to take a seat. Paul felt sure he knew the man, but couldn't attach a name to him.

The council official introduced himself as Gerald Kyle and asked Paul how he could help him.

The name was instantly recognised by Paul, who answered, "Would you mind if I ask you a personal question first, Mr Kyle?"

"Not at all – feel free to ask" was the reply.

"Did you attend CBS School here in Attanagh during your boyhood years?" Paul asked, and added, "And were you known at the time by the pet form of your first name, Gerry?"

The official smiled and replied, "Yes, I did; and yes, I was. How did you know?"

"My name is Paul Attanagh," Paul informed him, and he waited.

"That name strikes . . . yes, we were in the same class at school!" he suddenly exclaimed with a broad smile.

He offered Paul his hand and the latter grasped it and they both shook hands delightedly.

"I'm really glad to meet you again, Paul. It's been a long time."

"I am equally pleased to meet you again, Gerry. I hope you don't mind my using the familiar form of your name?"

"No, not at all. I wouldn't have it any other way. Gerald is merely the official version. I hope you have returned to stay,

Paul." Gerry expressed his wish.

"Well, that depends on the outcome of my visit here today, Gerry," Paul revealed.

"If I can help to fulfil your wish, Paul, you are more than welcome to it. So what is your request, Paul?" Gerry eagerly quizzed.

Paul explained his boyhood fascination with the thatched cottage on Valley Lane and his disappointment on just having seen its burnt-out ruin before arriving in town.

"Were you familiar with the cottage, Gerry?" he asked as a matter of curiosity.

"Yes, I was, Paul. I remember passing it on occasions and delaying to admire it, but then one Monday morning five years ago we learned that it had caught fire over the weekend and burned to the ruin it is today," Gerry sadly recalled, adding, "It certainly was a terrible tragedy."

"Tragedy," Paul repeated, surprised, and he asked, "Did some of the family members get injured, Gerry?"

"Worse than that, Paul. All the family members were consumed by the fire."

"What!" Paul exclaimed, shocked, and added with feeling, "My God! What a tragic accident! I was totally unaware of the family's premature demise and I really feel their loss. I knew the family members by sight, but only spoke to them in passing as a ten-year-old boy."

"Everyone in the town and countryside was likewise affected by their loss, and most were seized by verbal outbursts of anger when it was proved that the fire was not a tragic accident, but murder by arson," Gerry stated.

"Murder by arson!" Paul exclaimed. "You mean, Gerry, that someone deliberately set the cottage on fire, but—"

"It's a fact, Paul," Gerry interrupted. "Whoever carried out the heinous act did it in such a way that it was impossible for anyone to escape."

"How did the evil-minded devil manage to do that, Gerry?" Paul felt compelled to ask.

"The culprit soaked pieces of sacking with paraffin, pinned

them to the front and rear doors and windows and set them alight."

Gerry revealed the barbaric act of the arsonist.

"Goddam the insane evil of people on this planet!" Paul angrily condemned the atrocity and after a short pause he continued: "That evil, demonic-minded killer made sure that nobody escaped the holocaust of fire. What an unforgivable crime to even consider! It defies logic, and yet there must be a reason, even if it was the concoction of a deranged mind."

Paul tried to think of something plausible and fell silent until Gerry spoke.

"I can imagine how you must feel, Paul, but there was no easy way to relay the details to you."

"I understand, Gerry. I just find it so upsetting to know that such evil exists on a beautiful planet like Earth. It's beyond comprehension." Paul expressed his feelings.

"I entirely agree with you, Paul. I was similarly affected by the whole affair at the time, and I still think of it from time to time. I hope the truth will make itself known one day," Gerry concluded.

"Did the police manage to find the perpetrator of the atrocity, Gerry?" Paul posed the crucial question and expected a negative answer.

"Well, the police did arrest an itinerant traveller with a wife and young baby who had set up camp on the wide verge of the main road about fifty metres beyond the Valley Lane junction. He was charged with the crime, which he naturally denied. He pleaded his complete innocence of the inhuman crime, but nevertheless he was put on trial and, not convincingly, found guilty and sentenced to life in prison. He tearfully and angrily accused the prosecuting counsel of having perpetrated a crime against him by inventing false evidence. And even worse, he said they had also sentenced his wife and baby to the same term of punishment. He ended by saying, "Your guilty conscience will be your judge."

"It sounds like the plea of an innocent man," Paul remarked.

"Yes, Paul, and even I, having followed the trial through the press, felt he was innocent too. There seemed to be a lack of convincing evidence and there was no motive." Gerry stated his opinion and suggested, "You can ask for a photostat copy of the trial from the local newspaper office, the *Attanagh News Round-Up*. Better still, I can order a copy for you from here and you can call and pick it up later. The charge will be about €5. The office is in the same building as in our boyhood days. What do you say, Paul?" Gerry asked.

"Yes, I appreciate your offer, Gerry. You are just as genial-natured as you always were, and that's good to know too," Paul complimented.

"That's a pleasant reminder, Paul, and I get the feeling that your good character hasn't altered either." Gerry returned the compliment.

"Well, I must confess, Gerry, I have always tried to keep my principles intact," Paul stressed.

"That's good to hear. And now that you are aware of the sad end to the thatched cottage, what did you want to know about it, Paul?" Gerry enquired.

"Is the site for sale, Gerry, or is it already sold? That's my question," Paul revealed.

"Well, one thing I know for certain about the site is it belongs to the council, so there should be a document about it in my desk drawer," Gerry answered.

He began rummaging among a pile of papers in his desk drawer and withdrew one with the heading 'For Sale – Valley Lane. Spacious Site of Former Thatched Cottage'. Paul read the details of what was included.

"Do you intend buying the site, Paul, or renting it?" Gerry asked out of curiosity.

"My intention – sorry, *our* intention (that is my wife, Maura, and me) is to buy the site and apply for planning permission to build a family bungalow there," Paul revealed.

"So you found your true love, Paul, and decided to return to the homeland to settle down. Am I right, Paul?" Gerry asked.

"Exactly that, Gerry. We have just arrived in town in a camper van with two collie dogs, and Maura stayed in the camper to keep the dogs company," Paul informed his boyhood friend.

"Well, congratulations, Paul. And welcome home to all four of you. I remember your love of dogs, and that hasn't changed. Do you still want to fulfil your dream despite the bad news about the cottage and its former occupants?" Gerry asked, wondering.

"Yes, I do, Gerry, but I'm not sure how Maura will react to the tragic news. Did the police find any motive for the murder of the whole family?"

"No, the whole affair seemed to be a complete mystery and still is today. Nobody came forward with any rumour even of anything against any member of the family, and neither did anyone offer any convincing evidence against the itinerant traveller. The police had no record of any past criminality against him either. The only two items of material evidence against the traveller that the police produced were an empty five-litre-capacity paraffin can and a wicker basket the family used for collecting fruit and vegetables from the garden. Both were in the traveller's possession, but he told the police he had borrowed the basket from a member of the family to carry some damsons to his wife in their horse-drawn caravan. He said that was the reason the basket was in his possession; and the reason he gave why the paraffin can was empty you can read about later in the photostat copy of the trial report," Gerry informed him, adding, "So you can see why it's still a mystery, Paul."

"Yes, you're right, Gerry. The absence of a motive makes it a mystery, and yet the logic remains: there's a reason for everything. The problem is trying to work out what the reason might be, and to do that one sometimes needs a stroke of luck," Paul speculated.

"Agreed!" Gerry supported, adding, "But luck sometimes turns out to be the most elusive friend."

"Yes, true, Gerry," Paul endorsed, and asked, "Who was in charge of the police investigation of the crime?"

"Detective Chief Inspector Quinn, who came down from the city, but most of the investigative work was carried out by Detective Sergeant Luke Griffin, who had been transferred to Attanagh six months before the crime. Between us, Paul, he confided to me his personal belief that the traveller was an innocent man and he said he intended to make every effort possible to find the proof that would set the man free."

"That is commendable of him, Gerry. As a police officer he will have sworn to uphold the laws of the country and enforce them when the need demands, but the same laws may hinder and restrict him in his endeavour to find the evidence he believes exists. Would you agree, Gerry?"

"Undoubtedly, Paul. That's the main problem expertly highlighted. Where did you learn the art to be so precise?" Gerry asked, impressed.

"That's a long story, Gerry, but during the intervening years since our final schooldays I struggled through hardship to develop the art of writing. Suffice to say I became a writer, but I haven't reached the dizzy heights of success yet with my writing. Still, one never knows what's around the corner, so fingers crossed."

"So, you're a writer, Paul!" Gerry exclaimed with a broad smile, and he continued: "I remember at school that you used to love writing essays that were given at times as weekend exercises. You have developed that boyhood love and I hope you succeed in your quest. I congratulate you, Paul."

He offered his hand, and Paul grasped it and uttered, "Thank you, Gerry. I know you mean well. And you, Gerry? I expect you got married and perhaps you have one or two children now, unless I'm mistaken?"

"No, you're not mistaken, Paul. You are almost entirely correct. I married one of the three Shanahan sisters, namely Joan, and we have a two-year-old son. Joan is at present pregnant and the baby is due in the autumn," Gerry revealed with a broad smile.

"So, you are a happily married and settled man, Gerry. I'm delighted for both of you and your beloved son and his happily evolving sister or brother. The Shanahan family was composed of good people and I expect they have got better since you attached yourself to them, Gerry."

"Well, I'd like to think so, Paul, but, as the saying goes, self-praise is no recommendation. Still, I have no regrets." And he laughed his contentment and asked, "Have you and Maura got any children, Paul?"

"No, not yet, Gerry, and that's because we are not settled yet –

hence the enquiry about the cottage-ruin site." Paul returned to the object of his visit.

"So you are not deterred by the fate of the family that died there, Paul?" Gerry asked.

"No, Gerry. I don't believe the family was targeted simply because they lived there. I believe the reason has to be much deeper than that," Paul suggested. He asked, "Has anyone ever made enquiries with regard to purchasing the property since the tragedy, Gerry?"

"No, Paul, but that is understandable as, I suppose, suspicion would probably circulate if an interested party was a local. Another reason might be more off-putting – and that is the spread of superstition and a rumour that a malign force was involved. What do you say to that, Paul?" Gerry asked.

"Yes, I think you could be on target there, Gerry; but that wouldn't affect my scientific judgement, which doesn't allow for a destructive evil presence to have the power to perpetrate evil deeds with impunity, such as the murder of the family in the cottage. No, Gerry, I could never accept that, although I know that superstition is a powerful force and it's kept alive and cultivated in the mentalities of those who harbour it," Paul explained.

"Yes, I agree, Paul, and I'm glad that you are strong-minded where superstition is concerned. So that means that you still want to go ahead, at least on paper, at the moment, with the possible purchase of the site. If it turns out that your wife, Maura, agrees with your decision you will be entitled to a government building grant, and at the moment that is twenty-five per cent and possibly more," Gerry informed him.

"That's a generous helping hand for which we would be grateful should all go according to plan, Gerry." Paul expressed his feeling.

"If and when your plan materialises, Paul, and you want to secure it against any kind of criminality – such as erecting appropriate fencing – there are also grants available for such additions," Gerry reminded him.

"Well well, how times have changed!" Paul remarked, pleasantly surprised.

"Are you staying in a caravan park with your camper van, or are you parked privately, Paul?" Gerry enquired.

"Neither, Gerry. I was just about to ask you if there was a camp or caravan site where we could spend a few days or even a week not far from town."

"Yes, there is. It's only about two kilometres from the town on the forest road at the west end of town, if you remember."

Paul nodded and Gerry instructed him to turn left at the end of the town. "It's no more than a fistful of stone's throws away and it's highlighted by a large sign that reads, 'Forest Caravan and Camping Park'. As you have two dogs you won't want to be too close to other park users; so if you mention about the dogs to the proprietor, a man by the name of Sean Kavanagh, and tell him I recommended the site to you, I'm sure he will comply with your wish. In the meantime, Paul, I'll bring your request to buy the cottage-ruin site to the attention of the head of department and arrange a sale appointment with him so that he can explain all the details concerning the sale. How is that for a short cut to a quick deal?" Gerry concluded with a smile.

"You were always ready to help during our boyhood days, Gerry, and you haven't lost that trait. I'm sure you will be head of your department here one day soon too. So good luck in that field, Gerry," Paul complimented.

"Thanks for the assurance boost, Paul. If I were to describe your schooldays, I would be obliged to replicate your opinion of me, so there's the truth. And there's one other thing before I forget: to save you trouble and cost I will phone you to keep you updated with proceedings. Do you have a mobile phone?"

Paul nodded.

"Just write your number on that pad there and that's it for now. I don't want your wife, Maura, to get bored waiting. Give her my regards, Paul."

They both stood upright and shook hands again and Paul suggested, "We will have to meet again for a social get-together sometime, Gerry. I mean, of course, all four of us over a meal accompanied by a bottle of good French wine, like Chablis or Beaujolais. What do you say, Gerry?"

"Oh, I'm trying to think of the French word for *perfect*. Do you know it, Paul?" Gerry asked.

"Yes, it's similar-sounding, namely *parfait*. Have you got it now, Gerry?"

"*Oui, parfait*, Paul! I like French, but I don't practise it enough to remember. Are you into the language, Paul, or are you, like me – make a big effort and then let it lapse through a lack of practise?" Gerry confessed his guilt.

"No, Gerry, I must admit I am a keen student of the French language and I do practise it on a regular basis."

"Well now, Paul, that should be an incentive for me to get serious with the language and get involved with the task," Gerry reminded himself.

"I will give you some good news on the subject when we get settled, Gerry – that will definitely boost your interest in the French language. What do you say to that?"

"That sounds quite inviting, Paul, and Joan will be interested too. Is your wife, Maura, involved with the language as well?"

"Yes, she is, Gerry. We often have conversations in French at times."

"When I tell Joan she will be just as eager as I will be to progress," Gerry excitedly enthused.

"That's good to hear, Gerry. Grasp the nettle and don't let go. So, I leave you on a happy note and a deep thank you for your help with the task in hand. I am really pleased to have met you again by chance, Gerry. I'll go now and enlighten Maura."

With a final handshake the friends parted company.

CHAPTER FIVE

When Paul returned to the camper van Maura was still seated in the rear of the vehicle pampering the dogs and keeping them amused. When she noticed him approaching she stood upright, collapsed the chair and stored it away. She then returned to the front passenger seat just as Paul opened the cab door on the driver's side. He was eagerly greeted by Bonzie and Fleurie, who covered his face with a spate of affectionate licks.

This appealed to Maura's sense of humour, and she remarked, "Does your face feel like a sponge, Paul?"

He smiled and replied whilst fondling the dogs' heads, "That's a good analogy, Maura."

She detected an underlying tone of uneasiness in his voice and said, "You seem to be upset about something, Paul. Have you been unlucky?"

"Yes, you are right, Maura, but it's not about the site. That's ours for the taking if you still want to go ahead after I have related my findings to you." He went on to explain his surprise reunion: his former school friend, from primary school, was now a council employee in charge of land and property sales. He then related the story of how the thatched cottage became a ruin with the death of the six members of the family that lived in it in a fire that was started deliberately, and he described the method used to prevent any of the family members from escaping the inferno.

Maura was silent and remained so for a lengthy moment after Paul had finished, cradling her head with her hands before finally uttering, "What depraved, evil mind could even imagine perpetrating such a heinous crime on an innocent family without the slightest remorse for the wicked act?"

He noticed her teardrops as they trickled through the divisions of her fingers, and she exclaimed with a deep-felt pity, "Oh, God Almighty! The overpowering surge of pity I belatedly feel for that family in their desperate, hopeless plight! How they must have emotionally felt in their final moments is just impossible to imagine."

Paul placed a hand on her shoulder and spoke softly: "Don't use your imagination to torture yourself, Maura. That tragedy took place five years ago when the family were sadly forced to forfeit their lives prematurely. You must also remember that only their physical entities perished; their eternal spiritual selves, or souls, lived on and still do because they are immortal. I believe that their invisible spiritual selves regularly visit the cottage site to enjoy the flora and fauna that still exist there. That is how to imagine them today, Maura, and that, I believe, is the advice they would impart to us if they could communicate with us now, rather than reliving their tragic demise. Do you understand what I am trying to convey to you, Maura?"

She stopped weeping and went silent for an extended moment before answering, "Yes, I believe I do, Paul. And I also believe that you are right. I can see the joy in your description and in all the flora and fauna that you have previously drawn my attention to, and we together can restore the property to what it used to be to please the visiting spiritual selves of the family members – the family that created the original attraction that brought joy to your maturing mentality during your boyhood days. That's what you mean, isn't it, Paul?" she asked, emotionally inspired.

"That's it exactly, Maura. And what do you say about erecting a greenhouse on the site of the burnt-out cottage, where the spiritual family members could gather and enjoy the delightful beauty of the surrounding gardens with their damson and Victoria plum trees and the Bramley apple as well as all the fruit bushes and the wonderful diversity of flowers to keep the honeybees, bumblebees and butterflies supplied with their needs?"

Paul fired Maura's imagination to a point that prompted her to ask, "Have you decided to invest in the site, Paul?"

"Not unless I have your wholehearted approval, Maura."

"Well, you have it now, Paul, and I am with you every step of the way."

They reached over to each other and sealed their agreement with a loving embrace and kiss.

Before leaving the council car park Maura reminded Paul that they needed to do some shopping for themselves and the dogs, and Paul remembered a grocery store and a butcher's shop next door to each other. During his schooldays he had sometimes been entrusted by his mother to deliver a shopping list to each shop en route to school, and the items on the lists would be delivered by a teenage boy on each shop's 'messenger' bicycle and paid for in person by his mother on the following Friday.

"I believe those two shops might still be in business, Maura, but, of course, I could be wrong. We will find out in seconds."

He started the camper van's engine and guided the vehicle out of the car park. Then he turned west and stopped again about 100 metres further on by the side of the road, where his belief about the shops proved correct.

"Well, would you credit that, Maura? But no doubt the style of shopping has changed. Most items will be prepacked now with the price stamped on, and there will be no credit except for selected clients. And that doesn't include us!" He expressed his scorn at progress's deletion of trust.

"Yes, that's right, Paul. It's a strange fact that as humanity progresses poverty seems to increase," Maura remarked.

"Yes, correctly assessed, Maura, and the reason in my view is that progress feeds on greed."

"Yes, I see your point, and that's thought-provoking. I'll go and do the shopping now, starting with the butcher." With that thought in mind she fondled the dogs' heads, saying, "I'll see you all again in a few minutes."

Maura climbed out of the camper van, and Paul watched and waited until she had finished doing the bulk of her shopping in the grocery store and had approached the till. Then he fondled the dogs' heads, spoke to them reassuringly, slipped out of the camper van and joined Maura in time to bag her shopping and transport it to the camper van. He loaded it in from the driver's side and climbed in to be newly greeted by the dogs, having left them only a couple of minutes before. And when Maura climbed into her seat she was also affectionately mobbed as though she had been away for hours.

"My God, girls, I'm glad my flesh is not of lollipop texture or my face would be in a sorry state!" she remarked, and she laughed at the thought.

When she recovered from her loving greeting by the dogs, Paul told her their next stop would be at the local newspaper printing office to collect the photostat copy of the report of the murder by arson of the family in the cottage holocaust. His boyhood friend, Gerry, had ordered it on Paul's behalf. Then they would drive the two kilometres (or, as Gerry described it, five stone's throws) from the town to the caravan and camping park, and en route he would briefly stop at a supermarket to collect a couple of bottles of wine for the celebration later, which he hadn't forgotten about.

At the *Attanagh News Round-Up* office he made his enquiry concerning the photostat copy of the report of the five-year-old murder trial and was presented with a sealed envelope and a request for €5, which he readily paid.

"Mr Paul Attanagh?" The female assistant addressed him with a smile and asked, "Are you a member of the Attanagh family that used to live in Attanagh Cottage Row some years ago?"

"I am, ma'am, and I believe you are a member of the Brophy family that lived a few doors from us. Am I right?"

"Yes, correct!" the assistant replied, surprised. And she asked, "How did you manage to recognise me?"

"Simply by your eyes," Paul revealed. "Is that how you identified me?"

"No, it was your name. I hadn't thought about the eye factor, although I do now that you mention it. Your older sister, Alanna, and I were best friends and we attended the same school class in the convent. We kept in touch during our later life and still do, although she lives in the USA now – as you are aware, no doubt."

"Yes, I do write to her at times. It's a small world. I'm thinking about your name. Don't tell me yet – let me recall it if I can. . . . Yes, the name that's looming in my mind is Maureen. Is that correct?"

"Yes, exactly! You've got a good memory, Paul."

She offered her hand in friendship, and Paul responded. They shook hands and he remarked, "It's a pleasure to become reacquainted, Maureen, after all these years. We might cross paths in the future as my wife, Maura, and I are planning to settle here in Attanagh."

"Oh, that's good news. I'll be looking forward to meeting your wife. Give her my regards in the meantime. And I'm glad to have met you again too, Paul."

"The feeling is mutual, Maureen. By the way, there used to be a small supermarket a short distance from the town along Forest Road. Can you tell me if it's still there, Maureen?"

"Yes, Paul, it is, and it has been enlarged over recent years."

"Good. And thanks, Maureen. I'll pay a visit there next. Until we meet again I hope all goes well with you and your family. Farewell for now, Maureen."

"Best wishes to you – and your wife, Maura, too, Paul. Bye for now."

When Paul returned to the camper van he received another round of welcome licks from the dogs.

He informed Maura about his latest surprise, and she remarked, "Well well, that is a double coincidence! The first two people you speak to in Attanagh and you recognise each other from the past. If you continue in that vein you'll become reacquainted with all your former associates, or at least with all those that are still around; and through you I'll become well known as well, which should ease our settling into the community," Maura anticipated.

"I'm glad you said that, Maura, because by so doing I believe you have committed yourself. And if you have, I'm delighted that we are of one mind on the subject."

"From my point of view, Paul, it's all about being a bonded part of you, your unselfish nature, your devoted love, your love of flora and fauna, your special love of dogs (the most devoted best friends of human beings) and the scenery and atmosphere that surrounds us and everything else that ties us into the tapestry of existence. And . . . I just feel so happy in your company." And she spilled tears of joy.

Paul stretched his arm out to her and she responded and they embraced each other.

"I'm really pleased you feel that joy, Maura, because it inspires me to feel likewise and I believe we will fulfil our dream. Your joy just overflowed then, and your spiritual self and mine will bathe in its balm. We have to stop before the caravan park to collect the wine, and then we will prepare something to eat in the park, OK?"

"Whatever you say, Paul. Let's do that," Maura concluded with a smile as Paul started the camper van's engine.

CHAPTER SIX

All went smoothly at the caravan park when Paul made known the presence of the dogs to the proprietor and said they had come on Gerry Kyle's recommendation. As it was still early April there weren't many caravans or camper vans on the site. A secluded plot was offered to them close to a perimeter wood just beyond a small meandering stream. After receiving details of the toilet facilities and water supply, Paul signed in and paid the fee for the weekend initially. Then he steered the camper van to the numbered plot and parked it. The next fifteen minutes were spent by Paul and Maura unloading the necessary items to get their cooking equipment set up ready – table and chairs, cooking pots and pans, a large gas bottle and small cartridge stove, crockery, cutlery and condiments. The dogs pranced about playfully and indulged in hindering Paul and Maura, instead of helping, by catching hold of objects with their teeth and playing a game of tug of war with both, much to their innocent delight. Paul and Maura took it all in good spirit and played to amuse them.

Paul filled a kettle with water from a large container they carried in the camper van and placed it on the small gas stove set at a low flame.

Then, satisfied that Maura had everything under control, he kissed her and said, "I'll take the dogs for a ramble along the stream side whilst you organise yourself."

During the twenty minutes that Paul and the dogs were away Maura fried some scrap ends of meat in fat and mixed them with dog meal from a large sack they also carried in the camper van.

When they returned she greeted both dogs with a full bowl each of one of their favourite meals, and they gave her offerings their full attention, licking their bowls clean in a show of their appreciation.

Maura was also in the act of frying both Paul's and her meal, caressing the pork sausages, bacon rashers and tomatoes in a pan with a fork whilst a pot of baked beans was heating on a lower flame on the small gas stove. Thick slices of bread from an unsliced loaf, heavily buttered, were resting in a covered bowl on the table together with plates, pots, cutlery and condiments. The water in the kettle was simmering, and Paul poured the boiling water on to the tea in the teapot to brew.

He then poured fresh water from the tub into the dogs' bowls to wash down their food, saying, "If you don't drink some water there will be no tea later!"

They looked at him innocently and quietly lapped the water, either because they understood or, perhaps more likely, because they felt a little thirsty after their meal.

Paul and Maura enjoyed their meals too, and Bonzie and Fleurie disposed of their leftovers as well.

Tea and apple pie followed. The apple pie was one Paul bought in the supermarket when he stopped to buy the two bottles of wine. Neither Paul nor Maura would deny the dogs their share, which the latter always enjoyed – and likewise the cooled tea that followed, which was never refused.

The washing-up was placed in a basin of warm water to soak and be seen to later. It was then time to sit back and relax. Paul offered the dogs a new hide chew each, which they gently accepted, and the dogs sat down on their outdoor home-made rug with a waterproof bottom and concentrated on their pastime.

"I hope Gerry rings tomorrow, Maura, so that I can ask him if it will be OK to park on the cottage-ruin site and get started on restoring the gardens whilst awaiting the result of our application." Paul updated Maura.

"Yes, that's a good idea, Paul. We should make noticeable progress in a couple of weeks and that would boost our self-belief."

"True, Maura. You certainly have the determination to recreate the past – well, the scenic landscape at least – and that will generate the joy that waits to be summoned from every form of pulsating life."

"I interpret that as the glorification of unfolding spring, culminating in the colourful abundance of the riches of autumn," Maura anticipated.

"Yes, you are getting quite good at mind-reading." Paul commended her power of insight.

"Well, Paul, I must confess you do help a lot by making your ideas clear by the manner in which you express them, and from you I draw my inspiration." Maura paid tribute to her husband.

"Well, regardless of the honour you do me, you still deserve full credit for interpreting my train of thought, and I stand by my appraisal of your mental vision, Maura."

"I feel honoured by your belief in me, and I will try to live up to expectations. And now, to deviate a little, have we got enough tools to start the work, Paul?" she asked thoughtfully.

"Yes, I believe we have enough to make a start, and we can buy whatever additional tools we might need. There'll be a garden centre somewhere in the area, and supermarkets will also have a gardening section, so we needn't worry about that side of things. I was thinking, however, of having the bungalow constructed behind the cottage ruin in a rectangle shape with one long side facing south-east and the other side facing north-west so that we will have maximum light and sunshine from morning to evening all around the home. What do you think, Maura?"

"Yes, I understand the logic of that, Paul, and I am all for your idea. I can imagine the reality of it already, and I can even feel a rising surge of excitement," Maura enthused.

"Don't forget, Maura, you are free to suggest whatever comes to mind as well, and between us we can work out the most beneficial advantages and capitalise on them. For now though, we will have to restrict our efforts to what were the side and back gardens whilst the builder works on the construction of the bungalow. The field gate will be the entrance to our new home on completion of the project, but for now it will be the entrance to the site. Can you imagine it now, Maura, having seen the site?"

"Oh yes, Paul, I'm beginning, I believe, to see the evolving view of the continuous garden through your creative eyes, and I like what I see," Maura fantasised.

"Your creative imagination is starting to spread its wings too, Maura. I suggest we begin our work around and behind the damson tree, and when that patch of lilies of the valley, whose fragrant flowers are now in bloom, dies back I'll lift them. Then, after clearing the bed of invading couch grass and other smothering species, I'll reset the lily bulbs in their weed-free bed, and I think they'll be pleased by my thoughtful deed."

"Yes, I would certainly be grateful if I were one of the lilies of the valley, and I would make the effort to reward you with a stronger waft of fragrance," Maura remarked, and she added, "I like the way you think about flowers, Paul, as though you were in spiritual contact with them."

"How close you are to the truth, Maura! I could reveal the whole truth to you in a sentence, but alas, you wouldn't understand because the human psyche is designed on the principles of mental struggle, meaning the mind must indulge the process of mental configurations of thought to reach a solution. In other words one has to struggle mentally to solve problems, as you have already experienced," Paul explained.

"Yes, I get the gist of what you mean, Paul, and I am beginning to wonder if it's a blessing or a curse," Maura mused.

Paul laughed lightly and remarked, "Yes, I understand your quandary, Maura. Sometimes it feels like one and then the other, but the answer to the dilemma lies deep in the past. It is related to our ancestors' acquisition of creative intelligence, and that is another story within a story and all remote."

"So does that mean, Paul, that we are unlikely to ever discover the truth about what should be the golden key of knowledge that would lead to a harmonious and joyful existence for the human race without wars of any description?" Maura appealed.

"I think you are referring to the Garden of Eden theory and the sin of Adam and Eve, Maura. Is that right?"

"Yes, that's all tied up in it, Paul," Maura conceded.

"In my personal opinion, Maura, Adam and Eve and original sin are just a fantasy and far from the truth. All forms of life have to struggle to survive and, as I've said in the past, that is the only way that existence can survive. A more direct answer to your question is if the human race continues to exist, then, yes, it will eventually discover the truth about itself. And before you ask me, no, I don't believe that will be in our time," Paul explained.

"Yes, I suppose I would have asked you that out of curiosity, Paul," Maura honestly admitted.

"Have you ever considered the fact, Maura, that it might be better not to know about our creative-intelligence acquisition?" Paul asked.

"It might be better not to know," Maura repeated, and she asked, "Why, Paul? Do you know something that I haven't considered?"

"I think so, my love," he uttered, smiling.

"Oh, do tell, Paul, please, or I won't be able to put it out of my mind," Maura entreated longingly.

"OK, Maura, I'll give you something to think about, but we have to go back mentally one or two million years to a period in our history when our ancestors resembled apes. There was no technology then, so our species, no doubt, lived like apes, and the question remains: how did the species acquire creative intelligence?"

Maura was silent for a prolonged moment before speaking: "Yes, you are right, Paul – I haven't considered that fact before. The only answer I can concoct at the moment is that perhaps our primate ancestors came upon a new type of fruit or nut or berry, or some other new source of food that inspiringly activated a dormant gene, or genes, that instigated the acquisition of creative intelligence," Maura thoughtfully suggested.

"Wow! I must honour you with full marks, Maura, for your inspirational effort to explain the mystery. Though you've had no previous experience in the art, your theory is as good as any I have heard over the years, so congratulations! I feel really proud of your mental ingenuity." Paul expressed his praise and, standing upright, he moved two paces to where she was sitting and kissed her sweetly.

Bonzie and Fleurie stopped chewing, dropped their chews and moved close to Paul and Maura, responding to the call of nature.

"Shall we take a stroll along the stream with the dogs and mingle with the bluebells beneath the tall trees, Maura? And we shall toast your theory with Chablis when we return," Paul proposed.

"Yes, let's do that. The weather is ideal," Maura agreed, and after a brief pause she remarked, "My curiosity about our origin is put to sleep now, but no doubt something will spark it into wakefulness again as time progresses."

"You can be certain about that, Maura, because mysteries are magnetic fascinations to the active mind and are always good and interesting conversational topics," Paul ended.

As they strolled along at their leisure, Bonzie and Fleurie pranced around Paul in playful gesture as if reminding him of something, and Paul, suddenly remembering, produced the wooden baton from an inner pocket of his jacket. He threw it about twenty metres ahead for the dogs to chase, which they did delightedly and returned with it held in both their mouths for him to throw again. He kept them occupied in that game until he decided that they had exercised enough to expend their excess energy.

Then he quickly pocketed the baton again, saying, "That's enough racing to and fro for today, girls."

He fondled their heads and they seemed satisfied with their bout of running and began to indulge their scenting prowess.

Paul took hold of Maura's right hand in his left one as they ambled on to the end of the caravan park, where they crossed the stream on the small wooden footbridge. Then they sauntered slowly back towards the other end among the tall trees and the crowding bluebells whilst the dogs occupied themselves deciphering the odour-based language of the creatures whose scents they detected along the way. They crossed back over an identical bridge at the end and returned to the camper van.

"Would you prefer to sit out in the open, Maura, or sit inside the van?"

Paul left the choice to Maura, and she decided to sit outside as it was such a pleasant late afternoon.

"Fine. I'll get the wine, then."

He went to the camper van and returned with a bottle of Chablis, a corkscrew and two wine glasses. The dogs had settled themselves on their outdoor rug with their unfinished hide chews and they briefly glanced at Paul as the wine-bottle cork popped on its deliverance from the neck of the bottle. He poured the wine into both glasses, two-thirds full, and raised his glass to Maura; and she followed his example until the glasses clinked.

Paul uttered, "Congratulations! I think that's six times during the last week, and I will honour you more appropriately in due course." He sipped the wine and said with feeling, "Ah, the taste of love – or, as I should say, *le goût d'amour*."

And when Maura sipped hers she replied in like manner, "*Oui, c'est vrai, c'est le vin d'amour*."

"So you agree, Maura. Do you like it? Let's mentally bathe in the mystical essence of Chablis."

They sat relaxed sipping the Chablis and verbally designed the garden of the yet-to-be-built bungalow. Maura favoured Paul's previous idea of merging all the gardens into one sweeping half-circle garden, extending from one end of the intended bungalow to the other end, terminating at the field gate with all the fruit and all the other fruiting bushes and the rhubarb patch kept as they were and perhaps with other additions introduced.

"My God, Paul! I can picture the garden just as you describe it and as if it were already reality, and I really love what I see in my imagination. Perhaps the mystical spirit of the wine is playing a part and inspiring you too!"

"No doubt about it, Maura, because the spiritual ingredients of the Earth rise through the grapevines and gather in the grapes that develop on the vines. The grapes are harvested and pressed to release the spiritually changed liquid that becomes the wine, like this Chablis. It is stored in bottles, and when we consume it we allow the creative spirit of the Earth embodied in the wine to inspire our creative mentalities. That is the simplicity of it, according to me. So there you have it, Maura, free of charge, just as God intended." Paul philosophised from the heart.

"Well, that is just splendid, Paul. You never fail to evoke sleeping aspects of knowledge that bloom like new species of spiritual flowers in my mental Garden of Eden. I can't imagine how I would manage to survive without you, or perhaps I wouldn't even want to survive without you – and that is straight from my heart." Maura made known her deepest feelings.

"I believe you, Maura, and I feel likewise about you because you are a source of inspiration whose presence is the better half of me by virtue of the fact that your gender is the generator of our species and carries the light of truth into the future."

The Chablis was consumed within the hour, during which time Bonzie and Fleurie had dozed off with their chews protruding from their mouths. But when Paul suggested tea and apple pie to Maura, both dogs awoke as if by magic with wagging tails.

"I feel sure that somehow the dogs heard my suggestion in their sleep, Maura. That is, they heard it through their instinctive mentally developed mechanism. Would you agree?"

"The best answer I can give you, Paul, is I wouldn't disagree," Maura stated.

"Well, yes, that is understood, but it's something you might refer back to from time to time in thoughtful moments, and you might just be inspired to suggest a possibility. In other words, don't ever feel defeated because you feel unable to think of a suitable answer at any given time," Paul reminded her.

"Yes, that sounds like logical advice, Paul, and I'll keep it in mind," Maura agreed, impressed.

"And now for tea and apple pie, and I'll play the host," Paul said, rising from his chair and carrying out the simple operation of pouring water into the kettle, lighting the gas stove, getting the pots and bowls ready and fetching the apple pie and plates from the camper van. A slice of apple pie was placed in each bowl and sliced into manageable pieces before placing the bowls in front of each dog. The contents were devoured with haste, as is the nature of dogs, and they licked their muzzles clean and waited patiently for their cooled tea that followed, and each bowl was lapped dry.

Paul and Maura finished their snack at a more leisurely and equally satisfying pace, and Paul remarked, "That supermarket apple pie was pleasing, but not of the quality of your home-baked version, Maura."

"Well, I must confess I am of the same opinion, as are others that take the trouble to bake. But perhaps it's the acquired taste that we grew up with in our homes that is the deciding factor," Maura summed up thoughtfully.

"Yes, I think you may have struck gold there, Maura. I have never given that aspect of baking much thought before, and I believe, ipso facto, you are right. Well observed!" Paul spilled his rewarding accolade, much to Maura's delight, and to add to her jubilation he asked, "Would you say, Maura, that your observation was inspired by the Chablis wine?"

She laughed and replied, "Yes, I suppose it did mystically prompt me to make known my opinion."

"Yes, Maura, the mystical presence that manipulates the mathematical configurations of the psyche, and hence the inspiration," Paul concluded.

"If that means what I think it means then it's a magical concept of creation." Maura gave voice to her curiosity.

"Well and truly expressed, Maura!" Paul congratulated her, then remarked and suggested, "The sun is close to setting and soon the twilight will steal half blind, so shall we go for a final stroll as far as the toilets near the entrance and attend to our needs whilst the dogs can relieve themselves en route before we retire to the confines of the camper?"

"Yes, let's do that, Paul," Maura agreed, and she reminded him, "It's a bit inconvenient if one needs the toilet, don't you think?"

"Yes, it's one of life's necessities that can't be tuned in advance, but it's only sixty metres away; and besides, we are all likely to need relief during the night, so you won't be without company, Maura."

"Yes, of course, you're right, Paul, and the body gives adequate advance warning."

And a moment later the four moved in the direction of the toilets at a leisurely pace.

By the time they returned, darkness was closing in all around and roosting rooks kept alive their ever decreasing chatter from nearby conifer trees until darkness was almost complete. As silence fell over the land a robin sang farewell to day and a tawny owl softly hooted intermittently its welcome to night.

Having hastily tidied up outside the camper van, Paul and Maura and the dogs retreated inside the vehicle. Their sleeping quarters were two fold-up beds, one on either side of the van, and the dogs occupied the deep-pile rug in the central space. Conditions were a bit cramped, but it was much better than sleeping in a tent on the ground outside, especially when it rained, so there weren't any complaints. Both Paul and Maura sat on their opposite beds and spoke about events of the day whilst pampering Bonzie and Fleurie.

"We have had a fairly busy day's work when you think about it," Maura reminisced, and she added, "It seems more like a working week than a holiday. How would you describe it, Paul?"

"I have to agree with you, Maura. It has been more businesslike than relaxing, and I have to be honest too: the thought of the cottage tragedy has been plaguing my mind all day. I can't think of a reason for the killer's insane barbaric execution of the entire family, and yet I believe there has to be a reason, however twisted and complicated. Have you given any thought to it, Maura?"

"I find it very difficult to accept that a human being could even contemplate such a horrendous crime, Paul."

"I intended reading the photostat copy of the report of the trial this evening, but the lamplight falls far short of the luminosity of natural daylight, so I'll read it after we have breakfasted and exercised tomorrow morning. You can then, if you wish, read it after me and we can form our opinions of the guilt or innocence of the itinerant traveller. What do you say to that, Maura?"

"Yes, I'm looking forward to reading it, and I hope I will be able to make an honest decision concerning the man's guilt or innocence after having read it," she concluded in a thoughtful mood.

"Yes, I was thinking exactly the same," Paul concurred. Then, changing the subject, he said, "There's a natural-history documentary on the radio a little later, from eight forty-five until ten o'clock, and that should be interesting," he enthused. "Have you girls finished your old chews?" Paul addressed the dogs and they looked up at him innocently and expectantly, which meant they had. "You should have let me know sooner," he teased, and they wagged their tails as though agreeing.

Paul reached up to his jacket hanging from a hook above his bed and withdrew two new hide chews from a pocket. He presented them to the delighted dogs, and they at once settled down on their rug to indulge in their simple pleasure whilst Paul and Maura also settled down to listen to the natural-history documentary on their portable radio.

Later, during the early hours of the following morning, their sleep was disturbed by Fleurie pawing Paul's arm – an indication of the call of nature. Paul responded by rolling off his bunk and pulling on his jeans and a pullover. He woke Maura in the process, and she likewise hastily dressed. They left the camper van through the front passenger door with the dogs, and both decided to capitalise on the dogs' needs to visit the camp toilets.

On returning to the camper van and settling down again, the four eventually slipped into sleep again for a couple of hours. They were up and about again before sunrise.

After breakfast and a visit to the toilet facilities, Paul, Maura and the dogs went for a ramble through the woodland on the other side of the wandering stream. Bluebells spread in proliferation there, breathing their exotic fragrance that summoned the honeybees to service the bells and take their reward of nectar and pollen, from which the cells of their hives are constructed and in which the processed honey is stored – the very essence of their continuous survival.

"That in a nutshell, Maura, is the story of the honeybees."

"My, what marvellous knowledge! The very source of their unique survival is also the building material from which their home, the beehive, is constructed. That is next to miraculous. And how tirelessly dedicated they are to their survival! I just feel astounded by the fact." Maura expressed her enlightenment.

"I can't think, at the moment, of another creature that is so willing to sacrifice its life in defence of its home and the precious treasure it contains, and I am living proof of that fact. An incident occurred when I was seven years old, and it almost cost me my life. I will not trouble you with the details now as it would only make you cringe and probably disturb your sleep with nightmares, Maura," Paul decided.

"But you will at some point in the future, Paul, won't you?" Maura asked. "I will be tempted to ask you to relate your experience to me one day."

"Well, I suppose I will, Maura, when I decide that you are strong-minded enough to be able to mentally digest the foolhardy act I once indulged in," Paul cautiously replied.

"I can't imagine you doing anything foolhardy, Paul," Maura respectfully remarked.

"Well, you have to keep in mind, Maura, that I was only seven years old at the time," Paul reminded her.

"Oh yes, of course. We've all done foolish things during our childhood years," Maura agreed.

"Well, I am going to read that report of the traveller's trial when we return to the camper, but for now let's watch the wondrous honeybees endlessly toiling and seemingly loving their work," Paul remarked as both sat side by side on the mossy trunk of a fallen tree and the dogs rested by their feet.

CHAPTER SEVEN

On their return to the camper van Maura poured some water into the kettle and set the gas stove alight to boil water to brew a pot of tea, including a pint to be shared by the dogs, who had a particular liking for tea. There was no apple pie left to share, so they had three ginger nuts each – and that included Bonzie and Fleurie, who had developed a taste for ginger.

Before settling down to read the report of the traveller's trial Paul gave the dogs a partly eaten chew each and they sat down on their outdoor rug to continue their unfinished task. Maura passed the time perusing a magazine.

When Paul had finished reading the report of the trial he passed the copy to Maura, commenting, "You will find that thought-provoking, Maura, just as I have done, but I will save my comments until after you have read it. Then we can discuss our findings."

"I will try and give my honest verdict as if I were a member of the jury whilst keeping in mind the fact that I am a totally unqualified amateur," Maura reminded him.

"Don't highlight your negativity, Maura. Your opinion will be appreciated by me regardless of whether I agree or disagree. Have faith in your ability – and if it's any consolation to you, I do," Paul assured her, and he added, "To allow you to fully concentrate I'll take the dogs for a stroll alongside the stream." He then addressed Bonzie and Fleurie and suggested a walk whilst pointing in the direction of the stream.

They both instantly dropped their chews and pranced about excitedly.

Paul collected their lead from the front of the camper van, kissed Maura and said, "Try not to get upset with the reading ordeal, Maura," and he sauntered off.

The dogs hesitated a moment, expecting Maura to accompany them. Then, realising she wasn't, they planted a few affectionate licks on her face and took off after Paul. Both Paul and the dogs were in full view of Maura for the duration of the walk.

After about ten minutes, and having reached the footbridge, Paul's mobile sounded.

He withdrew it from his pocket, pressed the 'talk' button and said, "That must be Gerry. Am I right?"

"Yes, correct, Paul," the caller answered, and Gerry asked, "Did all go well at the caravan site, Paul?"

"Yes, Gerry. As soon as I mentioned your recommendation of the site everything went smoothly."

"Good! I'm glad to hear that. The most important question is how does your wife, Maura, feel about the tragedy involving the cottage family? I'm sure it must have upset her?"

"It did indeed, Gerry. She was really mortified by the murder and wept tears of sorrow for the unfortunate family. She was truly traumatised for a while. She finds it difficult to accept that a human being could even contemplate committing such a heinous crime. She fell silent for a long moment before asking me, 'And the site, Paul – was it for sale?' I told her what you said, Gerry – that the site was ours to buy if we still wanted it after learning of the tragedy – and she asked if I had decided to buy it. I told her I hadn't signed anything. 'Don't you want to buy it now, Paul?' she asked me, and I told her that I still wanted to buy it, but I needed to be sure her commitment for the fulfilment of my dream is as strong as mine; and if it isn't, the idea is a non-starter. 'I want you to buy it, Paul,' she pleaded tearfully, adding, 'We will restore the gardens to their former beauty, as you knew them. I want us both to fulfil your dream.'"

"Brave woman!" Gerry complimented, adding, "What a devoted wife you have, Paul! She is willing to make a sacrifice for the fulfilment of your dream. I congratulate her."

"Yes, agreed, Gerry. And I do truly appreciate her. I was really won over by her emotional plea and I tearfully embraced her and promised, 'I will buy it, Maura, for your sake, for my sake and for the sake of the souls of the family members who died in the flames.' And there you have your answer, Gerry," Paul concluded.

"My God, Paul, I have never heard such an emotional, heartfelt reason for buying a derelict site before. I didn't realise there was so much emotion tied up in that site. You must have been strongly attached to the setting since your boyhood days. I really felt tears welling up in my own eyes when listening to your description of your wife's effort to realise the fulfilment of your dream," Gerry added as an afterthought.

"Thanks, Gerry. And I'm glad you rang, for another reason: since we want to start on the task of restoring the gardens of the cottage ruin, would we be allowed to camp on the site to begin the work on the gardens to recreate the original attraction? If the answer is yes, we will need the key to the field gate to access the site."

"That's not a problem. I have already filled in most of the buyer's official contract in anticipation of a positive answer. I did inform you about the twenty-five-per-cent government building grant, but I am going to recommend it is increased to thirty-three per cent, citing extenuating circumstances, and I hope I can push it through. Have you given any thought to security fencing when the bungalow is completed?" Gerry asked.

"Yes, I have, Gerry. I am thinking of surrounding the property, along the garden perimeters, with one-and-a-half-metre-high galvanised fencing. That should be a good deterrent to criminal minds," Paul confided.

"That's a good idea, Paul. And just to remind you, there's a grant for that too. I will recommend a thirty-three-per-cent grant for that as well, plus you will receive a reduced quote on your house insurance. I will see a local builder friend today, Paul, and I can ask him, if you wish, if he can take the job on."

"Oh yes, I will appreciate that, Gerry. And thanks again."

"No problem. You're welcome, Paul. I will contact you later about it."

"One other question, Gerry: will the onus be on me to demolish the remainder of the ruined cottage?"

"Oh no, Paul. It always has been and still is council property, so that will be dealt with by the council, and the work will be carried out before the construction of the bungalow begins. So that will not be a worry for you, Paul."

"What I was going to suggest, Gerry, was leaving the base of the ruined cottage intact – the floor, that is. I could erect a greenhouse on it and mentally invite the spirits of the family who died in the fire to visit whenever they wish in their invisible form to enjoy the colourful contents of the gardens that they created during their lives. It's like a spiritual reminder that they are not forgotten. Do you understand, Gerry?" Paul posed the question.

"Yes, I know exactly what you mean, Paul. It's a very endearing and thoughtful gesture. I will make a note of that, Paul, and ensure that your wish is implemented," Gerry promised. Then, remembering Paul's question about the field-gate key, he added, "The field-gate key will be available for you at the town council reception on Monday morning next, from nine o'clock, Paul. I may not be around, and if I am not I might just call at the cottage site in the early afternoon with any useful information I might have. In the meantime, I hope you and your wife, Maura, and the dogs enjoy the weekend, which, according to the weather forecast, is going to remain fine. My regards to Maura, and happy gardening. Bye for now, Paul."

When Paul and the dogs returned to Maura, who by then had completed her reading of the report of the trial, his first thought was to let her know about the phone call from his boyhood friend and now council employee and relate the latest news to her.

"So we can officially camp on the cottage-ruin site," he enlightened her with a feeling of relief.

"Well well, that makes everything so much easier for us to start our gardening restoration project," Maura remarked, quite pleased by the news, and she continued: "And will the council remove what remains of the cottage ruin?"

"Yes. That came as a pleasant surprise, and I did confide to Gerry that we hoped the base of the cottage would be left intact as we planned to place a greenhouse on it to serve as a mental invitation to the spiritual members of the departed family to gather there whenever they wish to enjoy the company of the still-surviving plant species that they planted around the cottage during their lifetime as well as what we would add to the colourful scene. Gerry was deeply impressed by our thoughtfulness and assured me that he would make sure that our wish was granted."

"Well, that was quite good of him, Paul. He seems to have a caring nature too." Maura voiced her praise.

"Yes, he is a carer and sharer, Maura, just like he has always been." Paul characterised his friend and, changing the subject, he asked, "What did you make of the traveller's trial, Maura?"

"My overall feeling is that the supposed guilty man appears to have had absolutely no reason to commit such a heinous crime. So, unless he was a person with a mental problem that manifested itself in severe mood swings and violent outbursts that resulted in an insane act of dire cruelty, which the crime was, I would say he was innocent. I believe it was a travesty of justice. That's my verdict," Maura quite logically decided.

"I agree with you, Maura," Paul acknowledged, and he continued: "It is a fair assessment – well done to you. The wicker basket that was in the traveller's possession but belonged to the murdered family was only known through the traveller's admission and was simply explained by the convicted man. I believe his reason for it being in his possession. He had carried a half-filled bucket of crushed oats to the field where his pony was grazing overnight. The son of the farmer who owned the field had given the traveller permission to graze his pony in the field, and that was verified by the farmer's son. When the itinerant had fed his pony the crushed oats by the gate to the field, which was only twenty metres beyond the cottage-garden perimeter, he stopped to admire the crop of damsons on the fruit tree. That would have been in the month of August. At that same moment the eldest of the cottage-family siblings, a young lady of fourteen years, Mary by name, appeared in the garden carrying a wicker basket containing a mixed selection of food titbits for the songbirds and others. She emptied the contents of the wicker basket on to the bird table there. The traveller greeted her and remarked on how beautiful and tempting the damsons looked, saying, 'My wife loves damsons!'

" 'Well, why not pluck some for her? There's a ladder leaning against that shed over there, and you can place what you collect in this wicker basket,' young Mary invited.

" 'That's kind of you, Miss, but wouldn't I need the permission of your mother or father to help myself to what belongs to them?' the traveller respectfully asked Mary.

" 'Well, I'll go and get permission for you from my mamma,' the young lady replied.

"She retreated into the cottage and reappeared a moment later, saying, 'Mamma said yes, it's OK to take some damsons for your wife.'

" 'Well, that's very kind of her too, and as a mark of respect for her good nature I'll gather a basketful of damsons for your mamma, you and the rest of your family members first, and then I'll collect some for my wife after that,' the delighted man decided.

" 'Oh, no, mister, there's no need for you to do that,' young Mary replied.

"But the traveller gratefully insisted, stating, 'One good deed deserves another.'

"He went to the shed and returned with the ladder and fixed it in position against the damson tree. Mary passed him the wicker basket and he climbed up the ladder and soon filled the basket, and whilst he was thus engaged Mary went indoors momentarily and re-emerged with a second basket.

"When the traveller descended the ladder with the damson-filled basket Mary was waiting to relieve him of it, and she passed the empty one to him, saying, 'Gather all you want now for your wife. Thank you for your effort.'

"After half filling this second basket with damsons he returned to the ground, picked up the ladder and rested it against the nearby shed, saying, 'My wife will be delighted with these. I'll just empty them into the bucket and—'

" 'Oh no, don't, mister,' the young lady, Mary, interrupted, adding, 'Leave them in the basket and put the basket in the bucket. You can return the basket another day.'

"That's the story the imprisoned man told the court, and I have a strong inclination to believe it because it seems such an innocent, authentic account of how he came to be in possession of the wicker basket," Paul stated.

"Yes, my thoughts are in harmony with yours, Paul, regarding the wicker basket. There seems to have been no attempt to hide anything in his story and there's nothing to contradict it."

"And in addition to the empty paraffin container, Maura, they had an oil lamp for lighting and two Primus stoves for cooking, all with several days' supply of fuel in their tanks, plus a small gas stove and a bundle of candles as backup if and when they ran out of paraffin, which the traveller said they had on the previous Thursday, two days after arriving at their campsite."

"But he had no proof of that, Paul. It was just his word, even though his wife would have vouched for his innocence, I expect," Maura added.

"True, Maura, but what convinces me of his innocence is – and this seems to have been overlooked or ignored by the prosecuting and defence counsels – a guilty man would not have been in possession of an empty paraffin container. And I think that was his downfall," Paul concluded.

"Yes, I agree, Paul, especially after you have explained that. I hadn't actually considered the significance of him being in possession of the empty paraffin container, which, as you just highlighted, was the key piece of evidence that the prosecuting counsel used to condemn the man," Maura admitted.

"You had the honesty to confess your oversight, Maura, and that quality should always be applauded, but it begs another question: is it always wise to be honest?" Paul posed the question.

"But we were brought up to tell the truth always, and by so doing we would be granted absolution if we expressed regret for having sinned," Maura reminded him.

"Yes, but it's too easy, Maura, and I feel that I have to disagree."

Paul surprised his wife, who asked, "You wouldn't disagree unless you had a reason, Paul; so can you explain, then?"

"Yes, of course, Maura. In my opinion the counselling priest who hears the confession of a sinner plays the role of God or assumes a godlike role by granting absolution without divine authorisation, and that has to be wrong. In addition to that the act encourages the sinner to continue the forbidden act since the sinner knows that he or she is going to be continuously forgiven. That can't be conducive to honesty, but leaves it languishing in poverty. That's how I see it, Maura." Paul made his point.

"Yes, I understand your criticism, Paul, and I must say I agree as I have never given the subject any depth of thought before." And after a slight pause Maura asked, "Who gives the priest permission to grant absolution to sinners, Paul?"

"Well, I am not an expert in religious law, but I imagine it comes from the hierarchy of the Church the priest is an ordained member of," Paul replied.

"And do you have a personal suggestion of how a confession should be made, Paul?" Maura asked, her curiosity piqued.

"Yes, I do, Maura. I believe a confession should be in the form of a private mental supplication by the confessor direct to God."

"Oh yes, Paul, that is a suggestion I fully endorse," Maura strongly enthused, and she asked, "Is there a particular reason why you disagree with confessing to a priest?"

"Yes, Maura. I totally disagree with a sinner being allowed to grant absolution of sin to another sinner."

"You are stating that priests are sinners, Paul?" Maura probed tentatively.

"All human beings, regardless of their status, are sinners and always will be. Our instinctive origins underwent a change millions of years ago that resulted in our species developing creative intelligence; but our instinctive qualities remained intact out of necessity, and there is no way of escaping that fact, Maura."

"Well, would you believe it!" Maura exclaimed excitedly, and she continued: "I have learned so much more by discussing sin!"

"That just goes to prove, Maura, that everything on Earth is interesting. There is nothing that God created that isn't mysteriously thought-provoking."

"And that includes you, Paul," Maura remarked, smiling, and she added, "I sometimes wonder if God played a part in our accidental meeting; and if He did, I would like to be able to thank Him for His mysterious intrusion."

"You can do that, Maura, in the same manner as I do – by private mental conversation – and just as I still do when confessing my transgressions."

"Yes, of course. I must remember that. You said 'the same manner as I do' – did you mean you always do it that way, Paul?"

"Oh yes, Maura, every time I think I've transgressed."

"I would find it difficult to express my feelings in words, but I will try, Paul," Maura decided.

"I know how you feel, Maura. God knows how you feel too, and He understands," Paul assured her.

"How can we know we have been forgiven, Paul? Is there some way of knowing?"

"Yes, you will know by the feel-good factor you will experience. That is your assurance, Maura."

Whilst Paul and Maura were thus engaged the dogs dozed off on their outdoor rug.

"Do you fancy a stroll among the bluebells, Maura? Afterwards we'll have a sandwich and tea before we drive into town to do some shopping," Paul suggested.

"Yes, a walk among the bluebells might have an inspirational influence on our thoughts when we recall the nostalgic scenes from our memory banks at a later date," Maura anticipated.

"Yes, Maura, that is positive thinking. It's a sign that you are beginning to rearrange your mentality into a storage unit of related memories – the bedrock of inspiration. So you are heading in the right direction."

The dogs awoke as Paul stood upright and they sensed activity.

CHAPTER EIGHT

As soon as the four returned from their pleasant morning stroll all four climbed into the camper van and Paul belatedly suggested to Maura that she ought to drive the vehicle since it was a relatively short distance to the town and it would help her to acquaint herself with the area and the town itself. After a thoughtful moment she agreed and they climbed out again to swap seats. The dogs were at first a little confused and they welcomed them back on board with affectionate licks, having been momentarily shocked and then amused by their antics.

They were in the town centre in minutes, and Paul directed Maura around the streets and into a supermarket car park. She chose an easy parking space close to the entrance, where she brought the camper van to a halt, applied the handbrake and turned off the engine.

"I expect you have a shopping list, Maura?" Paul asked, and she nodded. He suggested, "I don't mind doing the shopping if you wish, Maura?"

"Thanks, Paul, but no," she responded with a smile, and she politely added, "A man is likely to overlook some essential items that a woman wouldn't, because her shopping instinct is more alert. I will look for a gardening section, and if there is one you can venture in on my return and decide on whatever we need for our gardening endeavours on Monday. How does that sound?"

"Inviting and very thoughtful of you, Maura. I will patiently wait with the dogs for your return – and remember, Maura, to take your time as there's no rush," Paul reminded her.

When she did return with a trolley containing mostly food items, Paul climbed out of the passenger seat and invited Maura to climb in. He passed the shopping in to her and she suitably stored everything.

"Women are very efficient at that art as well," Paul commended, smiling.

"Well, thank you for the compliment, Paul," she replied, smiling in turn as she unwrapped two little treats for the dogs – two ginger chews shaped like bones.

They accepted them with childlike delight and returned to their rug to gnaw at their leisure, but not before rewarding Maura with a spate of affectionate licks. On being informed that there was a gardening section, Paul left Maura with the dogs and ambled into the supermarket. He returned soon afterwards with a spade more suitable for a lady than a man and a small bow saw plus a couple of hand trowels and hand forks, a ball of string and a pack of pegs.

Maura viewed the spade with interest and remarked, "That's a dainty-looking spade, Paul."

"I'm glad you like it, Maura, because I bought it with you in mind. It's what is referred to as a ladies' spade, and I bought it especially for you," he revealed with a smile.

"Well, I hope that I live up to expectations!" she joked with a trailing laugh.

"There's nothing to worry about there, Maura. You won't be expected to do any more than you want to do, and only when you feel like it. First of all, what we do on the site will be a mark of respect for God, the Creator of all, who endowed us with creative intelligence; secondly, we'll assist nature in its self-expression of colourful beauty; thirdly, the garden will express our gratitude to the spirits of the departed family members who spilled their sweat to create the original haven of joy; and fourthly, we will have the satisfaction of having made the effort to restore this patch of beauty, which will appeal to the songbirds and other forms of wildlife again as it did in the past, and therein we will bathe in contentment. What more could one hope for on this beautiful Earth!"

"Now, that is a nostalgic picture you paint, Paul, and I am certainly happy to be part of it. I hope and pray that we will succeed in fulfilling your – no, *our* – quest. Is that appropriate, Paul?"

"Yes, exactly, Maura – our quest for harmonious contentment."

There was a moment's silence, after which Maura tentatively asked, "Do you ever consider things going wrong with the plan, Paul? I mean, do you ever have misgivings about the dream, and if you do how do you overcome them?"

"Yes, of course I do, Maura, as would anyone; but I have an unshakable belief that I will succeed, and I suppose that is my strength."

"An unshakable belief in what you are attempting, Paul, and I believe you have instilled that belief in me too. I can feel its surge of power within. It's a wonderful feeling that I will nourish," Maura stated with self-convincing dedication.

"It's really uplifting to know I have your support, Maura." Paul made his feelings known, and then, diverting, he asked, "Do you want to drive the camper back to the park, Maura?"

"No, Paul, I'm comfortable here now and full of thought. You drive whilst I think."

"OK, then. I'll call at that small supermarket on the way and collect an apple pie and a rhubarb pie if available. This is the rhubarb season. Do you like rhubarb, Maura?"

"Oh yes, I have always liked it. It has a unique taste that I find nostalgic. Does it affect you in that way, Paul?"

"Yes, I believe its taste conjures up nostalgic memories, as indeed does apple pie, but we must remember not to feed any rhubarb pie to the dogs. It has a disturbing effect on their bowel movements, for which they pay a price even though they like rhubarb pie," Paul explained.

"I wasn't aware of that, but I'll remember it as an item of importance for future reference." Maura made a mental note of the information.

Saturday afternoon was spent relaxing, reading, listening to the radio and exercising with the dogs on walks along the edge of the winding stream and wandering among the bluebells and trees on the other side. Paul had a pocket radio that allowed him to listen to commentary on football games. Maura could listen to a choice of programmes on the radio in the camper van whilst Paul sat outside with his radio in the open air. Paul always offered Maura the choice of venue – inside or outside – for listening to the radio, maintaining that he was at ease whilst lying down inside, sitting outside or walking with the dogs. Between walks, the dogs contented themselves gnawing on hide chews supplied by Paul.

"I expect you will want to attend church tomorrow morning, Maura," Paul reminded his wife during a relaxing moment, knowing what her reply would be.

"Oh yes, Paul, I'd hate to miss church without good reason. The dogs aren't allowed into the church," Maura reminded him, smiling.

"Yes, that's something I both agree and disagree with. I suppose it's a question of intelligence, both creative and instinctive, and it's the division between the two that defines the problem. Dogs rely on their natural instincts, their sense of smell being their guiding force, to survive, whereas human beings depend on the creative art of thought cultivation for their survival; but the bugbear of the success of humans is their instinctive root. Please don't ask me to explain that in detail, Maura, as it is a complicated aspect of deep thought."

"OK, Paul, so back to the dogs – do you think that our dogs should be allowed to enter the church with us?" Maura quizzed.

"In principle, yes, as long as I could reassure the priest that our dogs would be under control, well behaved and unlikely to need to relieve themselves during the service. Why not, since they would be doing nothing to offend anyone and certainly not God, their Creator? But I also know that it just wouldn't work, and that is why I agree with the rule not to allow dogs into the church. Does that answer your question, my love?"

"Yes, it does, Paul. I do understand the problem. I can imagine the chaos that would probably erupt among the congregation if they were allowed to bring their dogs into church," Maura agreed.

"I can tell you that your mentality is beginning to probe a bit deeper into the intellectual fabric of your mind, Maura, and you are being enlightened by aspects of truth."

"How can you tell that, Paul, without my confirmation of the same?" Maura was tempted to ask.

"I can tell from the decisions that you arrive at, including the deduction you have just come to. You can't do that without delving a bit deeper in thought."

"Are you ever tempted to criticise God for any reason, Paul?" Maura asked out of curiosity.

"No, Maura, I don't feel qualified to criticise God for any reason. The truth of the matter is I believe more in God now than I ever did when I was religious, and the reason is because I have discovered a lot of truth since I followed the scientific route to heaven, in which God is the supreme Guide," Paul concluded.

"So you are saying that God is the source of all knowledge and He answers all your requests. Is that how you interpret it?" Maura asked, her interest stoked.

"Of course, Maura. God is the source of everything, but He doesn't communicate verbally like you and I are communicating now. God's language is spiritual – that is, silent, through the process of thought, and inspiration is like a magic wand that illuminates aspects of truth that the mental processor fits into place like a jigsaw puzzle of facts. That is the simplest way I can think of to explain it to you, but the results free the mentality by degrees from the confusion of chaos."

"I get the gist of what you mean, Paul, but I imagine one would have to practise the art in order to master the method."

"Yes, correct, Maura. Nothing ventured, nothing gained. But you have the mental ability to flower, just as the cottage garden has."

"Thank you for the compliment, Paul. You appear to have great faith in my ability. I just hope and pray that I will fulfil your expectations."

"Remember this, Maura – whatever level of success you achieve, and however small, I will not be disappointed because

I am also a believer in that other old adage 'It's better to have tried and failed than never to have tried at all.' The truth of that is clear. Reflect on all you have learned during the process of having tried and treasure that."

"Have you ever failed in any of your ventures, Paul?" Maura asked out of curiosity.

He looked at her, smiled and replied, "The following is the truth, Maura. I have failed in everything I have tried. Failure has been my constant companion. I have gone through hell, suffered depression and heartbreak, contemplated suicide and had all my aspirations deleted. I have been plagued by poverty, roughed it through homelessness, starved, lived like a tramp, suffered physical and mental deprivation, but, strangely, I always believed that I would survive and that was what kept me going. What I have just told you, and I repeat, is true," Paul unashamedly confessed.

Maura was shocked by Paul's wretched past and remarked, deeply sympathetic, "You suffered all that and yet survived. I'm sorry I asked the question now. It must have been painfully embarrassing for you to recall your torturous past. I could really cry for you, Paul. I would never have guessed you suffered any of those traumas. You never told me anything much of your past life," she ended in a flood of tears.

Paul placed an arm round her shoulders and said, "I know you have a kind nature, Maura, and you are easily upset by sad events, but when you asked I felt it was best to tell you the truth so that you will know not to be overcome by any challenge. Always do your best; and if you fail, try again and again until you succeed. Dry your tears now. My past troubles are gone with the wind. What matters now is the slowly evolving future."

"And what about the present?" she asked thoughtfully.

"There is no actual present, Maura. There is only a future and a past. Your wristwatch tells you that. It fragments the slowly evolving future into seconds, minutes and hours. Do you understand now, Maura?"

She thought about it for an extended moment before exclaiming, "Oh, yes, I see now! Time would have to stand still to be the present, but it can't because evolution has to keep evolving in order for existence to exist. Is that right, Paul?" she appealed.

"Yes, that's it, Maura. You have just stepped on to the merry-go-round. Well worked out!" Paul agreed with complimenting words.

"I must be mentally digesting the scientific information you keep passing on to me and it's paying dividends, thanks to you, Paul," she credited him.

"Give yourself the credit, Maura. You had to mentally put all the bits and pieces together to spiritually visualise the reality. That's what I was explaining to you earlier," he reminded her.

"Oh yes, it all became clear when I put the facts in the right order and the illumination did its magic. I believe I am being tempted to delve a bit deeper each time I engage in a little contemplation. I suppose I'll have to explore different avenues of thought during the process, Paul."

"Yes, that's the way to do it, Maura. Do you remember the French adage '*Petit à petit l'oiseau fait son nid*'?"

"Yes, I do. 'Little by little the bird builds its nest.'"

"Good! Let that be your guiding light and remember patience is the key to solving all problems, and simplicity is usually the answer."

Paul, accompanied by Bonzie and Fleurie as usual, drove Maura to St Peter's Catholic Church at the east end of Attanagh town for the 11-a.m. service on Sunday morning and then drove to a nearby wild area to exercise the dogs and himself. He returned to the church car park just before noon to collect her again.

"How was your ramble with the dogs, Paul?" she asked on climbing into the passenger seat of the camper van and being greeted by the dogs.

"More interesting, enjoyable and thought-provoking than your imprisonment in a pew watching and listening to a boring sermon," Paul answered, smiling.

"Well, I feel obliged to agree, but it is part of our culture," Maura defended without conviction.

"Oh yes, Maura, I understand it is a necessity for young adults and their children to keep the tradition of the belief in God alive and to supposedly guide the children safely through life, but wouldn't you feel at a loss at not being able to logically answer their innocent questions concerning sexual reproduction and all the problems it generates? Our parents were faced with the same problem when we were young and nothing was explained then either. There doesn't seem to be any religious strategy in place to help developing mentalities to prepare for adulthood. Personally I believe the onus is on the parents to gradually inform and educate their children about puberty, including the rules involved and the pitfalls to avoid during the courting stage, plus the reason for marriage and the commitment of both parties. The fathers should instruct and advise the sons, and the mothers should do likewise with the daughters. What do you think, Maura?"

"Well, yes, I agree, but we haven't got any children yet," Maura replied, a little perplexed.

"I am aware of that fact, Maura." Paul laughed and his laughter induced Maura to laugh too, and Paul went on to explain that he believed pupils of a certain age ought to study the subject in schools, to prepare them in advance for puberty and everything involved with it, and religion should be seen to support it."

"Oh yes, I fully understand now, and I agree with you entirely, Paul. It is quite thoughtful of you to consider that aspect of school life."

"Well, I just think it's high time the human race came face-to-face with the instinctive process of life from a certain age." Paul made his feelings known and then suggested, "Shall we return to the caravan park or . . ."

"Yes, let's do that and enjoy a pot of tea and a slice of rhubarb pie, and apple pie for our beloved friends, and then a stroll by the stream and among the woodland trees where the wondrous bluebells spread their fragrant breath," Maura poetically suggested.

"That sounded like an idyllic description of an endearing setting, Maura. You might be developing a natural affinity with nature which will inspire your thinking process."

"What a delight that would be, Paul! Perhaps if you were to write a verse to get me started that might prompt my intellect to react. What do you think, Paul?"

"Yes, it might; and yes, I will. I hope it evokes the ability at present lying dormant in your cranium sanctum!"

"What's that, Paul? I can't recall having heard you use that phrase before."

Paul tapped the side of his head with his index finger and, smiling, said, "That's cranium, from the Greek word for skull, and sanctum, from Latin, meaning holy – the divine site of the spiritual self in the skull. Have I explained it well enough for you to understand, Maura?"

"Oh yes, I believe you have. What you are implying is that the cranium sanctum is the spiritual operations centre of the human body. Is that right, Paul?"

"Exactly that, Maura. Well done! You are learning fast."

And he smiled his compliment as he started the engine of the camper van and headed for the caravan park.

Sunday was a beautiful, warm sun-swept day, enjoyed by all four members of the family unit. Paul had also bought two solid-rubber balls the previous day in the supermarket for the dogs to chase, and he bowled them along the level ground whilst keeping in mind that dogs can't sweat. They pant instead to control their body heat. He also carried the wooden baton to vary their exercise, and he was always careful not to overdo it.

After their break for tea, rhubarb and apple pie the four strolled at their leisure along the edge of the placid stream, beneath the budding boughs of the awakening deciduous trees and among crowding bluebells bathing in their own fragrance. Golden dandelions proliferated along the fringes of the trees, adding their rich varying shades of gold to enhance the slowly changing scenery. Paul and Maura delightedly admired the joyous spectacle and mentally digested the seemingly endless servicing of the flowers by the tirelessly working honeybees, so dedicated to their task in their struggle for survival.

"How single-minded and yet collectively devoted to their work are the virgin worker bees under the auspices of their equally toiling queen, the sole generator of the hive's population! She continuously lays eggs, daily from spring to autumn, whilst the virgin toilers build up the honey store through summer that provides for the hive of bees over winter," Paul commented in praise of the honeybees.

"So that's how the bees exist – or should I say *contentedly* exist? By sharing their food store equally. What an example to the human race! What a shame we don't promote such a harmonious existence!" Maura suggested.

"It seems, Maura, that we are – or the majority of us are – instinctively driven by a force of greed that displaces God. But who would admit to their strangling sin when they are conveniently mentally blind to their waywardness?" Paul remarked in reflective mood.

CHAPTER NINE

On Monday morning after breakfast and their ramble with the dogs along the side of the stream, and among the woodland trees, Paul and Maura loaded all their equipment into the camper van and invited the dogs to hop in as well. They instantly obeyed. Paul then handed Maura the keys and suggested that she should drive the vehicle for the experience. She accepted the challenge, and moments later they were exchanging thank yous and farewells with the proprietor, Sean Cavanagh, and his wife. Maura then steered the camper van in the direction of the town, a couple of minutes' drive away, and into the town-hall car park, where she parked as close to the building entrance as possible, applied the handbrake and turned off the engine. It was then ten minutes past nine.

Paul kissed Maura and embraced Bonzie and Fleurie in turn, saying, "I'll see all three of you shortly."

He climbed out of the camper van and strode to the entrance of the council building, and once inside he went directly to reception, greeted the female desk attendant, gave her his name and asked if a field-gate key or keys had been left for him to collect.

The assistant greeted him likewise and glanced at a tab attached to a set of two keys. "Yes, Mr Attanagh. Mr Kyle, land and property sales manager, left them for you and asked if you would pop into his office as he has some information to impart to you."

"Yes, Miss, I will do that. Is it the same office that he occupied last Friday when I spoke with him?"

"Well, yes – the third door on the right in the corridor on the right just over there," the attendant replied with a smile whilst pointing the way.

Paul smiled too and remarked, "I thought for an instant that you were going to complicate the situation, but all's well. It's the same office."

"Yes, I understand. Complications do occur from time to time, and some are quite funny," she revealed with a slight recollective laugh.

"Yes, I can imagine. Some misunderstandings can be quite hilarious and deserve to be remembered for the humour. Well, I'll go and learn what's new. Thank you, Miss."

"You're welcome. And I hope it's good news," she ended with a smile.

Two light taps on Gerry's office door were answered by an invitation to enter and, when Paul did, Gerry greeted him with a smiling "Glad to see you again, Paul. I hope you, Maura and the dogs enjoyed a pleasant weekend?"

"It was indeed an enjoyable, relaxing couple of days. And you were right about the weather – truly blissful, Gerry."

Gerry laughed and remarked, "Don't credit me with the weather forecast, Paul. I was just repeating what I heard on TV; otherwise I wouldn't have known."

"Oh yes, I understand your meaning, Gerry, but I had missed the weather bulletin on the radio and I would have been wondering about the weather had you not reminded me. Is there anything new I need to know concerning the purchase deal?"

"Yes, Paul, there are advantages to you and Maura where grants are available, and I am going to try and get those grants increased as high as possible by stressing extenuating circumstances in your favour. One of those is the site price, which was initially €60,000 – I will try and get that reduced to half the price, if not better. The same principle will be applied to all the grants that you are entitled to apply for. Included in that strategy, Paul, I will stress the recent history of the derelict site and the haunting fear and superstition as well as the suspicion that the wrong man was convicted, as far as the local community is concerned. A man is serving a life sentence in prison for the heinous crime, but he is considered an innocent victim by many. Add to that the fact that you, the buyer, were born in the area and attended the local CBS school, plus the fact that you and your wife are intending to settle down and start a family there on that site. As you are probably aware, Paul, there are clauses attached to grants. For example, if you were to sell up and leave within a ten-year period you would be obliged to repay the grant, or part of it, and the house-building grant is no exception. Is that understood, Paul?"

"Oh yes, Gerry, I would expect to be penalised for reneging on the agreement. I would have no complaint about that, Gerry."

"Another thing, Paul: the price for the site can be paid over a number of years, to be agreed by both parties. One other thing, Paul: do you want me to continue to advise you, as a friend, during the process as to what's best to do and not to do regarding decisions if and when they arise?"

"Yes, Gerry, I trust you implicitly."

"Good, Paul! Your first step is to sign this site-purchase document, and then I'll get things moving as quickly as possible from here on. Is that OK with you, Paul?"

"That's fine with me, Gerry."

Paul placed his complete trust in his boyhood friend and signed the purchase document.

Gerry then produced an application form for planning permission for the bungalow and Paul signed it without hesitation. Gerry told him that the builder would discuss the building project with him during the week – the outer design and whatever additions Paul and Maura wanted to add or suggest – and the builder would pass on the details to the architect, who would include them in the plan for the building.

"It's better to get all these bits and pieces sorted out as soon as possible, and that includes removing the remains of the cottage, by the council. Then work can begin on the site. The builder will give you an approximate completion date for the bungalow, and I guess that should be September or October. Does that harmonise with your calculation, Paul?" Gerry asked.

"Yes, it does, Gerry. I was hoping it would be in the autumn sometime, and that would be fine with us," Paul agreed, and he felt obliged to add, "Our pressing problem at the moment is a fresh-water tap and toilet facilities. I was wondering if the builder might be able to set up a temporary toilet facility and maybe a fresh-water tap on the site?"

"Oh yes, I almost overlooked that. I'll speak to the builder this morning and see what he can suggest. But don't worry about it, Paul – I'll get that sorted out for you," Gerry assured him, adding, "I'll keep you informed on your mobile phone of all the changes as they are about to occur."

"I really am indebted to you, Gerry. It certainly was a stroke of good luck meeting you again in the same town that we grew up in, and I was especially lucky to meet you here in the council complex that holds the key to the fulfilment of my dream."

"All I can say to that, Paul, is how glad I am to be part of the human-race mechanism that makes the clock tick and helps you in the process. The most pressing need at the moment is the installation of a fresh-water tap and toilet facilities. I'll get on to that straight away, Paul. I expect the builder will contact you today, and he might even turn up in person on the site. If that's the case I will notify you in advance. I think that's everything covered for now, unless . . ."

"Yes, I believe it is, Gerry. The last thing I want to do is overburden you with worry for us, Gerry. You take it easy now – and remember, whatever can't be done today can wait until tomorrow as wise old Farmer Cowling used to say in our boyhood days," Paul reminisced.

"Yes, I remember that too, Paul," Gerry suddenly recalled, and he added, "He also said, 'God made time and plenty of it, but the human race developed a bad habit of trying to cram too much into each passing hour.'"

"Yes, correct, Gerry, and we are only beginning now, in this modern age, to realise, too late, that he was right in all his sayings," Paul endorsed.

"Yes, agreed Paul, so perhaps it's high time that we all slowed down and realised that we are blindly speeding to nowhere too fast."

"That's an inspired thought, Gerry, for one to think deeply about. Let's end on that note."

They shook hands in agreement before parting company with the phrase 'Until we meet again!'

Paul returned, content, to Maura and the dogs, the latter expressing their delight at his return by showering him with licks of affection when he embraced them. He related all the information to Maura concerning the site proceedings, and she responded by praising Gerry for the speed at which he was trying to finalise all the details relating to the purchase of the site and the construction of the bungalow, including applying for all the grants that were available and trying to have them increased as well.

"He certainly didn't forget the friendship of your boyhood days," she concluded.

"That's a fact, Maura. He was always a close friend ready to help in any way he could, and he has carried that quality into his adult years. I feel indebted to him, and I intend rewarding his efforts when the opportunity arises." Paul verbalised his intention.

"Are we swapping seats now, Paul?" Maura asked subserviently.

"No, Maura, you have only driven about a kilometre and a half and you need to drive on roads with which you are not familiar for the experience, so I suggest that you drive to the cottage site," he said, and then he added with a smile, "Please."

She understood the logic and agreed, also with a smile.

When they reached the site shortly after, Paul directed Maura into the opening leading to the field gate. There he climbed out and unlocked and opened wide the gate, then climbed back into the camper van to direct Maura past the ruin towards the end of the side garden, facing north. About ten metres before the perimeter hedgerow he instructed her to turn the camper van to face east and park it in that position, explaining to Maura that it was well clear of the construction area.

She understood the logical reasoning and agreed. Then she asked, "Is it OK parked as it is now, Paul, or do you want me to manoeuvre it a little more?"

"No, that's fine for me, Maura, unless you have a better idea."

Less than half an hour after their arrival on the site Paul's mobile sounded. It was Gerry informing him that the builder would be calling to see him before noon on the site to discuss the setting-up of a temporary flush toilet and a fresh-water supply tap for their convenience.

"Well, that is quite a pleasant surprise, Gerry. You lost no time sorting that out. Thanks a lot." Paul expressed his heartfelt thanks.

"Since it is a necessity, Paul, it needs special attention and I am happy to be in a position to be able to manipulate the means to fulfil your request. I hope it all goes well. I'll speak to you later."

Paul related the news to Maura, who was equally surprised and delighted.

"Your friend Gerry is a real doer, and not just a promiser," Maura commented.

"There's no doubt about that, Maura. He is a real friend," Paul endorsed.

The builder arrived just after eleven o'clock and was greeted by Paul accompanied by the dogs.

After introducing himself, Paul asked the builder his name and the builder duly obliged by answering, "Jack Kyley at your service, Paul."

He offered his hand and Paul responded with a handshake. Paul then asked the builder if it would be possible to have a temporary flush toilet close to the camper van.

The builder surveyed the terrain and said, "I've brought a Portaloo in the back of my pickup truck to tide you over for two or three days, Paul, until I excavate a sewer-pipe trench behind the ruin in the space between it and the proposed site of the new bungalow I've been informed about. It will be in a straight line between the south-facing gable end of the ruin and your camper van. Whilst I am engaged excavating the trench with a mechanical digger, a couple of my workmen will be dismantling the remains of the cottage, starting tomorrow morning, Tuesday. Mr Kyle – that is Gerry Kyle, who told me he is a close friend of yours, Mr Attanagh, Paul – informed me about the base of the cottage being left intact and in a suitable state on which to place a greenhouse."

"Yes, correct, Jack," Paul agreed, quite surprised, and he added, "Gerry is a man of action, there's no doubt about that. And yes, he is and always was a close friend, ever since our boyhood days. We spent years of our primary education in the same classes at the local CBS school that we attended."

"He is a good man to have as a friend, and he is well liked in the community," the builder, Jack, disclosed.

"From my knowledge of him, Jack, I can easily believe that; and he has a high degree of respect for you too," Paul revealed.

"Well, that's good to know, Paul. I didn't know you in the past, Paul, but I was acquainted with your father, Dominic. We worked together during our teenage years and we were good friends too. The tragic accident that abruptly ended his and your mother's lives and the lives of their two best friends, their neighbours, man and wife, twenty years ago now, really shook me badly, but obviously not to the same extent as it would have affected you and other members of your family. I still think of him at times and I still miss him." Jack recalled his past association with Paul's deceased father.

"Yes, Jack, it had a devastating effect on me and I found it really difficult to handle, even after going away to live with an uncle and aunt after the burial. But I never forgot the cause – alcohol and speed, the combination killers that ended their lives on impact with the innocent tree that fatal night. The lesson I learned from that tragedy was never drink and drive, and I never have, Jack," Paul concluded reflectively.

"Now that we are acquainted, Paul, where would you like me to put the Portaloo?" Jack asked.

"Just at the rear of the camper, if it's not too much trouble, Jack?"

"No trouble at all, Paul. I'll just drive over there and tip it into position. Just watch your dogs. I wouldn't want your best friends to get injured."

Paul called Bonzie and Fleurie to his side and took them to a safe area just beyond the Portaloo site. He kept the dogs close to him until the simple operation had been completed, which took no more than five minutes.

Maura then appeared from the camper van and Paul introduced her to the builder, saying, "This is Mr Jack Kyley, Maura – the man who is going to construct the bungalow. Before that he is going to remove the remnants of the cottage, starting tomorrow morning."

Maura offered her hand and, on its acceptance, said, "It's a pleasure to meet you, Mr Kyley."

The builder responded in kind, and said, "I admire the courage of both of you by buying this site and deciding to build a bungalow on it. Its recent history – that is, the tragic demise of the family that occupied the beautiful cottage until five years ago – is one of those mysteries that will not go to sleep. I think that's why nobody made an offer to buy the site until now. I suppose it was the fear of suspicion, or even superstition, but I'm glad both of you have invested in it. It is a beautiful setting and – who knows? – the truth might one day make itself known."

"Well, Jack, we believe we owe it to the tragic family to restore the gardens to their original beauty so that they can spiritually enjoy them with us again."

"Well now, Paul, that is a wholesome and thoughtful gesture. I will always be available with any helping hand you might need in your efforts, but for now I had better get moving as there is always something awaiting my attention. So until tomorrow I'll bid you both farewell, and I hope to see you both tomorrow," the builder ended.

"I will leave the field gate unlocked, Jack, just in case we are not here when you arrive. Bye for now."

A minute later, Paul and Maura were back to normal, with Paul bowling the rubber balls for the dogs to chase.

"He seems a pleasant and helpful man, Paul."

"Yes, he told me he was a good friend of my departed father's during their teenage years." Paul replied.

"Did he mention the tragedy that befell your parents?" Maura asked, interested.

"Yes, he did, Maura. The news of the fatal accident had a profound effect on him for a long time and he seemed to sorrowfully relive it."

"And you too, no doubt?" Maura suggested in a sympathetic voice.

"Well, yes, but only momentarily. I can't relive the past. It was just an abrupt, unexpected end to an unfolding future, and the aftershock was a lingering mental devastation that took a long time to dissipate and settle. Then you came tripping into my life like the accidental discovery of a rare and fragrant wild flower whose particles of fragrance infiltrated my very soul and mingled with it in a silent dance of love."

Maura stretched out her arms to him and he embraced her with loving tenderness.

She said in a flow of emotional teardrops, "That was a really beautiful description of our first meeting, and it was exactly how I felt too at that moment."

And they held each other in a warm embrace for a timeless moment until Bonzie and Fleurie stood upright on their hind legs and leaned their paws against Paul and Maura's bodies, holding their rubber balls in their mouths, waiting to be amused.

"Oh, sorry, girls," Paul responded, acknowledging their waiting presence.

He removed the rubber balls from their mouths and bowled them in turn across the grassy field for the dogs to chase, repeating this several times to relieve them of their excess energy. Then, on ending their exercise, he gave each a new hide chew to concentrate on.

CHAPTER TEN

Paul and Maura started working on what had been the end part of the cottage side garden, beyond and behind the damson tree, where the large rhubarb patch was still flourishing, but needed tidying up. It stretched across the back end of the side garden to the broken fencing that separated the garden from the field and where the camper van was parked from west to east. The broken fencing formed the north perimeter of the field. It was there in the rhubarb patch that Paul suggested beginning their restoration programme, well clear of the demolition of the cottage ruin, and the construction of the bungalow when the builder received notice to begin.

"What about that broken fencing, Paul? We will be doing something about it, won't we?" Maura asked, her curiosity compelling.

"Oh yes, of course. Haven't I mentioned the security fence that will be around the perimeter of the property when the bungalow is completed?" Paul asked.

"No, not before now, but you had a lot on your mind and you can't be expected to remember everything." Maura made the allowance.

"I meant to, Maura, but I suppose it's better late than never!"

He explained the plan for securing the finished dwelling with a metre-and-a-half-high galvanised fence, which would run alongside the field where the broken fence was at the moment, and that they would receive a council grant for the fencing too.

"Yes, I can see the logic. It's like a reward for securing the property against possible criminality. Everything seems to be clicking into place now," Maura enthused.

"Yes, that's right, Maura. We will just have to keep our fingers crossed and hope that all will continue to run smoothly, just as it has begun."

They began working on the rhubarb patch, removing nettles and brambles that had already established themselves among the rising rhubarb stalks.

That prompted Maura to remark, "We will have to get that baker out of hiding, buy some self-raising flour and start baking some rhubarb pies. We could have some stewed rhubarb as well with custard for dinner. That should stir nostalgic memories of not so long ago – agreed?" Maura asked.

"It already has, Maura. I have just been entertaining a memory of golden-brown rhubarb pie from last year, and I have even mentally savoured the taste," Paul nostalgically reminisced and Maura admitted that his description of the pie had affected her memory banks in similar fashion.

Bonzie and Fleurie sat on their outdoor rug, which Maura had remembered to spread near the rhubarb patch. There they settled, and they were busily demolishing their hide chews whilst Paul and Maura uprooted nettles and brambles and replanted them by the nearby hedgerow. Although the dogs were dedicated to the demolition of their chews, they were also aware of every move that Paul and Maura made. When Paul or Maura took the nettle and bramble roots to the hedgerow the dogs interrupted their chewing until they returned again.

It took the couple two hours to clear the rhubarb patch of the naturally invading plants, leaving the rhubarb stools free to spread and grow unhindered. They then took a break for lunch and, of course, the dogs joined them.

Maura placed some thick pork sausages in a frying pan, added fat and lit the Calor-gas radiant under the pan whilst Paul attended to the slicing and buttering of the bread and the brewing of the tea.

Bacon and eggs were fried too, and Maura also fried thick slices of bread for the dogs as they relished the fat. A hefty sandwich was prepared for each dog, containing bacon, sausage and fried egg, and these were placed in their bowls and presented to the dogs, who joyfully devoured the offerings. Paul and Maura then served themselves the same fare, but in more humanly presented form, and equally enjoyed their lunch. Rhubarb pie followed for Paul and Maura and apple pie for the dogs, and all was washed down with tea, the favoured drink of all four.

"Isn't it quaintly nostalgic to sit in the open like this, dining and listening to songbirds from near and far, and watch the colourful flowers bathing in the sunshine," Paul remarked in contented mood.

"Yes, it also evokes childhood days and fairy tales and playtime games of ring-a-ring o' roses and hopscotch – all the simple things of life," Maura fondly reminisced.

"And whipping tops along smooth tarmac surfaces, flicking marbles along the street gutter and gathering beech nuts and chestnuts in autumn from the tall trees – all fond memories that will never fade," Paul added.

"And now here we are in similar circumstances to those that existed in those days of not so long ago," Maura reminded him.

"Yes, true, Maura. I felt the same surge of excitement on being informed that we will be having a flush toilet installed this week plus a fresh-water tap – things that I took for granted during my early days. History can remind us that the past is not too far behind us as the future unfolds ahead of us and both are aspects of the same existence," Paul philosophised.

"Yes, how very true, Paul. It gives one the impression that we are towing the past behind us as we plod into the future. Would you agree?" Maura posed the question in inspired mood.

"Brilliant, Maura!" Paul congratulated her. "That is an inspirational description, Maura. The human race is a wandering band of scientific explorers, but the question remains: for what purpose?" Paul posed his question.

"Does there have to be a finality, Paul?" Maura asked, curious and intrigued.

"Yes, for the human race as we know it, Maura, but existence will continue without end because evolution has its ups and downs like the vagaries of life. Where life seems to struggle with extinction on one part of the planet it enjoys success on another part. Existence is a continuous balancing act and everything has to struggle to survive. Where one species dies, another one begins somewhere else. Every end has a new beginning."

"Do you have any idea what our new beginning might be, Paul?" Maura innocently enquired.

"I have a belief, Maura, that is too deep for you to understand in your present state of mental development. Your description of the human race was a brilliant breath of inspiration and is proof that you are tentatively probing into deep thought, but remember, Maura, not to delve too deeply too quickly. Always keep the French adage in mind and that will ensure that you progress by degrees," Paul advised, and he added, "So I think we ought to return to our present reality now: the temporary flush toilet and fresh-water tap that we are looking forward to before the week is out."

"Yes, we must keep our feet on the ground in the passing present. We have memories of the past and hopes for the future, and in between we have struggle. But as you have reminded me often, Paul, without struggle nothing would survive." Maura resorted to the simple truth.

"Yes, Maura, struggle is the foundation of our existence," Paul concluded.

The following morning (Tuesday) Paul, Maura and the dogs were up and about early. After breakfast all four wandered along the hedgerow surrounding the field for exercise and Paul bowled the rubber balls for the dogs to excitedly chase, but after an allotted time of chasing he pocketed the balls and let the dogs know that the energy-sapping chasing was ended. He knew from experience that the running was enough to activate the dogs' bowel movements, and so it proved because within minutes both dogs looked for a suitable patch of ground to relieve themselves.

Just after eight o'clock the builder's pickup truck arrived on-site. Paul had already unlocked and opened the field gate. The pickup, driven by one of the two workers in the cab, was parked close to the front of the cottage ruin, and minutes later a small version of a JCB excavator appeared, driven by the builder, Jack Kyley. It was initially parked behind the ruin until the builder marked out the proposed trench, assisted by one of his workers.

Paul and Maura, with the dogs, left around nine o'clock and had a few words with the builder before leaving to inform him that they would return before noon and that they would prepare some sandwiches for him and his workers at lunchtime unless they had other arrangements. The builder thanked them, but politely refused the offer, explaining that, just like himself, his workers always brought their own food supplies and flasks of tea or coffee; and besides, it wouldn't be fair, he said, to take advantage of the couple's generosity in their present circumstances. Nevertheless, he was grateful for their offer.

The two workers engaged in the demolition of the cottage ruin and reduced it to ground level by the end of the day. One reported to their boss, Jack Kyley, that the original doorstep of the cottage was intact and had the name, Valley Lane Cottage, carved into its face. The builder relayed the news to Paul and Maura and asked if they would like to have the step as a keepsake. They both agreed to the suggestion without hesitation.

"We will have it included in the wall of the bungalow in memory of the tragic family," Paul suggested.

And Maura agreed, saying, "I'm sure they will be spiritually pleased."

"Well, I congratulate you both. It's a fitting tribute and I will make sure your request is carried out," the builder assured them.

The sewer-pipe trench between the camper van and the original manhole, just beyond the south gable end of the cottage ruin, was excavated two-thirds of the distance the same day and was completed the following day. Whilst that job was in progress the two workmen removed the stones of the demolished ruin in their pickup – except the name-carved doorstep stone, which was safely housed in the camper van.

On the third morning (Thursday) the pickup arrived carrying the sewer pipes and some paving slabs to prepare a platform for the erection of a three-by-two-metre column to house the temporary flush toilet and a sink. Whilst the work was still in progress two water-company employees arrived to excavate a short trench to tap into the water main that ran beneath the edge of the lane, providing the water that would serve not only the flush toilet and sink, but the building site as well. The starter taps were positioned inside the field gate and to one side. All was completed that same day, except for the back-filling of the sewer-pipe trench, which the builder finished on Friday, much to the satisfaction of Paul and Maura. The bulk of the praise, of course, had to be given to Paul's friend Gerry, who got everything moving and prioritised every aspect of the work for the benefit of Paul and Maura. Gerry passed on all the details of the progress he managed to activate, including the granting of the application for the construction of the bungalow. He arrived on the site close to midday on the Friday, just as the builder was clearing up the back-filling of the sewer trench.

Paul greeted him and introduced his wife, Maura, who responded, "It's a pleasure to meet you, Mr Kyle. I feel as though I already know you from Paul's description of you."

"I'm pleased to meet you. My friends usually address me by the pet form of my name, and that is Gerry."

"If the speed of progress this week is anything to go by, it'll be no time before both of you and the dogs here will be settling in," Gerry remarked.

"The dogs are watching you, Gerry, waiting for your greeting before reacting," Paul pointed out, smiling.

"What are their names, Paul?" Gerry asked, eager to get to know them.

"Bonzie is the brown one and Fleurie is the black one." Paul identified them.

Gerry greeted both dogs: "Hello, Bonzie and Fleurie. What pretty names!"

The dogs instantly stepped forward, sat on their hind legs and offered a paw each to Gerry in greeting.

"Oh, how intelligent and cute you are!" Gerry responded, shaking their paws and fondling their heads, and the dogs somehow instinctively understood his nature and accepted him as a friend.

"You're a friend for life now, Gerry. They'll never forget you. That's how faithful dogs are." Paul characterised their best friends.

"I have always liked dogs, Paul, and I would like to have one, but I've never seriously thought about it. I would have to discuss it with Joan, and I'd be worried because if she agreed it would have to be a pedigree as our friends have pedigrees and arguments might follow, so I think it best to bide my time."

"Understood, Gerry. But still, if you ever do decide to become a dog owner, my advice is get two dogs, like we did – either two females, like ours here, or two males. Only get one of each if you want to try your hand at breeding dogs. The reason I advise getting two dogs instead of one is because dogs originate from wolves and the latter live in packs. A wolf wouldn't survive for long on its own, and likewise dogs don't like being left alone. So that's something to remember. The other thing is I wouldn't advise buying a pedigree dog – not because I dislike them, but simply because of careless and greedy breeders. Our two dogs are Border collies, the nearest to mongrels and the healthiest and most faithful companions. That's another fact to consider before taking the plunge, so to speak," Paul advised.

"I will certainly remember that advice, Paul. And if we do decide, I'll be asking for your assistance," Gerry replied with an appealing smile.

"I will always be ready to help you in any way possible, Gerry, so don't hesitate to ask," Paul assured him.

"I'll keep that in mind too, Paul." Then, suddenly deviating, he said, "Incidentally, there have been a number of enquiries about the site since you and Maura decided on buying it. One man even offered to pay above the agreed selling price, but I replied that the purchase price had been agreed and the contract signed and I said that was the end of the matter unless the buyer pulls out for some reason."

"Several enquiries, Gerry? I wonder if it was one person trying several times. Maybe someone doesn't want the site sold for some reason. What do you think, Gerry?" Paul asked.

"Yes, I see. I didn't think of that. But what could the reason be?" Gerry asked.

"That's what I have been trying to figure out since arriving home and learning about its recent past. And you, Maura – does it trouble you like it does Paul?" Gerry asked.

"What affects Paul rubs off on me, Gerry, since I am his wife. I imagine it would be the same with you and Joan." Maura made the comparison.

"Yes, I see your point, Maura. A married couple are like two halves of a whole – what bothers one bothers the other. I'll keep the mystery in mind. You know the old saying 'Many hands make light work', so we might work it out between us sooner or later unless one of you comes up with an inspired idea," Gerry ended.

The builder, Jack Kyley, approached them when he had completed levelling off the ground and silenced the engine of his excavator.

"Well done, Jack," Gerry greeted him, and added, "You'd be finished before Friday is out, you said, and you've kept your word."

"Well, yes, Gerry, but I did have two helpers and I have to share the credit with them. One has to be fair."

"Yes, indeed – that's thoughtful of you, Jack. Thanks to the three of you. I appreciate your efforts. Paul and Maura here will be likewise delighted." Gerry made his gratitude known, and Paul and Maura verbally applauded their efforts too.

"Jack, as soon as I am notified of clearance for the construction programme, I will give you the word to start. You can then liaise with the architect and pass on to him whatever design details and additions Paul and Maura might suggest to you in the meantime. And there we have to leave it for now. Are we all satisfied up to now?" Gerry concluded.

There were no complaints or questions as it was the cusp of the weekend.

Gerry rounded the day off by quoting old Farmer Cowling from their schooldays: "Let things rest till Monday."

They broke up with handshakes all round, including the dogs, and wished each other a pleasant weekend. Paul and Maura walked alongside the field hedgerow with the dogs, and Paul bowled the rubber balls several times to burn off any excess energy the dogs might have.

He then pocketed the balls again, saying, "That's it, girls – do a bit of scent investigating now. It will activate your instinctive brains."

Whether or not they understood, that is exactly what they did.

"Do you believe, Paul, that they understood what you said?" Maura asked, intrigued.

"No, Maura. That is what their instinct urges them to do in their daily existence. They have to build up an instinctive memory bank of scents that helps them in their daily survival quest, just like we build a memory bank of words and ideas that helps us in our daily struggle. I think it's as simple as that," Paul explained.

"Yes, I can see the logic in that, and I must bow to logic," Maura agreed. "Do you really believe what you suggested to Gerry – that you suspect the site enquiries were made by one person and not several?"

"Yes, I do, Maura. I believe there's only one person involved and that person is the same one who set the cottage ablaze and burned that innocent family to death. It's really frustrating to believe something strongly and yet not have a clue how to prove it. I feel really sorry for the traveller locked away for life in a prison cell. I personally believe that he is innocent. It must be torturous for him to be separated from his wife and child, and I hope and pray that he will not contemplate suicide."

"What makes you believe it's one person, Paul?" Maura asked, intrigued.

"Simply because there hasn't been one application to buy the site in the five years since the tragedy, and now that we have started the process of buying it there's suddenly a spate of buyers willing to jump on the bandwagon. That to me is illogical. That's why I believe it's a ploy by one person. His intention is to confuse. By making it seem as though the enquiries came from different people, he hopes to ensure any suspicion won't be focused in one place." Paul revealed his thoughts.

"Well, I understand your reasoning. Your theory is believable and therefore, in the absence of any other logical reason, I have to agree with you, Paul," Maura conceded.

"Well, I suggest we return now and have bacon-and-fried-egg sandwiches. What do you say, Maura?"

"Yes, I do feel a bit hungry. And what about you girls?" She addressed the dogs and they responded with a stifled bark that she took to mean yes.

CHAPTER ELEVEN

After their sandwiches and tea, enjoyed by all four, Paul and Maura relaxed on their collapsible chairs and Bonzie and Fleurie sat on their outdoor rug with a hide chew each to work on contentedly. The weather had remained fine for nearly two weeks and the forecast was for the fine spell to continue.

"Did you notice those primroses along the hedgerow bank – the way their flower stems seemed to leap out to greet the passing bees and butterflies and other flying insects with offerings of fallen grains and droplets of nectar for their pollinating endeavours?" Paul asked Maura as a belated afterthought.

"I am not adept yet at reading nature's language, as you are, Paul, but I did notice the quaintly beautiful primroses and now, as I recall, the flower stems did seem to stretch outwards. And on the wings of your explanation I can see the logic attached to the fact," Maura enlightened herself.

"It's just a morsel of knowledge to add to your growing bank of memories that constitute nature's encyclopaedia of life, Maura. And remember, there was a time when I didn't know about the facts either. We are all learners at varying levels of advancement, just as we were during our schooldays," Paul reminded her.

"Yes, all life forms are nature's encyclopaedia and our guidebook of knowledge. Am I right, Paul?" she asked excitedly.

"Exactly, Maura. And now that you have correctly interpreted your guide, you will never forget it," Paul assured her. And after a brief pause he remarked, "I've been wondering if there are any unusual or rare wild flowers growing in the field beyond the hedgerow on the other side of Valley Lane. That's the field wherein the imprisoned traveller had permission to allow his pony to graze the grass. I must get my binoculars and climb up into the branches of the damson tree. From there I will be able to scan the field and the surrounding area," he said.

"Do you think it's safe to do that, Paul?" Maura voiced her concern, adding, "I would imagine it's not as easy as it looks and I wouldn't want you suffering an accident."

"Oh, don't worry, Maura – I've been climbing trees since I was seven years old, and I'd become quite an expert at the art by my early teens," Paul assured her.

"I might sound a bit selfish, Paul, but I don't want to see you injured. I wouldn't know what to do should such an accident happen." Maura explained her fear.

"I will not fall, Maura. I am not a careless climber. In fact I am always aware of the necessity of being especially careful, so don't worry yourself needlessly." Paul convinced her of his confidence and ability.

When they had finished their break Paul entered the camper van and returned with a pair of binoculars. The dogs followed close behind him. He slung the strap of the binoculars round his neck and ambled to the damson tree with Maura. He sat on the ground and removed his work boots.

Then, looking at a worried Maura, he smiled, kissed her and said, "Don't worry – all will be fine. You'll see, Maura."

And he began to climb the tree, much to the surprise of the dogs, unable to follow. They whined and gave stifled barks of frustration.

Maura fondled their heads and tried to comfort them, saying, "It's OK, girls, he will be back down shortly."

They kept looking up at Paul and whining their frustration.

"It's OK, girls, I'll be down soon," Paul called down to the dogs to pacify them.

He used his binoculars to survey the field and countryside beyond the restricting Valley Lane hedgerow from the treetop, and relayed his findings down to Maura. After about ten minutes he carefully descended to ground level to be excitedly greeted by the dogs, delighted to have him back in their presence.

He embraced them and fondled their heads, and then put his boots on and laced them whilst informing Maura, "There's a farmhouse about 200 metres in a straight line west from the damson tree, and there's a hedgerow on the other side of the field bordering a lane leading to the farmhouse. There is also another gate near the corner on the western side of the field and quite close to the tarmac road. It is only about fifty metres from where the traveller, his wife and baby were camped on the verge. It strikes me as illogical," he remarked, still thinking it over.

"Why do you think it's illogical, Paul?" Maura's curiosity prompted her to ask.

"Because the gate on the other side of the field and close to its corner is only about fifty metres from where the traveller's caravan was parked, whereas the gate on this side of the field and, as you can see, just opposite us is about 250 metres from where their caravan was, going the long way round. Why make the man and his pony walk an extra 200 metres, mostly on the tarmac road, to gain access to the same field? Do you understand my reasoning, Maura?"

"Yes, I do now, I think. The traveller had to walk his pony 250 metres to access a field that could have been accessed within fifty metres of their caravan. Have I got that right, Paul?"

"That's it, Maura. It doesn't seem to make any sense. The farmer must have had a reason, but at the moment I can't think of one. Can you suggest something, Maura?"

"No, Paul, but I understand why it struck you as odd. One thing is certain though: as you said, the farmer must have had a reason regardless of how weird or illogical it might seem," Maura summed up.

"Yes, I agree, Maura. And another point worth mentioning: I can't remember having read anything about that anomaly in the report of the trial, can you?"

"No, there was absolutely nothing referring to it." Maura was certain, and she added, "Likewise, as you highlighted before, nothing was said about the empty paraffin container found in the traveller's caravan being more a sign of his innocence than of his guilt. It was portrayed as the condemning factor by the prosecuting counsel," she reminded him.

"If only we could discover some tangible clue to point us in the right direction," Paul remarked hopefully.

They both then concentrated on the garden and worked their way around gooseberry and blackcurrant bushes and raspberry canes, removing the crawling weeds and preparing clear patches for the planting of strawberries. They also prepared an area for the setting of onion bulbs using the remains of an old compost heap as fertiliser for the ground. After a couple of hours dedicated to their task, they called a halt and retreated to their chairs to relax over a mug of tea each with the remains of a bought rhubarb pie. The dogs had been equally busy, working on chews, and had fallen asleep in the process, but when Paul and Maura decided to cease their energy-sapping toil the dogs awoke as if by magic.

"I'm sure the dogs are somehow tuned into our thoughts, both awake and asleep." Paul repeated his previously stated belief.

"Yes, I'm beginning to believe the same. They are so precisely in unison with our thoughts," Maura agreed, and she added, "Perhaps they are tuned into the words 'tea', 'apple' and 'rhubarb pie'."

Paul laughed and verbalised his thoughts: "I feel sure of it. There's no doubt about that, Maura."

She placed a slice of apple pie in each of the dogs' bowls and cut them into smaller pieces and watched as they devoured their treats. When they had licked their bowls clean, she poured some cooled tea into them and they lapped the bowls dry of their favourite liquid.

"What are we having for dinner today, Maura? Have you decided or—?"

"Boiled potatoes in their jackets, boiled spring cabbage and boiled chicken is what I suggest, unless you prefer something else," Maura revealed.

"Oh, that will be fine with me. It's one of my favourite meals, as you know. Is that why you suggested it? Am I right?"

"Yes, Paul. I just thought you would be pleased with it, but don't forget it's one of my choice meals and the dogs love it as well; so it's a win-win-win meal to please all," she added with a smile.

"With the remaining bottle of Sauvignon Blanc we will celebrate over dinner the progress that has been made this week, including our efforts in the restoration of the gardens. It's not substantial, but it's a positive beginning. We will by degrees lovingly re-establish the garden in memory of the family who created it and then had their lives prematurely ended by an evil, callous, consciousless killer." Paul dedicated their effort.

"I'm sure not only will the spirits of the family appreciate our efforts, but they will appreciate the beautiful scene that we will recreate as well. Our sweat will be embodied in every aspect of the pulsating life forms that will express their joy in floral tribute and in their loud-appealing colourful fruits," Maura was inspired to add in a mental surge of delight.

"That was a poetical explosion of joy, Maura, that I will never forget. Congratulations!" Paul uttered in a burst of praise.

The pair ambled hand in hand, alongside the hedgerow that surrounded the field as a releasing conversational sightseeing exercise and to provide amusing, playful exercise for the dogs. Paul bowled the rubber balls for them to chase and thereby burn off some of their accumulated energy – an activity which they excitedly enjoyed – but he was careful, as always, not to overdo it and exhaust them.

"Do you still remember that day when we first met at the livestock market in Attanagh town not so very long ago, Maura, when you were with your mum? She was hoping to find a bantam with a clutch of chicks, but was disappointed," Paul recalled.

"Oh yes, I will never forget the day, Paul. It was the happiest day of my life up to that moment," she happily reminded him.

"It was mine too, Maura. I still recall the memory at times, and this time the following thought just crossed my mind: do you think your parents would like to live here?"

"I'm sure they would, given the chance. Why do you ask?"

"Because I was thinking of increasing the size of the bungalow. We could add an apartment to the end of the bungalow overlooking the garden and offer it to your mum and dad as a holiday and retirement home to use as they wish. I want you to make the offer to them and see what they think."

Maura looked at him dumbfounded for a timeless moment and slowly replied, "You want my parents to live here with us, Paul?"

"Yes, but only if they want to. Your father is restricted in his physical movements because of the arthritis he acquired after an accident earlier in his life, and your mother has to share his burden with him to some degree, so I just thought . . ."

"You not only want to share your dream with me, but with my parents as well," Maura interrupted, and she added, "I can hardly . . ."

She threw her arms around him and she was overcome by a surge of female emotion that broke her willpower and resulted in a flood of teardrops like a river overflowing its banks. He put his arms round her body and allowed her emotional flow to run its course until she regained her self-control.

Then she remarked, "Is there no end to your generosity, Paul? You would take on the burden of my mum and dad without even being asked?"

"Well, Maura, your mum and dad have always treated me well and I have always liked them, and neither one ever said or did anything to offend me in any way. With people like your parents I feel that I should show my caring and sharing qualities, and especially as they are your parents and are the cause of your existence, which has made my joy complete. And what more can I say?"

Maura spilled another flow of tears and then apologised for her weakness.

Paul was quick to defend her, saying, "There's nothing to apologise for. It's a natural relief for female emotion, helping to dissipate the pressure," he assured her.

"Have you seriously considered, Paul, that my parents might just accept your invitation without the slightest hesitation?" Maura asked him.

"I hope they will do just that so you can reunite with them. Would that please you?"

"Oh, I would be immensely overjoyed, but wouldn't you feel

disadvantaged at times, especially if you and I had a disagreement about something?"

"No, not really, Maura – not as long as we both work out a logical solution to the problem or, failing that, ask God's assistance in prayerful supplication. In other words, we should think how God might solve the dispute," Paul explained.

"Well now, I haven't considered the simplicity of that before, and I being a churchgoer too!" Maura confessed, and she added, "Nevertheless, I agree."

They both kissed the kiss of love whilst Bonzie and Fleurie sat on their haunches and quietly watched.

Dinner was enjoyed by all four participants, but Paul and Maura were careful when the dogs were fed chicken. The rule was no chicken bones were to be fed to the dogs because of their brittle nature and the danger of bone splinters causing internal injuries to their intestines. It meant extra work for Paul and Maura, stripping the edible flesh from the bones, but the good health of their best friends and the peace of mind of their masters were paramount; so the rule was always adhered to. The dogs' dinners, although essentially the same as Paul's and Maura's, were served in different ways. For the dogs the boiled potatoes and cabbage were chopped and fried in fat in a pot and then chopped. Boiled chicken was mixed in with it and then allowed to cool sufficiently before being served to the dogs in their bowls. Prepared in that fashion, the meal was lovingly devoured. A pan of fresh water was always provided for the dogs following their dinner. Tea was usually a breaktime treat.

Paul and Maura decided to have the wine later in the evening when listening to a radio programme.

An hour or so before dark Paul and Maura and the dogs went for an evening stroll alongside the field hedgerow, and, on returning, the four retreated into the camper van. Paul gave the dogs a new hide chew each, and they settled down on their rug to indulge in their favourite pastime. Maura searched on the portable radio for an interesting programme, such as a suitable documentary, but in the end she decided on a programme of relaxing classical music. Paul uncorked the Sauvignon Blanc and poured the wine into two glasses two-thirds full, and they both settled back in their seats to savour the soothing liquid.

"I would say this has an appealing bouquet and a taste to match, Maura. Would you agree?" Paul asked his thoughtful wife.

"Yes, it has a pleasant bouquet and an equally satisfying taste, and it seems to have a soothing effect on the digestive system." Maura stated her verdict.

"You are on course, Maura, to becoming a restricted connoisseur of wine," Paul remarked with a smile.

"Well, Paul, I must confess I have no wish to become an expert in wine tasting, but I do enjoy the relaxing effect of a favourite wine after a meal from time to time, such as now." Maura made her feelings known regarding alcohol.

"And glad I am to hear it, Maura, since I am of the same opinion. And I did say a *restricted* connoisseur, meaning restricted to a small number of quality wines that appeal to your taste and that you can savour now and then with a meal or after a meal whilst listening to a radio programme. You would agree to that, wouldn't you?"

"Alone with you like now, yes, of course – always, Paul. Your company is my joy."

"And now we have the pleasure of a toilet as well, and that's a real innovation."

"Yes, it most certainly is." And raising his glass he uttered, "And all thanks to Gerry and Jack Kyley and his team!"

They listened to several programmes during the evening and the dogs fell asleep over their chews, but were suddenly awake and alert when nature reminded them of their need for relief. Paul and Maura were likewise mentally activated. All four ventured out into the moonlit night with the moon playing peek-a-boo among the slowly passing wandering clouds. Maura visited their improvised flush toilet whilst Paul encouraged the dogs to fulfil their needs. There was another relief outing around midnight before retirement for the night. The peaceful silence of the darkness of the early morning was punctuated by the intermittent soft hoots of tawny owls, and the sawing calls of corncrakes from near and far helped to keep the night in tune, "And at the same time lulled the four occupants to sleep." But all was then suddenly and loudly interrupted by a staccato succession of barks from the dogs, which instantly woke Paul and Maura.

"What's wrong, Paul?" Maura asked nervously.

"I think maybe a stray pony or cow or even a donkey or a prowling fox. I'll take a look outside with the dogs," he said as he slid his feet into casual shoes and climbed out of the camper van through the cab passenger door.

But Bonzie and Fleurie slid past him and rushed towards the nearby hedgerow, barking and growling. Paul was close behind them and could just make out Bonzie's light-orange-brown coat in the slivers of moonlight that managed to faintly illuminate momentarily bits of the hedgerow. Fleurie was beside and slightly behind Bonzie. Paul guessed that Bonzie had hold of something by the way she was growling. He became worried then, as he didn't want either of the dogs injured by a possible kick from a large animal, so he called both dogs away from the source of danger. He was unable to identify what it was because it was hidden in the darkness of the hedgerow. The dogs didn't respond to his call, so he called again in a sharper tone of voice and they both obeyed. At that same moment the animal in the hedgerow broke free from the brambles, and whatever else was obstructing it, on the other side of the hedge.

The two dogs returned to his side, where he fondled their heads and praised them for their courageous efforts, and he then noticed Bonzie pawing at her mouth. He bent over and opened her mouth to check, and noticed something trapped between her teeth. He succeeded in getting a grip on the protruding part and, by gently manoeuvring it up and down, he prised it free from her teeth, for which he received a spate of thank-you licks on his forehead. He wasn't able to make out what the black substance was in the darkness, but he thought it might be a piece of animal harness and it might help in identifying the animal, so he placed it in his pyjama pocket, meaning to look at it again later.

He then detected a whiff of paraffin and checked the hedgerow where the incident took place, but darkness was his enemy so he decided to leave it until the following morning and have a look in the daylight. The darkness, however, didn't prevent configurations of thought from flashing through his mind, and he felt that whatever had become wedged in Bonzie's teeth would confirm or deny his suspicions. He called to Maura from outside that all was well, and told her that he would stay out for a few minutes to allow the dogs to calm down and relieve themselves if they needed to. Then, when he was certain that the source of the disturbance was gone, he went back inside the camper van with the dogs to relate the details to Maura.

"So, you don't know what was trapped in Bonzie's teeth, Paul?" Maura asked when he had finished.

"No, but I have it here in my pyjama pocket." And he retrieved it, saying, "You are about to see the object, as I am, for the first time."

He held it in the palm of his hand, by candlelight, and Paul realised instantly what it was.

He said to Maura, "That is a piece of the top part of a man's rubber boot, or wellington. Bonzie got her teeth into it and somehow bit it off. Its roughly half-moon shaped and about five centimetres wide and two centimetres deep."

"That means, Paul, that the dark shape was a man. What can have been his intention? Should we be worried?" she asked as fear cast its shadow over her mind.

Paul sat down beside her and placed an arm round her shoulders, deciding that he would have to share his suspicions with her.

"There's one other thing I have to tell you, Maura."

"Does it make the situation better or worse, Paul?" she nervously asked.

"Worse, I'm afraid, Maura. I can withhold it if you prefer."

She hesitated briefly and decided, "No, that would only make the worry worse, so I think it will be better if you tell me all."

"In the intruder's effort to escape Bonzie's hold on his rubber boot, he dropped something. I didn't see it, but I couldn't mistake the smell. It was the distinct odour of paraffin. I'll have to check it out in the morning's light and see what I can discover," Paul remarked, and he waited for Maura's response when she made the connection he believed she would make.

A long moment passed before the reality struck Maura and she exclaimed fearfully, "Oh, my God, Paul! He was intending to burn us to death like the family in the cottage. Isn't that so, Paul?"

"Yes, I believe now, Maura, that was his intention, but thanks to our beloved best friends here he failed."

Maura tearfully embraced Bonzie and Fleurie and thanked them repeatedly for their courageous intervention.

CHAPTER TWELVE

After a sleepless period following the disturbance during the early hours of Saturday morning, Paul, Maura and the dogs were up and about early. Paul and Maura felt a bit weary, but the dogs weren't burdened like the creative-thinking humans. Bonzie and Fleurie seemed unaffected by the ordeal. Paul took the precaution of putting the dogs on their double-chained lead before he and Maura accompanied them on an exercise walk round the field hedgerow. He explained to Maura about the possibility, but unlikelihood, of the potential killer arsonist having returned and thrown poisoned pieces of meat over the hedgerow in the vicinity of the camper van.

"I know that is unlikely to have happened so soon after the arson attempt, but one can never be certain how a killer without a conscience might act, Maura. I think he is getting desperate and will try again soon, but first he is going to make sure that the dogs don't interfere next time, so we have to remain alert – keep one step ahead so to speak."

"Oh yes, I understand, Paul. We must not let that happen. If they were harmed I would be truly heartbroken or worse than heartbroken. I can't imagine it, but I believe that is how you would be affected too."

"Yes, it would affect me really badly, Maura, but I don't want to think about that. Instead I want to concentrate and be aware of all the possibilities, and that is why I am going to buy a couple of muzzles for the dogs this morning – to prevent them from picking up any poisoned bait. But first we are going directly to the local police station, where I hope I will have a serious conversation with the police chief."

"I have just been thinking, Paul – whoever wanted to burn us to death must be the same person who burned the cottage family to death five years ago, and that means for certain that the traveller is innocent."

"That's right, Maura, and if we, including the police, can tempt the guilty person to try again by keeping this morning's attempt secret for a few days, we might be able to catch him in the act and that innocent man languishing in prison will be exonerated, released and compensated for having been wrongly imprisoned." After a short pause, Paul asked, "Are you having second thoughts about settling here now, Maura? If you are and you want to change your mind, we can still leave it all behind us. I mean that, Maura. I wouldn't want you to be a bag of nerves living here."

"I know you care about me, Paul, and the dogs, and this potentially beautiful site, and I am of the same nature. So I say let's struggle on and believe that we will win."

And they embraced and kissed.

After breakfast and before leaving to drive to Attanagh, Paul asked Maura to stay in the camper van with the dogs whilst he checked out something that was on his mind.

"I will only be a few minutes, Maura." He kissed her and embraced the dogs before she could agree or disagree, and he said, "I should have waited until you answered, but I knew you would say it was OK."

He smiled and slipped out of the driving seat and walked across the garden, past the rhubarb patch, underneath the damson tree, close to the perimeter hedgerow and on to Valley Lane close to the gate that led into the field next to the cottage garden. He climbed over the gate and checked a bramble bush in the corner of the field close to the gate. Standing there and abandoned was a rusty old spider-like hay gatherer. It was mostly covered by brambles, but its hollow interior was still mostly free of the brambles and that was where he was hoping to discover evidence that verified his theory. As he approached, he detected the odour of paraffin and felt a surge of positivity. He peered into the hollow interior and his eyes fell on a sack half filled with pieces of paraffin-saturated sacking. He realised then that it was the burden of the sack that had delayed the arsonist's quick escape in the darkness earlier that morning. He was also sure that the arsonist felt certain that he had escaped undetected and his plan had been merely delayed – hence the presence of the hidden sack.

'He intends to try again,' Paul thought to himself, 'and he is unaware that he dropped a piece of the paraffin-soaked sacking in the hedgerow when he was disturbed by the dogs earlier this morning. Advantage us! I must find that piece of sacking.'

He walked along the hedgerow to the spot behind the camper van and noticed the disturbed and damaged brambles, and almost instantly he noticed the piece of paraffin-soaked sacking attached to a thorny bramble.

"Success!" he exclaimed quietly. "We have got to catch him in the act."

He returned to Maura and the dogs with the piece of sacking, and the dogs greeted him enthusiastically as though he had been missing for an age.

"Were you satisfied with your check, Paul?" Maura asked with interest.

"Yes, and this is confirmation of my suspicion," he replied, opening a plastic shopping bag and exposing the piece of sacking smelling of paraffin. He didn't share his other find with her because of her nervous nature. "I have formulated a plan that I hope the police will agree with, but I can't discuss it with you now. I will share it with you at an appropriate time. Is that OK with you, Maura?" he asked.

"Yes, whatever you say, Paul. I trust you implicitly," Maura assured him.

Paul had unlocked the field gate on his way back, and he locked it again after steering the camper van through the opening. He then turned right instead of the usual left, and Maura reminded him of his possible mistake.

"Sorry, Maura – I should have told you in advance, but I've got so much going on in my mind that I am bound to overlook some things. I'm going this way to call at a farmhouse about 200 metres along Valley Lane, just next to a junction. I want to ask the farmer if he has any manure for sale for our garden project. If so, it's better to order a couple of trailer loads in advance so that it's on site when we need to use it," Paul explained.

"Yes, that's a good idea, Paul. I hadn't given it much thought, but then gardening is a responsibility of the husband, just like housework, cooking, washing and ironing are responsibilities of the wife," Maura reminded herself.

"Yes, I see what you mean, Maura. A man's main responsibility is outside the home, and a woman's is mainly inside the home. Agreed!" Paul said.

"Yes, I suppose that sums it up more or less," Maura conceded.

The opening leading into the spacious farmyard was about twenty-five metres from a junction. The large farmhouse commanded the left-hand side of the yard. A tractor and trailer were parked on the right and pointed towards the opening. Paul guided the camper van far enough forward so as not to obstruct the tractor's departure. As he brought the camper van to a halt and turned the engine off he noticed two men in conversation by a gate close to the end of the yard.

Paul engaged Maura with his childhood memories of the farm: "The residents will have changed, but the old farmhouse is just as I remember it. The only thing missing is the dogs and I'm wondering why," he mused.

"Maybe they're in the house," Maura suggested.

"No, Maura, they would be free to wander round the farmyard and announce the arrival of visitors with a staccato chorus of barks."

The two men ended their conversation and parted company. The younger one of the two came towards the camper van and passed. He was wearing a crinkled hat on his ginger-haired head and an arrogant, unfriendly expression on his face. As he walked past he was looking straight ahead towards the tractor. Paul watched him in the wing mirror of the camper van, and as he raised his right leg to climb up on to the tractor seat he noticed a distinct half-moon-shaped piece missing off the top back rim of his rubber boot. Paul struggled to control the sudden surge of revelation.

"The arsonist and murderer of the cottage family members! What a stroke of luck!" he quietly exclaimed to himself.

He stifled the urge to share the fact with Maura because he wasn't sure how she would react and it was best to remain calm. He climbed out of the cab at the approach of another man, who he thought must be the farmer. Paul greeted him in a friendly, easy manner and identified himself and his status as the owner of the nearly cottage-ruin site. He said why he had called.

"Oh, so you are the new owner of the site. I suppose you intend to settle there after you have had a house built, and no doubt you will raise a family," the farmer suggested.

"Yes, that's about the size of it. . . . I neglected to ask your name."

"Crowe – Frank Crowe – and this is my farmhouse, complete with wife, two sons and two daughters. At the moment my wife and eldest daughter are in town shopping. My youngest daughter is at the moment attending to household duties allotted to her by her mother. My two sons, still unmarried, are out in the fields preparing them for spring sowing. And that completes the picture," the farmer explained.

"Well, I must say that's a family neatly and precisely described, Mr Crowe. That's my wife, Maura, with our two dogs in the camper van. I hope you don't mind my remarking on it, but you didn't mention anything about dogs."

"No, I didn't. I suppose that's because I don't include dogs as family members."

"So you do have dogs, then, I expect?" Paul asked.

"Oh yes, we have two sheepdogs. They are both out in the fields with my sons."

"I am glad to hear that. I have never known a farm without a dog or two."

"You said your name was Paul Attanagh?" The farmer addressed Paul and invited the latter to address him as Frank, adding, "There's no need for formalities when socialising, as I am sure you agree, Paul?"

"Yes, Frank, that's exactly the way I like it," Paul responded.

"Did you recognise that man who just left, Paul?" the farmer asked; and on receiving a negative he said, "He is your nearest neighbour. He is also a farmer and lives about 200 metres as the crow flies west of the cottage ruin. He lives in the house alone at the moment. His name is Steve Rangton. His father died about three years ago and his mother had to be admitted to a nursing home just over a year ago with arthritic problems. He is a strange kind of man – not very sociable – and he has become interested in my daughter, my eldest child. He has actually proposed marriage to her once already, but she being of a kind nature and mentally, religiously restricted, so to speak, said she needed time to think about it since marriage is a lifelong commitment, and I am not advising her one way or the other," the farmer stated.

"Well, I am inclined to agree with your daughter, Frank. She knows to keep her feet on the ground and think deeply about the consequences of her decision. She has what I would describe as a sagacious mentality and therefore is a wise lady." Paul praised the farmer's daughter.

"Oh, I'm sure she will be mighty glad to hear that, Paul," the farmer happily concluded.

"I had better not forget the reason I called, Frank: I was wondering if you had any manure for sale. My wife and I are already in the act of mastering the gardens that the tragic cottage family created when they lived there. We want to replant the gardens in memory of them and for our own pleasure as well."

"Well, that's very thoughtful of you, Paul. And yes, I have a large pile of manure behind that barn on the south side of the farmyard. You can take all you need to complete your good deed, and it's free," the farmer informed him, adding, "I'll put a trailer beside the pile today or tomorrow. You will have to load it by hand, if you can do that?"

"Oh yes, I can do that, Frank. I feel that I should pay you since you and your sons will have had to pile it up there; and if you won't accept cash, perhaps I could pay you in kind somehow," Paul offered with feeling.

"I'll keep that in mind, Paul, and I will call upon your help if I need it. But in the meantime help yourself to the manure, and I will deliver it with the tractor when the trailer is loaded," the farmer stated.

They parted company with a friendly handshake.

When Paul returned to the camper van and climbed into the cab he was again excitedly welcomed by the dogs, and Maura asked him about the manure.

After he informed her of the farmer's reply, Maura commented, "That was generous of him. He sounds like a good neighbour to have, and he looks friendly too."

"Yes, he is, Maura. I could tell that by the conversation we had. That unfriendly-looking character that left just after we arrived is the farmer who gave the traveller permission for the latter's pony to graze in the field across from the cottage." Paul also told Maura about the farmer's status – a single man who had already proposed marriage once to the older of the other farmer's two daughters. "But she hasn't accepted as it is too sudden and she needs time to think before committing herself to marriage."

"Well, all I can say to that is if looks are anything to go by she ought to take a long time over her thinking. He looks like a distinctly unsociable character and I'm glad I am not in her shoes." Maura voiced her honest opinion.

"Yes, I agree, Maura. And just to boost your ego, her father made a similar remark about his possible future son-in-law, but he was adamant about not interfering with his daughter's decision whichever way she chose. That's the way with the farming community. Land, property and wealth discreetly displace God at the top of the ladder of life regardless of how it was attained, and such people try to convince themselves and others that they are representatives of God and are deserving of their temporary status in life. So let sleeping dogs lie, as the saying goes, and allow God to sort it out, which He will do in His own mysterious way," Paul philosophised.

On driving out of the farmyard, Paul turned right and then almost immediately turned right again at the junction.

He stopped on the verge and turned off the engine, and before climbing out of the cab he said to Maura, "Slide over, Maura, and drive, and I'll occupy the passenger seat. You still have quite a bit to learn about the local roads – and what better way!"

Maura accepted the suggestion as an honour. She was always pleased when Paul placed trust in her ability.

When they got moving, she smiled and said, "Do you like spoiling me, Paul?"

"No, my love. I don't ask you to drive just to spoil you, although I know you like to drive sometimes. I am a carer and a sharer and I know that by sharing the driving with you I am helping you to become more accustomed to the local roads. In that way you'll become more confident in your own ability and more efficient in making decisions. This will be especially useful when you have to drive alone. These are my reasons for encouraging you to sit behind the driving wheel at times. It's to boost your experience. But remember, Maura, never offer a lift to a man on the road when driving alone. Too many men interpret that as a sign of weakness in a woman," Paul advised.

"I'll remember that, Paul, and I want you to know that it makes me feel good to know that you trust me behind the wheel."

"Yes, I know you appreciate being trusted, Maura. I can feel the pheromone vibes that pass between us."

"That's a new one to me, Paul – at least, I can't remember having heard that expression before," Maura commented.

"I'll explain it to you sometime, Maura, but now is not the time," he concluded.

"OK, I'll be patient," she conceded with a smile.

A few minutes later they arrived in Attanagh town and Paul directed Maura to the police station, where she parked the camper van close to the entrance.

He then suggested a stroll round the perimeter for the dogs' benefit, and invited Maura to join them, saying, "It will exercise your legs and improve your circulation."

Maura responded positively, and Paul attached the lead chains to the dogs' collars.

During their ten-minute stroll, punctuated by momentary stops for the dogs' sake, Paul reminded Maura that what happened in the early hours of the morning had to remain secret except where the police were concerned. "Is that understood?" he asked.

"Whatever you say, Paul, I will abide by, I swear." And she held her hand aloft as confirmation.

On returning to the camper van, he undid the lead chains and the dogs climbed in and passed through the open half-door dividing the cab and the rear of the camper van.

He gave each a new hide chew each, kissed Maura and embraced the dogs, saying, "I'll remember to be as quick as possible. Don't forget to lock the doors."

Inside the police station he went directly to the enquiry desk and asked the desk officer if it was possible to speak to the chief of police. "It's urgent," he added.

"Your name, sir?" the desk officer asked, as was normal practice.

"Paul Attanagh," Paul replied.

"And the nature of your enquiry, Mr Attanagh?"

"Attempted murder," Paul replied.

The officer looked surprised and asked, "Who was the intended victim, sir?"

"My wife and I and our two dogs were the intended victims, officer."

"Have any of you suffered any injuries as a result, Mr Attanagh?"

"Thanks to our two dogs, no, but the threat is still alive."

"Do you know who the perpetrator or perpetrators were, sir?"

"No, and that is why I want to speak to the chief of police. Can you inform him or not of my request, officer?"

"He isn't here at the moment, but I will try and contact him and pass this information on to him. Can you call back later, sir?"

"Well, my wife and two dogs are awaiting my return in my vehicle outside in the car park. We have some shopping to do; so yes, I can call back later and I would like you to remind the police chief, if appropriate, that this meeting is of vital importance. It is connected to a serious crime that took place in the area some years ago. I will leave a phone number the chief can call to obtain a character reference of myself. When he dials this number, he should ask to speak to Detective Chief Inspector Gammon. That should simplify things. My mobile number is . . ." He wrote it out on a notebook page and passed it to the officer, saying, "Just in case you should contact the chief of police sooner than expected. I'll leave things with you now, officer, and I hope all goes well. Bye for now."

"Bye sir," the officer responded.

Paul returned to Maura and the dogs to be excitedly greeted by the latter and with a smile from Maura, who remarked, "That didn't take long, Paul. I was—"

"There is only the desk officer on duty at the moment," Paul interrupted her, and he continued: "Through him I have asked for an emergency recall. I expect to receive a phone call on my mobile sometime, to tell me when a meeting can be arranged." And, deviating, he asked, "When did you last speak to your parents on the phone, Maura?"

"Last Tuesday, when you were engaged in conversation with the builder, Mr Kyley. I intend calling my mum again today."

"Good – so all is going reasonably well at the moment. We will take the dogs for a ramble where I take them when you are attending church on Sunday mornings, and then we can do a little shopping. In case I should happen to forget, we need to buy two muzzles for the dogs."

"I'll make sure you don't forget, Paul. If you don't mind my saying, you seem to be more confident now than you were this morning – or, more precisely, since you spoke to the farmer, Mr Crowe, earlier. Am I right?"

He looked at her, smiled and replied, "You are right, Maura, but I can't share it with you now. It's what the police would call 'classified information', and if it were revealed it could easily jeopardise the plan I am formulating. But, just like the checks I made before we left this morning, I will share them with you at the appropriate time. For now, I have to concentrate on your safety and well-being, and likewise the safety and well-being of the dogs. Plus one other person is now included in the equation as well, and I can't name that person either. Do you trust me, Maura?"

"Yes, of course – fully. But what about yourself? You must be putting yourself in danger too, and who is going to look out for you?" Maura asked, concerned.

"My spiritual self will be my guide, Maura, and I believe that I have the advantage now over the murderer of the cottage family and would-be killer of us and the dogs. I also believe there is only one person involved, and that should make him more desperate."

"Well, have you any idea yet why he killed the family in the cottage fire and why he also wants to kill us and the dogs?" Maura asked in hope.

"No, not yet, Maura, but I feel sure we will find out. He cold-bloodedly murdered that innocent family in the cottage without any apparent reason, and he must have wallowed in his success as an innocent man was condemned to life imprisonment for the evil act. And this very morning he was intent on repeating the deed with our demise and without even being acquainted with us, which can only mean that he is either a lunatic hate killer or he knows something about the cottage site that he doesn't want anyone else to know about. That is the crux of the mystery."

"If the site is so important to him, why didn't he offer to buy it? Then he could have kept the secret to himself without fear of anyone finding out." Maura posed the question.

"Yes, that's an interesting question, Maura, and deserves a degree of deep thought. Since it has been derelict for five years, why has it suddenly become so important to one particular person? And why didn't that same person make an attempt to purchase the site? But that begs the question, then, why did the killer burn to death the cottage family in their home without any apparent reason unless he is insane and fascinated by fire. However, I still believe the reason for the killing of the cottage family and the reason he attempted to end our existence in like manner are the same. Whatever it might be, the mystery remains," Paul concluded.

He then directed Maura where to drive to exercise the dogs, and that was the wild area he used to explore in his boyhood days. It was only a few minutes away.

After parking the camper van the four ambled along the bank of a meandering stream admiring trout and minnows swimming against the flow of the central dancing current in rhythmic pulsation, but remaining in the same place. In the young meadows on the other side of the stream grasses were struggling to attain their appointed height by June together with the wild flowers that punctuated the mass of grass stems. The dogs detected new scents to investigate and perhaps matched other scents with those already stored in their instinctive memories.

On their return to the camper van, Maura drove to the supermarket they had visited the previous day and Paul went in first to search for muzzles. He succeeded in his quest, returning at once so that Maura could enter and shop at her leisure.

Paul fondled the dogs' heads whilst praising both for their alertness and courage during the dark early hours of the same morning. "I'll never forget your defence of Maura and me – and you, Bonzie, managed to get the evidence that has already identified the would-be killer. If only you could feel the huge surge of relief that I felt when I noticed that half-moon-shaped space on the killer's rubber boot top earlier in the Crowe farmyard. I had to struggle with my mentality to keep my emotions under control. And how grateful I am to you two wondrous, faithful friends for the preservation of all four of our lives! I owe you—"

He was interrupted by the ringtone of his mobile phone and retrieved it from his pocket.

He pressed the 'speak' button and said, "Hello. Paul Attanagh speaking."

The desk officer at the police station answered and informed Paul that he had managed to contact the police inspector, and a meeting with him and his investigative team of detectives had been arranged at the police station for twelve o'clock, noon, if that was suitable. Paul agreed, saying he would be there, but maybe a little late as his wife was, at that moment, in a supermarket shopping. He thanked the officer for his help.

"You are welcome, Mr Attanagh. It's all part of the job, and I am glad that I was able to help. I'll see you later, then, sir," the officer ended.

Maura returned a few minutes later and he related the news to her.

"Noon? That's only a little more than thirty minutes away," she reminded him.

"Yes, but it's time enough for all four of us to have some tea and a couple of ginger nuts. I'll get the small portable gas stove into action at the back of the camper, and our tea will be ready in minutes."

"It was, and after the dogs' tea was cooled by swirling it round in their bowls, and set down for them, Paul fed them a couple of ginger nuts each. They crunched and swallowed them and washed them down by lapping every drop of their tea, just as Paul and Maura were doing.

It was only a couple of hundred metres to the police station, where they arrived at eleven fifty. Maura parked the camper van close to the entrance.

Paul embraced and kissed her and embraced the dogs in turn and said to Maura, "I will keep you in mind while I'm in there, and if I think it's going to carry on a bit I will call for a ten-minute break after every fifteen minutes and I'll spend it with you and the dogs out here. Is that all right with you, Maura?" he asked.

"I can't imagine anyone being fairer than that, Paul. Good luck with your discussion."

CHAPTER THIRTEEN

Paul was greeted by the same desk officer when he entered the police station, and the officer then directed him to a door in a nearly corridor. After knocking on the door once, an invitation to enter was heard and the officer opened the door.

He entered and introduced Paul, saying, "This is Mr Paul Attanagh, Inspector – the man you are expecting."

The officer then retreated through the open door, slightly smiling at Paul, and closed the door behind him.

"Welcome, Mr Attanagh. I am Inspector Conroy," the Inspector introduced himself. He then introduced his three colleagues in turn: "This is Detective Sergeant Griffin, Detective Green and Detective Carey, who, as you can see, is a lady." The Inspector completed the introductions with a smile.

"Yes, there's no mistaking the lady, Inspector, and I say that with the highest degree of respect, ma'am," Paul remarked with a smile. After formally greeting all four, he anticipatingly said, "I expect you are all eagerly waiting to hear my explanation of the claim of attempted murder that I made earlier, and if you are ready I will begin."

The Inspector nodded his agreement and said, "We are all ears, Mr Attanagh. Please begin.

Paul started by explaining that he, his wife and two dogs were living in a camper van on the cottage-ruin site on Valley Lane, about three kilometres from Attanagh town. Paul told them he and Maura were in the process of buying the site, on which they intended having a bungalow built as soon as possible.

"I expect you are familiar with the recent tragic history of the site, even if you were not involved in its investigation," Paul said.

"Of the four of us, only Detective Sergeant Griffin was involved in that investigation, but we are all aware of the horrendous crime and the consequences, Mr—"

"Sorry for the interruption, Inspector, but I would prefer if all of you address me as Paul. I feel more at ease with that form of address,"

"Fine, Paul. We had heard that a new resident was camped on the cottage-ruin site and now we know who it is," the Inspector revealed.

Paul then described what had happened on the site during the early hours of that same morning – an occurrence that he believed would have resulted in a carbon copy of the inferno that wiped out the innocent family and destroyed the cottage five years previously but for their two alert dogs.

They raised the alarm with loud staccato barks – something the would-be assassin seemingly hadn't anticipated happening – and that was what saved us from being cremated in the early hours of this morning."

Before any of them could comment, Paul deviated by informing them that he had to check on his wife outside in the camper van "as I promised her I would. I hope you will excuse me for ten minutes, Inspector. The ordeal early this morning has unnerved her a bit."

"That's understood, Paul. We will discuss your ordeal among ourselves here until you return," the Inspector readily agreed.

On his way out Paul spoke briefly to the desk officer and told him he couldn't divulge anything about the attempted murder charge he made earlier as it came under the heading of 'classified information'. "Oh, I understand, Mr . . ."

"Just address me as Paul, as my friends and colleagues do. I'm just going to check on my wife and dogs."

When Paul rejoined Maura and the dogs she was talking to the latter like she would to children and fondling their heads, and when he climbed into the passenger seat the dogs welcomed him with joyful whines and affectionate licks.

"Have you finished now, Paul?" Maura asked, hoping he had.

"No, Maura. I have just related to them what happened in the early hours of this morning and I left them to discuss our experience among themselves. I know you are a bit nervous now about being alone, so I did mention that fact and they understand the necessity to check on you at regular intervals. I have a plan and I am going to suggest it to the police inspectors, but first I am going to explain it to you. I implore you to agree to it and try and see the logic in it, Maura. OK?"

"Well, what is it, Paul?" she asked nervously.

"I want you to phone your mum when I return to the police, and tell them that we will be visiting them today; when we do, I want you and the dogs to stay with your parents overnight, and possibly two nights. In the meantime the police, with my help, will hopefully catch the evildoer in the act, and that should give them enough evidence to hold him in custody and question him about his attempted murder and about the cottage-family murder five years ago too. The police will also have the opportunity to question the suspect about his motive for the murder of this innocent family and the attempted murder of us. What do you say, Maura?" Paul asked.

"You want me to stay with my mum and dad together with the dogs? And what are you going to do then, Paul?" she asked, a bit confused.

"I'll go back to the cottage-ruin site, where we were camped, and I hope, with the help of the police, to apprehend the potential killer."

"You mean that you are going to use yourself as bait to try and trap the killer in the act – a man you don't know anything about. You don't know him personally and you will be alone in the camper van if he should attempt to repeat what he intended to do this morning. What if you should fail and . . . do you realise how that would affect me and the dogs?" she reminded Paul with a surge of fear that generated a spate of tears.

"That won't happen, Maura, I can promise you that. It's for your safety and the safety of the dogs that I've decided on this plan of action," he tried to reassure her.

"But how can you be so sure that it won't end in failure? If it does and you die, then the dogs and I will die as well because there will be nothing left to live for." And she wept.

"I have no intention of dying, Maura. I want to live and enjoy life with you and the dogs and whatever babies we generate. But we can't be content living under this threat indefinitely, so please do as I ask. It's all for our future happiness together."

"You seem confident, Paul, but I am afraid of losing you," she tearfully remarked.

"I understand how you feel, Maura." And after a brief pause Paul suggested, "Let's take the dogs for a quick ramble round the car park on their lead in case they need to relieve themselves."

He connected the lead chains to their collars as they sat closely, and they clambered after him as he climbed out of the cab. Maura eased herself out of the driving seat, and they walked slowly round the perimeter of the car park a couple of times. Paul asked Maura if she needed to use the toilet and she decided she did.

Paul and she went directly to the entrance of the police station, opened the door and called out to the desk officer, "Are there ladies' toilets close by, officer?"

"Yes, just here on the left, Paul," he replied, gesturing with a hand.

"This is my wife, officer, and these are our two dogs and best friends," Paul informed him.

"Pleased to meet you, ma'am. And as for the dogs, there is nothing to compare with their bonding loyalty," the officer remarked.

Maura acknowledged the greeting and tried to smile, and when she entered the toilet area Paul said in a lower tone of voice, "She suffered a traumatic experience during the early hours of this morning and hasn't yet got over it, hence her timidity."

"Oh yes, I understand, Paul. She does look a little upset," the officer replied.

When Maura returned, the officer addressed her: "If you have any further need of assistance don't hesitate to ask, ma'am."

"Thank you, officer. That's very reassuring of you," Maura acknowledged.

When they returned to the camper van Paul led the dogs in through the passenger side and disconnected the lead chains from their collars.

He sat fondling their heads as he spoke to Maura, saying, "I am going to tell you something, Maura, that I hope will convince you of the soundness of my plan. This is information that I haven't yet shared with the police, and it must not be divulged to anyone – not even your parents. Is that understood, Maura?"

"I swear, Paul, that I will not repeat it to any other person. You have my word of honour." Maura swore to maintain her silence.

"I have worked out who the killer is and I know his name," Paul stated.

Maura looked at him, stunned, and slowly said, "You know who he is, Paul? You know the evil killer?" And after recovering from the shock she asked, "Well, why haven't you told the police and had him arrested, then?"

"Because I know there isn't enough evidence yet for the police to intervene and arrest and imprison him. That's the reason, Maura, and it's the same reason why I want you and the dogs to go to your parents' home for one or maybe two nights to keep you and the dogs safe. I have a feeling that he will try again if the opportunity is available, first by trying to silence the dogs and then by repeating his arson evil because he feels his secret is in danger of being discovered. I can't liaise with the police, watch out for you and the dogs and plan to catch the killer in the act all at the same time. Do you understand, Maura?"

"I don't like leaving you to face all the danger alone, Paul. I feel like I am abandoning you. It's that feeling of guilt that is crucifying."

"Yes, I can imagine how you feel, Maura, but you have to try and see the problem from my point of view. You are not abandoning me, but helping me and the police to bring the story of this five-year-old murder atrocity to a conclusion and release the innocent traveller from his lifetime prison sentence," Paul explained.

Maura was silent for a prolonged moment, after which she said tearfully, "OK, Paul, I agree, but reluctantly."

"Good!" he exclaimed with relief. "I believed you would see the logic, Maura, and now that I have your backing I feel successful already. We will speak again when I have finished with the police." He reached over, embraced her and kissed her, saying, "Dry up your tears, my love. I'll be as quick as possible." And addressing the dogs whilst embracing them, he said, "Our wonderful canine ladies, do comfort Maura." He kissed Maura again before leaving the three, saying, "Don't forget to lock the doors."

Then he returned to rejoin the police team.

"So, Paul, you've got your two dogs to thank for all four of your lives, but you didn't actually see any person," Inspector Conroy suggested to Paul.

"Yes, that's correct, Inspector, but I've got a piece of evidence that proves it was a human being and most likely a male. And as I am here not only as an intended murder victim, like my wife and two dogs outside, but also in a voluntary advisory role, I suggest that the early morning incident be treated as classified information for the time being. I have a gut feeling that the perpetrator of the failed murder attempt is intent on carrying out his evil intention to burn us to death, just as he did the innocent family in the cottage inferno five years ago," Paul stated with conviction.

"You believe it was the same person, Paul, that carried out that atrocity?" Detective Sergeant Griffin asked with interest.

"Yes, Sergeant Griffin, and, judging by my reading of the trial report recently, the exact same method of execution was to be used for the extermination of my wife and me and our two dogs. Complete destruction!"

"Well, I must confess I always had my doubts about the guilt of the traveller, but there was no evidence to prove otherwise." The Sergeant explained his opinion.

"You are implying, Paul, that the man condemned to life imprisonment for that horrendous crime is innocent?" the lady detective, Karen Carey, asked, impressed.

"Yes, exactly that, Detective. I believe arson was intended to bring about our demise in the early hours of this morning in a repeat of the cottage inferno of five years ago by the same killer," Paul stated. "The belief was triggered, Detective, by my detecting the odour of paraffin in the hedgerow early this morning. I called the dogs off whatever it was they were barking and growling at in the dark as I was afraid of them being kicked and injured by a donkey, a pony or even a cow. But then the odour instantly reminded me of the cottage tragedy I had read about. So at daylight I returned to the hedgerow and the paraffin odour still lingered. I looked around and found a piece of sacking caught in bramble thorns, and I thought where there was one piece there was likely to be more. So I wandered along the hedgerow, sniffing, and discovered the half-sackful of paraffin-soaked pieces of sacking. It was as simple as that, Detective. I then used my imagination and thought how I would transport the half-sackful of fuel, and I decided that I would use a bicycle and place the sack in the central area of the cycle, between the crossbar and the bottom bracket and push it along – not in daylight on roads or lanes, but in the dark along verges and behind hedgerows to avoid being seen. It seems the man is familiar with the landscape, which means he is probably a local resident. I also realised that if he was intent on trying again, he would first have to make sure that the dogs were silenced, and poisoned meat bait is the answer to that. He might even chance setting the bait today whilst we are away from the site, and if he does I will find it when I return. That will assure me that he believes he is one step ahead of us, and that might mean that he will try again tonight. And if not, then he'll try tomorrow night.

"Good thinking, Paul," the Inspector commended, and he recalled, "You mentioned earlier, Paul, that you found evidence that what you at first believed was a stray animal turned out not to be one. Can you share that evidence with us?" the Inspector asked.

"Yes, of course, Inspector, but I advise that it be treated as classified information for the time being," Paul requested.

"Yes, understood, Paul. We are all pledged to secrecy regarding such information," the Inspector assured him.

Paul then related how he came into possession of the piece of wellington boot.

"And that was when I realised the intruder was not an animal, but a human being, Inspector."

"So, you believe, Paul, that the killer will use poisoned meat bait to get rid of your dogs before making another attempt to cremate you?" Sergeant Griffin asked, adding, "But you don't know when?"

"That's my guess, Sergeant, and if he manages to set the bait today whilst we are away from the site I think he will try again tonight. I believe that this killer without a conscience will commit any crime necessary to prevent whatever secret he is hiding from being exposed."

"He sounds like a real evil, callous-hearted devil disciple, Paul." Inspector Conroy voiced his opinion.

"Yes, and he has already proved that with the cold-blooded execution of the totally innocent family five years ago. It's hard to imagine how a human being could stoop to that level of barbarity. There is no apparent motive, and yet there must have been a reason," Paul mused.

"Well, Paul, as you are aware, of the four of us only Sergeant Griffin was involved in that murder case five years ago. Judging by what you have divulged to us today, that case is going to have to be reopened and investigated again," the Inspector stated with intent.

"Yes, I agree, Inspector. Something must have been missed during the original investigation. It might have been a simple oversight in the rush to bring the trial to a speedy conclusion, and it might be well worth reading witness statements and the trial reports again," Paul suggested.

"Yes, I am going to make enquiries today, and I will try and get hold of the documentation of the case and trial. We will go over it again carefully. In the meantime, I'd like to know what you have in mind, Paul, and what advice, if any, you might want to pass on to us," the Inspector asked with meaningful interest.

"My intention now, Inspector, is to deliver my wife and the two dogs to the security of her parents' home, which is about fifty kilometres south-west of Attanagh in Tipperary. I had a difficult time convincing her to agree to my plan. It is primarily for her and the dogs' safety, and to provide me with the freedom to help the police – that is, you and your team – to hopefully tempt the would-be exterminator to make his move in again trying to eliminate us. If he believes that his hidden pile of incendiary paraffin-primed sacking remains undetected, he won't be able to resist the temptation. If the killer sets poison bait during the time I am away from the site, I'll find it when I return later. That might well mean that he intends to strike tonight – that is, I think, during the early hours of Sunday morning. I am proposing the police keep watch tonight and, failing that, watch over Sunday night and Monday, but that is a decision for you, Inspector. If you consider my suggestions inappropriate, I will respect your judgement, but it will not deter me from carrying out my own personal watch. I hope you understand my reasoning." Paul revealed his plan.

"Well, Detectives, you heard Paul's proposal. I would like to hear your comments, if any, before I decide," the Inspector invited.

Sergeant Griffin was first to respond, just as Paul expected judging by what Gerry had previously told him concerning the Detective's belief of the innocence of the traveller: "I believe Paul's plan is worth a try, Inspector, and I am willing to participate," the Sergeant declared.

"Count me in too, Inspector. I can't think of anything better." Detective Green cast his vote.

"Well, I can hardly spoil the party. I volunteer too, and I hope we succeed in apprehending the evildoer in the act," Detective Carey agreed.

"Well, all that's left to say is it will indeed be great if we succeed and then double our success by solving the mystery of why the cottage family were burned to death in the inferno five years ago," Inspector Conroy optimistically commented. "Since our job is investigating and solving crimes, we are going to make the effort to apprehend the attempted murderer of Paul, his wife and their two dogs in the early hours of this very morning. I'm glad you three detectives are of the same mindset as I am – positive. And regarding your suggestion, Paul, what time do you think we should begin watching tonight?"

CHAPTER FOURTEEN

Paul was delighted to hear that all four members of the detective squad were seriously committed, and he suggested a watch between midnight and 2 a.m. on Sunday morning, saying that was the time when he and his wife had been alerted by the dogs that morning.

"Right, Paul – if we visit the cottage site on your return after delivering your wife and dogs to the safety of her parents' home—"

"This afternoon, Inspector." Paul felt the necessity to interrupt in order to remind them.

"Good. We will be there about six o'clock, then, to familiarise ourselves with the layout, and then we will return later, and discreetly, before midnight to implement our stake-out. How does that sound to you, Paul?" the Inspector asked.

"Yes, that will be fine, Inspector," Paul agreed, and he added, "I will only be able to supply tea and coffee and biscuits, so make sure you have your dinner beforehand." And he laughed.

"I don't think we will be in the mood for much eating, Paul, so tea and coffee and biscuits will be fine," Detective Griffin agreed with a smile. "I think your wife might be getting a little restless now, Paul, so you go and attend to her and your dogs and we will get to work finding out all about the traveller's trial five years ago. Hopefully we will find something that was overlooked," the Inspector said.

"Well, thank you, Inspector and Detectives. That's a weight off my mind. I'll be able to think with a clear head after the concern for my wife and dogs has been eased. OK then; and until later, good luck with your search," Paul ended, and he departed.

On his way out he uttered a few words of thanks to the desk officer.

As he approached the camper van he noticed at once that Maura had moved over to the passenger seat, and when he climbed into the driving seat and was being excitedly greeted by the dogs he asked Maura, "Don't you want to drive?"

"No, Paul, my mind is upset and that would only interfere with my concentration. I'd rather you drove," she excused herself.

"Have you rung your parents?" he asked whilst fondling the dogs' heads.

"Yes, and they are delighted to hear about my surprise visit with the dogs. I'll have to explain the disappointing part later."

"The police inspector and his team of three detectives agreed to my plan to keep watch tonight, or rather in the early hours of tomorrow morning. If it works, we will catch the killer as he is about to activate his arson evil, and that will be the end of the worrying threat. Possibly the police will then be able to extract from him the answer to the mystery of why he murdered that innocent family, through questioning him whilst in custody."

Paul could sense her anxiety, and he suggested a walk round the perimeter of the car park again with the dogs to dissipate the tension. Maura agreed and Paul attached the lead chains to the dogs' collars and the four ambled round the grass verge of the car park.

"There's no need for you to worry, Maura. I'll be in the company of four police officers during the watch, and if nothing results from it then they are willing to do a second watch during the late and early hours of Sunday night and Monday morning. If both watches prove unsuccessful, I will drive to your parents' home on Monday morning, and after spending a few hours with your parents we will return to the site. How does that sound to you, Maura?" Paul asked optimistically.

"That will be fine, Paul, but it's the two nights between that worry me. I think I'll be biting my fingernails during our hours apart."

"Nothing bad will happen, Maura. There are five of us. I'll phone you before or around eleven o'clock, and again after the watch; or if the trap is successful and the evildoer is arrested I'll ring you immediately after. You don't ring, Maura, as that could complicate things. Do you understand?"

"Yes, Paul. I believe all you say and I trust you and the police. And I know the reason why you are trying to bring it all to a conclusion, but where a woman is concerned worry is like an unwritten prerogative. That might be due to the fact that the woman is the child bearer, so it's in a woman's nature to worry – and that is what a man has got to understand," Maura acquitted herself.

"Yes, I accept that, Maura, and I see the logic in it, so I won't press you any further on the subject," Paul conceded.

When they returned to the camper van and settled into their seats Paul gave the dogs a new hide chew each, and as they sat lengthways on the rug to work on their treats Paul started the engine and slowly guided the vehicle out of the car park. Then shortly afterwards he joined the main road and headed southwest. En route to their destination, he asked Maura not to divulge the reason for her and the dogs' stay with her parents until he rang her later, after which she would be free to share the details of the plan with them and fill them in on the story up to the present.

"I can only stay an hour before I have to leave again to get back by six o'clock, when the detectives will be arriving to familiarise themselves with the site. Then they will leave and return again before midnight to implement the plan for the night watch. Is that clear, Maura?"

"Yes, and you will call me at eleven without fail, Paul?" Maura stressed.

"Well, I am hardly likely to forget unless I fall asleep, and that is unlikely to happen whilst in the company of four police officers," Paul assured her, flashing her a smile.

Maura smiled in return and remarked, "No, I suppose not, but it's not impossible either." And she smiled again.

"I'm glad you still have a sense of humour, Maura – and no, it's not impossible." And he smiled.

They arrived at Maura's parents' home on the edge of a small village an hour and a half later.

"Rookcry Wood village – a haven of peace," Paul remarked as he parked the camper van outside the cottage where Maura's parents lived.

The four clambered out and stretched their legs. They were warmly greeted by Maura's parents – her mother, Maura senior, and her father, Frank. Bonzie and Fleurie were familiar with the couple from previous visits and were delighted with the attention they received. The hour that Paul allowed himself passed all too quickly, but he remembered to remove the bag of dog meal, the dogs' feeding bowls and meat supply from the camper van plus enough hide chews to last several days. He explained about his almost immediate return and the appointment he had for six o'clock.

"I can't disclose the reason to you as it is classified information and involves the police, but Maura will be able to inform you later tonight."

His parents-in-law understood and assured him of the comfort and well-being of Maura and the dogs. He told them if all went well at the meeting, he would be back the following day about noon; and if not, it would be Monday morning. Maura and the dogs accompanied him to the garden gate, where he embraced the dogs and told them to be good girls and ended with the words "I'll be back soon." Then, embracing Maura, he kissed her and asked her to try not to worry as all would go well.

He also reminded her to put the dogs' muzzles on when outside, and he reminded her, "One never knows where a rogue dog poisoner is operating.

"They will never be out of my sight, Paul," she promised.

He waited for the dogs to follow her inside the house, but they stood waiting for him to join them, so he had to go with them to the house door, and when they entered he quickly returned to the camper van, started the engine and departed quickly to minimise the upset.

When Paul arrived back at the cottage-ruin site he felt a sudden loneliness, already missing Maura and the dogs. The lack of their atmospheric presence caused a feeling of emptiness to linger over the site, and he realised what he would be faced with if he were to lose them. He instantly realised that Maura was experiencing the depressing fear of losing him, and the thought activated his mentality to overcome and dismiss the mood by reassuring himself that it wouldn't happen.

"They are safe now and I am going to make sure that they remain so by helping to bring the threat of a mental devil to an end!" he told himself.

After unlocking the field gate he drove the camper van to its parking place at the end of the long side garden and close to the perimeter hedgerow. After turning off the engine, he checked his wristwatch. It was five forty. He climbed out of the cab and decided immediately to take a look around for signs of scattered meat bait, but he couldn't find anything. As a last effort he checked the part of the hedgerow where the disturbance had taken place during the early hours of that same morning, and in the central area of this hedgerow his sharp eyes noticed something dark. On closer inspection he detected a pile of a reddish-brown meat-like substance, which he thought was most likely to be liver. At the same moment he realised why it was placed in this obscure location. The arsonist could have put it there without revealing his presence to any human eyes that might be watching in the vicinity, and although it was out of sight the dogs would have picked up its scent. That fact caused Paul's anger to surge, but he kept his feelings under control.

"What an evil, satanic monster Rangton is! If hanging were legal, he would be a prime candidate for the drop out of existence, but God will deal with him in His own mysterious way."

Still angry, Paul went to the Portaloo and returned with a plastic bucket and spade. He shovelled what he believed was poisoned liver into the bucket and searched around the hedgerow area for any more scattered pieces, but unsuccessfully. After securing the bucket containing the poisoned bait in the Portaloo, he walked about the site looking out for any other poisoned bait, simply because he didn't want any other species being poisoned either. It was whilst he was thus engaged that Inspector Conroy and his team of three detectives arrived on the scene in the Inspector's unmarked car. Paul directed him through the open gateway and gestured to him to turn right and park alongside the hedgerow that bordered Valley Lane. When the group climbed out of the car Paul informed them of the liver bait he had found in the hedgerow where the disturbance occurred that morning, and he said that he believed it had been treated with some poisonous substance.

"It's in a bucket in the cabin behind the camper van," he said, and he pointed to the Portaloo.

"I will take it in the boot of the car, Paul, when we leave, and I'll have it analysed," the Inspector said, and added, "Do you still believe the suspect will follow up with another attempted strike tonight, Paul?"

"Either tonight or tomorrow night, Inspector. He will know by now that the site is sold and he will be determined to undo that problem. By setting the poison bait he is displaying his intent to eliminate us and, by the same act, deter any would-be buyer from investing in the site in the future. That's how I anticipate his action now. The effort to poison the dogs and silence them shows there is a mystery about this site that he doesn't want to be resolved. I feel certain about that," Paul concluded.

"I can only agree with your logical assumption, Paul." Sergeant Griffin voiced his agreement and the others agreed.

"There is some important information that I haven't divulged to you yet, because of lack of evidence, but I feel sure you will agree to my decision not to reveal it yet. I believe I know the killer's name – I found it out by accident when we left the cottage site this morning and were on our way to the police station. We stopped at a farm to enquire about the purchase of some manure to fertilise the gardens of the cottage ruin...." He then recalled to the detectives what he learned during that brief visit to the farm, and he explained why he hadn't told his wife.

"Well, Paul, that certainly was a stroke of good luck!" The Inspector congratulated him and added, "And the fact that you learned his name without asking is quite advantageous."

"Yes, I could hardly believe my good luck, Inspector. But I have decided not to reveal his name until after our one- or two-nights' watch. Do you all agree with my decision?" Paul asked in hope.

"You believe, Paul, that if the suspect strikes tonight or tomorrow night and we succeed in apprehending him it will turn out to be the man you saw earlier this morning. Is that right, Paul?" the Inspector asked.

"Exactly that, Inspector," Paul agreed, and he added, "The one other fact about the suspect is he is a farmer, and I also learned that from the farmer I called on to ask about manure," Paul revealed.

"Well now, Paul, that piece of rubber from the wellington boot has suddenly become a very important piece of evidence if it can be matched to the man's rubber boot," the Inspector stated. He asked Paul if it was still in his possession, and, if so, would he surrender it to him.

"Yes, of course, Inspector. I have it here in my shirt pocket."

He produced a small brown envelope and passed it to the Inspector.

"Thank you, Paul – I appreciate that," the Inspector remarked as he slipped the envelope into his pocket.

"Something just crossed my mind, Inspector, before you and your colleagues arrived here. If the suspect decides to make his attempt tonight, I have a feeling that he will pay a visit first without the half-sackful of paraffin-soaked pieces of sacking – just to test the ground, so to speak. If he's satisfied, he will return to pick up his incendiary pile of destruction to complete his task. Do you all agree with that idea or do you think I am being overcautious?" Paul asked.

"No, Paul, it is not being too cautious. I speak for all of us when I say your thoughts are in line with our thinking, and we hope the watch ends in success." The Inspector commended him.

Paul then showed the police team around the site, pointing out the rusty old hay gatherer, now mostly covered by spreading brambles and still harbouring the arsonist's half-sackful of paraffin-soaked pieces of sacking. It was on the far side of the hedgerow that formed the north boundary between the cottage site and a field, and accessed by a gate on Valley Lane opposite the gate that led into the field where the now imprisoned traveller's pony had been allowed to graze. Paul suggested that it was from that direction that the suspect would approach later that night if he decided to make his move.

"So you've been trying to deduce the mindset of the suspect, Paul," the Inspector said, and he added, "You should have joined the police force and become an investigator. We can do with people like you."

"Thank you for the compliment, Inspector, but I prefer what I do and that is writing. I feel free to be creatively active in the field without restrictions. I don't mind helping the police in an advisory capacity when requested to, but I prefer the freedom of creative expression."

"Do you believe that the suspect is a cautious night prowler, Paul, using the land to his advantage whenever possible?" Detective Carey asked thoughtfully.

"Yes, Detective Carey, and since he is a farmer he will be familiar with the fields and able to find his way across them both in daylight and in darkness," Paul added.

He didn't elaborate on his belief as he was aware that things might not turn out as expected.

Inspector Conroy, Sergeant Griffin and Detective Green all agreed with Detective Carey and Paul regarding the suspect's advantageous familiarity with the land and his ability to find his way across it in the dark.

"Only a man who has a mental map of the area could operate efficiently in the dark," Sergeant Griffin stated, and he continued, "So he is likely to be not only a farmer, but a local one at that."

"Well worked out and described, Sergeant," Paul complimented him.

It was 7.15 p.m. when Inspector Conroy and his detectives,

satisfied with their briefing and familiarised with the anticipated crime scene, decided to leave the site.

"We will leave you now, Paul, and return between eleven thirty and midnight. We will be accompanied by a police van with four armed uniformed police officers. The van is dark blue, like my car, and both vehicles will be parked out of sight," the Inspector remarked.

"Yes, Inspector, park close to the hedgerow, where they will blend in with the darkness of the overhanging trees and bushes. I will phone my wife, Maura, at eleven o'clock and put her mind at ease. I have already told her not to phone me as that could jeopardise the situation. So the scene awaits ignition," Paul concluded.

"In other words, the stage is set, Paul," the Inspector remarked as he climbed into his car.

The other detectives followed in like manner with temporary farewells, and the police car was about to leave the scene when Paul remembered the bucket containing the liver bait set for the dogs by the suspect. It was still in the Portaloo.

"The liver bait, Inspector!" Paul exclaimed. "If you wait a moment I'll go and get it."

"Well remembered, Paul," the Inspector commented, and he nodded his agreement.

Paul departed and returned with the bucket containing its believed poisoned contents.

"I'm glad you remembered that, Paul, because the sooner it's sent to the forensic lab the sooner we'll get the results, the Inspector remarked. He added, "So, again, until later, Paul, farewell."

A moment later Paul was alone. He felt the loneliness without Maura and their beloved dogs, but he felt solace in the fact that before morning he, Maura and the dogs would be, hopefully, safe from the source of their distress.

CHAPTER FIFTEEN

Paul looked around the empty site as the echoing arrival of happy-sounding rooks among the forest trees 100 metres to the east reminded him that darkness would embrace the land within the hour. A robin sang heralding the approaching end of day from hedgerow brambles nearby and the lively hum of existence was already diminishing in the surrounding atmosphere. Paul ambled slowly past the cottage foundations, where he planned to erect a greenhouse in memory of the family members who lost their lives five years previously. He was heading for the damson tree, still displaying a few later-flowering blossoms, but he stopped several paces from the tree, knelt down and lowered his head to breathe the fragrance of a flush of lilies of the valley that still bloomed.

He spoke to them silently, believing that they might hear his thoughts: "Another week, my endearing lily bells, and I'll be able to lift you and clear your bed of couch grass and nettles and mix some fertiliser, in the form of manure, into the soil to nourish your roots."

He then moved five paces to the trunk of the damson tree, sat down and leaned his back against it to face the setting sun as it slowly descended behind the Sliabh Bloom mountains in the west, casting long shadows in the process stretching east. He visualised Maura and the dogs, there beside him among the gardening tools, a ball of cord, a fork, a spade, hand tools, pegs, posts and netting, and he allowed his imagination to play freely. He looked back over the exertions of the day from the disturbance during the early hours of that morning, causing the interruption of their night's rest; and the concerns of the day, including the drive to and return from Maura's parents' home, weighed heavy on his weary mind. He drifted into silent sleep.

When he next awoke it was as a result of a short dream, he recalled, in which a gentle female voice was appealing to his unconscious mind to awake. He responded to the appeal by suddenly opening his wide-awake eyes, and all his faculties were alert. He checked the luminous face of his wristwatch. It read ten thirty. He realised he'd been asleep under the damson tree for nearly two hours. He looked around the garden, but saw only shadows. It was a moonlit night interrupted by passing cumulus clouds. Shadows appeared and disappeared continuously. He heard a slight sound and looked towards the camper van, where he noticed a shadowy movement.

His first thought was that it was a stray animal, but he instantly banished the thought from his mind as he asked himself, 'Why would an animal be sneaking around the camper?' He guessed it must be the arsonist killer and thought, 'If I alert him to my presence he will simply disappear into the darkness of the night and he will remain free to threaten our existence, including the dogs, whenever the chance presents itself again. The Inspector, the detectives and the uniformed police officers won't be arriving until 11.30 p.m., by which time the arsonist will have carried out his evil deed and be gone, so I am going to have to try and apprehend him myself,' Paul decided.

He knew he was going to have to be as silent as the intruder. He placed the ball of brown cord in his jacket pocket and retrieved the trailing end, immediately. Then he made a loop at the end of the cord and passed most of the ball through the loop before returning it to his jacket pocket, where he also kept a penknife. He took hold of the garden fork, then, holding it halfway along its shaft, began creeping on hands and knees close to the ground using the shadows. He made his way past the rhubarb patch in that manner, and worked his way silently to within two paces of the Portaloo, which extended a metre beyond the end of the camper van. His eyes had become more accustomed to the darkness and he was able to make out the shadowy figure silently taking pieces of the paraffin-soaked sacking from a sack he carried and placing them under the camper van. Paul could smell the paraffin and he struggled to control his anger.

As the arsonist approached the front of the vehicle, facing east, Paul withdrew the ball of cord from his pocket and, when the killer went out of sight behind the front of the camper van, Paul quickly formed a large loop with the cord to cover the ground at the rear of the camper van. He then hid himself behind a bush in the shadows, praying that the would-be killer would not only not notice the cord, but would continue round the end of the camper van and into the loop trap. If he didn't, Paul would be compelled to strike, hopefully catching him by surprise and overpowering the killer with the help of the garden fork, which was still in his grasp. He must not fail.

He waited in a state of nervous tension as the arsonist continued to silently spread the pieces of paraffin-soaked sacking underneath and along the passenger side of the camper van. When he reached the end he stood upright and hesitated, and then moved a step forward as if to return the way he had arrived. But he hesitated again. Paul was on the point of launching his backup plan when the killer suddenly decided to round the end of the camper van. He stepped inside the loop of cord and Paul acted instantly, pulling the loop in with both hands at speed. The cord tightened round the arsonist's rubber-booted legs, causing him to lose his balance, and he fell headlong on to the ground.

Whilst he was still in a state of shock, Paul leapt forward, still holding the ball of cord, and continued in a frenzy wrapping the cord round the disabled arsonist's legs and holding the fork with the prongs pressed against the arsonist's back.

He snarled angrily at him, "Make a sudden move and I'll happily drive the prongs of the fork straight through your evil frame. Place your hands behind your back now, Rangton."

The shocked killer silently obeyed, suddenly gripped by fear. Paul wrapped the cord round the trapped man's wrists and then tied it to the cord binding the man's legs, and he knew he had him safely disabled. Paul's body was trembling with tension, anger and relief, and he thought of Maura, Bonzie and Fleurie and felt a great relieving surge of love for them. Then he thought of the danger he had been in: what if all had gone wrong and he had failed and died in his attempt, as Maura had feared?

'What would have happened to them? It would have been my fault, and I have no excuse because I know none of us are perfect. I've got to learn a lesson from this and be more aware of my bonded responsibilities in future and take no serious risks. Still though, I had to defend what I am responsible for, and I am especially grateful to the unknown lady in my dream. I'd like to be able to reward her for her help, but how?' He then thought about the arsonist/killer bound hand and foot on the ground at his mercy. 'This is the evil merciless killer who burned to death the innocent members of the cottage family five years ago, and he had the same fate planned for Maura and me this very night.'

He looked at his tied-up prisoner and asked him, "How do you feel now, Mr Rangton, being the victim rather than the victor?"

"It wasn't my fault. The devil controlled my thoughts," the captive whimpered, and he asked in a pitiful voice, "What are you going to do with me?"

"I'm thinking about that, but I have a question for you: how did you feel when you burned that family to death in the cottage five years ago? Why did you commit such a heinous crime? Answer that question," Paul angrily asked.

"I didn't want to do that, but the devil took over my soul and compelled me to do it," the captive pleaded, and he added, "I was powerless under the spell of the devil."

"Who was compelling you to commit this atrocity tonight and why? Was it the devil who compelled you to set the poisoned liver bait for the dogs earlier today?" Paul angrily questioned him.

"He doesn't tell me why," the captive cried. "He commands me in my mind to act and I must obey," he pleaded pathetically.

"You are a liar! Liar! Liar! Mr Rangton, you have no conscience. You are driven by the animal instincts of your primate ancestors, and in this age you are known as a monster lunatic. You should be either caged for life or executed. That should be your unenviable fate. Evil you are and evil you will always be, and now you had better pray to your invented devil to save you," Paul angrily concluded.

He then walked to the front of the camper van, where he noticed the cab's door handles were bound by a rope looped over the cab in a manner that prevented the cab doors from being opened from the inside.

"What depth of evil is this? This inhuman creature must be possessed," Paul told himself whilst keeping a wary on him all the time.

He checked his wristwatch. It read ten fifty-five. He decided to call the Attanagh police station.

A female police officer answered and he guessed it was Detective Carey.

He asked, "Is that Detective Carey I am addressing?"

"Yes, it is, and I believe that is Paul Attanagh?"

"Correct, Detective. I am calling to inform the team collectively that the suspect arrived sooner than expected, but I can't go into details over the phone. Suffice to say the suspect is now in my custody and this is an emergency, Detective. I need your help. Do you understand, Detective?"

"Yes, Paul, consider us on our way. And until we arrive . . ."

Paul then rang Maura, who answered almost instantly and asked, before he could speak, "Are you all right, Paul?"

"Physically, yes, Maura. And you, the dogs and your parents?" Paul enquired.

"Yes, all fine! Every sound from outside is interpreted by the dogs as your possible arrival. That's how expectant they are. What did you mean by 'physically'? Have you got some other ailment? Do tell me, Paul; otherwise I'll—"

"Just keep talking to me, Maura. It's an emotional problem, but don't ask me any questions. I'm waiting for the police to arrive. When they do, I'll hand this evil murderer over to them, Maura."

"Do you mean the plan worked and you have caught the killer? But why are you waiting for the police? Why aren't they there already, Paul? I don't understand."

"The police are here now, Maura. They are just driving on to the site. I will explain all to you later. First, I will have to go to the police station and give an account of the unexpected event and then I will drive to your parents' home. So be patient, Maura. The killer has been apprehended and that part of it is over. I love you and I'll see you in a couple of hours. Bye for now, my love."

Inspector Conroy's car stopped in front of the camper van and the Inspector and three detectives climbed out hurriedly. The police van following parked closely and four armed uniformed police officers emerged from it. Paul stood waiting to greet them.

"Are you OK, Paul?" the Inspector asked in a tone of concern, and before Paul could answer he followed up with "What's happened, Paul? Is our plan ruined?"

"No, everything has worked out fine now, Inspector," Paul replied, and pointing to the rear of the camper van he continued: "That heap at the end of the camper van is the killer, tied up and waiting to be taken into custody."

"What!" the Inspector exclaimed, and added, "How did you manage to do that, Paul?"

"If it's all right with you, Inspector, I'll explain all at the police station. That way everything will be clear and you will understand why I wasn't able to include you and the team in the concluding act."

"Agreed, Paul – that'll be fine." And addressing the uniformed police officers the Inspector said, "Sergeant Delaney, will you and your men see to it that the captive lying prostate there" – pointing to the bound arsonist – "has leg chains fitted as well as handcuffs and is placed securely under guard in the police van?"

"Yes, Inspector – your orders will be implemented immediately." And the Sergeant engaged his three colleagues in dialogue.

The Inspector then instructed the detectives to question the prisoner and get whatever information they could from him, and turning to Paul he remarked, "You have been through a tension-charged ordeal, Paul, but you came through it well." And offering his hand he said, "Really well done, Paul!"

"Thanks for the compliment, Inspector, but there's part of the story I still find strange. And I must admit, Inspector, between you and me, I was tempted to execute the evil demon and I had to struggle mentally to fight the urge to dispatch him after what I felt was his complete lack of humanity towards his victims. I was horrified when I saw what he did to prevent us, his victims, should we have awoken and tried to save ourselves from certain death."

"What did he do, Paul, to tempt you to commit such an extreme act?" the Inspector asked, and Paul pointed to the rope looped over the cab of the camper van from door handle to door handle to prevent the doors from being opened from the inside.

"That was his mocking goodbye." Paul interpreted the deed.

The Inspector took a closer look at the rope and checked it, uttering, "My God! He certainly was making sure there was no escape for the occupants. He is one of those evil people who deserve nothing less than the death penalty, and I would have no regrets about voting for it where such absolutely evil candidates are concerned. He is the epitome of evil, and I fully understand your feelings, Paul, especially when considering the fact that you and your wife, Maura, were the intended innocent victims. He is one of those human beings without a conscience. You have my sympathy, Paul, for what it's worth," the Inspector consoled.

"I'm glad now, Inspector, that I didn't give way to my feelings. And I didn't do so because I have a deeply thoughtful mentality that keeps reminding me that I am not God. That thought gradually overrides my feelings until they dissipate – that is the simple fact of it."

"I will keep that in mind, Paul, and try it myself at times when I am tempted with violent thoughts," the Inspector remarked. And after a short pause he asked, "Did the murdering arsonist set the pieces of paraffin-soaked sacking, Paul?"

"Yes, he did, Inspector. He placed them under the body of the camper on either side. You can smell the paraffin if you walk alongside the vehicle."

"Did you remind him of the cottage family five years ago, Paul?"

"Yes, and I charged him with the heinous murder of that innocent family, but he merely pleaded mental manipulation by the devil, whose power, he swore, compelled him to carry out a crime that he wouldn't have committed of his own volition. I got the impression that he was absolving himself of the blame. In a court of law, I expect my evidence would not be accepted without verification. Am I right, Inspector?" Paul asked.

"That's true, Paul. I believe it would be looked upon as insubstantial, like a ghost without a body. But I will make a good effort to get the truth out of him, Paul, and that's a promise," the Inspector assured him.

The uniformed police sergeant reported to the Inspector that the captive was secured in chains in the police van under armed guard and was being questioned by two detectives.

The Inspector thanked him and asked, pointing to the camper van, "What do you make of the securing, by the captive, of the cab doors of the camper van to prevent the occupants from escaping if they awoke during the inferno, Sergeant?"

"I would describe such an act, Inspector, as the work of an evil, demonic-minded member of the human race. It's difficult to understand how anyone would want to inflict such a horrible death on another member of the human race, or even on an animal." The Sergeant expressed his feelings.

"By the way, Sergeant, this is Paul Attanagh. Paul, meet Sergeant Sean Delaney. Both now greeted each other with a handshake, and the Inspector added, "Paul and his wife were the intended innocent victims of the arsonist killer tonight, Sergeant. As you now know, he is also the one who – I don't know how yet – managed to turn the event to his advantage. He is going to explain all to us when we return to the police station."

Sergeant Delaney offered his congratulations to Paul and both shook hands again. Then the Sergeant remarked, "Well done, Paul. I'll be looking forward to hearing your account of how you apprehended the demon in the act."

"Well, all I will say now is it was a mysterious happening that I don't fully understand myself yet."

"Well, Paul, that makes it even more interesting," the Inspector concluded.

"Inspector, can I undo that rope loop binding the cab doors of the camper as I have to travel south to see my wife and two best friends, our dogs, after the visit to the police station?"

"Yes, of course, Paul. That'll be fine. We need to collect all these paraffin-soaked pieces of sacking from under your camper van too as they are all items of evidence. If we all work together, we can clear up here in minutes and have all the paraphernalia stored in the police van."

It was 11.40 p.m. when Paul steered the camper van out of the cottage site behind the Inspector's car and ahead of the police van and headed east for the short drive to Attanagh town and the police station. There the captive arsonist was ushered out of the police van and into a secure cell supervised by two armed police officers to wait for interrogation.

Inspector Conroy, Paul, the three detectives and the uniformed police sergeant, Sean Delaney, together with his second in command, were invited into the conference room, where tea, coffee and biscuits were served. And when all were comfortably settled the Inspector called for order and asked Paul if he would like to begin to fill them in on events following their earlier departure from the scene up to their recent arrival that night. Paul duly obliged, explaining why he wasn't able to forewarn them of the earlier than expected arrival of the arsonist as he was asleep under the damson tree facing west when the criminal appeared on the scene through, he believed, the same gap in the hedgerow as he had entered by during the early hours of that same morning. The gap was about forty paces east of where he was sleeping. He must have come first to survey the scene and for some reason decided to activate his evil plan then, so he would have left again to pick up his half-sackful of paraffin-soaked pieces of sacking before returning, perhaps overconfident of success, to complete his evil plan. Paul reminded the listeners that he was still asleep under the damson tree twenty-five paces from the camper van. His tiredness was due to being awake since two o'clock that same morning plus the drive to and from his wife's parents' home fifty kilometres south of Attanagh. Paul went on to describe his awakening, which had not been caused by any sound the killer made, but, strangely, in a dream a female voice had spoken softly and silently, saying, "You need to awaken, Paul."

"I remember even now," Paul told them. "She spoke my name distinctly. But who was it? I still have no idea. He went on to relate that he awoke silently, suddenly wide awake, and he went on to describe what happened from then to the capture of his would-be killer. "I keep asking myself who could it have been in my warning dream? How did I know it was a female and how did she know my name? Since that experience I have been wondering if that spiritual lady was aware of the unfolding crime and was not only alerting me to it, but guiding my thoughts in the process of the killer's capture. I am now beginning to believe the latter the more I think about it. I don't know how the rest of you here interpret what I have just related to you, but I am convinced that my dream lady, whoever she was, might have been directing operations through my mind and ensuring success. That's it, for what it's worth. You are all free to interpret my little dream however you wish, but I will stick with my gut feeling," Paul concluded.

"Yes, I can understand why you were unable to alert us to the killer's manoeuvring, Paul, for fear of warning him of your presence. He might have killed you and bolted into the darkness of the night," the Inspector commented, and he added, "You took a big risk with a determined killer who could have been armed with a gun or knife or some other weapon," the Inspector reminded him.

"Yes, that's true, Inspector, but I felt fortified by the spiritual presence that was guiding my thoughts. That overrode my fear, and this is the result – a win for all of us and hopefully a quick release, a state apology and exoneration with compensation for the innocent traveller who has been languishing in prison for the last five years, separated from his wife and young daughter, who will be five years old now." Paul reminded all present of the injustice.

"They who played a key role in the itinerant's conviction are going to feel the weight of their guilt on their shoulders from tomorrow morning," the Inspector predicted, and he added, "Detective Carey, I'd like you to contact the local newspaper office, the *Attanagh Round-Up*, and if there's nobody available to make decisions try and get the home phone number of the editor or whoever is in charge and ask him or her to get a reporter down here to the police station at once. Put the word out to the dailies in the cities to do likewise and hold the front pages of tomorrow morning's dailies for a national scoop, or words to that effect. Is that understood, Karen?"

"Yes, Inspector. I'm on my way next door," the Detective replied whilst rising from the chair.

"I suppose your next move, Paul, is to join your wife and dogs down in Tipperary? Will you be OK for the drive? I mean by that, you are not likely to fall asleep, are you?" the Inspector asked, concerned.

"That is something I am quite unlikely to do, Inspector. I had about two hour's sleep under the damson tree earlier. I hadn't planned on falling asleep – but then, neither had I made the allowance for having been awake since two o'clock this morning. Plus the drive south to my wife's parents' home in Tipperary and the return journey must have added more weariness to my already weary mind – hence the two hours in dreamland. And that seems to have led the arsonist to mistakenly believe that I was asleep in the camper van and the way was clear for him to complete his murderous intention of burning me to death in a holocaust of fire. But, all thanks to the angel of the dream, it all ended in success for us and defeat and arrest for the cold-blooded, callous killer. And thanks for your concern, Inspector, but I believe I will be fine on my drive south, which should take no more than an hour and a half," Paul assured him, and added, "You've got my phone number if you wish to check on my arrival."

"Yes, I'll do that, Paul."

Both shook hands, as Paul did with the rest of the police team, and they departed with farewells. In the camper van he phoned Maura to inform her of his departure and his expected arrival time at her parents' home.

"Oh, I'm so relieved and delighted that all is well. The dogs are still cocking their ears at every sound." Maura voiced her joy.

"I have an interesting and intriguing story to relate to you, Maura – and your parents if they are waiting for my arrival."

"Oh yes, they are, Paul. We are all looking forward to seeing you soon. I love you."

"I love you too, Maura. And, until a little later, stay happy. Bye."

CHAPTER SIXTEEN

It was approaching 2 a.m. when Paul arrived at Maura's parents' home – a cottage on the edge of Rookery Wood village. Maura was standing by the garden gate with the dogs, waiting to greet him with a loving embrace whilst the dogs stood on their hind legs with their front paws on the gate top, whimpering, whining and prancing with delight. When he entered the garden they were so excited he sat on the garden bench and they swarmed all over him, delivering affectionate licks and whining their joy at his presence.

Maura sat beside him and she also received a deluge of affection, and she shed emotional tears as she held his hand, saying, "Oh, I'm so grateful to see you again, Paul, alive and well."

He reached out to kiss her as the dogs continued their greeting.

"I feel the same about you and the dogs, Maura. And what a tale I have to relate to you and your parents if they haven't gone to bed!"

"No, they haven't, Paul. They insisted on staying awake to greet you and, no doubt, are looking forward, as I am, to hearing about the fulfilment of your plan." After a slight pause she asked, "I expect you have had nothing to eat since you left here yesterday afternoon – am I right, Paul?"

"Well, apart from a couple of pots of tea and a few biscuits, no, I haven't," he agreed.

"Well, we have kept some dinner for you, having guessed right, and Mum and I have baked an apple pie and a rhubarb pie, so let's go in and I'll get your meal heated up for you," Maura suggested.

Paul kissed her again, and fondling the calmed dogs' heads he said, "Do you girls need to relieve yourselves?"

He took hold of Maura's right hand and ambled round the garden with the dogs to encourage them to urinate, and they did a couple of times each before the four entered the cottage to greet Maura's parents. Her mum had been known as Maura senior when Maura was living at home, and Maura had been addressed as Maura junior to avoid confusion.

Paul embraced Maura's mum and shook hands with her dad, Kevin, saying, "Sorry about my speedy departure yesterday afternoon, but I'm sure Maura will have explained as much as she knows to both of you."

"Yes, she did, Paul, and what an evil devil you had to contend with – a disciple of the devil wanting to burn both of you to death," Kevin remarked with a degree of disgust, and, hardly pausing, he continued: "The death penalty should be imposed on such heartless devils as he is."

Paul's mobile sounded then, and he excused himself, pressed the 'speak' button and said, "Hello! Yes, Inspector, I thought it must be you. Yes, I arrived about ten minutes ago. Yes, the roads were quiet as expected. How are things at the police station? A crowd of reporters already and more still arriving? I can imagine the noisy chaos and I can hear the voices and phones in the background. Yes, yes, Inspector, I'll relay your good wishes, and I hope you can escape home soon too. Yes, and thanks for checking. Bye for now."

He turned to Maura: "That was the police inspector in Attanagh checking to know if I had arrived safely. He sends his good wishes to all of you. The police station is being deluged with telephone calls from all over the country, and it is crowded with reporters arriving continuously. It seems like it's going to be a long night for him and his colleagues," Paul explained.

"That was thoughtful of him to check that you arrived safely, Paul," Maura commented as she placed a dish with what Paul considered was a substantial amount of food on it on the table by which he was sitting.

"I hope you and your mum won't be offended by my stating that I will not be able to eat all that food because of the tension my stomach has had to endure during the course of the night. I suggest sharing it with whoever wants to oblige, or else share it with the dogs."

"No, we have had our fill, Paul – and yes, of course, feel free to share it with our saviours. You always share some of your meals with the dogs anyway, whether you are hungry or not, and I remember you telling me when we were courting that you have always done so since you were a child; so there's no need to feel guilty since I am guilty of the same," Maura confessed, laughing.

She placed the dogs' bowls on the table, and Paul scooped a quarter of his meal into each. He then placed them on the floor for the dogs and they both gave the offerings their respectful attention and looked up at Paul on licking their bowls clean.

"Yes, I know what you are waiting to hear, girls – and yes, you can have a slice of apple pie later."

The dogs wagged their tales as if they understood.

"Those two dogs can almost talk," Maura's mother remarked, amazed, and she added, "They are held in high esteem now since they saved all your lives in the early hours of yesterday morning. They are well deserving too – aren't you, girls?" She praised them whilst sitting down to embrace them and received a spate of affectionate licks in return.

"Well, I have to say, Paul, I admire your willingness to share. Nobody could ever accuse you of being greedy. Your eagerness to share seems to be a natural trait," Kevin complimented him.

"I suppose it's because I have always been a carer and a sharer, Kevin – that's the only response I can make – and I believe I always will be."

"Does anyone ever care about you and share with you, Paul?" Kevin asked out of curiosity.

"Yes, Kevin, your daughter, Maura, your wife and you, plus the dogs are all caring and sharing with me now and I appreciate that," Paul replied.

"Well, yes, in a way I suppose, yes, I see what you mean. You don't expect much, do you?" Kevin asked, not sure what to say.

"Well, Kevin, I think you will agree with me when I say a little can seem a lot in a time of need."

"Yeah, yeah – wise words! A hunk of stale bread to a starving man is a lot better than nothing." Kevin agreed with his example.

"Yes, true, Kevin, and I would go as far as to say that all four of us have experienced that fact during our lifetimes," Paul suggested.

"No doubt about that, Paul – no, none at all." Kevin seemed to pluck memories from his memory bank.

Maura senior swept silently into the dining room carrying a large dish on which a golden-brown baked apple pie temptingly rested.

"Wow!" Paul admiringly exclaimed, and he continued: "That looks really appetising. I expect it was a dual effort."

"Yes, exactly, from start to finish," Maura senior confirmed.

"Well then, congratulations to both of you. I just know it's going to taste delicious," Paul enthused.

"How can you be so sure of that, Paul?" Kevin asked, intrigued.

Paul smiled and pointed to the dogs sat by his side, waiting patiently, and answered, "Bonzie and Fleurie here will shortly tell me, Kevin."

"How? Do they eat apple pie?"

"Well, your daughter, Maura, is just putting a slice of pie into each of their bowls and she will slice them into manageable pieces. And now the proof!"

Both dogs devoured their shares with rapid ease and licked their lips with satisfaction.

Paul smiled and said, "That's how I know it's delicious, Kevin, as you too will, no doubt, agree," Paul assured him.

Maura then poured cooled tea into the dogs' clean-licked bowls and they lapped the contents to the last drop and left their bowls spotlessly clean again.

When the four adults settled down to their apple pie and the tea, Kevin remarked, "Well, I never heard the likes before – dogs drinking tea and being expert apple-pie tasters!" And after tasting his slice of apple pie, he added, "And they're right too – it is delicious."

And mother and daughter smiled their pleasure.

"Now, Paul, do you feel ready to relate the events of the day after you left us yesterday afternoon?" his wife, Maura, appealed, eager to hear his account.

"Yes, certainly, just as soon as I give the dogs a hide chew each to keep them occupied. I always carry a few in my jacket pocket."

On completion of that act he began with his arrival at the cottage-ruin site the previous late afternoon or early evening at five forty, when his first task was to search for possible poisoned meat bait. He had thought it might be placed somewhere on the site, but he was unable to find it until he decided to check the gap in the hedgerow through which the killer had entered, or tried to enter, the site in the early hours of Saturday morning.

It was in the centre of that gap that I found a clump of liver hidden from human sight; but the dogs would have easily picked up its scent and eaten it without my knowing, and that would have been the end of their lives.

"Oh, I'm glad we didn't have to suffer that tragedy, Paul." Maura shuddered at the thought and embraced the two dogs sat on the settee between her and Paul.

"I won't tell you what I would have done if that demon had succeeded in his plan," Paul stated with conviction.

"I can guess, Paul, knowing how you feel about the dogs," Maura uttered, and she felt relieved.

Paul continued his account of the previous early evening up to the point when he dozed off under the damson tree and then his awakening at the request of a female voice in a dream. At first, I thought it was you, Maura, but as the words were spoken serenely, with concern and an element of fear, I thought it must be a spiritual presence. I couldn't understand who or what it might have been and I still have no idea now, but I knew it was gently entreating me to awake. It seemed to appeal to my very soul. When I did awake it was silently with my eyes suddenly wide open and my mind fully conscious. It was dark and silent, and even darker under the damson tree. I looked around trying to make out shapes, and whilst so doing I noticed a slowly moving shadow by the camper, about twenty-five paces away. I momentarily thought it was a stray animal, but almost instantly I put that idea out of my mind, asking myself why would an animal be wandering around the camper? At that moment I realised it had to be the arsonist killer. I checked my luminous wristwatch. It was just turned ten thirty. It was only then I realised that I had been asleep for at least an hour and a half."

"You must have been exhausted after that long day yesterday," his wife, Maura, suggested and, suddenly realising how things could have ended she exclaimed with a rush of tears, "You could have been murdered whilst you slept!"

Paul extended an arm to comfort her, saying, "Let's be grateful that I wasn't, Maura, and that, I believe, is because the spiritual presence of my dream was watching over me and guiding my thoughts and continued to do so during my wakefulness." Paul continued the story to its successful conclusion with the arrival of the police.

"By God, Paul! What an experience! And you managed to surprise and disable the murdering devil who was about to set your camper van on fire, believing that you and Maura were asleep inside. And he even tied the cab door handles in such a way as to prevent both of you from escaping if you had awoken. My God!" Kevin angrily denounced the heartless demon. "He deserves nothing better than to be burnt at the stake – God forgive me for saying so. You not only prevented the crime from taking place, but were forced by circumstances to tackle the killer alone and succeeded in bringing his reign of terror to an end. You deserve rewarding, Paul, for your night's work. Put it there!" Kevin said, extending his hand.

Paul grasped it.

"Well done, Paul! You deserve more praise than you are likely to receive, but I certainly admire your courage," Kevin concluded.

Paul acknowledged his father-in-law's accolade and modestly replied, "I am not a glory seeker, Kevin."

Both Maura and her mother were weeping, affected by the reality and significance of what they had heard, and Paul was moved to apologise for having related the events of the previous night to them, not realising the effect his account was going to create.

"Don't apologise, Paul," Maura appealed. "We all wanted to hear the revelation of your ordeal and the risk you took to keep me and the dogs safe from the murderous intent of the insane killer,"

Maura reminded him. She continued: "My tears and my mum's – and dad's too, if he sheds any – are tears of gratitude to you. It's the only way a woman can release the emotional build-up, and we certainly don't want you to be sad because of it," Maura tried to reassure Paul.

"Yes, I appreciate the feelings of all three of you, but I would like you to understand that I do not enjoy being hero-worshipped simply for having made a decision, fuelled by love, to reluctantly carry out the agreed plan of a group single-handed. That I had to tackle him alone was due entirely to the unpredictable thinking of the opportunist killer. Added to that is the fact that I believed I was being assisted by the spiritual presence that was silently guiding me," Paul explained.

"Yes, we understand your feelings, Paul," Maura senior commented, and she added, "We, by spilling our tears, are not only celebrating the joy of your success and survival, but we are also relieving tension caused by the build-up of fear for your safety that we have experienced since you left yesterday afternoon. Can you digest that aspect of it, Paul?" Maura senior asked, in tears.

Paul bent his head in thoughtful contemplation for an extended moment and then apologetically replied, "Yes, Maura, I can see clearly the logic of your explanation and I'm sorry. I should have thought more deeply, but I do now appreciate the extent of the emotional release of your tension. I too felt the other side of that tension, and when I had that evil demon tied up and at my mercy I felt the rising anger that was pressing me to execute him. That was why I asked you to keep talking to me on the phone, Maura, until the police arrived; otherwise I feared giving way to the temptation."

"Knowing now what both you and Maura have been through, Paul, had I been in your shoes I think I would have succumbed to the urge and put an end to the murdering devil there and then – God forgive me," Kevin confessed to his desire to take the law into his own hands.

"Thousands would have agreed with you, Kevin, and I certainly wouldn't have condemned you," Paul remarked with a smile. Then, after subduing the memory of his temporary anger, in a different mood he revealed, "On my return to the cottage-ruin site I called at that small supermarket in Attanagh and bought two bottles of Chablis, Maura, to celebrate the hoped-for success of the original plan; but the unexpected change of circumstances galvanised me to see the plan through with the help of the unseen spiritual presence in my dream that ensured success was achieved. So what better time to celebrate that success than now, with the four of us! What do you say?" he asked.

"Yes, why not!" Maura agreed, and she added, "It's a shame the dogs can't join us."

"Well, they can indeed, and they'll settle for cooled tea and a new chew to work on," Paul said, and addressing Bonzie and Fleurie he added, "Won't you, girls?"

He received affectionate licks and tail-wags in response.

"Well, I've heard this wine mentioned before in telephone conversations, and now we are going to actually taste it. That is an experience I'm looking forward to," Maura's mother enthused.

"And what about you, Kevin? Are you religiously against it or agriculturally in favour?" Paul tempted.

"Well, since the fruits of the vines are agriculturally nourished by the soil it would be against my religious belief to refuse to drink the wine." Kevin excused his decision to join the wine tasting.

"Good. And now, Maura, will you accompany the dogs and me to the camper van and help to carry a bottle?" Paul asked with a smile.

"At your service, Paul," Maura volunteered, standing upright. And addressing the dogs: "Are you coming, girls?"

They wagged their tails, cocked their ears and looked at Paul, and as he stood upright they dropped their chews and pranced about excitedly.

"We will only be a few minutes, or just long enough for the dogs to relieve themselves," Paul announced on departing.

They returned within fifteen minutes and the dogs chose their positions on the rug alongside the settee after lapping the cooled tea Maura provided, and recovered their unfinished chews in the process. Maura senior had thoughtfully provided four wine glasses in anticipation of the celebration.

"I can see where your daughter got her thoughtfulness from."

Paul commended Maura senior, and the latter replied with a compliment for her daughter: "She didn't need much reminding, Paul. She just seemed to adopt that trait by observation."

"Yes, I can well believe that because I have noticed her powers of observation too, and now she is going to teach you both something about wine that you might not already know," Paul suggested.

"Well, a few aspects of knowledge you, Mum and Dad, might not be aware of, such as the pronunciation of Chablis, which is shab-lee. Paul refers to it as '*le vin d'amour*'." Maura pronounced it several times and encouraged her parents to repeat it until they could copy her quite well.

"That's what Paul calls it, and it means 'the wine of love'. Whether you agree or disagree with him, the wine is French, if you hadn't already guessed. I usually reply to his saying in French – '*Oui, il a le goût de l'amour*', which translates as 'Yes, it has the taste of love', with which you are also free to agree or disagree. There are two other expressions you might like to know. One is '*l'esprit de la vigne*', meaning 'the spirit of the wine', and the other is '*bonne santé*', meaning 'good health' or 'cheers'. I will write them out for you later and we can practise the pronunciation," Maura concluded.

"Well, what do you say, Maura!" Kevin exclaimed. "We have two French speakers in the family."

"Yes, and I am pleased to know that because it might be an incentive for us to become involved. Would you ask Paul something in the French language, Maura," her mum appealed, adding, "to see if I have a feeling for the challenge?"

"Yes, I will, Mother, just for you," and addressing Paul she asked in French, "*Avez vous un tire bouchon pour les bouteilles de vin, Paul?*"

Paul replied, "*Oui, bien sûr, j'ai lui ici dans une poche, Maura.*"

"That sounded fine. What's the translation?" Maura senior asked, impressed.

"I asked Paul if he had a corkscrew for the bottles of wine, and he replied, 'Yes, of course, I have it here in a pocket,'" Maura translated.

"Very good, both of you," Maura senior complimented them and suggested to her husband, Kevin, "I think you'll be able to handle a bit of that language, Kevin. What do you say?"

"Oh, I'm certain to be a success if I were to have an operation that could persuade my tongue to contort itself into any shape to deal with foreign words," Kevin declared with a burst of laughter that struck a chord and ignited an outburst of laughter from the other three. Even Bonzie and Fleurie joined in with a series of whines and stifled barks.

"You've even touched the funny bone in the dogs with that remark, Kevin," Paul managed to compliment him amid the laughter.

"Well, I don't know if I've reached a new high or a new low by making the dogs laugh," Kevin replied, and that generated another bout of laughter, but Kevin was left feeling unsure whether to feel elated or deflated.

Paul was still bubbling with laughter as he poured the wine to the customary two-thirds level in the glasses, and his wife, Maura, explained about tasting with their noses first by sniffing the bouquet and then allowing the first sip to trickle down their throats to their taste buds to identify the fruits embodied in the wine, followed by the first taste. After the tasting Paul asked Maura's and Kevin's opinion of the Chablis.

"Oh, I must say I found that soothingly satisfying, Paul, and quite pleasant too." Maura senior voiced her verdict.

Kevin found the taste welcoming and remarked, "I could get really attached to that, Paul. Yes, no doubt about it, I find it quite appealing."

"Well, my dear, I wouldn't get too fond of it if I were you because poverty's presence isn't far from any of us." His wife smiled her reminder.

"Well, Maura, I have strong willpower when temptation is afoot," Kevin assured her.

"Oh yes, I believe you have, Kevin, especially when the door is closed to prevent draughts." Maura hinted at her suspicions.

The first glasses of Chablis didn't last long and Paul refilled the glasses to the usual limit.

He then commented on the wine: "I find the essence of Chablis really relaxing, and that might be because of the tension I was under earlier last night. But it also creates an overall mental and physical state of contentment. Am I alone in feeling that effect, or are you three feeling likewise?" he asked.

"Yes, that's exactly how it affects me, Paul," his wife, Maura, agreed, and she continued: "It seems to wind down all the mental and physical tensions of the day, just like a clock slowly releases its energy to mark time, like sitting on a summer evening watching slow-winging rooks heading homeward to their rookery across a fiery sky as the sun is setting."

Paul kissed Maura and added, "Or even listening to you, Maura, painting a picture of the sunset with creative words that colourfully weave a feeling of nostalgia."

"Wonderful, Maura!" Maura senior exclaimed. "And beautifully summed up by you, Paul," she complimented him, adding, "How did you learn to do descriptions like that?"

Her daughter, Maura, smiled and said, "Paul inspires me to express my natural feelings with words, Mum."

"Now, don't go praising me, Maura. You put that nostalgic statement together and you deserve the reward," Paul reminded her with a loving embrace.

"It was indeed a nostalgic poetical statement of fact," Maura senior remarked proudly.

"Yes, it was a thought-provoking description that evokes memories of boyhood days," Maura's father, Kevin, was moved to remark, adding, "And, yes, the Chablis seems to have the power to magically recall nostalgic settings and moods."

"It certainly does! And as Paul said, that inspiration must be generated by the state of contentment this wine creates," Maura senior suggested.

"I believe you have struck gold there, Maura." Paul complimented her and continued: "It's the contentment of the spirit of the Earth that rests in fragmented form in the particles of the soil and is collected in mineral substances by the roots of the vines and embodied in the fruits of the vines, the grapes, where they are stored, fortified and nourished by the all-embracing sun until September or October. Then the mature grapes are gathered and are put through the process of being pressed to extract the spirited juice, which is stored and later bottled and put on sale to be sampled like we are now doing. The spiritualised ingredients circulate round our bodies through our blood-flow system; and as they do so the spiritual contentment of the Earth caresses our organs and our mentalities – hence the satisfying contentment. That is the history of Chablis in a nutshell."

Paul concluded by raising his glass, and the others followed suit. Then they all clicked their glasses together and finished off their second glass of Chablis with a '*Bonne santé!*'

Paul had already uncorked the second bottle of wine before they had emptied their glasses, and he refilled them to the customary level, two-thirds full, for the third round.

"I hope I am not overloading your taste for the Chablis, am I?" he asked with a serious concern for their sobriety.

"Well, where I'm concerned, Paul, not at all," Kevin was quick to reply, and he added, "I am just getting into second gear – mentally speaking, that is – but I'm happily under control, thanks to the wine," he assured him with a contented smile.

"Well, well, after all these years I've finally found out how to control you, Kevin. I must put that Chablis on my shopping list in future," Maura senior commented with a smile.

Paul's wife, Maura, laughed aloud, as did Paul, and Maura reminded her father, "It seems as if the Chablis has made an honest man of you, Dad!"

"Yeah, I have to concede," Kevin confessed. "The bait was too tempting to ignore and I allowed honesty to circulate freely through my mentality, but my weak point was when I said earlier that I could get quite attached to the wine."

"You'll admit, then, Kevin, that you fell victim to the old adage 'Fools rush in where wise men fear to tread'," Paul reminded him, and then added, "but the opposite would apply to you, Kevin."

"What's that, Paul?" Kevin asked, puzzled.

"Well, since the Chablis had a good influence on you, the adage should read, 'Wise men rush in where fools fear to tread,'" Paul suggested.

Kevin thought a moment, mentally digesting the significance of the reversed adage and then erupted excitedly, "Exactly! Without a doubt, Paul, that's a fact. Chablis and Maura have won the day, and I'll have to toe the line to save my blushes." Kevin capitulated and laughed off his defeat in a happy, thoughtful mood as though he had been victorious over a self-considered personal weakness. He considered this for several minutes before suddenly posing the question "What do you think that murdering arsonist will receive for his evildoings, Paul?"

"As things stand, Kevin, I would expect him to be given life imprisonment without parole, and that is what he deserves, but if he pleads insanity, which I believe his counsel will advise him to do, by stating that he was possessed by the devil and was following the latter's instructions (and I also believe he will do that), then his term in prison will be determined by the psychological and psychiatric assessment he receives while he is in custody and the relevant reports of any progress he may make. That could be the deciding factor as to how long he remains locked up," Paul explained.

"Do you believe his devil excuse, Paul?" Maura, his wife, asked with a willingness to be influenced by her husband.

"No, Maura, absolutely not. Some people are just born with an evil instinct and will always be evil when the opportunity presents itself. They interpret life solely through an instinctive trait that is passed on, and they are locked into that tunnel-vision perspective."

"Are you saying, Paul, that a person like that will never change?" Maura senior asked.

"Their tactics might vary, Maura, but their instinctive trait never changes and prayer does nothing to alter their kind."

"Well, God is merciful to all, Paul, so we are brought up to believe, and I suppose God knows best how to deal with His sinful followers even if we don't," Maura senior summed up.

"Yes, I would agree with you on that, Maura, and I think it's best left between God and the sinner." Paul capitulated out of respect for Maura senior's religious principles.

"I couldn't forgive an evil person like him." Kevin made his feelings known. "The man who set out to murder two innocent people and their two wonderful dogs by burning them to death whilst they slept. No, I could never forgive that, especially when one considers that he did it for no apparent reason other than his own evil satisfaction."

"Yes, I understand how you feel, Kevin. And that is still the mystery: he has to have had a reason. I feel certain of that. Inspector Conroy and his team of detectives I hope might prise that information from him. We will just have to wait and see what develops from the investigation. In the meantime, we had better share the remains of this inspiring wine," Paul suggested, and he did the honours, making sure that Kevin and Maura senior received a greater share of the remaining wine than his wife and himself. He verbally added, as a bonus, "After this Chablis, Kevin, you and Maura are certain to enjoy several hours of peaceful relaxing sleep. And when you awake you will feel totally refreshed," Paul predicted.

"Can it really do all that, Paul?" Kevin asked, surprised, and then on reflection he stated good-humouredly, "Don't sell me any, Paul, or I might become really addicted to it. I'll surely be in trouble then," he added with a burst of laughter.

His wife, Maura, was quick to retaliate with her own prediction and roll of laughter by stating, "Yes, you will be in trouble, Kevin, because all you would succeed in doing would be to cause me to become addicted too, and how would you deal with that?"

"Well, we could sympathise with each other, humour each other and fall asleep singing. At least we would be happy in our misery," Kevin joked.

"And when we ran out of money to buy the source of our contentment, what then?" Maura pointed out the dilemma.

"Well, Maura, my love, if it came to that we would just have to comfort each other with my mother's favourite song, '*Que Sera Sera*'," Kevin answered with another burst of laughter, and Paul, Maura and her mother joined in.

Bonzie and Fleurie had fallen asleep over their chews, but awoke abruptly at the sound of laughter. Both stood upright and looked at Paul, indicating they wanted to go outside.

"You know what that means, Maura?" Paul addressed his wife.

"Oh yes, of course. Do you want to go out, girls?"

The dogs responded with tail wags and put their paws on the edge of the settee.

Paul stood upright and asked Maura if she had the muzzles, and she nodded, saying, "I feel the same as you do now regarding the danger after that evil devil set poison bait for them."

"Yes, it only takes one evil act to spark a fear syndrome. Where are the muzzles, Maura?"

"On a hook in the hall," she said, pushing herself upright, and Paul steadied her. "I feel a bit dizzy after the Chablis," she admitted.

"Yes, perhaps it's the sudden surge of blood when you move from one position to another. I felt the same when I stood upright. Are you coming with us, Maura?"

"Oh yes, the pure night air, or morning air, will sort out my head. Besides, I don't want you getting lost in the dark," she laughed. Then she asked her mum, "Are you and Dad getting ready for bed now, Mum?"

"Well now, it's hardly worthwhile seeing as it's pushing five o'clock. And what about you and Paul?" her mum asked.

Maura looked at Paul and he shook his head and remarked, "I agree with your mum. Besides, I expect to receive some phone calls early in the morning, but you go to bed when we return, Maura, if you feel like it. You will have exhausted yourself worrying about me yesterday and you might sleep," Paul thoughtfully suggested.

"Well now, that's a show of concern, Paul, isn't it, Maura?" Maura senior commented.

Maura looked at Paul, smiled and answered, "Yes, I know he is caring, Mum, but I'll stay awake too. We can nod off on the settee if our minds decide. What about Dad?"

"His mind has already decided and he is in dreamland," her mum informed her.

"OK, Mum, we will be back as soon as the dogs have completed their needs."

"I'll put the kettle on a slow boil and await your return," Maura senior remarked.

CHAPTER SEVENTEEN

Paul's mobile erupted into life in his pocket and woke him from the sleep he had descended into on the settee. The noise also woke Maura and her parents as well as Bonzie and Fleurie. It was just after 7 a.m. A succession of yawns and stretches followed, including those of the dogs.

"Hello and good morning," Paul greeted the caller. "Yes, this is Paul Attanagh. Oh, good morning, Inspector. I didn't instantly recognise your voice. Is it? Well, it might be raining here too, but I can't hear any raindrops peppering the roof or the windowpanes. Still though, I expect it will be heading this way. A plethora? Well, that's a lot more than enough, Inspector! Yes, yes, I can't say I'm surprised by the request. I suppose I'll have to face them sometime. Yes, I agree, Inspector. Yes, she and her parents and the dogs are all fine. Yes, I'll do that, Inspector. Did you manage to get any sleep overnight? Two hours? The same here, but a little is a little better than none, I suppose. Yes, Inspector, ring any time you feel it necessary. Thanks for keeping me up to date. Until later, then. Bye for now."

Paul turned to Maura: "Inspector Conroy asked me to pass on his regards to you, Maura, and to your mum and dad."

"That was kind of him, Paul. You must have told him about my concern for you?"

"Yes, I did, Maura, and of my concern for you and the dogs, and he was very understanding." Addressing Maura's parents, Paul continued: "He also asked me to ask you, Kevin and Maura, if you could tolerate us for another few days as reporters are requesting permission to visit the cottage site where the arsonist was apprehended in the act of preparing to cremate us in the camper van. But if we are a bit too much we can sleep in the camper van," Paul suggested.

"No, you will not sleep in the camper," Maura senior adamantly stated, adding, "There's a room ready for both of you and the dogs for as long as you wish to stay. We are glad to have your company – isn't that so, Kevin?" She asked for her husband's blessing.

"Certainly so – in fact, you can stay permanently as far as I'm concerned," Kevin invited them.

"Now, don't tempt us, Dad, or we might just take up your offer," his daughter joked with a trill of laughter.

Kevin laughed too and remarked, "Well, we could change our drinking habit from lager or Guinness to wine." And as an afterthought he added, "You're right about that wine, Paul – it doesn't leave you with a hangover in the morning."

"That's what Maura and I discovered, and now you have discovered the same effect, Kevin. What is your verdict, Maura senior?" Paul asked.

"Yes, I must agree. My head is as clear as the morning air." Maura senior boosted the endearing effects of the Chablis.

"I think that might be due to the amount we each drank. I don't know how we would feel after drinking two bottles each. That would, no doubt, have a more detrimental effect on our minds and bodies," Paul reminded her.

"Oh, I would agree entirely, Paul, and in more ways than one," Maura senior added with a laugh.

"In case you are alluding to me, my dear, I'll just remind you that I have never made a spectacle of myself." Kevin defended his past intoxicated behaviour.

"That's true, Kevin, but you have often struggled to keep your balance," his wife reminded him.

"Well, that was simply because I wanted to prematurely sleep instead of walk and I was struggling to stay awake."

Kevin tried to excuse aspects of his past, and that provoked an outburst of laughter from all four.

"Congratulations, Kevin! That was an ingenious defence of your struggle to keep upright on occasions in the past." Paul applauded Kevin's attempt at plausibility. "You deserve top marks for your effort. Wouldn't you agree, Maura senior and junior?"

"Oh yes, I'll have to give him credit now. He isn't slow in trying to convince us, despite his own lack of confidence in his argument, as we have just witnessed." Maura senior agreed, and she added, "I suppose he is a unique character in his own right."

"And how would you describe your parents, Maura?" Paul asked his wife.

"I have to say that my mum and dad are loving, caring, sharing and understanding parents," Maura stated without hesitation.

"And I would say that you are a close-knit, happy family and an example to others, and I am pleased to be a member of it now as well." Paul stated his affiliation.

"Well, welcome to our family circle, Paul. We couldn't have wished for a better addition." Kevin voiced his pleasure and offered Paul his hand in friendship, and they shook hands to seal the affinity.

"I'll put the dogs' muzzles on now and take them for a stroll," Paul decided, and he asked Maura if she would be accompanying him.

"But of course. I've been looking forward to that since we arrived here – and that was only yesterday afternoon. Would you believe so much has happened during that short space of time! What could be better than an early morning in the surrounding woodland and fields with you and the dogs, Paul, and listening to the songbirds singing?" she expressed her feelings of joy.

"I have no wish to dampen your spirits, Maura, but Inspector Conroy told me it was raining in Attanagh," Paul informed her, and he added, "And it might be raining here too. We haven't had a look yet."

"Oh, I hope not, Paul – at least not until we have had our walk with the dogs." And she parted the living-room curtains to check.

"Cloudy, but no rain yet, so let's get going and pray that it doesn't rain until we get back."

"What would you like for breakfast when you return?" Maura senior asked.

"Oh, don't worry about breakfast for Paul and me, Mum.

We always have organic oats made into porridge with muesli, a tablespoonful of honey and a little milk. You and Dad are welcome to share some as well. We have all the ingredients except the milk in the camper van. We follow up our cereal with a hefty slice of bread from an unsliced loaf of bread, toasted, buttered and finished with a covering of tangy marmalade. So don't worry about us, but join us if you wish. As for the dogs, they share the porridge with us and a thick slice of bread fried in fat with one or two slices of bacon or a couple of fried sausages cut up and mixed with the fragmented bread. If you can prepare some of that, Mum, they will really appreciate it and never forget your generosity," Maura told her.

"I will do that for you wonderful heroines," Maura senior agreed whilst fondling the dogs' heads and embracing them.

She received a spate of affectionate licks in return as a grateful reward, much to the amusement of Paul and his wife.

"I can imagine how a lollipop might feel if it were a living thing," Maura senior remarked, unable to avoid the affectionate attention of the dogs.

"I know of no other creature that shows its gratitude like a dog. It is supreme in this, and, there's no doubt about it, it is a human being's best friend." Kevin announced his feeling for dogs.

"Absolutely true, Kevin, and that's exactly how Maura and I feel about them too," Paul endorsed.

"And what about me?" Maura senior reminded him.

"We don't have to remind you, Mum, because you show your love for the dogs more than words can describe," Maura junior stated with feeling.

"I expect you are all attending church this morning?" Paul said, and he asked if there was a church in the village.

"Yes, St Theresa's, at the other end of the village. It's a small church and Mass is celebrated by a priest from one of the larger towns at noon on Sundays, when a priest is available," Maura senior revealed.

"And when a priest is unavailable, what then?" Paul asked.

"In that case, the caretaker – the villager who lives nearest to the church – leads the flock in reciting prayers and singing hymns for a half-hour or so, after which we have a conversation about the latest news of the parish, and religious matters, before dispersing and returning home again," Maura senior explained.

"Well, I suppose that's fair enough to fulfil your obligations," Paul agreed, and he suggested, "I will drive you there for the noon service and wait around to take you home again, or take you to wherever you might want to go. Dogs are not allowed into churches, which is understandable, so I will stay outside with them and take them for a stroll round the churchyard, where I will have a private conversation with God in his Garden of Eden." Paul revealed his thoughts.

"Well now, Paul, that sounds fine with me," Kevin remarked, and he continued: "You are of sound mind, aren't you, Paul?" And he erupted in laughter.

Paul instantly saw the funny side of the remark and burst into laughter too, and they were both joined by the half-smiling, half-laughing women, still unsure of what it was that caused the laughter.

"What are we supposed to be laughing about?" his wife, Maura, naively asked.

Paul looked at her, smiling, and said, "Oh, it's just a light-hearted joke between your dad and me. It was his interpretation of what I audaciously stated was a private conversation with God in the Garden of Eden whilst you three were in church, where God is supposed to reside and listen to your confessions and supplications," Paul explained.

"I still don't see what's funny about it," Maura admitted, and she asked her mum if she understood the joke.

Her mum said, "No, but somehow your dad and Paul do."

Paul tried to clear up the mystery by slowly explaining, "It was the manner in which your father remembered the biblical Garden of Eden, and Adam and Eve, that prompted him to jokingly ask if I was descending into fantasy or, in other words, going potty. Is that right, Kevin?" he asked for clarification.

"Yeah, that's it exactly, Paul, and you were quick to pick up the meaning and see the funny side of it," Kevin agreed.

"Well, I have to give you full marks for stimulating my mental response, Kevin." Paul credited his father-in-law and added, "And you haven't forgotten your biblical knowledge either. So now, ladies, you will realise that it's impossible to have such a conversation with God since my supplication would have to be a mental one, just like yours in the church."

"So, it was a private joke that my dad made about you, and the audacity of you having a conversation with God that was just fantasy?" Maura worked out the puzzle to her satisfaction.

"Don't men sometimes laugh over the simplest things?" Maura senior remarked to her daughter.

"You know best, Mum. Since you have more experience than I, I have to be subservient to you in such matters." And turning to Paul she asked, "Are we ready to go now, Paul?"

"Yes, let's go, Bonzie and Fleurie. See you later, Maura and Kevin."

On their return, Maura senior had the dogs' breakfast waiting for them. They relished the fried bread, sausages and bacon, and when she asked them if they liked it she was rewarded with a deluge of licks, and she could only grin and bear it whilst the other three enjoyed the amusement.

When the thank-you gesture ended, Maura senior remarked affectionately, "My God, girls, you two would lick a person to the bone in your eagerness to express your thanks!"

Her daughter commented: "They will never forget your act of generously, Mum. You're a friend for life."

"Well, I suppose I should be grateful for their exuberance since it's an instinctive response." Maura senior smiled her satisfaction.

Paul and Maura didn't offer them any of their organic oats and muesli, and the dogs didn't show any sign of wanting any. Their breakfast had satisfied their hunger.

The rest of the morning went well. The priest turned up for the Mass, and Paul and the dogs went for a stroll round the 'Garden of Eden' (which to him was the Earth or any part of it) and he had a private conversation with God. The sky remained cloudy, but the rain was held in abeyance perhaps by the hand of God or, more likely, by the lack of wind to push the clouds along.

After the church service the four plus the dogs returned to the cottage for a light lunch, which consisted of apple and/or rhubarb pie with custard. A slice of apple pie and custard was given to each dog, washed down with cooled tea, and their bowls were licked spotlessly clean.

"Those dogs are ideal diners – they never leave anything to be cleaned up or washed up after eating their food." Kevin commended the dogs. "We should learn a lesson from them."

"Well and truly stated, Kevin!" his wife agreed. "And now you can set an example, Kevin, by tidying up and washing up after us," she suggested with her checkmate reply and a smile.

"Oh, there now! You are very quick-witted this morning, dear. It must be the belated inspiration of the Chablis from earlier this morning manifesting itself in your mentality, and I walked innocently into the trap," Kevin remarked and admitted.

"That was a masterstroke by you, Maura," Paul congratulated her. "And it was graciously uncontested by you, Kevin. That deserves congratulating too. And now would both of you like to go for a drive anywhere in particular?" Paul suggested.

"Well, since Sunday is traditionally a day of rest," Maura senior reminded him, "and we will soon begin preparing the Sunday dinner, why not enjoy an interesting conversation together instead?"

At that precise moment Paul's mobile erupted into life and interrupted proceedings. Paul apologised as he retrieved the mobile from his pocket and pressed the 'speak' button. He said hello and was answered by his boyhood friend Gerry Kyle.

"Hello, Paul, and congratulations! I can hardly believe what I am reading." Gerry spoke in an excited tone of voice.

"Hi, Gerry – glad to hear from you. What do you mean you can't believe what you are reading. I don't—"

"Haven't you read the morning paper?" Gerry interrupted.

"No, we are not in Attanagh at the moment, Gerry; we are in a small village in Tipperary, at the home of Maura's parents, and I don't think there's a newsagent's shop here," Paul informed him.

"Well, I'll just read the headlines of the copy I have here, Paul: 'Itinerant Traveller Serving Life in Prison for Murder Five Years Ago Declared Innocent'. It goes on to name you as the hero who risked his life to prove the man's innocence. You are the talk of the town – no, of the whole country – at the moment. I can imagine how the innocent man and his wife and young daughter feel this morning."

"Oh, I don't like hero worship, Gerry. I was bound by the police rules about classified information in order to keep the plan of action secret, but circumstances changed and I was forced to act alone to bring the affair to a successful conclusion. All worked out well. I will explain in detail when we meet again, which won't be for a few days according to the advice of Inspector Conroy of the Attanagh police force. Is all well with you, Gerry?"

"Yes, fine, and even better now thanks to your success. I will keep you updated until you get back. The planning permission for the bungalow has been passed and the construction preparations will begin shortly. There is a buzz of excitement around the region now, Paul. I will keep you in touch with anything you need to know. I hope you, Maura and the dogs enjoy your break. Bye for now, Paul."

"Bye, Gerry. And thanks for calling."

"Is there a newsagent's shop in the village or do you have to go to the nearest town for a paper?" Paul asked.

"No," Kevin replied, "but there is a house-to-house paper-delivering service on Sunday afternoon at around two o'clock, which is soon."

"Are you on the delivery list, Kevin?" Paul asked.

"Indeed we are, Paul. They never fail to deliver, although sometimes they are late. But there again, as the old saying goes, it's better late than never."

"True, Kevin. One can't argue with that."

Paul expressed his satisfaction, and a few minutes later a copy of the Sunday paper was passed through the letterbox. Paul's wife, Maura, en route to the kitchen picked it up and glanced at the headlines.

"Wow, Paul! Listen to this: 'Arsonist Killer Surprised and Disarmed by Brave Intended Victim as Police Team under Inspector Conroy of Attanagh Closed in on the Potential Murder Scene!' How is that for the main headline!" Maura exclaimed in excitement whilst sitting down beside Paul and embracing him, adding, "But best of all is the fact that you are safe and well, Paul, as are the dogs and as I am. And it's all thanks to you too."

Paul embraced and kissed her and fondled the dogs' heads, saying, "That is what I am most content about, and I really hope the police will extract the truth about that demon's motives from him. That would complete the unravelling of the mystery still surrounding the murder of the family in the cottage five years ago."

"I remember reading about that murder at the time. You must remember it as well, Kevin," Maura senior said.

"Yes, I do remember it. You read it aloud to me," Kevin reminded her, and he continued: "I remember thinking to myself, and sharing my thoughts with you, Maura, about the arsonist's reason for setting the cottage on fire and killing the innocent members of that family. He either wanted that land for some pressing reason unknown to anyone else, or he was afraid of the occupiers discovering something that he didn't want to be discovered. I can't think of any other reason for the killing," Kevin recalled.

Paul began thinking of other possible reasons, and suddenly he reacted aloud: "I've got it! Why didn't I realise that before?"

"You made me jump then, Paul," his wife Maura declared, startled.

"I'm sorry, Maura," Paul apologised, and he explained: "It was something your dad said that made me rethink about the past. The killer didn't want the occupiers discovering something – that's what you said, Kevin, wasn't it?" Paul asked.

"Yeah, either that or he wanted the land – one or the other," Kevin repeated, and he asked, "What's important about that, Paul?"

"Well, the question I asked myself, Kevin, was what could it be that he didn't want to be discovered? Something five years ago prompted him to commit the heinous murder of an innocent family to prevent whatever it was from being exposed, and now five years later, when Maura and I decide to buy the site and have a new house built on it, both of us and the dogs are targeted. Our execution was planned to prevent the truth, whatever it may be, from being exposed. Whatever the secret is, it must have been known five years ago," Paul decided.

"That's good thinking, Paul, and I believe you are on the right track. The police, I hope, might get to the bottom of it," Kevin suggested.

"Well, I hope so, Kevin, because I don't like loose strings dangling. Still though, it's an interesting idea and I'll put it to Inspector Conroy when I next see him. And I'll remember to mention your contribution in the process, Kevin."

"Oh, I only mentioned what I thought of the crime, Paul, not more than that," Kevin reminded him.

"Well, you prompted me to rethink the situation, Kevin, and that is something I won't forget."

Paul didn't want to get involved in a conversation about the Sunday paper's coverage of the previous night's drama concerning his exploits and the surprise arrest of the killer arsonist who had attempted to set the camper van on fire believing that Paul and Maura were asleep in it. He suggested a game of Scrabble between the four of them to divert their attention.

"I have a Scrabble board and tiles in the camper. I'll go and get them and it will keep our minds occupied, concentrating on something more amusing."

The other three agreed and Paul stood upright and excused himself. He left the room with Bonzie and Fleurie following closely at his heels. He delayed a few minutes in the garden for the dogs' benefit, sitting on the garden bench. After a while Maura joined him and held his hand.

"You don't want to talk about your heroic act, do you, Paul?" she asked sympathetically.

Paul shook his head and answered, "No, Maura, I'm sorry, but I don't like hero worship and I do not relish being the centre of attention. I find it all too embarrassing, to an extent where I just want to hide myself away until it has all died down. I understand how people feel, but I feel at a loss to know how to respond to people's congratulations every time I am recognised. Do you understand, Maura?"

"Yes, I can imagine how it affects you, Paul, and I feel sorry about your state of mind. You did what you felt you had to do for my sake, for the dogs' sake and for my parents' sake too. Let's go in and get lost in a game of Scrabble and joke about other things."

He smiled, kissed her and said, "Yes, let's do that, Maura."

CHAPTER EIGHTEEN

Paul gave Bonzie and Fleurie a hide chew each to keep them occupied whilst the four family members indulged in their game of Scrabble. The game generated as much laughter as thoughtful endeavour for more than an hour, after which mother and daughter broke off to prepare the late-afternoon dinner. They still managed to engage the men in broken conversation during the process, which was also punctuated with laughter. The meal itself was composed of roast chicken, roast potatoes, mashed potatoes and swede with boiled cabbage chopped and fried. It was enjoyed by all, including the dogs, but without chicken bones for the dogs because of their brittleness and tendency to splinter when chewed and the likelihood of splinters causing gut problems for the dogs. Dessert was looked forward to by all in anticipation of home-baked apple pie and custard, and the dogs by force of habit licked clean their bowls as a sign of love and gratitude and planted affectionate licks on mother and daughter each time the opportunity presented itself.

"*Felicitations, mère et fille, les chefs suprêmes,*" Paul congratulated them with a broad smile.

"You had better do the translation, Maura," her mum suggested.

"Paul said, 'Congratulations, mother and daughter, the supreme cooks!' And we should reply with '*Merci bien, Paul – vous êtes très gentil*', which translates as 'Thanks a lot, Paul – you are very kind.'"

Maura senior was quite pleased with the compliment and she repeated each French phrase several times until she got them almost perfect.

"It's a shame we didn't have any wine with which to celebrate the final meal; but then, a few French words were an acceptable substitute and the tea caressed us with its flavour," Kevin made the effort to contribute.

"Now, that was quite a quaint way of honouring tea, Kevin. Its source is the tea plant, just like the vine is the source of the wine, but the history of the tea plant isn't widely known or appreciated; so just in case you are not familiar with the history of the tea plant, I'll enlighten you about it as a matter of interest. Tea has been known in China since at least 2735 BC and wasn't introduced into Europe until AD 1610, where its spread was restricted to those who could afford it. It was at that time priced at £16 sterling per pound in weight. The manufacture of the tea was a closely guarded secret in China, hence the exorbitant price for the refreshing drink. Then in 1825 the tea plant was accidentally found growing in a tree form in the wild in India and the secret was out. Soon after, tea plantations spread across India and other neighbouring countries and the exorbitant price of tea rapidly fell to a level where ordinary people could afford to buy it. That is the simple story of the humble tea plant, for what it's worth," Paul enlightened his listeners.

"Well, Paul, I'm glad I mentioned tea now since I knew little or nothing about its origin, but now I do and I find it interesting."

"Don't feel bad about that, Kevin. There was a time when I didn't know about it either." Paul tried to make Kevin feel at ease about his lack of knowledge.

"So it has been known in China since 2735 BC. Have I got that right, Paul?" Kevin asked.

"Yes, Kevin, that's ancient," Paul agreed.

"My God," Kevin exclaimed, "what a length of time! That makes it over 4,500 years old. It existed all those years before the arrival of Christ!" Kevin exclaimed, and he added, "So China had the monopoly on tea until the tea plant was accidentally discovered in India in . . ."

"1823," Paul reminded him.

"That is a mighty long time to have a monopoly on a product," Kevin remarked.

"One has to remember, Kevin, that trade in ancient times was at walking pace and often took months and even years to complete. No doubt at times goods never arrived. When one looks back from our advanced situation today it's hard to imagine how lethargically slow progress was in our ancestors' time," Paul summed up.

"Well, I find those facts about tea quite interesting too," Maura senior chipped in.

"And so do I," Paul's wife, Maura, admitted, and she added, "So in Jesus' time tea can't have existed in the countries associated with Jesus. I can't remember tea ever being mentioned in the Bible. Would you agree, Paul?" she asked.

"That is very observant of you, Maura, and I must agree with you. Full marks! The only reason I can think of why tea isn't mentioned in the Bible is because wine was drunk with their meals – wine is often quoted in the Bible. Still, tea, it seems, is almost as old as the hills and is as popular today as it ever has been, I believe, since the beginning of its use. I can't ever see it losing its appeal."

The others agreed on that concluding point.

After the meal was finished, Paul and Maura volunteered and insisted on doing the washing-up; and on completing that task, Paul put the dogs' muzzles on and took them for a rambling exercise for half an hour. The walk was enjoyed by all four of them. Not long after returning it began raining at a steady pace. There was no wind, which meant its passing would be a slow process, and the dogs settled down to work on their hide chews whilst the four family members demonstrated their Scrabble skill.

Most of the evening and overnight were affected by heavy intermittent rain showers, and Paul and Maura had to chance their luck when the dogs needed to respond to the call of nature. Although they were caught out a couple of times, they accepted the hits and misses as part of the vagaries of life. Apart from trying to avoid the rain showers, they passed the evening playing Scrabble and discussing thought-provoking subjects that all four learned from and the game provided plenty of laughter.

Monday, Tuesday and Wednesday were unsettled days with rain, hail, sun and wind at times annoyingly gusting. But all unsettled weather dissipated during the early hours of Thursday morning and high pressure followed with fine weather in tow and higher temperatures with long sunny periods. Paul and Maura decided to take Maura's parents to the nearest town and restock their depleted supplies, which included buying six bottles of wine – two bottles each of Chablis, Sauvignon Blanc and Beaujolais. Paul suggested to Maura not to hold back on anything that her parents might need, and that included two ten-packs of a lager of their choosing.

"And make sure they have enough of everything they need over the coming two weeks at least," he added.

Whilst the family members shopped in the supermarket Paul took the dogs, with muzzles fitted and a double-chained lead attached to their collars, on to a stretch of wasteland adjoining the supermarket car park.

His boyhood friend and council official, Gerry Kyle, phoned to say that Jack Kyley, the builder, would be moving machinery on to the cottage ruin site on Monday to begin preparing the ground for the construction of the bungalow, and the council would be holding a special meeting over the coming weekend. Paul was the subject of the meeting, and Gerry felt it would benefit Paul in some way. He said if he discovered what transpired at the meeting, he would let Paul know immediately.

Inspector Conroy also phoned and asked Paul to call at Attanagh police station on their return as he had some information that Paul might be grateful for.

He was back from the ramble and waiting by the open rear doors of the camper van when the shoppers returned with the dogs still on the lead. The dogs greeted the family members as soon as they recognised them from a distance with whimpers and stifled barks of excitement.

Paul handed Maura the lead and charge of the dogs whilst he stacked the shopping in the camper van.

"Now, Maura, you have to allow us to pay for this shopping. It's just too much to reward us with. It might be ten times the amount of food and drink you, Paul and the dogs have consumed over the four days you've been here," Maura senior reminded her daughter.

"But, Mum, it was Paul's bank card that paid the bill, and I was only doing as instructed. Paul will verify that."

"Yes, Maura, I asked her to restock your kitchen and fridge and freezer with all that you and Kevin might need; and yes, she paid with my bank card. It's a gesture to show our gratitude to you both for housing and feeding us and the dogs since last weekend, and it's small payment for your generosity. I fear to think what you are going to say or do when we offer to reward you financially for your hospitality," Paul explained.

"What!" Maura senior exclaimed. "You want to add payment to all these provisions you have paid for? My God! But – but – but it would have been far cheaper to book all four of you into a first-class hotel" was all that Maura senior could think of to say.

Paul laughed and replied, "In that case we would have deprived ourselves and the dogs of the pleasure of your and Kevin's company, and that was what we needed most of all. So what's wrong with rewarding both of you in return for your generosity?" Paul concluded.

"Because you and Maura are not only family members, but guests as well in our home, and it would be sinful to charge my own daughter and son-in-law for the pleasure of your and your dogs' company for a few days." Maura senior defended her principles.

"Well, I do admire your moral outlook and your consideration for family members, relatives and friends, Maura, but couldn't you just ease your grip on the reins of your moral ruling for the sake of our sensitive feelings? We are grateful to you and Kevin, and we would like to express our thanks to you both. We can afford the outlay, and we are merely showing our appreciation. Besides, your daughter, Maura, will be rewarding you with a far greater reward in the course of time," Paul appealed.

Maura senior looked at her daughter, surprised by Paul's remark, and instantly smiled, saying, "Well, yes, allowances have to be made in such cases, and under the circumstances I suppose we should accept your generosity."

"Great!" Paul exclaimed. "Let's get these provisions home unless you want to call somewhere else."

"Home direct, Paul," Maura senior stated, adding, "before we allow you to bankrupt yourself."

Paul's wife, Maura, didn't get the opportunity to ask him what he meant by what he had said to her mum, because she had respectfully surrendered the front passenger seat of the camper van to her dad. So she had to bide her time until after lunch.

When they took the muzzled dogs for their exercise, Maura seized the opportunity: "What did you mean, Paul, when you told Mum in the supermarket car park that I would be rewarding her with a greater reward in the course of time?"

Paul looked at her, smiled and explained: "I meant that you would be surprising her with a grandson or granddaughter, which I hope you will be, won't you?"

"Well, hopefully, yes, but I believe that my mum interpreted what you said as meaning that I was already pregnant."

"She did!" Paul exclaimed, and asked, "And is she right, Maura?"

"Not that I am aware of, but that's beside the point. My mother believes I am now, and that is why she softened to your generosity."

"Yes, I believe you are right, Maura. I should have been more careful in the way I expressed myself. I'll have to correct my mistake, but not today. We will be leaving tomorrow morning, so I'll write a note of explanation and put it in the envelope with the money, and she will read it after we have left. Do you agree, Maura?"

"What money are you referring to, Paul?" Maura asked, her curiosity piqued.

"The money for having accommodated us and the dogs, and for the pleasure of their company as well as for sharing their food with us and the dogs. I would like to reward your parents for their efforts on our behalf. I'm sure you agree with that, Maura?"

"It's not how I feel that concerns me, but how Mum is going to react. You heard what she said when you mentioned *reward*?"

"Well, yes, but I'll explain in the note and take the blame for having raised her hopes. How does that sound?"

"Well, that's thoughtful of you, Paul, but . . . How much money do you intend putting in the envelope?" Maura asked.

"Two or three hundred euros. What do you think, Maura?"

"Knowing my mum, I would suggest 100," Maura advised.

"I'll say 200, then, as there are two people involved. They can buy themselves a present each at our expense. As you already know, Maura, I don't like getting into disputes over money, so can we agree on that?"

"It's your money, Paul, and I—"

"Correction, Maura," Paul interrupted her: "it's *our* money. It's as much yours as it is mine. That's how I feel about it. Do you have enough cash to cover that, Maura?"

"Yes, we have sufficient cash to cover that, Paul," Maura agreed.

"So is that settled, then?" Paul asked hopefully, and he came to a halt, as did Maura. Bonzie and Fleurie, with muzzles on, stopped alongside them. Paul took Maura in his arms, embraced her and kissed her, and she willingly responded.

"Have I told you lately that I love you, Maura?" Paul asked, smiling.

"Of course, Paul. We tell each other every day that we do, and I hope we always will." Maura smiled her joy.

"I'm sure we will, my love, and our bosom friends here as well," Paul added.

"Who could not love such truly faithful friends?" Maura concluded.

"There's something I neglected to tell you, Maura. Gerry Kyle rang whilst you were in the supermarket and told me that planning permission for the bungalow had been granted and the builder, Jack Kyley, will be moving machinery on to the site on Monday to begin preparations for construction, so I think it's time to inform your parents of our plan to have an extension apartment added to the garden end of the bungalow as a holiday or retirement home, or whatever they want to call it. They can use it as they wish. Can I leave it to you, Maura, to break the news to your parents and ask their opinion on the proposal? I hope they will accept the offer, but they are definitely not under any obligation to accept."

"My personal opinion is that they will be delighted, Paul, with the offer to use it as their second home any time they feel like it, and even permanently if they decide to. When my mum hears that offer, she won't be able to bring herself to chastise you for your generosity," Maura enthused.

"Oh, don't worry yourself about that, Maura. I won't be upset whatever your mum decides. I know she means well and I admire her for standing by her godly principles. So can I depend on you, then, to invite your mother into the kitchen and explain our proposal to her, Maura? It will have to be decided by Monday, when I hope to speak to the builder, Jack Kyley. He will then advise the architect on the extension to be incorporated into the building plan."

"Yes, I will do that, Paul. I just know she will be delighted, as will my dad and as I am. My deepest thanks to you, Paul," Maura said, putting her arms around Paul's neck and kissing him passionately.

When they relaxed their loving embrace, Paul remarked, "The sooner we get settled and generate a baby the better it will be." And after a thoughtful moment he added, "Of course there is the possibility that we could end up bankrupt if circumstances turn against us, but if that were to happen we would somehow find ways of negotiating our way through the vagaries of life even if it means having to live as wanderers indefinitely." Paul accepted the unknown future.

"Yes, we will survive together even if poverty were to rule our roost." Maura expressed her devotion.

Bonzie and Fleurie led the way back to the cottage, where they all had apple pie with tea – and that included the dogs.

After their favourite snack Paul gave the dogs a hide chew each, and they settled on the rug to ply their art whilst Paul engaged Kevin in conversation and mother and daughter retreated to the kitchen to do the washing-up. Maura junior related to her mum Paul's proposal concerning the apartment extension to the new bungalow for her parents' pleasure.

"Free? Wow!" Maura senior's exclamation echoed from the kitchen.

"My daughter must have told the wife something exciting," Kevin remarked during his chat with Paul.

"Well, I suppose, Kevin, just like us, women find the simplest things exciting too," Paul reminded him.

"Yeah, that's true, Paul. Life would be very dull without

amusement, and there are people who are quite amusing without even trying."

"Yes, and some are very quaint in their verbal expressions and naturally generate laughter and are a joy to be in conversation with," Paul agreed.

They were soon joined by mother and daughter from the kitchen, and Paul suggested a game of Scrabble.

The other three voted in favour and Kevin remarked, "It sounded like you two were enjoying your chat in the kitchen?"

"Oh, we certainly were, Kevin," Maura senior confirmed, and she added, "It concerned you too, Kevin, but I'll explain later. For now, let's concentrate on the game."

Bonzie and Fleurie stopped chewing momentarily until the four settled down to their task, and then they resumed their chewing interest again.

The game progressed in a relaxed mood with jokes and laughter generated by innocently misspelt words that had to be corrected. They were into the second game when Bonzie dropped her chew and approached Paul, placing a paw on his knee, indicating the call of nature, and Fleurie joined her in the action.

"Well, we have to call a temporary halt and resume when we return," Paul announced, and he asked his wife if she felt like accompanying them.

"But of course. I wouldn't feel right if I didn't, and our saviours would, I'm sure, miss me too, wouldn't you, girls?" And she embraced them.

"And I would miss you too," Paul reminded her.

"Yes, I know you would, Paul. Thanks for reminding me." Maura planted a quick kiss on his lips.

After the muzzles were fitted over the dogs' jaws and the lead chains were attached to their collars, Paul addressed Kevin and Maura, saying, "As soon as the dogs have satisfied their needs we will return without delay."

And the four departed.

"I expect that exclamation your mother made in the kitchen, Maura, was her reaction to what we have planned for both of them," Paul said.

"Yes, that was her delighted reaction to the news. I thought for a moment that she was going to rush into the sitting room and embarrass you with her exuberance, but I put a finger to my closed lips and moved my head from side to side and she instantly understood," Maura explained. "She will most likely tell Dad whilst we are out. You understand, don't you, Paul?" she appealed.

"Yes, of course I do, Maura. I'm pleased that she is delighted and I hope your dad will be too." Paul made his feelings known.

"Oh, I'm sure he will be just as overcome as my mum. Both will struggle to express their pleasure in appropriate words." Maura excused their excitement.

"As long as they are satisfied with the offer, they can express their thanks in whatever way they wish." Paul smiled.

On their return, Maura senior greeted them with "Anyone for tea or coffee and apple and/or rhubarb pie?"

"I guess that we are all agreeable. We accept your offer, Maura, as I hope you and Kevin will accept our offer," Paul replied, smiling.

"Well, I'm sure I speak for both of us, Paul, when I say we have never been so joyfully shocked as we are by your and Maura's wonderful offer. we just don't know how best to express our gratitude." Maura senior confessed their lack of suitable words.

"No more thanks needed since you declared that you have never been so joyfully shocked. I couldn't have done any better than that and might not have even equalled it. I am glad that you are both pleased by the offer."

Paul managed to make them both feel at ease, and after the snack of apple pie, which the dogs also enjoyed, the four family members decided to finish their game of Scrabble whilst the dogs returned to their chewing endeavours. The remainder of the day was enjoyed by all, and their final act before bedtime was to take the dogs for their customary outing.

CHAPTER NINETEEN

The following morning, Friday, as the sun lit up the May-time sky, Paul and Maura awoke after a memorable night in bed together to find Bonzie and Fleurie sat on their haunches beside their bed waiting to greet them with affectionate licks. Paul's first thought, after fondling the dogs' heads and greeting them, was to haul himself out of bed and open the rear door enough to allow the dogs access to the garden so that they could relieve themselves if necessary. They returned within minutes and followed their masters from bedroom to bathroom as they hastily dressed in casual clothes for their early morning ramble. On returning to the cottage, they found that Maura senior and Kevin were up and about in active mood.

Maura senior addressed Paul and her daughter: "Why don't you both have fried bacon, sausage, egg and tomatoes for a change, seeing as you are leaving us after breakfast?"

Paul looked at Maura and said, "Perhaps we should do as your mum suggests to prove to her that we have nothing against her cooking skills?"

"Yes, why not for a change?" Maura agreed. "I'll slice and butter some bread." And just for fun she added, "Are the dogs included in the invitation, Mum?"

"Certainly so!" her mum stated. "You didn't think I would leave those wonderful members of the family out, did you?"

"Oh no, I'm only joking, Mum. I know you would give them yours if you didn't have enough, and that's not a joke."

"Well, would you believe it, Maura, I would." Her mum surprised herself.

After breakfast Paul and Maura loaded their and the dogs' supplies into the camper van along with their personal items, and then they took the dogs for a second ramble before departure. Maura senior and Kevin reminded them that accommodation was permanently reserved for them whenever they wanted it. Embraces and handshakes were exchanged by all members of the family, including the dogs, just prior to parting company.

"We will see you soon again, Mum and Dad." Maura tearfully spoke whilst embracing her parents as Paul and the dogs climbed into the camper van.

Minutes later, they were rolling towards the main road, heading in a north-east direction. After fifteen minutes Paul steered the camper van into a lay-by and stopped.

He turned the engine off and asked, "How do you feel now, Maura?"

"I'm fine, Paul. It's always sad parting company with loved ones."

"Oh, I know that, Maura, and parting company with loved ones prematurely, suddenly and permanently is the worst of all," Paul recalled sadly.

"I'm sorry, Paul – I should have realised that parting company is a painful reminder to you."

"Don't be sorry, Maura. It's not your fault. You have to bid a temporary farewell to your parents, but you know you will see them again. It's a natural occurrence, but it's hard to recall being woken from my sleep and being told that my parents, alas, had departed without a farewell. I felt abandoned in a pool of sorrow," Paul reminisced with tearful eyes.

Maura leaned across and placed an arm round his neck, saying, "Don't torture yourself like that, Paul."

"What upsets me, Maura, is I didn't know how to say farewell to your parents in a meaningful way. That's how that tragedy has affected me. So please explain to your parents when you speak to them again."

"Yes, I will, Paul, and they will understand," Maura assured him.

"I was going to ask you if you would like to drive, if you feel in the mood, Maura."

"Yes, I will if you think I'm capable, Paul."

"Yes, I do. I'll climb out and go round, and you just move yourself across."

Paul slipped out of the cab to the surprise of the dogs. They welcomed him back with licks of affection when he climbed into the passenger seat.

An hour later they arrived in Attanagh Police Station car park and Maura parked as close as possible to the entrance.

"I'll take the dogs on their lead for a stroll around the perimeter of the car park, and I suggest that you join us, Maura, to exercise your legs."

"I was just about to suggest the same," Maura replied, undoing her seat belt.

They spent fifteen minutes on their walkabout, and on returning to the camper van Paul advised Maura to lock both doors from the inside and to speak to any possible enquirer through a slightly open window.

"If any suspicious activities should occur beep the horn repeatedly," he said.

"Understood, Paul," Maura answered, and after kissing Maura and fondling the dogs' heads and asking them to be good Paul walked the few paces and entered the station.

The desk officer recognised him instantly: "Mr Attenagh, glad to see you again. Inspector Conroy asked me to look out for you." And he pressed the intercom button.

"Yes," the Inspector's voice answered.

"Mr Attenagh has just arrived, Inspector."

"Good. Send him right in, Donal."

"So that's your first name – Donal – but I will always address you respectfully as officer. Is that OK, officer?"

"If that's your wish, it's fine with me. It's the second door on the right, Mr Attenagh. It's a more spacious office."

Paul uttered his thanks and strode towards the office, where Inspector Conroy was standing by the open door waiting to greet Paul with a handshake.

"I hope you, your wife and dogs enjoyed your few days' break?" he asked.

"Yes, we did, Inspector. My wife's parents were great fun to be with, and it was the ideal therapy after our ordeal. How did you manage all the news media enquiries?"

"It has been a hectic week, Paul. I have never been so busy in my life before, but I must confess it was also an interesting experience. And incidentally, the piece of wellington boot that your brave dog managed to secure and got wedged in its teeth proved to be the missing piece of the arsonist killer's boot. It places the culprit at the intended murder scene on the previous night. He did as you expected. He tried to lie his way out of trouble until we placed the evidence under his nose and read the forensic-science report to him. He then resorted to blaming the devil for his crime, and not himself. He admitted preparing the holocaust of fire that was to consume not only the camper, but the occupants, and we questioned him about the murder of the innocent family in the cottage five years ago. He answered, 'Yeah, the devil was using me as his tool of destruction.' He did it, but he says he had no say in it."

"So he is using the devil as his excuse for his evil crimes, which means he will be pleading insanity at his trial. Is that right, Inspector?" Paul asked.

"That's how it looks at the moment, Paul, unless some other revelation comes to light, but the killer has woven a cocoon of lies around his mentality at the moment," the Inspector stated.

"Did you find anything on your reading of the court report relating to the murder case of five years ago, Inspector, if you found the time during your hectic week?" Paul asked.

"Yes, I did manage to read the report and other important documents, but found nothing unusual about the Foley family of six members living in the thatched cottage at the time. There was the father, Frank, the mother, Mary, the eldest sibling, a girl of fifteen also named Mary, and two sons, Dominic, aged thirteen, Frank, eleven, and the youngest, a girl named Angela, nine years old. On a Saturday morning five years ago the father, mother and three youngest children travelled by van to visit the father's parents about twenty-five kilometres south in Kilkenny, and the eldest child, Mary, cycled five kilometres east to visit her mother's parents. That fact was confirmed by the father's parents, and it was stated then that all the family members met at their cottage home again later that same afternoon or evening. Then, during the night of the following day, Sunday, the cottage was consumed by fire. You know the rest, Paul," the Inspector said.

"The grandparents on the mother's side, then, I believe, weren't interviewed, Inspector?" Paul asked.

"Well, it would seem not, but I suppose it wasn't considered relevant enough to have any bearing on the outcome," the Inspector speculated, and he asked, "What would you have done had you been involved in the case, Paul?"

"To be honest, Inspector, I believe I would have felt compelled to pay them a visit to commiserate with them on their loss. I think they would have had a special relationship with their granddaughter, since she was the eldest and probably the first one in their lives, and she may have been a regular visitor to them, taking into account the short distance between their homes."

"Yes, I see your logic, Paul, and I understand your caring nature. I will pay them a visit if it's not too late. What do you think?"

"I think they'll be pleased by your consideration, and you will get to know a little about their relationship with what might have been their favourite grandchild," Paul suggested.

"Incidentally, Paul, we received the results from the forensic laboratory concerning the liver bait you found, and you were right – it was laced with poison. That's another charge for which he will pay the price," the Inspector commented.

"I wonder, in his twisted mind, what the devil might have against dogs, Inspector?" Paul remarked.

"Yes, what indeed! I'll remember to put that question to him in the next interview," the Inspector noted.

"If he had succeeded in killing the dogs, Inspector, I believe that I would be in prison now awaiting sentence." Paul expressed his feelings.

"I can understand how you might have reacted, Paul, and in your shoes I imagine I would do exactly the same without regret," the Inspector agreed, and he asked, "I expect Maura and the dogs are waiting for you in the camper van outside?"

"Yes, they are, Inspector. We are heading to the cottage-ruin site to continue our work on the gardens and we will be staying for a while. The builder is moving excavating machinery on to the site on Monday to prepare it for the construction of the bungalow, and we are hoping it will be completed by September. If you ever need access to the site to carry out any police investigative work, Inspector, feel free to do so," Paul invited him.

"I will keep that invitation in mind, Paul, and when I get the chance I will call to keep in touch. But for now happy gardening, Paul, and my regards to your wife, Maura," the Inspector ended.

Paul returned to Maura and the dogs, having engaged the desk officer in a brief, friendly conversation en route.

He related the information he had received to Maura, and her first remark was "So that evil devil believed he had disposed of our two beloved best friends. He doesn't deserve the least morsel of mercy from anyone." She made her anger known.

"They are alive and well, Maura. Let's be thankful for having been aware of the danger and let's be alert to the danger at all times – hence the muzzles."

"Yes, you are right, Paul. We must be wary of everybody with whom we come into contact. That's the mindset to adopt, I think," Maura suggested.

"Yes, I agree, until we establish trust in friends like Gerry, for example," Paul decided, and he asked, "Where do you want to start in the Garden of Eden today, Maura?"

"Wow!" Maura exclaimed. "That's quite an inspirational name, Paul. Let's adopt this title for our garden. What do you think, Paul?"

"Why not, since that is what we are trying to recreate anyway – our own Garden of Eden!"

"Great!" Maura sounded her delight, and said, "I have already decided to give the rhubarb patch my attention to begin with," and she added, "because after all that rain during the week the rhubarb stalks will be like saplings and I am going to attempt to bake a rhubarb pie or two and even some stewed rhubarb. What do you say, Paul?"

"Hooray for that!" And, addressing the dogs, he said, "Sorry, girls, but we will pick up an apple pie at the small supermarket on the way. What do you think of that, girls?"

The dogs reached over the top of the barrier with wagging tails to reward Paul with affectionate licks as if they had understood.

"You always seem to have a great rapport with the dogs, Paul. I wonder if it's your tone of voice or the words 'apple pie' that they react to?"

"I think you may have struck the right note with one or the other, or even both, Maura, so you will have to start addressing them as I do and with excitement in your voice and see how they react."

She smiled as she started the engine and guided the camper van out of the police-station car park.

"Don't forget to stop at the small supermarket on the way, Maura, and I'll pick up an apple pie and a couple of bottles of wine as well."

On arrival at the cottage-ruin site, they both felt an endearing attachment to it and the trees, bushes, plants and flowers. They had developed an affinity with the site even before Paul had brought the threat of the arsonist killer to an abrupt end by his inspired unexpected heroism instigated by his strange dream.

"How do you feel now, Maura, about settling here after what's happened?" Paul asked after Maura had parked the camper van by the Portaloo and turned off the engine.

"Well, I still feel a strong affinity with the site and the plants and animals that are thriving here. I feel that I have developed a harmonious relationship with them, and that includes your queen of all the wild flowers, the dandelion. Do you understand, Paul?" she asked.

"Yes, absolutely because you have just described my feelings as well. What we feel so too will the dogs, and hopefully your parents when the bungalow has been completed, and add to that the spirits of the departed cottage family members," Paul commented.

"Yes, and it sounds marvellous, so let's go and greet all the members of the plant families, including the rhubarb plants," Maura suggested.

"Yes, just as soon as I put the dogs' muzzles on."

When Paul had done that, all four climbed out of the camper van.

"My, my! Look at the size of those rhubarb stalks, Paul!" Maura exclaimed. "They seem to be calling out to be turned into rhubarb pies or stewed rhubarb."

"Yes, I can imagine them singing a pie song if they had a voice, Maura."

"Yes, so can I, and we will have to honour their wish as soon as we have finished the rhubarb pies that Mum and I baked yesterday morning for us to take with us this morning."

"It was thoughtful of your mum to put herself to the trouble after providing for us and the dogs for several days," Paul gratefully remarked.

"She wanted to show her appreciation in some way as a thank you for the wonderful gift of a private apartment attached to the new bungalow. She said it was an unimaginable gift that will be like a dream come true when it becomes a reality, and my father was like-minded about it," Maura revealed.

Whilst they were admiring the rhubarb and the proliferation of other plants and flowers, Paul's mobile phone sounded. It was his boyhood friend Gerry Kyle on the other end, asking, "Are you on the cottage site, Paul, or—"

"Hello, Gerry," Paul interrupted. "Yes, Maura and I are on the site. We arrived only fifteen minutes ago. And how are you, Gerry?"

"I'm fine, Paul, and you sound likewise. It's nearly lunchtime and I wonder if it will be OK to call and have a chat with you and your wife?"

"Certainly, Gerry. We are here for the rest of the day. You are welcome any time – you don't have to make an appointment."

"Good. I will call within the hour. I have some good news for you. So I'll see you soon, OK?"

"Yes, Gerry, I look forward to seeing you. Until then, bye for now." He turned to his wife and said, "I expect you overheard that conversation, Maura, so you'll know it was Gerry. He is calling to see us shortly with good news. We had better get the table and chairs set up and we can offer him some tea or coffee and a slice or two of rhubarb pie," Paul suggested. Then he addressed the dogs: "You girls will be having cooled tea and apple pie and you'll be meeting a friend who is calling to see us. Do you understand, girls?"

The dogs pranced about excitedly with whines and stifled barks, giving the impression that they understood – or was it their instinctive interpretation of his tone of voice, Paul wondered.

"I'm sure they can detect the excitement emanating from your mind, Paul," Maura said, thinking likewise.

"That's exactly what I was thinking, Maura. My thought processes must be covalently bonding as our minds are interacting." Paul speculated on the connection.

"Well, I believe you even though I don't grasp the significance of what you mean," Maura confessed.

"It just means, Maura, that the atoms of our thoughts are magnetically interacting with each other and causing us momentarily to think alike. Does that make it clearer, Maura?"

"I think the dogs' instinctive mentalities and your creative mentality at times fuse and act like a single unifying force. Am I near, Paul?"

"Yes, as near as you are ever likely to be, Maura. Congratulations! And welcome to the realm of science, mind over matter," Paul concluded with a kiss for his delighted wife.

CHAPTER TWENTY

Less than half an hour later Gerry arrived, drove through the open gateway and steered his car in a half-circle to where the camper van was parked. He came to a halt alongside it. As soon as he climbed out of his vehicle the dogs recognised him, and as Paul greeted him both dogs joined him with wagging tails to offer their greetings too.

"Hello, Paul and Maura. Glad to see you both in good health, cheerful and welcoming after your worry-filled experiences – and you girls too," he added, addressing the dogs. You hadn't forgotten me," he reminded them as he fondled their heads.

"We are just about to have some home-baked rhubarb pie with tea or coffee. You will join us, Gerry, I hope?" Paul invited.

"Oh yes, I certainly will," Gerry accepted without hesitation. "It's quite a while since I had home-baked rhubarb pie."

"This pie is courtesy of Maura's mother down in Tipperary," Paul declared.

"I bet it tastes perfect," Gerry anticipated.

"Well, our beloved friends here" – pointing to the dogs – "would be the best judges of that had it been an apple pie, but alas rhubarb affects their bowel movements far differently from those of humans. We have some bought apple pies for them, and you can also sample apple pie too if you wish, Gerry."

Maura placed a slice of apple pie in each of the dogs' bowls and sliced them into more manageable fragments for the dogs to enjoy. She placed the bowls on the ground in front of the dogs, and they made short work of devouring the contents and licked their bowls clean. Maura then poured cooled tea into each bowl and the dogs lapped the tea to the last drop and licked their snouts and lips clean.

"Well, well, I have never known dogs to have a penchant for apple pie and tea before. And if the bought apple pie tasted so good, what's the home-baked rhubarb pie going to taste like!" Gerry commented, adding, "I can hardly wait to taste it."

Maura ended his wait by placing a fairly large plate on the table beside him containing a hefty slice of rhubarb pie accompanied by a spoon and a mug of tea. "*Bon appetit*, Gerry," she said.

"Well served, Maura. All I can say in reply is '*Merci beaucoup, madame.*'"

"*C'est approprié*, Gerry," Paul added.

On tasting the rhubarb pie, Gerry exclaimed, "Wow, Maura! My compliments to your mother when you next make contact. She is certainly adept in the art of baking, and I believe your effort will be equal to your mother's." Gerry congratulated her.

"Exactly so, Gerry – I can vouch for her skill in the art." Paul intervened to save Maura from any embarrassment, and added, "Maura's rhubarb, apple and gooseberry pies are indeed as excellent as her mother's, since the latter was her teacher. You will probably discover the truth of that from time to time."

When all three had finished their tasty snack, Maura asked Gerry out of common courtesy if he would like another slice, and although he admitted that he could easily eat another he declined the offer, saying, "I'd better not as it might deter me from eating my dinner later, and that would require an explanation."

"Take some rhubarb with you, Gerry, when you leave. We have a large patch that we were admiring when you rang," Paul told him.

"Well, yes, I suppose I could if you don't mind. I just hope that Joan hasn't forgotten the art of baking," Gerry remarked.

"It should all come back to her as soon as she starts preparing the ingredients," Maura assured him.

"Well, that should encourage her to engage with the culinary art again, Gerry."

Paul supported Maura's advice and then seized the opportunity to relate the story of how the identity of the arsonist killer was exposed, including the encounter and capture of him that same night. When Paul finished his intriguing recollection Gerry was quite impressed.

He remarked, "What a tension-filled, dangerous, unanticipated, nerve-racking encounter you found yourself accidentally involved in, Paul, and you believe it was inspired by the spiritual female presence in your dream acting as your guardian supervisor. What a worrying ordeal you experienced with Maura and the dogs safely housed in her parents' home fifty kilometres away!" And, addressing Maura, he said, "And what a worrying mental ordeal you must have suffered waiting for news, Maura! I'm glad it all turned out well for all of you. I mustn't forget the dogs, who set everything in motion by their alertness. Which is the one that helped to identify the killer, Paul?" Gerry asked.

"The orange-brown one with the white paws, white throat patch and white tail tip," Paul described Bonzie.

"What an intelligent girl you are, Bonzie!" Gerry praised the dog whilst fondling her head. "You are not aware of the fact, Bonzie, but you are famous – a real heroine." He fondled Fleurie's head too and said, "You played your part as well, Fleurie, and you are equally admired – another heroine." Addressing Paul and Maura, he said, "You have only been here two weeks and you are both famous already, and all because of an old thatched cottage you fell in love with during your boyhood days, Paul."

"Yes, that's true, Gerry. Strange, isn't it, how the past has a bearing on the future! Would you agree, Maura?" Paul posed the question.

"I wouldn't argue against it, Paul, especially where you are concerned. You seem to have some kind of insight into the future." Maura voiced her opinion.

Paul laughed and answered, "Possibly accidentally, but by design definitely not. *Que sera sera* – that's near to the truth."

"Well, I can't comment on that," Gerry remarked, and remembering the reason for the visit he exclaimed, "The good news! I had better tell both of you before I forget. It concerns the meeting of the council members I mentioned to you, Paul – you were the subject of the meeting. Well, the result of the meeting was the waiving of the site price, so it's yours now and you have nothing to pay. It has been gifted to both of you," Gerry revealed with a smile.

"Well, that is a truly unexpected and welcome surprise," Paul enthused. "Wouldn't you agree, Maura?"

"That's mentally uplifting – a really pleasant shock, like a blessing in disguise. I think we ought to compose a letter of thanks to the council for its collective benevolent gesture," Maura suggested.

"Yes, I believe that would be appropriate. Would you agree, Gerry?" Paul asked his friend's opinion.

"Yes, but wait until you receive official confirmation. Since you haven't got an official residential address yet, I will put myself forward to deliver the communication personally. Is that OK, Paul?"

"Oh, certainly, Gerry. That will be fine. And thank you for your help." Paul expressed his gratitude. He then placed the muzzles over the dogs' mouths, saying, "You will understand now, Gerry, why we keep the dogs muzzled when they are free to wander around the site."

"OL., yes, I do, Paul, and I agree entirely with you. I also believe the arsonist killer should receive a separate lengthy sentence for the attempted murder of the dogs, if he is still alive after he has served his prison term for murdering the family." Gerry made his feelings known.

"Yes, agreed, Gerry. I believe there ought to be a really stiff sentence for any person who ill-treats innocent animals, and there should be a life sentence for the killing of a truly faithful animal like a dog." Paul emphasised his belief.

"Yes, I would agree with you on that, Paul." Gerry supported him and then brought the conversation to an end by saying, "Now I'm sorry to say I must leave you both and your wonderful faithful friends. Thank you for your hospitality. My compliments to your mother, Maura, on her excellent baking skill. I'd like to stay longer and help you with the gardening, but duty compels me to return to my line of work."

"Come with me, Gerry, and I'll pull and top some rhubarb stalks for you to present to Joan. If she is not in the mood for baking, she can chop them into pieces and make some stewed rhubarb instead. That is equally tasty," Paul said.

"Yes, I had forgotten that method for the moment, and I do like rhubarb in that form too," Gerry agreed.

After parting company with Gerry, Paul and Maura sat a while digesting the good news that Gerry had brought.

"It's difficult to realise the significance of the good news, Paul. Do you agree?" Maura asked.

"Yes, it is, Maura. I suppose it will take a bit of time to realise the significance of the reality that we are now the actual official owners of our Garden of Eden. We are like a modern-day Adam and Eve. It's like we've been told it's ours now and we can do what we want with it, and I suddenly feel an even greater respect for it. We will feel the same affinity with it as we do with the dogs. Its happiness and well-being are our responsibility now, and we and the dogs are lovingly embraced by our Garden of Eden."

"Yes, that's it. That is exactly how it is now, and it is on us to maintain the harmonious atmosphere. Oh, I love it all!" Maura joyously exclaimed.

"What we have achieved, Maura, must mean a lot to the local community and beyond," Paul speculated.

"Yes, I believe you are right, Paul. It seems to have generated consequences of lasting importance and we will probably receive some official notification of ownership from the council. And as your friend Gerry suggested, he might be used as the delivery agent since we don't have an official residence at the moment," Maura also speculated.

"Well, we will find out soon enough, Maura. In the meantime, do you feel like continuing with the gardening or would you rather rest for the remainder of the day?" Paul thoughtfully asked.

"I would feel more at ease gardening than doing nothing, Paul. Knowing that I am helping to restore the gardens to their previous beauty is rewarding in itself. It generates a feel-good factor. How do you feel about it?" she asked.

"Exactly the same as you, Maura. I will start by digging out a square-metre bed closer to the damson tree and then I'll lift the lily-of-the-valley plants and set them in a temporary prepared bed so that I can clear their present site of nettles, thistles and couch grass. I will replant some lilies of the valley along the edge of the hedgerow at the end of the garden before adding some fertilising compost to the original bed and replanting the rest of the lily-of-the-valley plants in it. That will encourage the plants to reward us with a rich profusion of fragrant flowers next spring," Paul explained.

"Oh, yes, Paul, I can already imagine the scene in the springtime of next year. We are sitting beside them and breathing their exotic fragrance. What a nostalgic setting they will create, bathing us in a mysterious, inspiring spiritual embrace! I can hardly wait for the moment of reality," Maura felt the urge to poetically utter.

"That was an inspired description of angelic innovation that deserves remembering and recording in writing, Maura," Paul suggested, impressed.

"Well, if I can remember it I will, Paul," Maura hopefully enthused.

"The best time to write it down is as soon as you have mentally composed it. If you leave it you are most likely to forget it, Maura," Paul reminded her.

"OK then, I will heed your advice and go into the camper and write it out."

A few minutes later she re-emerged and remarked in French, "*Aussitôt dit, aussitôt fait.*"

"Good. Every time you are inspired by a poetical phrase or verse, let that saying be your reminder," Paul advised.

"Yes, I'll try and remember that, Paul, because I want to make the effort to emulate you." She humbly expressed her devotion to the accumulation of knowledge.

"Are you going to work clearing the fruit bushes of weeds as before?"

"I am indeed, Paul. We want to sample gooseberry pie, blackcurrant jam and raspberry jam, don't we, now?"

"Certainly, but not at the expense of you suffering painful wounds from the vicious thorns of gooseberry bushes, so be careful, Maura."

"Yes, I will be careful. I wonder if the gooseberry bushes resent our stealing their gooseberries?" Maura posed the innocent question.

Paul laughed and replied, "I can imagine your mother telling you that during your childhood years to prevent you from having your fingers stabbed by gooseberry thorns – and rightly so too, but the truth is the thorns are not to protect the gooseberries. They are merely a defence against animals eating their leaves, which are essential to the well-being of the complete bush. Without leaves the bush would become barren – no leaves, no fruit," Paul explained.

"Well, my, my, I never would have guessed!" Maura confessed her lack of knowledge.

"Don't feel guilty, Maura. Just to enlighten you a bit more, the same applies to any thorn bush or tree, including roses. And here's something that may raise your confidence: there was a time not so long ago when I didn't know either, and the same applies to every other human being on Earth," Paul reminded her.

"Thanks, Paul, you always play down my ignorance with aspects of truth and diminish my embarrassment with factual comments."

"We are all learners regardless of our status in life, and the truth is we will always be learners because of the evolutionary process. So let's put evolution to work in the gardens," Paul suggested, removing the muzzles from the dogs' mouths before pouring some cooled tea into their bowls from a jug that had been left standing and covered.

"There you are, girls – tea break."

The dogs lapped the contents and wagged their tails as a thank-you gesture. Paul then called them to him and they instantly responded.

"I have to put your muzzles on again, girls, for your own safety, because I fear that the evil man who tried to poison you might have left other pieces of poisoned meat scattered about for you to find and—"

"Oh, I dread to think of that happening." Maura expressed her feelings, and she added, "I'm glad you anticipated that possibility, Paul. I'm sure I wouldn't have considered the fact."

"I remember during my boyhood years how I lost my best friend, a young Border collie only six months old, the victim of a pub owner, landowner and religious zealot who legally set poisoned meat discreetly along the headland of a ploughed field. What evil there is embodied in the human race! How anyone could stoop to kill innocent creatures is beyond understanding as far as I am concerned. I have never forgotten that godless act nor the tear-soaked heartbreak of my premature parting from a beloved faithful friend." Paul recalled the vivid memory from his childhood that was seared into his mind.

You seem to have suffered a lot of heartache during your boyhood years, Paul," Maura remarked in a sympathetic tone of voice.

"Yes, I have, Maura, and that's why I am so careful now and my trust in mankind is very tenuous." Paul expressed his feelings as he placed the muzzles over the dogs' mouths and said, "There you are, now, girls – safely attired. You can relax and have a snooze as you watch us work." And he laughed lightly at his own suggestion.

When they started work on their chosen tasks, they were still able to converse with each other, being only ten paces apart. Paul dug out the square-metre bed close to the damson tree and then he began digging up and transferring the lily-of-the-valley plants from their original site and setting them in their temporary bed. When he lifted the last one, Fleurie ambled over to the now empty bed and began sniffing the soil, digging with her front paws and growling softly at the same time.

"What's Fleurie growling at, Paul?" Maura asked, looking across.

"She probably detects a bone buried by the cottage family's dog years ago, or perhaps one buried more recently by a fox." Paul speculated on the reason.

"What a wonderful sense of smell dogs have!" Maura remarked, impressed.

"Yes, indeed, that's an animal's guiding light throughout its life," Paul commented, equally impressed.

"OK, Fleuric, I'll dig down and find the bone for you," Paul assured the dog whilst fondling her head.

Bonzie then wandered over for a share of the attention and had her head fondled as well. Fleurie then growled lightly again and caught Paul's shirt cuff and pulled it gently in her excitement. Paul responded by digging another fifty centimetres into the soil. The spade struck something not solid, but obstructive, like some kind of fabric, so he cleared the soil from around the obstruction, which he soon realised was sacking and partially decayed. Fleurie was whining frustratedly, seemingly concerned.

"It's OK, Fleurie, I'll just clear the area around it. It might be a bag of bones." He placated her by fondling her head again, and said, "You are a real canine detective, Fleurie."

He kept clearing the soil from around the sacking in the empty bed until he found an overlap in the partially rotted fabric, and he managed to roll the flap back with a garden fork and stared, shocked by the sight before his eyes: the top half of the skeletal remains of a human being. Remnants of clothing were still clinging to the skeletal remains, and entwined in the finger bones of the skeleton's right hand was a chain with a medallion attached. Both seemed to be in good condition. Paul turned the medallion over with a small hand fork to see if there was anything engraved on it and was rewarded by a name clearly visible that read, 'Steve Rangton'.

'That's the arsonist killer,' Paul thought to himself, shocked again.

As he stared transfixed, Maura's voice called out, "Have you found the bone, Paul?"

"Yes," Paul answered, and he embraced Fleurie, now quiet and sad. "You are wonderful, Fleurie," he said.

Then he did likewise with Bonzie, who was sitting on her haunches next to Fleurie. He then stood upright with thoughts racing through his mind and paced slowly and thoughtfully across to Maura with Fleurie and Bonzie in tow.

Maura straightened her posture into an upright position and, noticing Paul's sombre look, asked, "Are you all right, Paul?"

"Shocked, but OK, Maura. Fleurie has just – or should I say *almost*? – solved the mystery of the cottage-ruin site."

"She has!" Maura exclaimed, stunned, and asked, "But how? You said she must have detected a bone."

"That bone turned out to be a collection of bones in the form of a human skeleton which I believe is the remains of a young woman," Paul revealed.

"God Almighty! How can you be sure, Paul?"

"Entwined in the skeletal fingers of her right hand is a chain, probably of stainless steel, with a medallion attached. The name engraved on the medallion is 'Steve Rangton', the arsonist killer and farmer who lived in the farmhouse 200 metres north-west of the field gate opposite this site."

Maura's mind was suddenly in turmoil. She embraced Fleurie and asked her, "How did you know, Fleurie?" And she embraced Bonzie too, saying, "You might have known as well, Bonzie." She embraced both dogs for several minutes and then asked Paul, "Can I see the remains, Paul?"

"If you are sure it won't result in you having bad dreams, yes; otherwise don't," Paul suggested.

"But I want to, Paul. I want to speak to the spirit of the young woman privately and express my sorrow for the loss of her young life and all the joys she missed out on in life, and I want to thank her for watching over us. Do you understand, Paul?"

"Yes, of course," Paul agreed.

He held his left hand out to grasp her offered right hand and, together with the dogs, who seemed sadly affected too, they walked the few paces to the emptied lily-of-the-valley bed, where the upper part of the skeletal remains of the body lay exposed with some hair still attached to the skull and the chain with medallion held in the fingers of the skeleton's right hand.

Maura gazed on the remains and exclaimed, "Oh, God Almighty!" She made the sigh of the cross over herself and openly wept, and whilst weeping she said, "How could anyone attack a young, innocent lady, force their wicked intentions on her and then violently and brutally end her existence and leave her in a state of humiliation? It's a crime that cries out for the ultimate penalty to be carried out without the slightest thought of mercy for the evil perpetrator." After a period of silence to calm her emotions, she asked, "How do you know for certain it was a woman, Paul?"

"At first I formed the opinion when I noticed the remaining hair was long, and then I decided the skeletal fingers and hands were shorter than a man's, but the convincing fact is that the medallion has the killer's name engraved on it. I believe it was torn from round his neck by the young woman as she struggled to defend herself," Paul explained. "I also believe the spirit of the young lady has been trying to make spiritual contact with me over a period of time. Do you recall my telling you, Maura, of my recurring dream about the presence of the lily-of-the-valley flowers close to the damson tree and my surprise when we first arrived and I saw them blooming here? But I couldn't remember ever having noticed them there during my boyhood years."

"Yes, I do, distinctly, and I found that quite strange too," Maura confirmed.

"And when I fell asleep here a week ago today, on returning after having delivered you and the dogs to your parents' home in Tipperary, it was a female voice in my sleep that gently told me to awake. That was followed by the unfolding plan when I was guided by the spiritual inner voice that inspired me to devise a trap for the killer. And here again, only minutes ago, it was Fleurie's frantic behaviour that encouraged me to dig deeper into the soil. She was almost begging me by her actions to uncover for her whatever it was that she had detected. I believe the spiritual self of the young lady was yet again the inspirational driving force that urged my creative mentality and Fleurie's instinctive mentality to expose the remains of a woman holding a chain and medallion bearing the name of her killer. Do you begin to see how it all fits together like a jigsaw puzzle, Maura?" Paul asked, and he added, "When her identity is finally discovered we will have solved what I will call the mystery the lily of the valley. It's an example of what is considered as the psychic paranormal."

"Yes, I follow what you mean, Paul, and I can believe in the mental prompts from the spirit of the young woman, whoever she may have been. What has occurred also proves to me the immortality of one's spiritual self," Maura stated, having cast her doubts aside.

"I'm glad you have convinced yourself about the immortality of spirituality, Maura. It will help you to have a better understanding of existence, including the temporary life cycle of the pulsating species of life, of which human beings are a part," Paul concluded.

"Yes, I'll be giving that subject a lot of thought from now on, but I'll have to lean on you for support, Paul," Maura reminded him appealingly.

Paul looked at her, smiled, placed an arm round her shoulder and said, "I will be your pillar of support, Maura, as will the dogs, our heroines, and we will be assured by the spirit of the young lady whose unidentified remains are resting in the empty lily-of-the-valley flower bed. There is something else you need to know, Maura, which is that we are going to have to leave the site again today because of this discovery. I have to phone Inspector Conroy, and we will have to wait for him and his team's arrival. I think they'll be here within an hour, and after that the site will be swarming with police forensic officers, uniformed officers, newspaper reporters and reporters from radio and TV networks. We don't want to be caught up in all that excitement today, so I will arrange with Inspector Conroy to meet the reporters tomorrow morning in the police station in Attanagh if he agrees – and that includes you and the dogs as well, Maura. What do you say?"

"If you think that's the best way, Paul, I will be as obedient as our devoted heroines," she replied, still in his embrace.

"Good, Maura!" Paul uttered.

He kissed Maura warmly, disengaged himself from her embrace and withdrew his mobile from his pocket. He dialled the police station number and the desk officer answered. Paul introduced himself and asked if Inspector Conroy was available.

The friendly officer recognised Paul's voice and replied, "Sorry, Mr Attenagh, but the Inspector is conducting an interview with a couple and he is accompanied by Detective Carey. If it's urgent I'll keep trying to contact him until I succeed."

"Yes, I appreciate that, officer. If you manage to contact him please give him the following message: 'There has been a dramatic twist in the ongoing murder investigation. Please come to the cottage site as soon as possible.' Have you got that, officer?"

"Yes, Mr Attenagh, and I will keep trying to contact him until I succeed, starting now."

"Thanks, officer – much obliged. Bye for now."

CHAPTER TWENTY-ONE

Paul, Maura and the dogs retreated to the camper van, where Paul brewed some tea for all four of them. The muzzles were removed from their dogs' mouths to allow their beloved pets to drink their cooled tea, and then Paul gave each a hide chew to keep them occupied and not likely to wander about as he was still conscious of the possibility of them finding a piece of poisoned meat.

Inspector Conroy, accompanied by Detective Karen Carey, arrived within fifteen minutes and drove through the open gateway and on to the site, coming to a halt close to where Paul and Maura were sitting. When they climbed out of their car Paul greeted them and introduced both to Maura. She responded in a welcoming manner and offered the visitors tea or coffee. Both settled for tea and Paul invited them to sit down. When they did, the dogs broke off from their chewing endeavours momentarily to greet them with wagging tails, and Detective Carey cuddled them fondly.

"I took your advice, Paul, and went to visit the grandparents, on the mother's side, of the children who died in the cottage inferno five years ago and we did learn something more about the trial. The eldest child, who was named Mary, after her mother, was aged fifteen, and she was expected to visit the grandparents on the Saturday morning prior to the Sunday-evening tragedy, but she never turned up. The grandparents thought she must have changed her mind for some reason and gone with the rest of the family members to visit the grandparents on the father's side."

Thoughts flashed through Paul's mind at high speed, and within seconds he suddenly exclaimed, "That's it, Maura! That's who it is that Fleurie discovered – Mary, the eldest sibling of the family!" Addressing the Inspector and Detective Carey, he apologised and declared, "You have just solved the final piece of the mystery, Inspector."

"Has that got something to do with the message you left, Paul – the dramatic twist to the mystery?"

"Yes, Inspector, everything to do with it." He called Fleurie to him, lifted her up on to his lap and said, "Fleurie is the heroine who has solved the mystery of the cottage-ruin site." He embraced Fleurie and said, on putting her gently down, "Go and enjoy your chew, Miss Wonderful."

She returned to her chewing with a wagging tail.

"I will relate the dramatic discovery to you both now if you are ready."

"We are all ears, Paul," Detective Carey enthused.

Paul explained in detail how he and Maura, with the muzzled dogs in close proximity, watching, indulged their gardening skills and how his removal of the lily-of-the-valley plants from their bed led Fleurie to investigate and begin digging deeper with her front paws, appealing to him with urgent whines that he, Paul, interpreted as an appeal for help. He responded, thinking it was a buried bone she had detected. After exposing some partially rotted sacking, and not knowing what to make of it, he dug the soil out surrounding it, turned a flap over and was confronted by the skeletal remains of a human being with the chain with medallion attached entwined round the finger bones of the skeleton's right hand.

"The name engraved on the medallion is that of the man you are holding in custody, Inspector."

Paul also informed the Inspector that he had no idea who the young lady was until the Inspector told him of his visit to the grandparents on the mother's side and what he had learned about their granddaughter's non-arrival five years previously. Paul was now convinced she didn't die in the cottage fire, but had been murdered sometime on the Saturday, before the Sunday-night inferno. The reason for the latter was to create the false belief that Mary died in the fire with the other members of her family. Rangton thought he would be safe from suspicion as long as the remains of Mary were never discovered, and he was willing to commit murder to keep the secret sleeping.

"What do you think, Inspector?" Paul posed the question.

"I go along with your theory, Paul, and I believe that you, your wife, Maura, and your two wonderful dogs have solved the mystery of the cottage murders. The murder of Mary Foley, the daughter, was followed by the murders in the cottage fire and the attempted murders of you, your wife, Maura, and your two wonderful beloved dogs. Congratulations to all of you!" The Inspector applauded them all. "Can we see the site of the discovery now, Paul?" he added politely.

"Certainly. I'll just put the dogs' muzzles on, Inspector. I am still fearful of the evil devil having spread pieces of poison bait about as a backup strategy."

"Oh, yes, Paul, in your shoes I would be likewise cautious," the Inspector agreed.

"Are you joining us, Maura?" Paul asked, and before she could answer he added, "Please do, since you are part of the team now, as are the dogs."

And she smiled, pleased, and agreed.

Inspector Conroy and Detective Carey stared solemnly at the exposed upper torso of the skeletal remains and each made a sign of the cross as a mark of respect for the soul, or spirit, of the young maiden who might have been a happy young mother by now had she survived.

"So this is what the evil devil didn't want to be discovered, and why he so callously murdered the rest of the girl's family. He wanted to keep his heinous murder of this young lady secret," the Inspector sadly commented, and Detective Carey dabbed her tear-filled eyes with a handkerchief.

Fleurie and Bonzie were sat on their haunches between Paul and Maura, and Fleurie whined as though lamenting over her discovery. Paul fondled her head as a source of comfort.

"There's a hand trowel and fork there on the edge, Inspector, if you wish to satisfy your curiosity about the medallion on the chain," Paul remarked.

"Yes, I'll do that, Paul," he agreed, and he stepped into the flower bed beside the exposed remains and used the hand fork to turn the medallion on the chain and read the name of the killer held in the finger bones of the skeletal remains that five years previously were the living body of the young maiden Mary Foley.

"I will have to have the site officially cordoned off by uniformed police, Paul, and I'll request the police forensic team from the city to carry out their investigation. They will have to exhume the remains, and there will have to be a squad of police officers camped here for the duration of the task, which will be several days," the Inspector informed Paul, and he asked, "How will that affect you, your wife and the dogs, Paul?"

"That won't be a problem, Inspector. We will depart and take up temporary residence in the caravan park on Forest Road, close to Attanagh town."

"Well, that's very generous of you, Paul. I didn't expect to be given total command of your property for the duration of the investigation." The Inspector expressed his gratitude.

"I'll do anything possible to help bring the process to a conclusion, Inspector. I understand the complications involved and you are welcome to our assistance. We will help in any way we can," Paul assured him.

"Are you of the same mind, Maura?" the Inspector asked, out of respect for her opinion whatever it might have been.

"Yes, totally, Inspector. Just like the dogs, wherever Paul leads I follow faithfully." Maura declared her loyalty.

"Well, that's very kind of both of you, and I am truly indebted to you," the Inspector concluded.

"Mr Jack Kyley, the builder," Paul recalled, "is due to arrive on the site on Monday to begin levelling the ground with machines for the construction of a bungalow, but I'll call into the town hall when we leave here and ask Mr Gerry Kyle to ask the builder to suspend work on the site until the police investigation of the crime scene has been completed, Inspector, if you wish."

"Well, yes, and thanks again, Paul. That is another task I won't have to remember. If there's anything I can do in return, don't hesitate to ask, Paul," the Inspector invited him.

"Apart from the following suggestion I have no requests, Inspector. We have to face the media reporters sooner or later, so I suggest a meeting with all of them in your police station tomorrow morning, when we will try and answer their questions. What do you think of that, Inspector?" Paul posed the question.

The Inspector thought for a moment before answering: "Yes, I will arrange that, Paul. Let's say for ten o'clock tomorrow morning, Saturday. Is that agreeable to you, Paul and Maura?"

Paul glanced at Maura for her approval and she didn't falter, saying, "Yes, I think that will be ideal."

"We will have to be accompanied by the dogs all the time, Inspector. I hope you understand."

"Yes, that's fully understood, Paul. They are certainly welcome to make their appearance in the police station," the Inspector stated whilst fondling the heads of both dogs. "What a wonderful pair of canine detectives they have proved to be. It almost borders on the miraculous," he continued, and he added, "They will go down in history as legendary canine heroines."

"One other reminder, Inspector: can we rely on you to make sure that those lilies of the valley, in the bed over there, are not disturbed? I dug them out of their original bed, which is where the remains of the young lady lie exposed. We intend to replant them there after the police forensics team has completed its work. If Mary's living relatives agree, we would like her remains to be reinterred in the bed where Fleurie was somehow inspired to detect them, and for the site to be consecrated by the local parish priest or bishop of the diocese. I believe the soul, or spirit, of Mary would be pleased for her remains to rest among the flowers, shrubs and trees where she passed her short life. We hope that will be her final resting place." Paul made his feelings known.

His words brought tears to the eyes of Maura and Detective Carey, and the Inspector struggled to hold his composure.

"We will be liaising with the coroner's office and the tragic young Mary's family," the Inspector stated, adding, "And as for the lily-of-the-valley plants, I will make sure your wishes, Paul, are adhered to."

Shortly after, Detective Sergeant Luke Griffin and Detective Green arrived on the site. They were closely followed by a large police van containing a number of uniformed and armed police officers led by Sergeant Sean Delaney. The Inspector filled them in on the latest dramatic development, and they were not only surprised by the discovery, but amazed by the part played by Fleurie. They were solemnly saddened by the sight of the exposed remains of the young lady, whose family members had been burned to death by the arsonist five years previously to keep his murder of the innocent girl secret. He had attempted to do the same to Paul, Maura and their dogs only a week before, but Bonzie, the slightly older dog, supported by the younger dog, Fleurie, not only thwarted his effort by her alertness, but she managed to secure enough evidence to identify the killer. Now Fleurie, the younger dog, had solved the cottage-fire murder mystery. Paul and Maura and the dogs were congratulated by all the police officers.

A little later, after farewells to the Inspector and his colleagues, Paul, Maura and their dogs left the scene before the arrival of the police forensic team and the news reporters.

Paul steered the camper van off the site, and outside the entrance he stopped and swapped places with Maura, saying, "Sorry, Maura – just an aberration of thought. You drive – you still need experience to familiarise yourself with the locality, the roads' bumps and hollows as well as the scenery. We are heading to Attanagh, and our first stop is the town-hall car park."

Maura smiled and moved over to the vacated driving seat. Paul climbed into the passenger seat and was greeted by the dogs again with affectionate licks.

"Does your mind ever rest, Paul? I get the impression that it's always active."

"Yes, it does rest when I am asleep; otherwise, yes, it is always active, but not as active verbally as it is mentally. That is the story of my life. Do you find that interesting and intriguing, or would you prefer me to be endlessly talking?"

"I am quite pleased with your natural demeanour. It's like a haven of contentment with which I can harmonise and I can therefore be a part of it. I believe that is love. Am I right?"

"Now, I can hardly deny the truth, Maura, can I?" he replied, and he smiled the smile of love.

Paul informed Maura that he not only wanted to tell Gerry about asking the builder to delay the preparations for the bungalow construction, but he also wanted to inform Gerry of the dramatic discovery so soon after his departure – otherwise he might not hear about it until he read the Sunday morning paper, and he might wonder why Paul hadn't enlightened him about it sooner.

"Yes, I'm sure he would, Paul, and possibly he'd feel offended, though he might later understand that restrictions had been imposed for good reason," Maura suggested.

"Yes, that's how Gerry would interpret the silence, I'm sure," Paul decided.

Maura drove into the town-hall car park, parked as near as possible to the entrance and turned off the engine.

Paul embraced and kissed Maura and reminded her to lock the vehicle doors when they parted company. He told her he would be as quick as possible, adding, "If Gerry's not available I will leave a message asking him to phone me urgently." He suggested that Maura should phone her parents and bring them up to date with the latest news and the possibility of a second visit sooner than expected.

He then slipped out of the passenger seat and closed the door. On entering the building and enquiring, Paul learned that Gerry was in his office; and on being informed that Paul had requested a brief urgent conversation with him, Gerry replied, "Direct him to enter at once."

Paul received a warm, smiling welcome, as always.

"This is a pleasant surprise so soon after parting company with each other. Sit yourself down, Paul, and tell me what's so urgent – nothing worrying, I hope?" Gerry asked.

Paul related the story of his dramatic discovery of the remains of the young lady through the instinctive efforts of Fleurie, the younger dog. He described the shock, the effect on Maura, and the chain with medallion attached, on which was engraved the name of her killer, Steve Rangton, the man who was now in prison awaiting trial for multiple murders and attempted murders. Paul went on to tell Gerry about the arrival of Inspector Conroy and the vital piece of information he brought that helped to identify the remains of the young lady.

"I now believe the remains are those of Mary Foley, the eldest child of the Foley family. She didn't die in the cottage inferno five years ago, but was murdered sometime during the Saturday before, after the other members of the family had left to visit the parents of the father. These details have to wait for verification. As it isn't classified information, I decided to come and inform you of the changing events, Gerry. What do you think?"

"I am really dumbfounded, Paul. It's more than dramatic! You and your wife, Maura, and your two wonderful heroic dogs have not only solved the murder of the cottage family five years ago, and identified and captured the killer, but you have now also solved the mystery of the killer's motive. You risked your own lives in the process, and all within a few weeks of arriving in the town. Your actions have also guaranteed the overturning of the life sentence imposed on the innocent traveller five years ago. I am amazed by what the four of you have achieved in such a short period of time. This latest dramatic conclusion came so soon after I had tea and rhubarb pie with you both. What's next, Paul? It's hard to take it all in. It's like a dream," Gerry said, not knowing what to say he was so emotionally overpowered.

Paul smiled and said, "The next is, Gerry, can you ask Jack Kyley, the builder, to delay the bungalow start day until Inspector Conroy and the police forensic team from the city have concluded their investigation of the crime scene and exhumed the remains of the young lady for further examination in their forensic laboratory. I have given Inspector Conroy complete occupation of the site until they have completed their work, which will be spread over several days. The Inspector will give you the all-clear to inform the builder when he is able to begin work on the site."

"Yes, I will gladly do that, Paul. What are you going to do in the meantime?" Gerry asked, concerned.

"We are hopefully going to stay overnight at the caravan park on Forest Road, and we will be meeting newspaper and TV reporters tomorrow morning at the police station. Afterwards we intend to drive south to Tipperary to stay at Maura's parents' home for a few days," Paul revealed.

"You shouldn't have to go to all that trouble, Paul. For what you, Maura and the dogs have achieved here in your home town the council should be providing you with the appropriate accommodation reserved for VIPs. I am going to remind the officers of their duty and the embarrassing criticism that will follow in the wake of the fact being made known to the public, as it is bound to be." Gerry verbalised his feelings.

"Well, I know your intentions are good, Gerry, but we don't want to make a fuss. The caravan park will suffice for now. I don't like drawing attention to myself," Paul stressed.

"Yes, I can well understand that, Paul. In our boyhood days you were always willing to help others and yet you never burdened anyone when you were in need. I have never forgotten your good nature. You demonstrated it here again during these last few weeks," Gerry reminded him.

"Well, Gerry, I recall you being of a similar nature. You have exercised your good traits to benefit us since we arrived here, and I don't forget it either. So I'm asking you to let sleeping dogs lie for the time being," Paul appealed.

"How could I refuse a good friend, Paul? It's done, but if the subject is raised, I'll have to speak my mind, Paul, OK?"

"Yes, fine, Gerry. I wouldn't deny you that, and now I had better rejoin Maura and the dogs."

"I'll ring Sean Cavanagh and let him know to expect you, Paul. Thanks for filling me in on the latest dramatic development. I'll let you know what's going on locally whilst you are down in Tipperary," Gerry ended.

"Thanks, Gerry, and farewell for the moment," Paul uttered on parting company with his friend.

When Paul rejoined Maura and the dogs he was, as usual,

excitedly welcomed by the latter. He then told Maura of Gerry's shocked surprise when he heard the dramatic news of what had taken place in the hour and a half after he had left them.

"He was really impressed by Fleurie's canine instinct, which encouraged me to dig deeper into the flower bed."

"Yes, I can understand his interest. It was as if she had been inspired by something or someone," Maura enthused.

"Yes, that is exactly what I believe and I'm convinced it was the spirit of Mary Foley, the daughter of the tragic family. I believe they will be able to prove it was her by examining the DNA in her remains. I also believe her spirit was the cause of my dreaming of lily-of-the-valley flowers, as I mentioned to you before, Maura, and it was she too who inspired me to follow a plan that led to the capture of her murderer. Her spirit has been watching over us, and she perhaps played a part in my decision to come here to begin with. What do you think of my theory, Maura?" Paul asked.

"You make it sound logical, Paul, and therefore beyond reproach. I feel obliged to believe you." Maura pledged her support with a smile.

"Do you remember asking me, Maura, if I would write a verse or two of a poem to help activate the creative aspects of your mind?" Paul asked.

"Yes, I do. Are you going to do that for me?" she asked with an air of excitement.

"I already have, Maura, and it's here among my scribble," he said, picking up a folder and withdrawing a page of handwritten script.

"You never scribble, Paul. You write very legibly," she reminded him.

"Yes, true, but anything I consider unfinished I usually refer to loosely as 'scribble', Maura. So here it is. Do you want to read it, or do you want me to read it to you?"

"I would prefer it to be read to me. That way I'll know if I have a feel for it and hopefully it will inspire me," Maura decided.

"Fine, then. It's entitled 'Spring'.

SPRING

By forest fringe and
Softly sounding stream,
We wandered hand in hand
With faithful friends contentedly
Along,
Amongst proliferating bluebells
that bathed us in their exotic
fragrance,
Whilst songbirds spilled
Their exquisite notes of joy
In unwritten song.
Oh, what wondrous, colourful
Scenes,
That loudly appeal to admiring
Eyes,
Evoking nostalgic memories of
Childhood days in the
Fields of home.
Among daffodils, daisies, dandelions
And buttercups in wild delightful
Stray,
Whilst listening to the cuckoos'
Calls from near and far.
And oh, how joyful to embody
The memories in a poem!

Does that appeal to your creative longing, Maura? And if so, are you going to try and compose another verse, or possibly two?" Paul asked.

"Oh, wouldn't I just love to, Paul! But I doubt that I could emulate you. I promise though that I will try." She committed herself to the task.

"That is all that you can do, Maura, and that is all I expect you to do. Failure is merely a stepping stone to success. It will compel you to try again and again, and so on. . . . I know because I was a failure at everything I tried. I never let it deter me completely, although if I had known about a problem earlier in my life I would never have tried to begin with. Still, I am glad now that I didn't know. So you take as long as you like and don't give up," Paul stressed, and he added, "You can drive off when you are ready, Maura, and don't forget to stop at that small supermarket, where hopefully I can pick up an apple pie." Then, turning to address the dogs, he said, "Did you hear what I said, Bonzie and Fleurie?"

Both dogs stretched to deliver their thanks with licks of affection on his neck.

"I knew you would let me know you understand," Paul remarked, and turning to Maura he said, "I'll pick up a bottle of Chablis too if they have any; and if not, a Sauvignon Blanc or a Beaujolais."

"What are we celebrating, Paul?" Maura asked naively.

Paul looked at her and smiled, saying, "We are celebrating Fleurie's discovery, which solved the mystery of the cottage ruin and the murders of the innocent family members that the killer committed to hide the separate murder of Mary, and our escape from his overeager attempt to murder us as well to cover up his evil crimes. We are celebrating the success of good over evil. Both Fleurie and Bonzie played key roles in that success as did the spirit of Mary Foley, the innocent teenage girl whose life was ended prematurely at fifteen. Her spirit orchestrated the exposure of the killer and his capture and guided Fleurie when she found the solution to the mystery."

"Yes, that's very thoughtful of you, Paul. It's an angelic gesture of our gratitude to this tragic young lady, who I hope will always be close to us – that is if your request, Paul, for her remains to be permanently interred in the lily-of-the-valley flower bed where she was found is granted."

"Yes, Maura, I hope it will be. And the remains of her family members, if their relatives agree, could be interred with hers. We will have to wait and see what transpires, but nevertheless I believe they know that their spirits are welcome to share the site and all its attractions with us," Paul concluded.

"Yes, and with that let's get going," Maura remarked.

She started the camper van's engine and steered it out of the town-hall car park.

CHAPTER TWENTY-TWO

Sean Cavanagh, the caravan-site owner, was waiting to welcome Paul and Maura. He informed them that Gerry Kyle had rung and forewarned him of their coming and that the site they had occupied previously was still available if they wanted it. Paul gratefully accepted the suggestion.

"The terms are the same as before. You can settle the fee on leaving, Paul," Sean reminded him, and with a hand gesture he invited them to drive in.

When Maura had parked the camper van, they both, together with the muzzled dogs, went for a stroll along the gently wandering stream and woodland edge. The dogs looked at Paul appealingly, expecting him to produce the two rubber balls and bowl them for the pets to chase, and Paul was aware that they would feel frustrated. They couldn't grasp the balls with their teeth because of the muzzles, but he was still unwilling to make an exception to the rule he had adopted because of his love and concern for the two beloved dogs. He therefore didn't disappoint them. When he bowled the balls the dogs showed their frustration at first, but soon came to terms with the temporary restriction.

After an adequate period of exercise Paul fondled their heads and said, "You'll have to satisfy yourselves with scent investigation for the remainder of the walk, girls."

Whether they understood him or not, that was what they indulged in.

"Do you think they understood what you said, Paul?" Maura asked, her curiosity aroused.

"The truth is, Maura, I believe they are adept at deciphering voice tones to distinguish between positive and negative remarks."

"Yes, I see the logic in that. You may well be right," Maura agreed, and she asked, "Do you feel hungry enough for a cooked meal today, Paul?"

"I am not starving, Maura, but I could eat a salad sandwich or a bacon-and-fried-tomato sandwich. And you?"

"Likewise, a sandwich will suffice, but it will have to be bacon and fried tomato, as you suggested. And you girls?" She addressed the dogs. "You will have diced fried meat mixed with dog meal – one of your favourites! What do you say?"

They both barked their approval, or so it seemed.

On returning from their pleasant walk both Paul and Maura prepared their and their dogs' meals. The dogs were always served first, and they usually cleared up any leftovers from their masters' meals. The diced meat was fried in fat, and when cooked it was left a while to cool sufficiently before Paul spooned it on to the meal he had placed in the dogs' bowls. Then he mixed the contents together whilst Maura fried the bacon and tomatoes for their sandwiches. Paul removed the muzzles from the dogs' mouths and placed the bowls on the ground in front of each dog. They eagerly devoured their meals, licking their lips and snouts on finishing.

"I've got some tea cooling for the girls. You don't mind waiting, do you?" he asked, and they wagged their tails in agreement. Paul buttered some thick slices of bread and covered them with a bowl to protect them from any interested flying insects, and at that same moment a car approached them from the entrance and stopped quite close to them.

Gerry, from the council office, climbed out smiling and remarked, "Wow! The smell of frying bacon is so appealing."

"Well, this is a pleasant unexpected surprise indeed, Gerry," Paul greeted him.

Maura asked, "Can you manage a bacon-and-fried-tomato sandwich, Gerry?"

"Well, the truth is, Maura, I shouldn't, but I can't resist the temptation even though I don't want to impose on your kindness.

So I will say yes against my better judgement if you have enough to spare." And addressing the dogs he said, "And hello, Bonzie and Fleurie."

The dogs responded with wagging tails and licks of affection on his hands as he fondled their heads.

"You will be both wondering, no doubt, why I've arrived here so unexpectedly, so I had better explain why I am here as we wait for the sandwiches. It concerns what we spoke about a little earlier – the accommodation I said you should have been offered. Shortly after you left my office, Paul, I was summoned to the council chairman's office, and the subject he wanted to discuss was you, Maura and the dogs. He wanted to know if you had arrived back from Tipperary, and when I told him you were back and what had happened and that you had surrendered the site to the police and forensic-science team from the city for the duration of their investigation of the crime scene, that being the reason for you being where you are right now, he was for an extended moment lost for words."

Paul poured the tea and placed the mugs on the table, and before sitting down he poured the cooled tea into the dogs' bowls. Whilst he was thus engaged, Maura served the bacon-and-tomato sandwiches on plates and sat down herself.

Gerry bit into his sandwich and said, "Wow, Maura! They are not only really tasty sandwiches, but hefty too. They are like a dinner in composition."

"What was the council chairman's remark then?" Paul asked, interested.

"The chairman was suddenly a worried man, Paul, and he stammered, 'But – but – but we can't allow that to happen, Gerry. What will the public think and what will the government say? We will be disgraced if it gets out. We have reserved properties, haven't we?'

"'Yes, Mr O'Leary, but—'

"'Don't call me Mr O'Leary, Gerry. Call me Donal in private, like now. We are friends, aren't we?'

"'Yes, of course, Donal,' I replied hesitantly, so I didn't have to push my point forward on your, Maura's and the dogs' behalf.

Instead I was patient, believing he would ask my opinion.

"Eventually that was exactly what he did, asking me, 'What do you propose we should do, Gerry?'

"'Well, to be completely honest, Donal, I believe the council should do now, before it's too late, what it should have done a week ago, and that is offer Paul, his wife and the dogs temporary residence in one of your reserved properties, and without delay to save yourself and the council serious embarrassment.'

"'Yes, I believe you are right, Gerry,' he stated, and he added to my surprise, 'I am giving you carte blanche, Gerry, to complete forthwith the needlessly delayed process. You can take responsibility and I will deal with those who dragged their feet in dealing with the matter. Please extend my apology to Mr Attenagh and his wife for the lethargic reaction of the council to their need.'

"That's the reason for my presence here now," Gerry explained.

"So we are going to be temporarily housed by the council until the police have concluded their investigation. What do you say to that, Maura?" Paul asked, pleased with the news.

"I'm delighted!" Maura beamed, and she added, "It will be a welcome relief not to be on public display for a while."

Paul asked, "Who's for another mug of tea and a slice of bought apple pie? The suggestion was accepted with nods, and even the dogs barked their approval.

"Did Bonzie and Fleurie really understand what you said, Paul?" Gerry asked, amazed at their apparent intelligence.

"Yes, Gerry, they know exactly what apple pie and tea means," Paul assured him.

Maura slipped a slice of apple pie into each dog bowl and sliced them into manageable pieces before presenting the bowls to the dogs, and she watched as each consumed the contents and licked their lips. Paul poured some leftover cooled tea into each bowl and the beloved pets lapped the bowls dry.

"They are without doubt two exceptional dogs. One identified the arsonist killer, without a conscience, of the cottage family, and the other exposed the secret that the killer was willing to brutally murder to keep hidden. They will be made famous by those deeds alone. Apart from that they are loved by both of you for their wonderful natures." Gerry defined their value.

"Will we be moving into the house tomorrow, Gerry?" Paul asked out of curiosity.

Gerry smiled and answered, "No, today, when you are ready. You won't have to leave as soon as the police complete their work, but you can stay indefinitely – perhaps until the bungalow is ready to move into. There's no need to rush. I'll help you with the loading and then lead you to the house. It's about a mile north of the town and about a mile east of the cottage site in a quiet cul-de-sac. There's quite a spacious, completely fenced-off garden at the rear with several fruit trees. It's ideal for the dogs, and I believe you both will really like it," Gerry assured them.

When all that had been unloaded from the camper van had been reloaded, Gerry led the way in his car to the exit from the caravan park. They stopped briefly by the gateway, where Gerry exchanged a few words with Sean Cavanagh, the proprietor. Paul wanted to settle the bill and apologise for any inconvenience they might have caused, but Sean told him that all was understood and the bill had been settled by Gerry. He ended by wishing Paul and Maura good luck, and he said he hoped to see them again sometime in the future.

The country house they were to occupy was in a secluded setting half surrounded by a wood at the rear. It was only a kilometre east of the cottage-ruin site, so it was ideal for going to and fro to continue their garden restoration work. Everything about the spacious bungalow was roomy. There were two toilets, two bathrooms and two garages (one at either end of the house), and a metre-and-a-half-high fence surrounded the premises to ensure privacy.

"That is an impressive building," Paul remarked to Gerry on their arrival, and he added, "I was aware of its presence during my boyhood days, although I have never seen it because of its wooded seclusion."

"Well, if you prefer, Paul, you can cancel the proposed bungalow and apply to the council to occupy this property instead permanently. I'm sure your application will be granted," Gerry said.

"Well, I think not, Gerry, because of the one thing that didn't appeal to me about it when I was a boy, and that is I always felt the trees were too close. I still do, but at the same time I wouldn't want them removed." Paul made his thoughts known.

"Yes, I agree, Paul," Maura remarked. "The wood seems to have a claustrophobic effect, being so close to the house."

"That would be my only criticism too." Gerry voiced his opinion too, and continued: "But whoever had it built originally must have had a love for the nearness of the trees."

"Still though, it's a quiet, relaxing setting and I'm grateful for your determined effort to get us housed, Gerry." Paul expressed his gratitude and Maura added her appreciation too.

"You are both very welcome to my humble effort and— Oh, I almost forgot to mention the perimeter fencing round the new bungalow. You have been granted a 100% grant for the fencing, so you will have nothing to pay." Gerry surprised them both.

"Well, Maura, what do you say to that? The site fee has been waived and now the fee for the security fencing has also been waived, so we've only got the bungalow to pay for," Paul enthused.

"Well, all I can think of to say is what my grandmother used to tell me when I was a little girl, which is the fairies are watching over the Earth for God and they always reward good deeds. Need I say more?" Maura recalled a childhood memory.

"Your grandmother must have been a very wise lady, and I wish I had been acquainted with her, Maura," Paul commented thoughtfully.

"I can harmonise with both of you where fairies are concerned. I still read fairy tales whenever I come across any." Gerry confessed his interest.

After a look around the inside and outside of the property, and winning the approval of both Paul and Maura regarding his choice of accommodation for them, Gerry parted company with his friends and their playful dogs. He returned to the council offices to report to Mr Donal O'Leary, the executive chairman, regarding the successful outcome of the task.

After manhandling their food supply and the dogs' from the camper van, which they'd parked just outside the front entrance of the house, they decided to have another bacon-and-tomato sandwich each. The dogs had the same, washed down with tea. Afterwards they sat on a bench in the porch at the front of the house facing west, and the dogs sat on the wooden floor of the porch beside them busy with a hide chew each. They watched the sun on its slow descent to the Sliabh Bloom mountains about three kilometres away, and Paul commented on the beauty of the ever changing cumulus clouds, like the embers of a log fire. The blue sky was continuously being altered by the fiery glow of the setting sun as if there was a giant unseen artist painting the ever changing scenery at the same speed as the sun was setting and sucking all the colour variations back into itself as it sank beneath the horizon.

"Oh, what a wondrous spectacle of magical splendour! Homeward-winging happily vociferous rooks in lengthy queue and unhurried flight are sounding their gratitude to fading day and God as they head south to their rookery nest, content." Paul voiced his praise.

"That's a poetical description of a marvellous sunset, Paul. We will be able to enjoy similar fiery scenes from the cottage-site bungalow every time one occurs through the years," Maura prophesied.

"Yes, they are joys to look forward to, Maura," Paul agreed, and after a brief pause he asked, "Have you phoned your mum?"

"No, but I will a little later – about nine o'clock."

"I'm glad we don't have to burden them again with our presence so soon after leaving them. I'd feel a bit guilty putting pressure on them like that." Paul made his feelings known.

"Oh, they wouldn't be put out by that, Paul. They enjoy our company and the dogs' company as well – and even more so now," Maura assured him.

"Well, Maura, I can't help feeling guilty about it. I suppose it's because of the respect I feel for them, and that has become a habit. But enough of that! Let's go inside and retrieve the Chablis I picked up earlier today and left in the fridge just before we wandered out here."

"What are we celebrating this evening, Paul?" Maura asked, her curiosity piqued again.

"Our good fortune today, Maura – the unexpected news of the 100% grant for the security fencing, and this tranquil accommodation. They are worth celebrating, don't you think? Plus I wish that the spirit of the tragic Mary Foley will join us to celebrate with us."

"That is thoughtful of you, Paul. I wish she will too, and she is welcome to join us any time she wishes." Maura mentally invited her.

"That's thoughtful of you too, Maura, and she might let us know of her presence in some mysterious way."

They both then pushed themselves to an upright position and the dogs followed their example. Paul looked down on the dogs and invited both to bring their chews indoors and they seemed to understand and followed obediently with the chews held in their mouths.

Paul and Maura passed a pleasant evening with the dogs in the living room of the comfortable house, with the addition of the cooled Chablis. They sipped their drinks at their leisure, recalling the unfolding events of the previous two weeks.

"It seems so unreal all that happened during the last two weeks, Maura. It seems like a dream. Do you get that impression?"

"Yes, I do," Maura agreed, and she continued: "It is like the stuff of dreams; but, like people say, truth is stranger than fiction at times."

"Yes, that's true, Maura, but then life itself is a mystery too, and the struggle to solve it is the ultimate challenge," Paul suggested.

It was during their discussion on that subject that both drifted off to sleep, as did Bonzie and Fleurie over their slow demolition of the chews.

All four sleepers awoke instantly at the echo of a loud report from a trumpet on a music radio programme. The dogs growled angrily, but were calmed by a few words from Paul.

"I think it's time that we had something to eat," Maura suggested, and she asked, "Are you hungry, Paul?"

"My hunger is just enough to be placated by a slice of rhubarb pie, if that's available; and if not, a slice of apple pie; and if that's off the menu, then a few biscuits will suffice."

"Yes, there's enough rhubarb pie for both of us and enough apple pie for the dogs."

The dogs cocked their ears and dropped their chews at the mention of apple pie.

Maura consumed the remaining Chablis from her glass, commenting, "That wine is pleasantly satisfying and relaxing."

"My sentiments exactly, Maura. You are beginning to develop a connoisseurship of wine, which to me is simply a memory bank of tastes. One shouldn't become too attached to wines, but treat them as casual friends," Paul remarked.

"Now, I like that description, Paul, and I will certainly remember it," Maura stressed, impressed.

After their evening snack they both indulged in interesting conversation again, broken by visits to the rear spacious garden of the house, where Paul amused Bonzie and Fleurie by bowling the rubber balls for them to chase until he felt they had been adequately exercised, but far from exhaustion. The last outing was at 11.30 p.m. Bedtime followed. The dogs bedded down on their large rug in a corner of the bedroom a metre from Paul and Maura's bed – a double bed, into which they rolled. They conversed in subdued voices, uttering loving dialogue to each other, and that led to a natural outpouring of passion, which culminated in an exciting copulation – the fulfilling sex act of relieving union.

During the night Bonzie and Fleurie came to Paul's side of the bed to alert him to their call of nature. Each had her own way of rousing him from sleep. Bonzie would nuzzle under his hand or arm until he awoke, whereas Fleurie would paw at his hand or arm and whine lightly. Both would activate their tails when he awoke, and lick Paul's face as though grateful for his attention. He would respond without hesitation and roll out of bed, slip his feet into sandals and escort his beloved friends to the rear of the garden. He would wait for them to fully satisfy their needs and investigate whatever scents they encountered.

Maura was awoken by Paul rolling out of bed, and when he and the dogs returned she asked, out of curiosity, "Why do the dogs always go to your side of the bed to rouse you when they want to go out, Paul, even when my side of the bed is nearest to them?"

Paul laughed lightly and replied, "That is a logical question, Maura, and deserves a logical answer. The following is how I see it. When we first got Bonzie as a pup I wasn't working in a regular job, but was self-employed for a while; you were employed full-time. I took Bonzie everywhere with me and I carried our food and drink in a backpack. She bonded with me and became instinctively dependent on me. Then when she was six months old I decided she needed a play pal and companion, and I knew a friend whose female dog had a litter of pups. I went to see them one day. Whilst I was wondering which one to choose, one in particular wandered over to where I was kneeling on the ground. It placed its two front paws on my right knee and looked up with innocent eyes at my face, as much to say, I thought, 'Take me, please.' I was smitten by its angelic expression and I felt compelled to bow to fate even though I was reminded by my friend that it was a female. I believe it adopted Bonzie's habits, and the latter was delighted with her new friend. Whatever Bonzie did, Fleurie followed her example. Does that explanation satisfy your curiosity, Maura?"

"Oh, yes, Paul! Not only is it logical, but it's an endearing little story too. Yes, I can believe that is the reason why they disturb you at night when nature calls."

"Maura," Paul said, suddenly remembering, "did you ring your mother and let her know that all was well?"

Maura answered, yawning, "Yes, I rang her just before getting into the bath earlier, and I explained about the offer of the temporary accommodation. I also told her to be sure to read the Sunday paper as there had been a sudden dramatic conclusion to the cottage-ruin mystery, but I didn't go into details."

"I'm glad you didn't, Maura, because it might have caused embarrassment if the news had got out before publication."

"Yes, I remembered what you said in the past about classified information, Paul."

"Very good. You certainly are growing wiser, Maura." Paul complimented her, followed by a yawn, and shortly after they fell asleep again in each other's arms.

Bonzie and Fleurie settled down to sleep as well.

At sunrise both dogs were again at the bedside on Paul's side sitting on their haunches waiting for him to awake.

When he did, he immediately noticed them and stretched an arm out to fondle their heads, saying, "Good morning, Bonzie and Fleurie, our precious friends."

They licked his face in greeting, and Paul's voice woke Maura. When she greeted Paul, both dogs scurried round to the other side of the bed to greet Maura in like manner, and Maura greeted them and fondled their heads too. After kissing Maura, Paul slipped out of bed, pushed his feet into his sandals, which he preferred to slippers, and still in pyjamas he accompanied the dogs into the rear garden. He was joined there fifteen minutes later by Maura, washed and casually dressed, and they sat side by side on the garden bench admiring and commenting on the plants in the surrounding flowerbeds and the songbirds passing over into other gardens.

"Offerings are no doubt set up to attract them," Paul remarked, and he added, "We need to buy some seed, peanut and fat-ball containers to hang out round the garden, Maura, so that the songbirds will visit our patch too."

"Yes, of course, we mustn't encourage them to ignore us. That would be sinful, especially when we have their welfare at heart," Maura stressed.

When the dogs had exhausted their scouting investigations they returned to Paul and Maura and nuzzled up beside them on the bench. A few minutes later Paul stood upright and announced that it was time for him to wash and shave. Maura decided to prepare their cereal breakfast in the meantime. The dogs followed them indoors and trailed after Paul to the bathroom, where they waited patiently for him to complete his refreshing morning routine.

After breakfast Paul and Maura with the dogs spent more than an hour in the rear garden. Paul amused the dogs by rolling the rubber balls across the short-cropped grass of the garden. This light exercise induced them to relieve themselves of their waste products, which were then placed in a bucket set aside for that purpose.

"The caretaker lady's husband is the gardener for the house, then, so we had better not interfere with the set-up," Paul decided.

"Yes, I suppose that is the arrangement, and I agree with your suggestion, Paul, but I feel sure we are free to hang out some songbird containers on the pretty Bramley apple-tree branches and others."

"Yes, I imagine that would be left to our discretion, Maura, but no doubt we will be informed in some way if the habit is not encouraged," Paul assured her.

The four left in the camper van at 9.30 a.m. for the kilometre drive, to Attanagh police station. Maura was asked to drive and she agreed with a smile.

Paul fitted the dogs' muzzles whilst talking gently to them: "I have to do this, girls, because I can't risk you nipping someone's fingers when they attempt to fondle your heads on being introduced to you. That is your natural reaction regarding certain people. I understand such behaviour, but those who are resented don't. Is that understood, girls?"

The dogs wagged their tails, giving the impression they understood.

"I wouldn't have thought of that, Paul," Maura remarked, acknowledging the fact.

"You will from now on, Maura. That's how we all learn – through experience and tuition. And one other piece of information: never trust anyone that a dog doesn't trust."

"Well, good advice. I will make a mental note of that, Paul, and I won't forget," Maura assured him.

When they arrived at the police station, they were met by Inspector Conroy, who, on welcoming them, introduced them to a man with whom he had been in conversation – Mr John Fitzpatrick, a reporter for a newspaper syndicate.

He had a proposition to put to the couple and the Inspector suggested, "I will leave you with Mr Fitzpatrick for a few minutes and he will explain."

After shaking hands with Paul and Maura, the reporter remarked, "These must be the two wonderful dogs – the already famous heroines that identified the real killer of the family in the cottage inferno five years ago. Which one discovered that fact, Paul?" he asked.

"Yes, that's true, Mr Fitzpatrick, and it was Bonzie, the orange-brown dog sitting beside me here, that identified the killer."

The reporter invited Paul and Maura to address him simply as John, and he stooped down to speak to Bonzie.

"I would like to shake your paw if you're willing," he said, and he offered his open hand.

Paul urged Bonzie to give the man her paw, and she duly obliged.

The reporter was quite pleased by her response, and he said, "And that means that this other wonderful dog is the heroine that solved the mystery of the cottage-ruin site only as recently as yesterday. And her name is . . . ?"

Paul looked at Maura and said, "Your turn, Maura."

Maura's eyes lit up delightedly, and she smiled and answered, "Yes, this is the beloved mystery solver – Fleurie."

The reporter stooped again and offered his hand, saying, "Delighted to meet you, Fleurie."

Maura urged Fleurie to offer her paw, and she followed Bonzie's example and lifted a paw to engage the reporter's hand.

John was also pleased by the second introduction and remarked, "They certainly are two wonderful dogs to be proud of, and I am glad to have personally met both. And now the proposition: I have been asked by my editor to make a deal with you both for the story of the cottage-ruin site. I have also been informed that both of you are now the official owners of the site and you are in the process of having a bungalow constructed there. I don't know at the moment what the exact offer for your story will be, but I know from experience that it will be larger than the cost of building the bungalow. In addition I have been told, Paul, that you are a writer. Is that true?"

"Yes, but I am not an established force yet," Paul confessed.

"Well, don't worry about that. We can arrange a commission for you to write the story, and the newspaper syndicate will promote your book and help to make it a success if you agree to write it. What do you think of the proposition, Paul?"

"I am pleasantly surprised by the proposition, John. All I need now is my wife Maura's opinion." Paul extended his respect to Maura.

"I am as pleasantly surprised and pleased as you are, Paul, by the offer, and I endorse your decision." Maura declared her support.

"Good, good! I'm glad you've accepted the offer. I will make arrangements with you to write your story. We'll complete the contractual details involved early in the coming week. Thank you for sharing your time with me and for introducing me to your two wonderful and already famous dogs – the heroines of the story. I hope you enjoy your meeting with other media representatives too. Until we meet again quite soon, be happy."

Paul and Maura thanked him and were then rejoined by Inspector Conroy, who asked, "I hope that proposition was to your liking, in the plural?"

"I expect you know what the proposition was, then, Inspector?" Paul asked.

"Oh, yes, before I left I made sure that any deal would be beneficial to both of you and the dogs. Short-changing you in any form will not go unpunished," the Inspector assured them. Call it a small reward for the enormous help you have given us in the continuing investigation. And a bit of good news to cheer you up as well: we interrogated the arsonist killer and confronted him with the medallion and chain entwined in the skeletal fingers of the young lady's remains, which your dog, Fleurie, discovered in the empty flower bed. Although the medallion bears his name, he tried to lie his way out of trouble, stating that he lost it somewhere, but when we told him where it was found he went to pieces and admitted his guilt. He said that he never meant to kill her and if she hadn't struggled violently and screamed he wouldn't have killed her.

"'I didn't mean to do it; I just lost my self-control,' he said.

"He deliberately and without feeling burned the remaining members of the young lady's family to death in the cottage inferno to lead the police and others to believe that she too died in the fire, and he created an atmosphere of fear, suspicion and superstition among the community to deter anyone from buying the site, but you bravely decided to buy the site and build a home there. He decided to eliminate you to deter anyone else from attempting to do likewise, and he even tried to poison your two dogs, but he failed and those dogs are the heroines that exposed his evil to the world. He cowered before me, and when I mentioned the innocent traveller who was convicted and sentenced to life imprisonment for his crime (but he will now be set free), he broke down again and bawled, 'Why don't you just find me guilty and hang me and I'll be free too?'

"I said to him, 'And let you go unpunished? Oh, no, Mr Rangton, you will have to suffer the full punishment for your evil deeds, and you can shout and rant all you want for the remainder of your natural life. Now sleep on that and let your friend the devil comfort you.'

"I believe you guessed right about the identity of the young lady's remains, Paul, before the killer's confession and before the legal identification too," the Inspector concluded.

"Well, it was merely an inspired or instinctive speculation on my part, Inspector." Paul played down his prediction.

"Nevertheless, Paul, you seem to have developed an art for following the slightest clue to a conclusion. The police force could do with more of your kind in its ranks, if you should ever be tempted," the Inspector suggested.

"I'll keep the thought in mind, Inspector, and I will always make myself available to help when requested," Paul remarked.

The meeting with the newspaper and TV reporters was a lively affair. Bonzie and Fleurie were showered with accolades as they sat between Paul and Maura throughout the press conference, which was restricted to thirty minutes and was overseen by Inspector Conroy. He intervened on behalf of Paul and Maura when he felt the necessity to enforce the rules to save them from any form of embarrassment. Paul, Maura and the dogs would be on all the front pages of Sunday's newspapers and on Saturday evening's television news.

The press conference ended in a cacophony of vocal sounds from the crowd of news-hungry reporters as they dispersed, and they wasted no time before getting their brief stories to their hometown news offices in time for the evening papers. Paul wrote down his temporary address on a page of a notebook, added his mobile phone number and gave it to Inspector Conroy to pass on to John Fitzpatrick, the reporter, then he, Maura and the dogs exited the police station through a rear door and wandered round the secluded area with the dogs so that the latter could relieve themselves if necessary. When they eventually emerged from the premises and into the car park they were confronted by the Inspector and Mr Fitzpatrick in conversation and apparently awaiting their appearance.

"I gave Mr Fitzpatrick your contact details, Paul, but he had already decided to wait and confirm a day and time for your meeting," the Inspector informed him.

"Yes, I missed you in the exit confusion, Paul, but all's well that ends well, as the saying goes. How does ten o'clock on Monday morning sound to you?"

"Yes, agreed, John. That will be fine. I'll be standing by the avenue entrance on Green Road, about two kilometres north of the town centre – otherwise you might miss the opening."

"I'll remember that, Paul. Until then I hope you, Maura and the dogs enjoy the weekend. Farewell for now – and that includes you, Inspector. Thanks for your help."

Seconds later they all parted company.

CHAPTER TWENTY-THREE

Both Paul and Maura embraced Bonzie and Fleurie when they climbed into the camper van, and congratulated them on their behaviour during the question-and-answer ordeal that Paul and Maura and the dogs successfully had endured from the intrigued reporters.

"You two girls are famous now, and everybody in the country and beyond will know about you and your intelligent exploits. How do you feel about that, girls?" Maura asked, curious to see their reactions.

She was rewarded with an excited spate of affectionate licks, and Paul was likewise treated. He offered each dog a hide chew, and the dogs gratefully accepted and settled on their rug to work on their treats.

"Now, Maura, wasn't that proposal an out-of-the-blue, totally unexpected and rewarding surprise? The fee will more than pay the cost of the new bungalow plus I've received a guaranteed commission from a publisher to write a book that will be promoted by the newspaper syndicate. That is a guarantee of some sort of success. What do you say?"

"I am still mentally frazzled by the possible consequences to come in the unfolding future, Paul. I find it difficult to mentally digest, but at the same time I feel delighted. Do you understand what I mean, Paul?"

"Yes, of course, my love. I too feel the evolutionary unfolding reality. I think you should phone your mother when we return to our temporary home and update your parents on events, but now let's go and do some shopping."

Maura started the camper van's engine and headed for the largest supermarket in Attanagh.

On arriving back at their new address, and unloading their shopping, Maura decided to call her parents and Paul busied himself by filling the songbird containers with birdseed, peanuts and fat balls. He hung them from branches of the Bramley apple tree, just beyond the central area of the garden, and on completion of that task he amused Bonzie and Fleurie by bowling the rubber balls across the lawn for them to chase.

On finishing her phone conversation with her mum, Maura put some fat in a frying pan, fried some slices of bacon and eggs in the kitchen and made four hefty sandwiches, including one each for the dogs, which she sliced into manageable pieces in their bowls. When ready, she called Paul and the dogs in and placed the dogs' bowls on the floor ready for their attention.

"I hadn't expected that!" Paul exclaimed, pleased with Maura's effort, and he rewarded her with a kiss.

The dogs showed their delight by giving the food their undivided attention, and Maura poured their cooled tea into their emptied bowls. The sandwiches were followed by rhubarb pie with custard for Paul and Maura, and apple pie and custard for the dogs. Both pies had been bought at the small supermarket. Maura had also bought some imported cooking apples and the other ingredients needed to bake apple pies in the house. Paul and Maura sat out on the patio garden bench, and Bonzie and Fleurie sat close to them on their outdoor rug and concentrated on a hide chew each.

"The songbirds have already noticed the stuffed containers hanging from the Bramley branches, Maura, and they are sizing up the situation from the safety of their vantage points. As soon as one or two decide to venture on to the scene the others will be tempted to follow their example."

"Yes, I see. As soon as one breaks the ice the splashes will follow, and we might even have some rare visitors appearing at times," Maura suggested.

"I hope we don't get a fast-flying visit from a sparrowhawk

in the mix. Although nature designed them to predate on smaller birds and other creatures, I don't like to witness the act of violence. I do understand the necessity, but still, I must confess, I do find it emotionally difficult to accept. I suppose that is related to our primatial root." Paul exposed a mental weakness.

"Yes, I agree with your feelings, Paul, for the songbirds and other little creatures, but surely God, through evolution, must be somehow exonerated from guilt for creating what seems to me to be a cruel existence." Maura defended God's role although she didn't understand the spiritual complexity of such a mysterious subject.

"Oh, yes, Maura, you are absolutely right to defend God. I know the reason why God is blameless and I promise that I will explain it to you when I am sure that you are mentally mature enough to understand the simplicity of the complexity," Paul assured her.

"Well, I will certainly be looking forward to being enlightened by that knowledge in the unfolding future," Maura remarked with hopeful satisfaction.

"There's something we have to do concerning Gerry, Maura." Paul changed the subject.

"Like what, for example?" Maura asked naively.

"He is the person who has helped to change our lives dramatically, and he deserves rewarding. I have an idea that I think you will agree with. I will contact him after we have finished with John Fitzpatrick, the newspaper reporter, on Monday, and you will witness the unfolding of my idea thereafter. Is that OK with you, Maura?"

"It's just like I told the Inspector, Paul – I am as faithful as the dogs, and wherever you lead I too faithfully follow."

Paul put an arm round her shoulders, kissed her and said, "It's very satisfying to have a bonded attachment like ours, Maura."

"Yes, I agree, and we will need to look after it very carefully. We need to beware of any hairline fractures that might threaten the delicate fabric of our bond. Do you agree, Paul?"

"Exactly! Disagreements, for example, and their root causes! But then, we are both adept in the art of honesty, so I see nothing to worry about." After a thoughtful moment Paul suddenly remembered and remarked, "The thought just crossed my mind, Maura, that the traveller wrongly imprisoned for life is to be set free on Wednesday next. What a joy that will be for him, his wife, his young daughter or son and all his other family members! I'm sure that will be a big celebration."

"Yes, and if anyone deserves to celebrate, he and his wife are worthy candidates. I hope they both enjoy a wonderful new life together too. And good luck to them and their children!" Maura expressed her wishes for them and then decided to go indoors and phone her mum again as she had promised. The dogs stopped chewing and looked up when Maura stood upright, and then stooped down to fondle their heads, saying, "See you in a little while, girls."

She received a flurry of tail wags in acknowledgement as she departed. The dogs – out of force of habit, no doubt – decided to stay put with Paul. He continued to sit and watch the comings and goings of the songbirds to the food containers on the apple-tree branches whilst the dogs continued their chewing endeavours.

During Maura's absence Paul's mobile erupted into life. It was his friend Gerry asking if all was well with their accommodation, and he received a positive reply. Paul decided then to put his plan into action by asking Gerry if there was a car sales company somewhere in the vicinity of the town.

"Yes," Gerry replied, "there is one a couple of hundred metres out on the Dublin road. I am going there with Joan tomorrow morning after church to have a look as my car is three years old next month and I am thinking of exchanging it. And you, Paul? Are you thinking of investing in a car?"

"Well, yes, not for myself, but for Maura, and not until the autumn, when the bungalow is completed. I want her to see in advance what might be suitable for her, and she will have plenty of time to think it over and change her choice if she wishes," Paul revealed.

"Yes, I see, Paul. That's a good idea. Did all go reasonably well for all four of you this morning? I rang Inspector Conroy to inform him of your new address from yesterday in case you needed to be visited, and he told me about your meeting with Mr Fitzpatrick, which was ongoing as he spoke. That's about all I know at the moment."

Paul apologised for not having informed him sooner. "So much was happening, Gerry, that I was beginning to be besieged by voices, but I'll fill you in on the details now whilst they are fresh in my mind." He related the important aspects of the meeting to Gerry, and the latter was pleasantly surprised by what he heard.

Gerry remarked, "And you are going to be commissioned by a publisher to write the story? Wow! That is good news, Paul. You will soon be projected into the limelight in a literary sense and showered with accolades. Attanagh will be proud of you. Congratulations, Paul!" Gerry concluded.

"Gerry, I have to confess I am not looking forward to accolades and wild success. All that is beyond me. A quiet contented existence is my dream and Maura's, and I can safely include the dogs' wishes in my dream.

"Yes, I understand, Paul. You were never one to wallow in wild bursts of excitement during our boyhood years either. The town will be better for your presence and your name will attract tourists, so be happy, Paul. I'll see you in the car park outside the car showroom tomorrow after church, OK?"

"Yes, I'll do that for you, Gerry. Until tomorrow."

Maura reappeared shortly after with news that her parents were fine and they were eagerly looking forward to seeing what was on the television news programmes that evening and to reading the Sunday newspaper tomorrow.

"I told them we might be calling to see them during the coming week, and Mum said that we and the dogs are always welcome."

"That's good news, Maura. Gerry rang whilst you were engaged with your parents. He was delighted by the news of the proposal offered to us. I asked him about a car sales company in the town and I was informed there was one on the Dublin road just outside the town. We will meet him and his wife, Joan, there after the church service tomorrow morning. Are you in favour, Maura?" he asked. "It will be advantageous to you."

"I don't quite follow you, Paul. How will it be advantageous to me?" Maura asked, her curiosity aroused.

"Because I am inviting you to have a look at the cars and decide which make and model you would like to have for your personal use when the bungalow is built," Paul explained.

"You are saying, Paul, that you are going to buy a new car for me?" Maura uttered, surprised.

"No, Maura, I am suggesting that you and I should buy a new car for you if you agree. You will need one to drive into town when necessary to call at shops, the church and the hairdresser's, for example, and to take your mother or both your parents with you."

"But what about you, Paul? Won't you be—"

"Well, the truth is, Maura, the camper van is going to become too well known and there wouldn't be enough room in a car for the dogs. And even if there was, they could easily be seen and that would attract attention and upset the dogs. And nasty people may plan to steal the car and dogs and demand ransom money. That means we are going to have to be very careful where the dog's security is concerned from now on. Do you understand the danger?" Paul asked her.

Maura was silently subdued for a long moment before commenting: "Yes, I can see your logic, Paul. The great mystery that hung over the cottage site has been solved, but it has generated another problem," she suggested.

"Yes, you are right, Maura, and so it will always be. We must be continuously alert and vigilant and we will survive the vagaries of life," Paul said.

"You are sacrificing a lot for my welfare and the welfare of the dogs, and I feel—"

"Don't say it, Maura," Paul interrupted her. "All three of you are my responsibility and are worth more than any sacrifice I make. That's your value to me." Paul made his feelings known and then changed the subject to Gerry. He explained to Maura that he intended to reward Gerry, without whose help nothing would have transpired. "I suggest that we pay for the new car that he intends to trade his present one in for, when he decides. After we have met Gerry and his wife, Joan, after the church service in the car park outside the showroom tomorrow morning. I will excuse myself at some point and seek to make a deal on Gerry's behalf with the manager of the car company in secret. What do you think, Maura?" He asked her opinion.

"I think that is very thoughtful and generous of you – I mean *us*. But how are you going to know which model of car he has decided on without asking him, Paul?"

"That's simple, Maura. I'll just ask him if he were in my shoes which car would he choose to buy? That will give me the answer, Maura."

"Yes, I see – clever!" Maura agreed, and snuggling up to Paul she said, "Have I told you lately that I love you, Paul?"

"Yes, of course," he smiled, adding, "Last night in bed. And I'm telling you now that I love you too, Maura."

They embraced and kissed lovingly for a timeless prolonged moment, after which Maura decided to prepare and bake a couple of apple pies whilst Paul amused the dogs with the rubber balls in the rear garden and watched the songbirds flitting to and from the containers on the apple-tree boughs! As he watched he suddenly realised that he should have bought a drinking tub for the birds to have a drink when needed, plus a birdbath to amuse the onlookers with their bathing antics. Paul made a mental note of the extras as priority purchases on Sunday. He returned indoors with the dogs as Maura was about to place the apple pies in the oven to bake, and after filling the electric kettle with water he plugged it into the socket and turned it on to brew enough tea for the two of them and the dogs.

"It's time you had a break, Maura," he reminded his wife thoughtfully.

He placed two slices of rhubarb pie on a plate and a slice of apple pie in each of the dogs' bowls and sliced them into smaller pieces and put them on the floor for the attention of the dogs, who devoured the contents with wagging tails that were an indication of their joy.

He then poured half a pot of cooled tea into each bowl and this tea was lapped with tail wags of pleasure. He poured his own and Maura's tea as well and sat at the kitchen table beside his wife and said, "A woman's life is far more important than a man's, Maura."

Maura looked at him, smiled and said, "You say things at times that amaze me. I have never heard of a woman being complimented like that before, Paul."

"I am merely stating the truth, Maura. The fact that the woman generates the babies is proof of that apart from being a willing slave to her offspring for most of her life and all the stress and strain of caring and worrying about them and demanding nothing in return. To me, that is the ultimate sacrifice of life. I love you because of all that and I hope that compensates you in some way."

Maura was emotionally piqued by Paul's declaration. She shed a spate of silent tears, saying, "That is the most gracious compliment I have ever received from a feminine point of view. It is something I will never forget, Paul."

He put an arm round her shoulders in a reassuring manner and replied, "I was only stating the truth about women and motherhood, and it should be more widely acknowledged, Maura."

"And men? Where do they stand in the frame, Paul?" Maura enquired.

"Men, I would say, are meant to be the guiders, providers and protectors, but the manifold vagaries of life are often their downfall and both joy and sorrow always follow in their wake. Still though, chance appears on the scene from time to time to delight or disappoint, and the result is decided by the toss of a coin, so uncertain is the route through life. And bon voyage, I say!" Paul concluded.

"You are optimistic, Paul, I would say." Maura formulated her opinion.

"Yes, you could well be right, Maura, because I have always harboured the belief that when things get so bad that they can't get any worse then they are bound to get better."

"Yes, that sounds logical, and anyway it's better to be optimistic than pessimistic, for misery follows the latter," Maura concluded.

"Although we have finished our little snack, Maura, I am going to help you with preparations for dinner. Whilst you prepare the chicken for roasting, including stuffing it, I will see to the spring cabbage, potatoes, frozen garden peas and sweetcorn – or vice versa, if you wish. The choice is yours. How does that sound?"

"Fine, Paul. Thanks for the offer, but you don't have to because I can take it all in my stride."

"Why should you, Maura? It would only encourage me to become dependent on your efforts, and that's not fair."

"Well, yes, I see. That's thoughtful, and I agree. Thanks." Maura accepted the arrangement.

"I believe a husband's duty is to treat a wife with respect, protect her mentally, spiritually and physically and help to make her life a contented existence, Maura."

"Now, I am emotionally moved by that statement, Paul, and I believe in doing the same in return." And she spilled tears of happiness.

The rest of the afternoon went well and all relaxed in each other's company. They listened to some radio, music and documentaries, and watched a little television through the evening after dinner. The dogs were kept amused by exercise, chasing the rubber balls across the garden lawn, and lulled themselves to sleep after wearing their chews down.

On Sunday morning after driving Maura to church Paul drove to the wasteland site of his boyhood days to exercise Bonzie and Fleurie and himself along the bank of a wandering stream, nostalgically recalling adventures of not so long before. He returned to collect Maura at the church and drove on to the car sales company, where he parked the camper van close to the sales office. Here they were able to keep an eye on the camper van, with the dogs inside, from every part of the sales park.

Gerry and his wife, Joan, had been on the lookout for them. They approached and Gerry introduced his wife, Joan, to both friends. The two women got into a chatty acquaintance at once, and whilst they were busily engaged Paul asked Gerry the question he had said he would ask.

Gerry pointed to a car nearby, saying, "That's the one Joan and I have decided on, Paul."

Paul smiled and glanced at Maura, who returned the smile.

After the four moved over to admire Gerry and Joan's choice of car, Paul asked what trade-in price Gerry was hoping to get for his present car.

"Five or six thousand euros, I expect. I'll just have to wait until I decide to make the deal and come to an arrangement," he revealed.

Paul then excused himself to visit the toilet just a few paces from the camper van and (ideally) next to the sales office. Paul discreetly went and asked a sales assistant if he, Paul, could speak to the manager, who was summoned by mobile phone. Less than a minute later the manager appeared in person, greeted Paul and introduced himself as Matt Dempsey.

He asked, "How can I help you, sir?"

Paul explained his planned surprise for Gerry, stating that he wanted the trade-in price of his friend's present car to be paid in the form of a cheque to his friend, and he, Paul, would pay the full sale price to the company with a bank draft. I hope I have made myself clear enough for you to understand, Mr Dempsey," he concluded.

"Yes, understood, and that's fine. I can arrange that deal. And the name and address of your friend, sir?"

"Well, at the moment I can only give you the client's name, and that is Gerry Kyle."

"Would that be Gerry Kyle, married to Joan, who works for the town council?"

"Yes, that's him exactly. Are you acquainted with him?"

"Yes, I know Gerry quite well. He is a good friend and I know his address, which makes it even easier. And your name, sir?"

"My name is Paul Attanagh and my address – well, at the moment I am not certain of it, but Gerry knows it well," Paul embarrassedly replied.

"Paul Attanagh," the manager repeated. "I'm sure I've heard that name." And then he exclaimed, "You are the hero who captured the killer of the family who died in the cottage inferno five years ago! It's a real pleasure to meet you in person, Mr Attanagh."

He offered his hand, and Paul grasped it and shook hands with the delighted manager.

Whilst glancing about, he said in a low voice, "I am not a publicity seeker, Mr Dempsey. I hope you understand."

"But you are a national hero now, Mr Attanagh. Everyone in the country is talking about you, your wife and the two heroic dogs," the manager said excitedly.

"Just address me as Paul, Mr Dempsey," Paul requested.

"And please call me Matt, Paul," the manager invited him. "I think there will be a special deal for you, Paul. I feel sure there will be. Is this some kind of thank you to Gerry for help he may have given you, Paul? It won't go beyond me, I promise."

"Yes, it is, Matt. Without Gerry's help early on, the mystery would never have been solved."

"The mystery has been solved, Paul, you say! I didn't know that," Matt remarked, surprised.

"Yes, but you wouldn't know, Matt, as it only happened early yesterday afternoon. It is the headlines of today's paper."

"Did you solve it, Paul?" Matt's interest was aroused.

"Not exactly, Matt. It was my dog Fleurie who really solved it."

"Your dog Fleurie solved the dark mystery. My God, Paul, your two dogs will be famous worldwide. I am really delighted for you, your wife and you two wonderful dogs. All four of you will make Attanagh famous. I can hardly wait to read today's paper. And you are asking us to do a deal for you when we should be asking you, Paul. Will you leave your phone number with me, Paul, and I will ring you later after I have spoken to the proprietors of the company? Will you do that, Paul, please?" Matt pleaded.

Paul wrote his mobile number out and gave it to Matt, then he asked for a brochure for his wife to browse as he intended buying her a car in the autumn.

Shortly after, he rejoined Maura, Joan and Gerry.

"We thought for a moment there that you got delayed by someone who recognised you, Paul," Gerry remarked with a smile.

"Oh, thank God, no! I just decided to ask for a brochure for Maura and I had to wait for a few minutes. Since you and Joan have set your sights on your next car, I suppose we can no more than offer you coffee or tea and biscuits in the camper van with the dogs, but I'm sure that wouldn't be to everybody's liking," Paul invited.

"Oh, but I would love to meet your two dogs – two heroines, I should say. Gerry has told me a lot about them," Joan said, and she added, "Half of the front page of the Sunday paper is devoted to the four of you, and the headlines state that Fleurie has solved the mystery of the cottage-ruin site."

"Well, we did have to have an interview with the press, and I suppose it was only fair that we did, but I, well . . ."

"I think what Maura wants to say is she feels a bit concerned for my opinion due to the fact that I don't like publicity," Paul interrupted her, and he continued: "But what's done is done and one has to live with the consequences, so let's climb into the camper van. I'll go first and take the dogs to the rear, and then you, Joan and Gerry can enter unhindered. Maura will take up the rear position as she knows where everything is."

The dogs recognised Gerry at once and greeted him with wagging tails as he sat down on one of the side bunks and Joan sat alongside him.

Maura introduced Joan to the obediently waiting dogs: "Are you going to give Joan your paw, Bonzie and Fleurie."

Both dogs seemed to understand, and each dog lifted a paw to greet Joan. She gently grasped their paws and she was delighted with the gesture, saying, "Oh, you are beautiful and loving, Bonzie and Fleurie, and I can see why you are so loved."

She fondled their heads and they licked her hands affectionately in return. Paul poured four mugs of coffee and poured some into the dogs' bowls as well. Then he left the bowls on a shelf for the contents to cool sufficiently. Maura produced a large plastic container half filled with a biscuit selection and told the guests to help themselves. She reminded them that the dogs had a liking for ginger nuts, but they only allowed them to have three each so that they didn't get too fond of them from a sweetness point of view as that would have an adverse effect on their health. But the dogs, of course, wouldn't be aware of that.

"Aren't they just like children!" Joan remarked, impressed.

"Yes, but with many differences, Joan, and one in particular," Paul reminded her. He explained: "Because of a dog's shorter lifespan they naturally mature much more quickly than a human does. By two years of age they are fully mature adults, and because of that they prefer the company of adult humans, which is only natural too."

He was hoping that both Gerry and Joan would realise that a puppy dog was not merely a pulsating toy for a child. A fast-maturing animal would become a burden to the child and the child would become a bigger burden to the dog. He hoped they would see and understand the logic in what he was saying and not make the mistake so many people make.

A half an hour later they parted company in good humour after an enjoyable conversation, and Maura said she and Paul would like to invite Gerry and Joan over to their temporary home one evening when they were settled in. Joan and Gerry expressed their delight at the invitation and said they would be looking forward to the occasion.

That afternoon Matt Dempsey rang to inform Paul that the company director of Attanagh Motors Ltd was delighted that he had visited the showroom and had associated himself with the company by purchasing one of their vehicles. In recognition of Paul's role in recent events, the director had instructed Mr Dempsey to reduce the price of the car by €5,000 and increase the trade-in price to €7,000.

"Now, what do you say to that, Paul?" Matt asked.

"Well, that is indeed very generous of your company, and I am grateful to you, Matt, for the part you played, which I feel obliged to reward."

"Oh, absolutely not, Paul. It's a privilege for me to be able to show my appreciation to you, your wife and dogs for the good publicity you've brought to the town, the region and the country."

"Well, I don't know how best to express my thanks to you, Matt, but I'll think of a way."

"Don't concern yourself with that, Paul. And where Gerry is involved, I will work out a pleasant surprise for him on your behalf, if that's OK with you, Paul?"

"Yes, that's fine, Matt. Do you know the make of the car Gerry has set his sights on, Matt?"

"Yes, I certainly do, Paul – no problem there."

"I appreciate your help, Matt, and I am indebted to you again."

"Think nothing of it, Paul. I will see to all the details and I will inform you accordingly. Until we speak or meet again, good luck, Paul, and bye for now."

"Well, what a good friend he has turned out to be!" Paul spoke aloud, and he was interrupted again by the mobile sounding.

When he answered it, it was Matt Dempsey that spoke: "Sorry, Paul, but I forgot to mention in the excitement that I read the story in the Sunday paper regarding the solving of the mystery surrounding the cottage-ruin site – how your beloved dog Fleurie prompted you to dig deeper until you found the remains of the young lady who had sadly been murdered. That really was mysterious how the dog somehow knew something. That's a mystery in itself."

"Yes, Matt, I understand how you feel, but there is a bit more to the mystery that wasn't in the paper. I will reveal that to you when I call again, so if you can be patient until then . . ."

"Yes, I certainly can, Paul, and I will be looking forward to hearing that mystery. Until then, Paul, bye for now."

"Who was the good friend you revered, Paul?" Maura asked.

Paul explained to her all about the car sales manager he had been speaking to, and he outlined the dialogue between Matt and himself.

"So he is going to arrange the surprise for Gerry secretly. He just rang to tell me the company had offered me a better deal because of the fame now associated with our name. They are reducing the cost by €5,000 and raising the trade-in price to €7,000, which means that Gerry and Joan have nothing to pay. In addition they will receive a cheque for €7,000. I think they will be pleased with that, Maura."

"Oh yes, Paul, no doubt about it, and well deserved too!" Maura replied. Then after a brief pause she suggested, "Should we reward the car sales manager too, Paul?"

"Yes, of course. I suggested that to him, but he said no and that it was a pleasure to have been able to help. Nevertheless we will reward him, Maura."

"Yes, I agree, Paul. His good deed deserves that."

"What are we having for dinner today, Maura?"

"The same as yesterday unless you prefer something else. What do you say, Paul?"

"Oh, that's fine with me. Have we got enough for the dogs as well? As you know, they like to eat what we eat."

"Yes, we have enough for our beloved VIP dogs – or I should say VIPs. Isn't that right, girls?" Maura addressed the dogs sat on their rug busy with chews.

They cocked their ears and wagged their tails as though they fully understood.

"And Mr John Fitzpatrick will be our guest tomorrow morning. What can we offer him for lunch?" Paul enquired.

"We have some frozen haddock that I will move from the freezer to the fridge to thaw out overnight, and we can offer him fried haddock with chips or mashed potato, garden peas and sweetcorn. If he doesn't like fish, there's sandwiches, and failing that there's home-baked apple pie with custard and excuses, of course." And she laughed at the thought.

They both sat out on the back garden patio after dinner with the dogs in close proximity and a mug of tea each. The dogs didn't linger over their cooled tea – they just lapped it until their bowls were dry and then concentrated on their chews and eventually fell asleep.

CHAPTER TWENTY-FOUR

On Monday morning Paul left Maura and the dogs at nine forty and strolled the fifty metres from the front of the house to the entrance of the cul-de-sac at the edge of the main road. He stood in plain view to await the arrival of Mr John Fitzpatrick, and just before ten o'clock an approaching car flashed a right-hand indicator, slowed to a crawl and turned into the cul-de-sac. Both men greeted each other with hand gestures, and Paul pointed towards the house. Maura welcomed the newspaper reporter into their temporary home, and Bonzie and Fleurie wagged their tails in recognition and offered a paw each to the visitor. John Fitzpatrick crouched down, shook the paws gently and spoke to the dogs in a soft tone of voice whilst fondling their heads.

"Would you like something to eat or drink, John?" Maura asked.

The guest answered, "I wouldn't refuse a mug of coffee, Maura, and if that's not available then tea will suffice."

"Coffee it is, John. With or without sugar?"

"Without sugar, Maura, thank you."

Over the drinking of the coffee John told them that he had a recording apparatus in his briefcase, and what he wanted Paul to do was to tell his story in his own words from start to finish with slight interruptions from him, John – mostly for clarification. That was about the size of it.

After the coffee break John and Paul sat in the dining room whilst Maura took the dogs into the rear garden and amused them by bowling the rubber balls for them to chase and burn up their excess energy.

Bonzie and Fleurie kept breaking off from their exercise to take a look inside the house to check on Paul's presence before returning to join Maura, and that extended to their chewing endeavours. When Maura decided that they had done enough ball chasing, she sat and watched the coming and goings of the songbirds to and from the food containers hanging from the apple-tree branches.

The recording session lasted an hour and twenty minutes, and afterwards John Fitzpatrick remarked, "That is a fascinating story, Paul, and well described. I can imagine what a good read it will be with the addition of background settings and descriptive scenery. When the story is in book form, I believe it will be a success."

"Well, thanks for your positive anticipation, John. I hope it will live up to expectations."

"I believe it will, Paul. Be brave and accept the challenge," John said to him.

"Oh, I will give it my best effort, I promise. My wife, Maura, was wondering if you would be lunching with us? If not, at least have some home-baked apple pie with custard and tea or coffee. What do you say, John?"

"Home-baked apple pie", John repeated, "with custard! How could I refuse that? Yes, I would love to taste home-baked apple pie." John readily agreed to the pie as though evoking nostalgic memories of the past.

Paul went to the rear door and called to Maura, "We are finished, Maura; and yes, John would love to sample your home-baked apple pie with custard." Turning to John, he said, "I only have to mention apple pie to raise the expectations of the dogs."

"Do the dogs really like apple pie, Paul?" John asked, surprised.

"They love it, John. It's a favourite treat for them as you will see."

Maura entered behind the rushing dogs, who pranced around Paul in excited greeting.

"That ended quicker than I expected. So it's apple pie and custard all round. *Aussitôt dit, aussitôt fait!*" she remarked, smiling, in French.

"That sounded like French. Was it?" John asked.

"Yes, John, it was and it translates as no sooner said than done," Maura explained.

"So, you study French, Maura. Is that right?" John asked.

"Yes, we both do, but Paul is more advanced than I am. We often use set phrases like that so that we don't lapse."

"Well, good. That's the way to quicker learning. Two heads are better than one, always." John complimented them.

Maura, as usual, served the dogs first, and John watched as they lovingly swallowed the pieces of apple pie and custard washed down with equally loved cooled tea.

He said, "I see what you mean by their love of apple pie, Paul." And on tasting his slice of apple pie and custard he exclaimed, "Wow! Yes, you certainly know how to bake, Maura. I have to award you top marks. It's truly delicious."

"Have another slice if you wish, John," Maura invited him.

"Well, I don't want to seem greedy, but I am tempted," John confessed.

"There you are, John," Maura said, placing an extra slice on John's plate and adding some custard.

"Thank you, Maura. I'll never forget the taste of your apple pie. I understand now why the dogs love it." John complimented her, and on finishing he spent several minutes fondling the dogs and praising their exploits he already knew about.

The dogs responded with hand licks.

"Are Bonzie and Fleurie friendly with all strangers, Paul?" he asked.

"Oh no, John. There are certain people they don't take to. They don't react to them in a friendly manner regardless of how friendly they try to be, and they will bare their teeth and growl deeply to let them know how they feel. I usually excuse their unfriendliness by saying the dogs are very wary of strangers, but at the same time I don't trust people the dogs reject. I believe they are unknowingly releasing pheromones that the dogs instantly detect and display their aversion to," Paul explained.

"Well, well, I didn't know that, but it's something I won't forget," John remarked.

Shortly after the break John made his reason for departure

known and shook hands with Paul and Maura. Then he shook paws with the dogs, wished Paul and Maura well, and good luck with the writing of the book, and thanked them for their hospitality and particularly the unforgettable apple pie. He was waved off outside the front of the house by Paul and Maura accompanied by the dogs.

"Well, that's another task completed. I am looking forward to starting the book, Maura. You will be my assistant and secretary, won't you?" Paul asked.

She looked at him, smiled her delight and said, "Of course I will! How could I refuse? Thanks for the invitation."

Then they kissed and waltzed around the dining room to the music of Mozart followed by the prancing, playful dogs.

During the afternoon Inspector Conroy rang Paul to inform him that the police forensic team had completed the exhumation of the skeletal remains of the young lady, and they were already en route to their laboratory in the city for further examination. He also revealed that Paul's identification of the young lady was correct – the head of the forensic team had confirmed it after comparing DNA from the bones with DNA from one of Mary Foley's surviving relations. The other news that the Inspector imparted to him was that he, the Inspector, and Detective Carey had visited the grandparents of the murdered young Mary Foley, north and south of Attanagh, and they had agreed with Paul and Maura's request to have their granddaughter's remains reinterred in the lily-of-the-valley bed where her killer had buried her body. The Inspector also said that he had been in contact with the local parish priest to have the burial site consecrated, and that would be done at the same time as the reburial of the girl's remains. The police would make arrangements for the relatives of Mary Foley to be present for the burial ceremony.

"I hope you are both pleased with the news, Paul, and now I place the site back in your hands. I also remembered to notify Mr Jack Kyley that he is free to begin the construction of your bungalow. Thanks for all your help, Paul," the Inspector concluded.

"We are delighted, and we're very grateful to you, Inspector. It has been a rewarding experience working with you and your team. Thanks to all of you for your help. It is appreciated. I hope to see you again soon, Inspector."

Paul made known to Maura all that the Inspector had related to him, and commented, "I'll have to phone Jack Kyley and arrange to meet him at the site tomorrow to discuss the perimeter fencing and the separate section reserved for the remains of Mary Foley complete with a bench at one end for visitors who might like to pay their respects. We could include an outer gate in the fence to access the grave site from the lane and another gate to allow us access to carry out maintenance work. What do you think, Maura?" Paul asked.

"Oh yes, Paul. I believe the spirit of Mary Foley – the Lily of the Valley, as you affectionately call her, will be very pleased that she has been lovingly remembered by all of us. I am also sure that she will always be here with us together with the other members of her tragic family too." Maura made her plea.

Paul asked Maura to brew some tea, and not to forget the dogs. He went out into the rear garden with them to make a call to Jack Kyley, the builder, but before he could dial the number his mobile erupted into life. When he answered it, he was surprised by John Fitzpatrick's voice – the newspaper reporter who had left only a half-hour before.

"Hello, Paul. I'm sorry I forgot to mention your fee for the story, and I imagine you forgot too."

"Truthfully, John, the thought never entered my mind. I suppose that's an indication of how trusting I am. Perhaps I shouldn't be, most people might say, but that's how I am."

"Well, yes, having got to know you a bit I can well believe that. But anyway, the news is your fee for the newspaper version of your story is €160,000. I hope you are satisfied with that, Paul?"

"Oh, I'm delighted, as Maura will also be, John. Thanks for your belated pleasant surprise. We will speak again soon, John, I hope."

"Yes, Paul, I will check with you from time to time to ask how you are progressing with the book. Until then, Paul, good luck to you, Maura and your two wonderful dogs. Bye for now."

Maura appeared with two mugs of tea and placed them on the

patio table. She left again momentarily with the two dog bowls, filled them with cooled tea and set them down on the concrete path for the dogs.

She asked, "So you managed to contact Mr Kyley, then?"

"No, Maura. Before I had a chance to dial his number I had a call from John Fitzpatrick, who left less than an hour ago. He told me that he had forgotten to inform us of the fee for the newspaper story, but it's €160,000. What do you say to that, Maura?"

"Wow! That's a wonderful surprise – a really good starter in life. That means the bungalow is paid for and we'll have more than the price again in the bank as well. Do you believe that we did right to face the danger of the challenge?" Maura asked cautiously.

"Yes, but we weren't doing it for money. We simply wanted to help to free the innocent traveller and expose the heartless killer of Mary Foley and all her family. We didn't even consider any monetary reward. The rewards were simply the after-effects of our dangerous experience, and we have the joy of knowing we have proved the traveller's innocence and he has been united with his wife and young daughter again. We had no idea that we were going to benefit in any way from the strange catalogue of events that culminated in the solving of the murder of the innocent family in the cottage inferno five years ago and the capture of the killer, who also turned out to be the killer of Mary Foley the day before the cottage fire. Fleurie's discovery of the young girl's remains helped to solve the whole mystery hanging over the site. We have no shadows hanging over our consciences to haunt our mental equilibrium. We were two potential victims destined for the same fate as those five years before, but we were saved by our two precious sentinels. We are indebted to them, so smile, Maura, and be eternally grateful to Bonzie and Fleurie and the spirit of Mary Foley, the Lily of the Valley." Paul summed up the story of their survival.

"Yes, you are right, Paul. If we are guilty of anything it can only be of putting our lives at risk by investing in the cottage-ruin site. And now, after the haunting fear of being killed, I am glad that we did persist and eventually won the victory over evil, helping to put right the wrongs of the past."

"That's the spirit, Maura. We have to help to shape the future by sowing beautiful seeds in people's minds, and now I'll phone Jack Kyley and arrange to meet him on the cottage site tomorrow around lunchtime."

Followed by the dogs he walked around the garden hand in hand with Maura and he spoke to Jack Kyley. The meeting was agreed and Paul returned with Maura, trailed by the dogs. He and Maura sat down side by side on the patio bench and conversed about the cottage gardens and the flower-scapes they wanted to create. Bonzie and Fleurie settled on their outdoor rug alongside their beloved masters and concentrated on the chews that Paul had given them.

Maura drew Paul's attention to the comings and goings of the songbirds to the food containers and the amusing antics of the birds as they queued on branches waiting for their chance to bathe in the birdbath that Paul and Maura had remembered to get (plus a drinking tub) at the local garden centre on their return to their temporary home the day before, Sunday.

"Isn't it marvellous how the birds can give themselves a real shower with their wings? And it's so fascinating to watch them perform!" Maura enthused, mesmerised by the spectacle.

"Yes, one could watch them continuously without getting bored. It's a natural art that different species of birds use in a variety of bathing habits," Paul commented, impressed. After a momentary pause he asked, "Did you thaw that haddock out overnight as you intended, or did you forget?"

"Yes, it's thawed out, which means, I think, that you would like fried haddock and chips. Is that so?"

"Exactly that, Maura. If you are in the mood we can follow that with a hefty slice of apple pie with custard, and I believe the dogs will have the same, won't you, girls?" he asked.

The dogs stopped chewing, looking up at him, wagged their tails and excitedly barked their answer with three barks each.

"There's your answer, Maura – you can't deny that." Paul acknowledged the fact.

"Yes, I'll take your word for it since I can't translate their responses as efficiently as you." She then added, "Is there anything else on the agenda, Paul?"

"Oh yes, I've just remembered," he responded, and he continued: "Your dad used to drive, I remember?"

"Yes, he did, but it became a burden when he retired and he was reluctantly forced to part company with his car," Maura revealed.

"Well, I suggest we pay your mum and dad a visit tomorrow, if that's OK with you, Maura. And if it is, you had better phone your mum later and make sure that we are not going to be an inconvenience to them," Paul suggested.

"Oh, I know what she is going to say, Paul, but I'll ring anyway to please you!"

"I don't want you to do it to please me, Maura, but because it's the thoughtful, polite and respectful thing to do."

"Yes, Paul, I can see it from your point of view and I agree, it is the correct procedure to follow. Nevertheless they will be delighted anyway." Maura was certain.

Paul was silent for a moment and then suggested, "You and I, Maura, are going to buy your parents a new car so that they can get out and about and it will deter your father from developing a temptation to drink. What do you say, Maura?" Paul asked on the spur of the moment.

Maura was dumbfounded.

On recovering her composure she replied, "Whatever you decide will be fine with me, Paul, and I'm certain my mum and dad will be delighted and shocked – over the moon, so to speak."

"Good! I'm glad you agree, Maura, because I want you to announce the news to them that you and I decided together to reward them."

"But you thought of the idea yourself all alone, Paul, so that would mean I will be lying," Maura reminded him.

"Well, yes, I see what you mean, Maura, but it's an angelic lie and that's the difference."

"Would you mind explaining that to me, Paul?" Maura asked, naively confused.

"Yes, an angelic lie is the bending of the truth slightly to highlight a heavenly trait in another. In this case the other is you and the heavenly trait in you was first waiting to be awoken, and I did that. So there it is. I hope that explains the angelic lie."

"Does that mean then that not all lies are sins?" Maura asked, still confused.

"Yes, an angelic lie is not a sin by virtue of the fact that it's angelic and therefore heavenly," Paul concluded.

"I've never heard of an angelic lie before in my life, Paul," Maura stated.

"Well, you are not alone in lacking that piece of knowledge, Maura, so don't feel bad about not having known about it. Just feel glad that you know about it now."

"I'll have to give that some thought over the coming days – an angelic lie," she repeated to herself.

"So you will agree to break the news to your parents, then, Maura?"

"Yes, if you think that would be best, Paul," Maura agreed.

Paul put an arm round her shoulders, kissed her and said, "Yes, I do think so, Maura, because I want your parents to know that you are an important part of our relationship." Then, changing the subject, he suggested, "After dinner, let's listen to that natural-history documentary that I recorded on a cassette three weeks ago. It asks questions about why there were dinosaurs present on the Earth for millions of years, and then for some reason over a period of time went extinct."

"Yes, that should be interesting. I feel sure it will be worth listening to, so let's get the dinner started. I'll get the haddock ready for frying," Maura said, heading for the kitchen.

Paul followed her, saying, "I'll get the chips ready for frying."

The dogs excitedly followed in close pursuit.

CHAPTER TWENTY-FIVE

On Tuesday morning the weather was fine and the sun spread its warmth all over the land just like the previous days. After exercising the dogs and breakfasting, Paul and Maura loaded their necessities into the camper van both helped and hindered by the excited, playful dogs, which sensed an outing. They also made sure to restock the songbird food containers and both sat and watched a blackbird showering itself in the birdbath.

"The blackbird always amazes me by its bathing technique, Maura. I often wonder how it manages to give the impression that it is being showered by a real shower-head. Does it affect you that way?"

"Yes, it does, now that you've drawn my attention to it. It seems so effortlessly lifelike. Like you said before, Paul, one can't get bored watching them," Maura ceded, and she added, "Even the dogs seem to enjoy it."

When the birds finished their bathing, Paul asked Maura, "You don't mind being chauffeuse, do you?" he smiled.

"*Pas du tout*," she replied, and she asked, "Is that the word for a female chauffeur?"

"Yes, exactly that, Maura. You were quick to make the connection."

Maura smiled her pleasure.

"At the main road turn left and almost immediately turn right on to that unmade byroad. That will take us to the cottage site, which is only about two kilometres distant." He handed her the keys.

Five minutes later Maura turned left into the entrance leading to the field gate of the cottage site, and stopped in front of the closed gate. Paul climbed out and unlocked and opened the gate, gesturing to Maura to drive through and continue to the parking place close to the Portaloo.

Paul joined her there and muzzled the two dogs whilst apologising, "I'm sorry girls, but we can't take a chance on losing you now."

It was then 11.45 a.m. and the four wandered over to the damson tree, from beneath which the remains of the young, tragic Mary Foley had been removed. Her resting place had been covered over to deter sightseers from trampling all over it.

Fleurie sniffed around the site and Paul reminded her, "Yes, Fleurie, that's where the remains of Mary that you discovered lay." He fondled Fleurie's head, adding, "But she will be coming back to be with us again soon."

The dog seemed to understand and stood on her hind legs with her front paws resting against Paul's midriff.

Paul fondled her head with both hands, saying, "Yes, I know you miss her, Fleurie, and so do we." Bonzie joined Fleurie and Paul fondled her head too. "Yes, I know you both miss her, but she will be coming back to stay soon."

"Paul, I believe, as you suggested, that Mary has been in spiritual contact with Fleurie. She may have possibly seen Mary's spirit. Do you think that might be so?" Maura asked.

"I can't say she didn't, Maura. Spirituality is mysterious and in that psychic world anything is possible."

At that moment Jack Kyley, the builder, drove on to the site. He parked alongside the camper van and approached Paul and Maura. The dogs recognised him and wagged their tails in greeting.

"Well now, apart from good morning – if indeed it is still morning – I don't know how to address dogs. Since all four of you are suddenly famous, I can congratulate you on how you not only identified the killer of the family burned to death in the cottage inferno five years ago, but also trapped the same killer and thwarted his attempt to burn you, Maura, to death in your camper van as well (or so he thought). And then you solved the mystery of why the family was murdered. I can't think of words to express my feelings, Paul and Maura," Jack confessed.

Paul pointed to the dogs, smiling, and said, "These are the real heroines of the solving of the crimes, Jack. Bonzie here, on my right, identified the killer; and Fleurie, on my left, discovered the remains of the young girl buried under this covering, Jack. Her remains were exhumed yesterday for further tests in the police forensic laboratory in the city."

"My God, what truly wonderful faithful friends dogs really are! After hearing that, I will from now on treat all dogs with the love and respect they surely deserve. And there's you and Maura, Paul – but for those precious dogs, all four of you would have, most likely, burned to death. And added to that, the killer tried to poison your beloved dogs and returned to finish you and Maura off in his second attempt, and you, Paul, single-handedly turned the tables on him, catching him in the act and overpowering him. It's a miraculous story of survival," Jack concluded.

"There's one thing I would like you to know, Jack – I was not alone," Paul revealed.

"But it said in the newspaper—"

"Yes, I know, Jack, but how does one explain to the news media that spiritual help was involved?"

"Spiritual help?" Jack repeated, and he said, "I don't understand that, Paul."

"I'll explain it to you, Jack. I'm talking about the spirit, or soul, of the young lady, Mary Foley. As you now know, she was the eldest child of the family that died in the cottage inferno."

Jack nodded his agreement.

"I believe her spirit was guiding me mentally, and it was also her spirit that inspired Fleurie here to almost beg me with whines, scraping the earth with her front paws, trying to excavate something. That induced me to dig deeper, resulting in the discovery of Mary's mortal remains."

Paul then drew Jack's attention to the faded lily-of-the-valley plants in a bed a couple of paces away and explained that he had removed the plants from the flower bed that was Mary's now empty grave. He then related to Jack that he and Maura had requested that the remains of Mary be reinterred in the grave where her remains were discovered, subject to the approval of Mary's surviving relatives. They had agreed, and Inspector Conroy and his team of officers had arranged to have the site consecrated by the local parish priest. Paul's intention after the reburial was to replant the lily-of-the-valley plants on the grave, which was their original site."

"Well, I must say that was very thoughtful, caring and respectful of both you, Paul, and Maura." Jack expressed his feelings.

"So can we depend on you to ensure the safety of those plants, Jack?" Paul asked.

"You can, Paul. I will be their guardian," Jack promised.

"We have two other requests to make, Jack, and one is we have decided on a green fence to surround the property about a metre and a half high. Can you take that on, Jack? And if so, can you complete that first? We will leave it to your discretion, Jack," Paul suggested.

"There's an old saying, Paul, that goes 'Great minds think alike.' Your suggestion is exactly what I was going to suggest and I expect your reasoning is the same as mine, and that is to give the site some privacy and prevent trespassers from trampling all over it. Am I right, Paul?"

"Exactly the same, Jack, and it proves that some people do think alike. We would also like the area around the grave to be fenced off, with a gate from the lane for people wanting to pay their respects, and an inner gate for us to access the grave for its maintenance. Is that OK, Jack?" Paul asked.

"Yes, I've got all that in mind, Paul, and it will be done. And now the other request?" Jack asked with a smile.

"Maura and I have decided to have a retirement apartment built on to the bungalow at this end, for Maura's parents to use for holidays and to retire to when they decide, and to be alone in when they choose to be. Can that be arranged, Jack?" Paul asked.

"My God, Paul! You and Maura can ask anything you want and it will be done. You and your dogs are celebrities now. Can I be any clearer than that?" Jack stressed, smiling.

"No, not really, Jack. That's fairly comprehensive," Paul agreed, and he added, "It almost strikes me as an invitation to be greedy, but I could never be that, Jack." Paul stated his nature.

"Oh, I know, Paul. But still, don't hesitate to ask when you need anything." He scribbled a few notes on a pad and declared, "All will be faithfully done, Paul. If there are any alterations to your plans, just phone me and I will see to it. I could spend a couple of hours asking questions of you both, but I haven't asked you anything, Maura. I must apologise to you for that."

"Oh, there's no need to apologise, Jack. I understand. I'm a good listener too." Maura dispelled any shortcomings.

"Before we part company, Jack, as we are now in private accommodation provided by the council we intend to spend Saturdays and Sundays working in the cottage-site gardens when we return from a few days' break with Maura's parents down in Tipperary. Is that likely to interfere with your working routine or not?" Paul asked.

"No, Paul, since we work a five-day week as a rule. That will be fine – no problem," Jack assured him.

The three of them ambled back to their vehicles with the dogs leading, and after a brief chat they shook hands and Jack fondled the dogs' heads, saying, "You two canine ladies are super dogs the best."

The dogs wagged their tails in friendship.

"Bye now, Paul and Maura. I hope you all enjoy your break in Tipperary."

They climbed into their vehicles, and Jack moved away with a hand wave. Then Paul climbed out of the camper van clutching a plastic bag and was followed by the dogs.

"I'll only be a minute, Maura." He addressed Maura with a smile, and ambled back to the rhubarb patch and pulled a number of stalks. He snipped off the large leafy tops with a pocket knife and rejoined Maura in the camper van, ushering the dogs in ahead of him.

"There should be enough there to bake several pies, Maura."

"Yes indeed. The thought escaped my mind as I was so interested in the conversation," Maura excused herself guiltily.

"Don't belittle yourself. Everyone is guilty of mental deviation at times. I was guilty of the same until the last moment, but better late than never," Paul reminded her, and he continued: "We have two tasks to complete before heading south. The first one is to call on Farmer Crowe to let him know that I haven't forgotten about the manure. You need to turn right on the way out, and I believe you remember the rest, Maura."

"Yes, right on the way out and right again into the farmyard just before the lane junction," Maura recalled.

"Good, Maura! Quietly confident – and just as I expected, since you do everything well."

"Well, thanks for the compliment, Paul," Maura responded, and she added, "Come to think of it now, I can't recall you ever saying that I did anything badly, Paul."

"Well, Maura, my philosophy is, when one puts effort into doing something even if it ends in failure it can't be described as bad, can it, now?"

Maura thought for a moment and answered, "I see the logic in that and I have to agree, although many people see failure as a weakness and seem to ignore the effort applied."

"Yes, that's true, Maura, but every failure is merely a stepping stone to success, and success follows in the wake of failure," Paul reminded her.

"Yes, I see, and you did say in the past that the vagaries of life are unpredictable," Maura mused.

When Maura steered the camper van into Farmer Crowe's farmyard Paul asked her to stop close to the farmhouse.

Then after pacifying the dogs he climbed out, and after looking round the area he was about to approach the house when the farmer appeared at the half-door and came out to greet him with outstretched arms, saying excitedly, "Delighted to see you again, Paul."

He offered his hand in greeting, and Paul accepted it and shook hands.

"I don't know how to thank you enough, Paul, for saving my daughter from certain suicide had she decided to give her hand in marriage to that evil hell-bound murderer. My daughter, wife and I are so relieved that you and your faithful dogs not only captured him and exposed his ungodly nature, but put an end to his evil as well. You saved my reluctant daughter, who was so close to giving way to pressure to marry that multiple murderer of innocent people plus the intended murderer of yourself, your wife and your heroic dogs, which saved all of you. And you were the hero who overpowered him on his second attempt to burn all of you to death." The farmer shed emotional tears of relief that his beloved daughter's life had been saved from certain suicide. And that is a fact, Paul," he declared, drying his tears with a handkerchief.

"Don't upset yourself, Frank. Just thank God that your daughter was saved from the fate you feared. I had intended writing a letter to your daughter beseeching her not to accept Rangton's proposal of marriage under any circumstances. I'd have sent it if things hadn't worked out as they did," Paul revealed.

"You were going to do that, Paul, were you?" the farmer asked, surprised and relieved, and he asked, "How am I going to reward you, Paul, for saving my daughter's life? Tell me. Ask me anything."

"Is the manure still available, Frank?" Paul asked politely.

"Manure!" the farmer exclaimed. "You can have all the manure you want, but that is not a suitable reward, Paul," the farmer reminded him.

"It is to me, Frank, and I am grateful for your generosity." Paul thanked him and continued: "Your friendship, kindness, sociability and willingness to help and share are qualities I value, Frank, and they generate contentment. Is your wife at home, Frank?"

"No, Paul, she and our daughter are in town shopping. If they had been at home, they would have been out here thanking you for keeping us all safe from the tragic effects of what might have been."

"Well, pass on my fond regards to them and the rest of your family members. I'll call again in a few days to load some manure on to the trailer if it's in place, OK, Frank?"

"The trailer is loaded, Paul. My two sons volunteered to do that job and they will deliver it if you wish," the farmer offered.

"Well, do convey my gratitude to them, Frank. The field gate is closed, but unlocked, and if they have the time to deliver it I would appreciate their effort. There's a small cabin at the end of the garden, with the hedgerow behind it. They can tip it there by the hedgerow; but if they are busy with work in the fields, I will see to it in a few days – probably over the weekend," Paul suggested.

The farmer replied, "It will be delivered today or tomorrow, Paul – no trouble."

"Well, thanks again, Frank, and give my regards to all the members of your family. And tell your daughter, Frank, that God was watching over her welfare. Tell her not to dwell on her experience. Until we meet again – which I hope will be soon, Frank – cheer yourself up and think of the good side of the event."

Both parted company with a friendly handshake as teardrops welled in the farmer's eyes. Paul climbed into the camper van and made a hand gesture of farewell to the farmer.

"Turn right as you leave, Maura, and then right again at the lane junction only metres away. The farmer was emotionally upset, Maura, and that deterred me from introducing you to him as it might have turned into a tear-filled encounter. Did I do right or wrong?" Paul asked.

"I believe you made the right decision, Paul. It probably would have caused him more distress and I would have felt guilty then, but what was he distressed about, Paul?" Maura quizzed.

"He said I'd saved his daughter's life because she was feeling the pressure to reluctantly accede to the killer Rangton's next marriage proposal, since farmers' daughters are expected to marry within the farming community. If she had done so, her father believes she would have committed suicide when the truth was exposed, especially as she was acquainted with Mary Foley. He asked me how he was going to reward me for saving the whole family, including himself, from the consequences of a tragedy which I, you and our beloved dogs prevented from happening. 'How am I going to reward you, Paul?' he pleaded, in tears."

"And how did you respond, Paul?" Maura asked.

"By asking him if the manure offer was still on; and if so, could that be the reward? He told me we can have all the manure we want, but he wants to reward us more substantially than that. I said no, the manure will be our reward, and we are happy with that."

"Were his wife and daughter in the house?" Maura asked.

"No, they were in town shopping, and I am glad because it would have been a trying ordeal for me to witness all three of them emotionally upset."

"Yes, I understand, Paul, but I think the root of their emotional expression would have been their joyful relief, and that is the difference," Maura summed up.

"Yes, that may well be true, Maura, and I hadn't considered that, but nevertheless I would have felt the embarrassment of having been the generator of it," Paul remarked.

"We are approaching the lane-end junction, Paul, so am I turning right there?"

"Yes, unless you want to call at our temporary home for anything you might have forgotten."

"No, there's noth—" Maura momentarily hesitated and decided, "Yes, there is something."

She indicated left and, on this main road, immediately signalled right. She drove into the short cul-de-sac and turned the camper van sideways in front of the house, stopped and turned the engine off.

She then turned to face Paul, who asked, "What have you forgotten, Maura?"

"I forgot to tell you, Paul, that I am pregnant!"

Paul looked at her, stunned, and said, "You did? I mean, you are? Are you sure?"

"Of course!"

"I'm delighted! Overjoyed!" And he embraced and kissed her. "This is the best news since I don't know when. What better news to bring to your parents!"

"I think you should drive, Paul, as I am not sure how the physical change is going to affect me mentally."

"Yes, that's a thoughtful consideration. Let's climb out and change places."

And the dogs followed them.

"What do you want from inside the house, Maura?" Paul asked.

"Nothing," Maura replied, and she added, "I just thought this was the more appropriate place to tell you."

"And what wonderful news it is! Life is suddenly like a flower-filled meadow of joy."

After several minutes to recover his mental composure, Paul addressed the dogs: "Come, Bonzie and Fleurie – all on board for our journey south."

The dogs rushed to the camper van and clambered into the rear, and Paul gave each a hide chew and started the engine. He kissed Maura again and steered the camper van out to the main road and headed towards Attanagh town.

"We have two – no, three – stops to make in town: one to the supermarket to pick up a pack of six bottles of wine to accompany a cheque for €1,000 for Matt Dempsey at the Attanagh Motor Company as a reward for his help; secondly a visit to the bank to collect a draft for €10,000 to cover the cost of the new car for Gerry; and the third stop is at the Attanagh Motor Company to complete the transaction with Matt Dempsey. We will also collect six bottles of wine for your parents and us to celebrate your pregnancy, Maura, and then it's south to Tipperary for a few days of relaxation. I think Lady Luck has smiled on us today, Maura, and all that's left to say is '*Vive bonheur!*'"

"Oh yes, I agree entirely, Paul: *Vive bonheur!*"

"There is no end – only an endless beginning."